EXILES OF
CONOTA

EXILES OF CONOTA

STRANGER MAGICS,
BOOK TWELVE

ASH FITZSIMMONS

EXILES OF CONOTA. Copyright © 2021 by Ash Fitzsimmons.

Print Edition ISBN: 978-1-949861-30-3

Cover design by BespokeBookCovers.com

www.ashfitzsimmons.com

CHAPTER 1

In Iroja, the dead are *noisy*.

This was among the first lessons I learned upon coming to the so-called mortal realm, and one altogether unexpected. In Conota, the realm of my birth, the dead are well behaved—relatively, I suppose. They can be demanding when displeased, but in general, they seldom nag. Then again, the Conotan dead are few in number. Cynaeli are immortal, after all, and death comes to us only by attack or accident. Growing up in my father's tower in High Vale, I had glimpsed the spirits of his parents (he the victim of battle, she of one of her husband's opportunistic concubines) and his father's parents before him, along with a smattering of uncles, aunts, cousins, and concubines, but their appearances were infrequent, their messages brief. Some were content to watch me from the shadows as I worked in the great barn, cleaning up after Father's prized chinols and tending to their young. Others—my grandfather in particular—made it a point to criticize my work when my efforts were less than perfect. I remember him huffing one morning after I, having been awake all night with a difficult birth, tripped in my exhaustion and dropped a tray of ointments into the straw. "I suppose it's too much to ask for a half-breed to show a little competence," he'd said as I picked myself up and gathered my supplies. "On your feet, lazy girl!"

At times like that, I'd wished that the dead were *slightly* more corporeal—just enough that I could administer a good slap across the face. Instead, I'd apologized to him for my clumsiness and returned to work. Had I been disrespectful, he might have complained to Father, and I had no desire for a beating. Father's wife and his favorite concubines could protect their children, but I was a half-blooded female likdenfi—a concubine's child—with no one to advocate for me, and his blows came hard and fast when he was angry.

As a child, I'd thought that our family's dead lingered around me for the sport. I presented an easy target, and if it pleased them to watch me learn by trial and error how to convince the magic around me to make the chinols' waste disappear, well, at least no one was yelling. When I visited another tower, or even a settlement beyond High Vale, I often found the local dead watching me with mild curiosity, perhaps intrigued by my Irojan blood. I wasn't unique in that regard—I knew of a handful of Irojan concubines, and I heard whispers of a place in one of the deep caves where male and female Irojans alike were kept for sport—and yet, I tended to find myself with a spectral audience wherever I went.

Not until I fled to Iroja did I understand the cause of their interest in me, and learning the secret almost cost me my life.

Like most cynaeli girls, when I was young, I dreamed that my father would arrange for me to become a wife. That he would eventually give me to a man was understood, but I desperately hoped that I'd have a marriage instead of being passed on as a concubine. Even with my shortcomings, I thought my odds were decent. Father was the paramount lord of High Vale, and I, therefore, was a highborn lady. Granted, I was the lowliest of his children, but I thought I could give an aspiring man certain prospects. Father had only three sons to his fourteen daughters, and though daughters usually didn't inherit, Father owned land enough to parcel off small tracts as an incentive for suitors. Several of my eldest sisters were made wives to lords—elder sons of Father's peers, promising matches.

As for me, I never looked so high. Once I began working in the stables, Father took me along to help with the chinols when he traveled into the Triple River settlement, far beneath the peaks of Heluweya. My presence on these trips wasn't intended as a gift to me—chinols can be wonderfully sweet to the people they know, but they can also bite off a finger or worse if they feel threatened, and many longtime stable hands lack a digit or two from a visiting chinol who didn't like the accommodations.

The Irojans of my acquaintance who had seen chinols didn't seem to understand my fondness for the beasts. Personally, I found their Irojan counterparts—horses—to be far less impressive. A well-bred chinol was black as night, scaled like a dragon, surefooted on stone, and swift on the plains. Blessed with a second pair of eyes to widen their field of vision and a nasty bite, wild chinols lived and hunted in packs—dangerous to a lone traveler caught by surprise—but their tamed cousins made excellent mounts.

But I digress. Father visited Triple River every season with a small herd of chinols to meet with his counterpart there, Ketulm. The two would discuss the chinols available for trade and the persistent problem of the raiding jinoda, a nomadic people who liked nothing more than to steal our herds. Though untalented with magic, the jinoda were dangerous: pale, thin creatures with claws and teeth that put a chinol's to shame. They kept to their own kind and spoke their own tongue, and though they could occasionally be hired as a mercenary force, they usually just made themselves a nuisance to us.

While the lords traded and plotted arrangements for defense, I made the acquaintance of one of Ketulm's likdenfi, Arikol, a boy two years my senior. Like me, he was half-blooded, but there was barely a trace of his Irojan mother about him. The only obvious gift she'd bestowed on him was his height, as Arik was a full head taller than most of his brothers—all but Fikwed, who also bore Irojan blood. Arik was broad-shouldered and toned, kind to me and quick to laugh, and my heart soon fluttered whenever I caught his smile, a flash of white teeth cutting across his pale violet face. Some of my sisters thought our subterranean neighbors appeared strange with their comparatively washed-out complexions, but I found Arik handsome, despite the fact that he looked like he'd never even peeped out from the caverns—and gradually, I came to understand that what I felt for him wasn't mere friendship. Though I dared tell no one, I was in love.

When I was sixteen and nearing an appropriate age for marriage, I waited until Father was in a good mood, then approached him about the possibility of making an arrangement with Ketulm. It was a solid plan, I thought—a marriage of likdenfi would cost neither father greatly. But to my dismay, Father chuckled and shook his head. It was impossible, he told me. Ketulm had seen to it that Arik would never take a wife. When my face fell, Father chided me to smile. He'd made a better match for me, one that would come with far more status than a marriage to a half-blooded likdenfi. On my twenty-first birthday, I was to be given to Warohn, one of the lords of High Vale, as his tenth concubine.

Father never took me back to Triple River, and Arik never accompanied Ketulm when he visited High Vale. I had no way to send him a message in secret, and it would have been improper for me to do so openly. My future had been arranged for me. And so I smiled, even though I saw the walls closing in and could almost feel the concubine's choker closing around my neck. It was the best I could hope for, I told myself, considering the taint on me. Warohn's household was wealthy and his family respected, and I would be treated well, especially if I gave him sons. Yet something within me rebelled at the notion of my predetermined placement, and a wild idea came to mind.

What if I could find a way to Mama?

I knew precious little of my mother when she was ripped away from me. She was Irojan, obviously, with hair as dark and thick as mine but skin the color of sand, and her accent was strange, her vowels stretched like the sticky candy she used to sneak me from the kitchen. She left me with her exotic name—Hayleigh Lozano—a few words of her native tongue, and a necklace before Father tired of her and sent her back to Iroja, presumably to the land of Oklahoma, from whence she'd come. I knew nothing of the place but its name, which felt funny in my mouth and sounded almost magical when Mama said it. But I had loved my mother dearly, and I mourned her departure.

Even as a small girl, I vowed to visit the other realm someday and find her. To that end, I repeated the words she'd taught me over and over, terrified that the strange syllables would slip from my memory. And while Father had named me Imaranta, I called myself by the name Mama had used: Hope.

After I turned twenty and my impending concubinage neared, I began to quietly panic. Surely Warohn would never allow me to travel to Iroja, even if I swore to return. I knew better than to ask Father's permission. He was in a foul mood much of the time that season, as the jinoda raids were becoming more brazen. Every time his chinols went missing, I was sent into the wilderness with a handheld tracker, instructed to follow the jinoda and return with the chinols if possible. But I've never had a great gift for magic, and there was only so closely that I could follow the jinoda without risking an arrow through the chest. My expeditions were failures, as no two bands of jinoda ever went the same direction with their prizes.

Then came the dawn raid. I awoke to the sound of the ward alarms and ran out to find twenty chinols missing, the pasture empty. Throwing a little food and water into my bag and saddling my mount, an endurance runner if I ever knew one, I set off after the sound of distant snorts and whinnies.

Coaxing a chinol out of High Vale is a task best left to the experienced. My mountain-reared girl was as surefooted as if she were traversing the wide plain below us, but the jinoda had a head start and generations of thievery to expedite their escape. By the time I descended, the tracks led out through the grasses toward the southern horizon, and all I could do was follow. I rode until my mount was exhausted, then bedded down for a few hours of rest, the little I could afford.

By morning, they were long gone. The projection from my tracking disc showed me a view of the jinoda in the far distance, riding hard. I pursued them as fervently as I dared, pushing my chinol to her limits, but I couldn't close the gap. And then, in the afternoon, I saw a chance: the jinoda were no longer running, but rather had turned their attention to hunting. A small herd of nikots fled before them, the jinoda racing behind on their stolen mounts—

No. Not nikots—*kadalin*. And a hunting band, presumably, not a herd.

It's difficult sometimes when one comes to understand that the truths one has been taught are in fact untruths. As a child, I used to play in the shadow of the two nikots that Father had hunted and mounted as trophies for the tower's entry hall. They were huge beasts, their top halves much like ours, though with exposed skin browner than Mama's, their lower halves covered with reddish hair, their front hooves raised as if to strike. I'd contemplated them, considering how brave my father had to have been to bring down such fearsome creatures.

But as I grew, I saw how much better our weapons were. The nikots had spears and bows and short knives, but we fought with magic, and Father was sufficiently old and experienced to fling killing bolts. His hunt of the nikots had been for sport, not because they were a threat. Still, I let the matter go. Men hunted nikots on occasion— it was almost a rite of passage in certain families.

And then I met one. A transformation bind had made him smaller, almost Irojan in appearance, and he was unarmed, but I've never seen such burning fury directed at me as I did on the day I encountered Kip. I learned then, at ear-blistering levels, that the nikots—kadalin, rather— had their own language, that they weren't beasts, but rather an intelligent people...and that Kip hated me on sight because my kind murdered his.

It's nauseating to realize that you're the villain of the story. I've tried to amend my thinking since then and refer to the kadalin by the name they call themselves, but childhood lessons are like bedrock, firm and difficult to change. Still, I do try. I owe them that courtesy.

To continue: the jinoda were chasing a band of five kadalin across the plain, and I saw a chance. Assuming they brought down their quarry, the jinoda would have to stop and deal with their kill. They'd have the carcasses to carry, and they'd be slower. Perhaps they would make camp, and then, I reasoned, I could sneak close enough to free and retrieve my father's chinols.

But the dragon found them first.

I watched the tracking disc projection as a white dragon—a male, I assumed, judging by its size, though I was no expert—swooped down upon the jinoda, spitting fire into their midst. The tracker began to beep with alarm as several chinols' collars ceased to transmit, victims of the blaze. The system compensated with the remaining enchanted collars, showing me how the dragon rose and banked for a second pass...and how the jinoda prepared to fight back. I saw the giant crossbow bolt embed itself in his shoulder, followed by the rain of smaller arrows, and I heard the dragon roar with pain. One of the chinols turned just in time to catch his final blast of fire, and then the projection ceased as the last of the chinols and jinoda were burned alive.

The carnage was enough to make me queasy, but I was too stunned to do the sensible thing and retreat to High Vale. Before the projection had died, I'd seen that the dragon had a *rider*—and even at a distance, I believed that rider to be Irojan.

An Irojan, alone in Conota. On a *dragon*.

Forget prudence—I had to investigate.

It was full night before I came upon the dragon, a hulking mass darker than the sky, coiled in the grass. Dismounting, I bade my uneasy chinol to stay, then created an orb to light my way and slowly neared. Though I'd chosen a dim red light, however, the injured dragon woke and noticed me, and he growled, a sound like grinding boulders deep beneath the earth that I felt in my bones. The message was abundantly clear, but I'd come too far to run.

When the Irojan appeared, she was armed and bearing a much brighter light. She flashed it in my eyes before lowering the beam, and as my vision cleared, I got my first decent look at her: perhaps my age and size, her skin beige, her hair almost white and pulled back in a messy tail. One cheek bore odd red stripes, presumably an impression of her bedding. In her right hand was a long sword that glittered like cut diamonds in candlelight.

So as not to give her the wrong idea—and hoping that she would calm her mount—I raised my empty hand in greeting as Mama had once done, then called upon my shallow reserve of the Irojan tongue and bade them, "Howdy!"

The Irojan, to put it mildly, was confused.

Fortunately for my poor linguistic recall, there was power enough in the sword that its wielder could produce a translation. Her name was Kitty Connolly, the dragon was Frank—and talkative, to my surprise—and when I asked if they knew anything of the land of Oklahoma, Kitty assured me that they did. They'd come to rescue Artur, Kitty's long-enchanted sister, but thanks to Frank's fresh injuries, they were stranded in the wilderness.

We made a deal. I doctored Frank's wounds and brought Kitty to Warohn's tower, where Artur had been locked in sleep for centuries. The next day, when Kitty broke the ancient enchantment on her, we escaped from my intended lord, climbed aboard Frank's back, and flew through a gate between realms into the Irojan night.

Looking back, I can't fully encapsulate that moment with mere words. The air on the other side of the gate was far warmer and heavy with moisture—we'd come in over a tropical sea, I later learned—and the brilliance of the magic I knew was dimmer, mixed with a shadowy ether. But above me—oh, the wonder!—the dark dome was studded with twinkling lights and a brighter white face, an almost complete circle. Stars, I know now, and a nearly full moon. But I had no frame of reference then, and the sight of thousands of lights in the darkness after a lifetime of perpetually overcast skies was enough to take my breath.

I wish Arik could see this, I thought, and then I was stabbed with a pang of guilt. I'd escaped, I was flying across an unknown ocean beneath impossible heavens…and he remained in Triple River, consigned to an abhorrent fate.

I hadn't said goodbye. I hadn't even *tried*.

It hit me then that I would probably never meet him again. Arik, the man I loved above all others, whose face and voice and arms my imagination still conjured in my sleep…he was lost to me. I couldn't help him, couldn't free him, couldn't undo what his father had done to him.

Even stunned as I was by the alien majesty of the moment, my heart cried out, but I had no time to process my convoluted feelings. Within seconds, Kitty opened a second gate, and we passed from Iroja straight into the daylight of a place I'd hoped never to find myself.

Faerie.

Any cynaeli with half an education knows of the three realms: Conota, our homeland; Iroja, the realm beyond, a place of strange people and less magic; and Faerie, a bizarre, dangerous land accessible only from Iroja. As I was taught, there were three peoples in Conota— ourselves, the tennuwaya to the south, and the raiding jinoda—though the jinoda recognized no authority but their own, and the average cynaeli would be reluctant to consider them our equals. Other species, like dragons, might show intelligence, but they fell on the other side of the line diving "people" from creatures that one could kill without being considered a murderer.

Beyond our borders lay Iroja, whose inhabitants—or those I'd seen, at least—were short-lived and untalented with magic. They were considered a curiosity more than a true people, and those who entered Conota by accident or force were used as the cynaeli and tennuwaya liked. I don't know who among my people first discovered that Irojans could bear half-cynaeli children, but most lords kept at least one Irojan concubine around for variety.

And then there was Faerie, whose natives might look Irojan but were far deadlier. *How*, exactly, they were meant to be so dangerous was never explained to my satisfaction when I was a child. After all, magic was what made us powerful, and the common thought was that if Iroja's magic was weaker, Faerie had none at all.

As I learned, this was true, but only in a fashion. Faerie, as it turned out, was a source of a kind of magic, but not anything recognizable as such to my people. If Conota were a bright flame, Faerie was its shadow, similar in shape but inverted. The clouds of color I'd known all my life, the constant currents of untapped magic, were instead replaced by swirling shadow. While I saw lovely homes and parks and—to my surprise—was treated well, I found the overall atmosphere disquieting, not least because even the simplest enchantment was impossible in that magical desert.

The natives were quite comfortable, however, as were the Irojan adepts—"wizards," they called themselves, Irojans with magical abilities. What I saw as magic was like shadow to them, and whereas I groped in vain for potential, they practically swam in useable magic. Considering their skewed perspective, I suppose it makes sense that they called Faerie's ether "magic" and Conota's "dark magic"; I could have offered the cynaeli term, but we had more pressing matters at hand than linguistics. Still, it rankled slightly that their term for Conota was "the Gray Lands," as if my home realm were nothing more than the formless unknown.

Thankfully, I didn't linger long in Faerie. Kitty was half fae, but she resided among wizards in an Irojan settlement called Glastonbury. She was as good as her word, and two days later—after I'd glamoured myself to blend with the Irojans, giving myself extra digits and shifting my skin tone from purple to beige—she'd delivered me to the land of Oklahoma, to Mama's home settlement of Pauline. After a moment's disbelief, Mama had welcomed me, and I'd settled into my new life in her quiet farmhouse, anticipating a fresh start. I had much to learn. Though Kitty had been considerate enough to give me the rest of Mama's language, my accent was unfortunately distinctive, and I knew none of the Irojans' customs.

Humans, not Irojans. Habit is a difficult ravine to escape.

Mama tried to help me find my footing. We had long talks when she was home from her store, and when I was alone, I spent hours staring at screens, attempting to process a lifetime's worth of missing information. (The technology was bizarre. Having grown up with projections powered by magic, I struggled at first to understand how humans could accomplish a similar effect without it.) Mama cautioned me to go easy on myself, to take my time—there was no great rush, after all. I looked to her for guidance, and she led me wisely, even as she grappled with the strangeness of having a grown daughter in her house. Mama was strong, *so* strong, but there was a brittle quality to that strength, and I felt it when she hugged me too tightly and lingered on the threshold of my bedroom, watching me as I pretended to sleep.

But Mama never warned me about the dead of Iroja, who soon came to me in droves.

I arrived in Pauline on a rainy Tuesday, and Mama took the day off. She stayed home with me on Wednesday, too, but by Thursday, she needed to put in an appearance downtown. "It's just me running the store," she explained. "If I'm suddenly gone, people will worry, and one of the biddies from church will stop by to check on me, and—"

"And I'm not ready to be introduced yet," I concluded. We were still working on our cover story, a way to reconcile Mama's apparent mental breakdown with my existence that didn't involve Conota. I hadn't realized how few humans knew of my people—the Arcanum, the Fringe, the Minor Arcanum, and the Dark Company knew at least *something* of us, but the mundane population were clueless. When Mama had returned from Conota years before, telling everyone where she had been held captive and what had happened to her, she'd been deemed insane. Intense therapy and drugs had nearly convinced her that she *had* snapped…and now I'd appeared. While Mama seemed happy to have me back, we had some creative explaining to do.

So Mama left for work that morning, closing the blinds to keep the glaring sun out of my unaccustomed eyes— Conotan skies were constantly cloudy, making the sun a painful novelty for me. I sat with her computer, picking through the information sites she'd shown me while a nature documentary played on the television as background noise. I still didn't understand the system, so Mama had left a series on autoplay for me, giving me a welcome distraction from my reading. Nestled in Mama's leather recliner with a cup of sweetened coffee, I'd just glanced up to watch a segment on sloths when I saw that I was no longer alone.

The man and woman standing between the television and me were dead. *That* was easy enough to tell, but as for the rest, I was at a loss. Though I had little experience with the rapid human aging process, I guessed they were older than Mama, but I couldn't have begun to be more specific. Both had thick heads of hair, dark but heavily shot through with silver. They were dressed casually, he in a blue golf shirt and khakis, she in a purple tunic top and jeans—all terms I would learn to assign later, of course, as I had no knowledge of local fashion beyond what I'd seen in Mama's closet.

That there were spirits in Mama's house didn't bother me. I'd grown up with the curious dead around, after all, and I assumed that what I'd find in Iroja would be similar to what I'd known at home. The primary difference would be language, I surmised, but that was hardly a problem. For most cynaeli, it's simple to have a conversation with a spirit, as it's much like talking to a living person. But there's a trick in our arsenal: even if we can't speak the spirit's language, we can still communicate via a specialized form of telepathy. When two living people speak mind to mind, they need to have a common tongue between them, but for the dead, there's no such limitation. Indeed, I once had such a conversation with a long-dead tennuwaya who hadn't known a word of Cynaeli in life. (Our tongues are similar enough that the parallels are obvious with study but too divergent to be considered mere dialects of each other.) Perhaps it's just a quirk of the cynaeli brain, but it's a useful one.

Still, I tried out my new English first. "Howdy," I greeted them, putting the computer aside and popping the footrest back into the delightful chair. "Looking for someone?"

The woman slowly shook her head in disbelief. "You really *are* purple."

I frowned and glanced at my bare arms, but the glamour that masked my true skin tone seemed to be intact.

"It's still hidden," she said, divining my concern, "but not to us. Oh gosh, I'm sorry," she continued in a rush, "that was *really* rude, but we just—"

"It was a shock," the man interjected, "learning that you weren't a product of Hayleigh's imagination. Actually seeing you…"

I put my coffee on a coaster and folded my hands. "Forgive my ignorance, but I've only been here two days. I'm Hope, and you are…"

"Your, uh…your grandparents," the woman replied. "Hayleigh's mom and dad."

She seemed unsettled, which was odd; in my experience, the dead were comfortable making themselves known whenever they chose, no matter how inconvenient their interruption might be.

"Ah," I said, unsure of how else to respond. Something told me that the formal greetings used in High Vale might not have direct translations. "Again, forgive me, I mean no disrespect. Mama told me to read this," I said, gesturing to the computer, "but if there's something else I'm meant to be doing…"

"Oh, no, honey," said my grandfather, taking a step closer to me. "We didn't…I know we're interrupting, but, uh…"

"We wanted to meet you, that's all," my grandmother finished. "So, um…are you settling in?"

Their discomfort was evident in their attempt at small talk, even if their expressions didn't give it away. Though it stung a little, I reminded myself that they had been mundane in life, and now they were face to face with the granddaughter they'd thought to be nothing more than the product of their daughter's break with reality. "I'm fine," I told them. "Mama's been very kind."

"Did I hear you two discussing a cover story?" my grandfather asked.

I rubbed the back of my neck and nodded. "Any suggestions?"

"Say you're a cousin from Arizona. I've got some people out there," he replied, folding his arms. "Maybe you grew up abroad, huh? That'd explain the accent."

"A cousin?" I asked, taken aback.

"Yeah, yeah, maybe Hayleigh's second or third cousin, come to town to help her with the store. That'd work, wouldn't it?"

My grandmother, at least, understood my unspoken question. "Hayleigh's been through so much, you know, with her...her *incident*," she said, drawing out the word, "and it would be easier for her if she didn't suddenly have a grown child to explain."

I tried to keep my tone light, though forcing a polite smile took every bit of my willpower. "Understood. I'll tell her your suggestion when she comes home. Or if you'd like to tell her first, she should be at the store."

To my surprise, my grandfather chuckled. "She can't hear us. Can't see us."

"No one can," my grandmother added sadly. "You'll tell her for us, won't you?"

"Sure," I replied, puzzling through that. The tennuwaya couldn't speak with the dead...did humans share their shortcoming?

My grandmother started to pat my shoulder, then seemed to remember the limits of incorporeality and withdrew her hand. "When you see Hayleigh, could you tell her that we're sorry we didn't believe her? Please?"

I nodded. "I will. Nice to meet you," I began, but they

were already gone.

Mama was shocked that night when I relayed our conversation. "You *still* see dead people?" she asked, her eyebrows arching toward her hairline.

"Why wouldn't I?"

"I mean, I figured you'd grow out of it." She frowned at her porkchop and sawed off another bite. "Enogi could do it, but you…"

"All of us can," I mumbled, concentrating on my rice. "All of Father's children. But that's normal. It's the rare cynaeli who can't sense the dead."

"You're only half," she said in a clipped voice, as if my talent were a betrayal.

"Every half-blood I've met can do it. I'm nothing special." I shoveled rice into my mouth, my tongue complaining about the odd sensation of the soft grains. "Mama," I began when I could stall no longer, "if it's too hard having me here, just tell me. I'll understand."

Mama dropped her knife and reached across the table to clasp my wrist, her grip as firm as a manacle. "I want you here," she insisted. "Where you belong. And if you're listening," she added, raising her voice and glancing toward the ceiling, "I am *not* passing my daughter off as some distant cousin, got it?"

"They're not here."

"Just in case." She released me and glanced at my plate. "Let me get you some seconds, baby. Enogi didn't feed you enough." Mumbling curses about my father, she pulled another porkchop off the platter for me.

At first, the dead gave me a wide berth. There are few things secret to them, and my carefully maintained glamour didn't blind them to my true form. But by Monday, having realized that I, unlike the rest of Pauline, could see them, they came to visit me.

And came.

And *came*.

Spirits dropped in from the next town over, then from the rest of the county. By Friday, I was learning Oklahoman geography piecemeal with the aid of an old atlas and a steady parade of visitors, spirits who'd heard of me by word of mouth and tagged along with those who knew where I was hiding. I was barely sleeping, so eager were they to speak with me, and I constantly carried a notepad to jot down messages to loved ones and addresses. Not wanting to worry Mama, I kept my conversations telepathic when she was around and during the long, sleepless nights. I was much obliged to one spirit, a great-grandmother from Stillwater who stood guard outside the bathroom on Sunday while I took my first shower in two days. I told myself that the press would subside, that they were only coming for the novelty, but I heard the lie in my own thoughts.

Then came Tuesday and a predawn visit from Kitty and Toula Pavli, grand magus of the Arcanum. My flight from Conota hadn't been subtle, and Father, for reasons beyond my comprehension, wanted me back. Lady Nath was prepared to conquer Iroja and war with the fae to secure my return. Though I was terrified at the news, I gladly threw on clothing and accompanied them to Faerie, where the dead of Iroja couldn't follow. That night, even with my roiling stomach, I had my first decent sleep in a week.

For six days, Mama and I were guests of Lord Valerius, protected from the skirmishes in Iroja, the natural battleground between our realms. Our host was absent, busy in Glastonbury, but his aides tended to our needs and reassured us that there was no need to worry—all, that is, but one called Bonnie, who returned to the villa long enough to check on us and quietly tell me of the casualties. People were *dying* because of me, and I was a realm away from the war I'd inadvertently sparked.

I wanted to be sick. I wanted to do *something* to help.

I didn't realize just how much would be asked of me.

As I've said, communication with the dead is possible for almost every cynaeli, even those of us with impure blood. But there's a step beyond that: one of sufficient age and talent can *channel* energy into spirits. While this has the side effect of making said spirits visible and audible to non-cynaeli, its primary purpose is to allow our dead to defend us.

Long ago—I've never heard anyone put a firm date on it—the tennuwaya discovered the ability to make scintol, catastrophic weapons. A scintol is an undead abomination, a creature born of magic and made solely for the purpose of destruction. While I can't speak to the precise technique, I do know that the tennuwaya construct them by ripping apart and amalgamating the spirits of their own dead. The result resembles a cloud of living smoke, perhaps five times taller than a man and as wide as it is tall, with a ring of red eyes roughly around its equator. Appealing to its component spirits is pointless; the scintol's intelligence, though limited, is purely its own, and all signs suggest that it remembers nothing of its previous personalities. It understands basic commands, and it seems to exist in a state of blood lust, as anything that comes within its reach is killed with talons of hardened smoke.

Eventually, and perhaps by dumb luck, my people realized that the only weapon useful against scintol is the energized dead. While a spirit so empowered is still unable to interact with flesh, it's highly effective against incorporeal threats. But there are two problems in producing this defense. First is convincing the dead to fight. No one, living or dead, wants to square off against a scintol, and appeals to altruism and mercy are ineffective when dealing with cynaeli. Instead, the best way to recruit spirits is to remind them that if their descendants fall in battle and their line is ended, their glory will likewise die, and they'll become afterthoughts, if not completely forgotten. As an incentive, the energizing process is apparently quite pleasant for the dead, and so some veterans of previous wars can be recruited with that bonus alone.

The second problem is finding cynaeli capable of channeling a sufficient quality of energy. It's not simply a matter of tapping into ambient magic—that would be easy. No, empowering the dead requires drawing upon one's own life force as well, which is why it's a technique reserved for the aged with strong, proven talents. It's difficult to perform properly in Conota, and even harder in Iroja, with that realm's more limited supply of magic.

Some fifteen hundred years before my birth, Lady Morgen, one of Warohn's ancestors, managed to empower the dead of Iroja, giving strength to an army that beat back three scintol. But Morgen was a talent among talents, mature and well instructed in the use of her gift. I, on the other hand, was twenty when scintol returned to Glastonbury, and I was quite sure that I wouldn't leave the field alive if I tried to replicate what Morgen had done. Still, there was no one among the humans or their fae allies who could accomplish the necessary feat, and so I lied to Mama about my chances for success and prayed that my death wouldn't be too painful.

Maybe, a small voice within me suggested, once I was dead, I could find a way to reach Arik.

A stupid notion, that. The dead can't cross between realms. If I died in Iroja, I would remain there...and considering the task before me, that appeared to be much closer to a likelihood than a mere possibility.

But to my surprise, I didn't die in the first few minutes. That day, sitting in a downpour and shaking with the strain as an army of the dead defended their homeland, I discovered why I was so intriguing to the dead in Conota: I had a rare gift. For more than an hour, I made a conduit of myself, giving my all to force back Nath's creatures. But though I had a natural talent for it, I was inexperienced and foolhardy. When I finally cut the connection and passed out, I didn't wake again for four days, as I'd pushed myself to the brink of death. While I recuperated, part of my consciousness floated above my bed in the Arcanum's infirmary, watching the doctor comfort Mama and hoping that the thread barely tethering me to myself wouldn't snap.

The doctor proclaimed that I'd made a full recovery, but I felt hollow, drained, as if the reservoir I'd discovered within myself had run dry. Still, I smiled and nodded in the appropriate places, and I didn't tell Mama how close to the edge I'd come. Back in Pauline, I pretended to be stronger than I felt so that she wouldn't worry—and I didn't tell her that the house was packed to the walls at all hours with needy spirits. Mama's brittleness carried with it the constant threat of breaking, and I couldn't let that happen.

I'd heard her yelling and whimpering in her sleep, mumbling in Cynaeli and begging someone to stop. It didn't take a genius to understand that she was having nightmares about my father. Mama never spoke of those dreams, and she refused to tell me everything that he did to her, so I did what I could not to exacerbate the problem. I refrained from speaking about Conota, didn't press Mama to seek out the Fringe for support, and continued to smile as if I weren't exhausted from my spectral guests. Mama was happiest when life was mundane, and she'd earned what little comfort I could give her.

As for me, I quietly struggled on as the dead poured through the house, fearing that I'd never have a peaceful night or a solitary shower again.

That is, until Flora came to town.

CHAPTER 2

By early August, I was about to drop from exhaustion. The spirits were persistent, and worse, as word of what I'd done in Glastonbury spread, they began asking me to do the same for them. Thankfully, I had no means of transportation—I wasn't strong or talented enough to make gates, especially not with the more limited magic available in Iroja—and so I had a legitimate excuse when tearful mothers begged me to let them speak to their children one last time. But that didn't slow the requests, the pleas that I write messages on behalf of the deceased, the nagging when I hadn't sent those messages weeks after receiving them. I had an excuse for that, too: it took me a little time to understand how e-mail worked and why I needed it, and as for physical letters, all I knew was that they required a special sticker before they went in the mailbox. I researched the matter on my own, as Mama would surely have wanted to know why I was in search of several thousand stamps.

Weary, worn down by the requests and demands, and still weakened from my time in Glastonbury, I buried my head beneath the blankets one night and curled up on myself, trying to eke out an hour or two of sleep before a persistent spirit woke me. The visitors had been bad that day, however, and even as I made it clear that I needed rest, they crowded close to the bed, a few shouting for me to listen to them. I squeezed my eyes closed in my cave of bedding, intending to wait them out and wondering if leaving Conota had been a terrible mistake.

And then a woman's voice cut through the cacophony: "Get back, you damned ingrates! Do you want to kill the poor girl?"

The other voices subsided to muttering, and I risked peeking out from beneath the quilt. The spirit who had spoken stood by the bed with her arms folded, glaring at the room. I hadn't seen her before: my age or a little older, I guessed, with large, dark eyes, brownish-beige skin like Mama's (I'm terrible at the subtleties of human skin tones), thick brown hair coiled into a low bun, and a simple off-white dress. Noticing my movement, she glanced down and gave me a tight smile. "Rest," she said. "I'll keep the crowd at bay."

"Message?" I mumbled, reaching for the notebook on my nightstand.

"*Rest*, Hope."

I paused, one hand still hovering over the table, as my exhausted brain tried to understand what I was hearing. Eventually, enough of the meaning got through that I groaned in agreement, rolled over to face the wall, and fell asleep within seconds.

When I awoke, it was to full sunlight glowing through the gaps between my shade and the window frame. I wiped the gunk from my eyes and sat up, expecting to see my visitors waiting. Instead, I found the room empty—well, almost. The woman had remained with me, sitting at the foot of my bed, and she smiled as I rubbed my face. "Your mother left for work. You were sleeping soundly, and she didn't want to wake you. There's a note on the table downstairs—I assume it's something to that effect. I can't read it," she added with an apologetic shrug.

"You can't read?" I asked, yawning. She looked at me blankly until I understood the problem and repeated the question mentally.

"No, not that language," she replied, and stood as I stretched. "The note will wait. You should bathe."

Catching a whiff of myself, I concurred and rose.

Incidentally, I'm Hope.

"Call me Flora. I'll guard the door."

Only a few spirits roamed the upstairs hallway, and no one interrupted my bath. I stood under the warm jet until the mirror fogged to opacity, then toweled off, willed my hair dry, and threw on a robe. "Flora?" I called through the door.

"Yes?"

Is everything all right?

"Clear."

When I emerged, I wasn't mobbed. I descended to the kitchen, poured a bowl of cereal—Mama insisted that it tasted better with milk, but the notion disgusted me—and took two bites before my stomach roared to life and demanded to be filled. Flora sat beside me as I stuffed myself, keeping a sharp eye on any intruders. Finally, I asked, *How did you manage to make them stay back?*

"Practice," she replied, "and logic. You can't help anyone if you're dead, correct?"

Presumably. The cereal was bland, but I would have gulped it straight from the box, had I been alone. *What can I do for you?*

"Nothing."

Nothing? I repeated, incredulous.

She shook her head. "I came to see whether you would like some help. Don't take this the wrong way, but you seem like you could use it."

I was too relieved to even think of being insulted. *That would be amazing. Can you keep the crowd down?*

"Yes. And so can you," she added. "I trust that you're unaccustomed to saying no." I made a face, and she chuckled. "You're not the first. Let me assist you, at least while you're recovering. What you did in Glastonbury..."

You saw that?

"I did. Incredible. The fact that you're still breathing is miraculous, you understand."

Nodding, I swallowed another spoonful of bran flakes.

But if you don't want anything from me, then why—

"You did a very good thing when this realm needed help," said Flora. "It's only fair that someone return the favor."

Part of me—the part that had grown up around cynaeli and knew that nothing was given without payment—insisted that I should study her until I found her angle. The louder part of me that was rested, clean, and fed for the first time in days told me not to be stupid.

Thank you, I told her. *Where do I go from here?*

While Flora spoke little of herself, I gleaned a few facts quickly, most pertinent among them that unlike the majority of my visitors, she wasn't native to Oklahoma. When she appeared while I was watching television, I found myself explaining the shows to her, and we puzzled through the less obvious storylines together as mutually confused strangers. But she was a quick study, and after a month or so, she had learned the geography of Pauline as well as I had, even if her attempts to read the signs often ended in mangled approximations of the text.

More importantly, she was an excellent gatekeeper. I did want to help the many spirits who sought me out—I just couldn't handle all of them at once. Flora stood guard at first, holding the aggressive ones at bay, then coached me into setting boundaries. I owed the Irojan dead nothing, and unlike the ones at home, none of them could complain to Mama if I displeased them. The balance of power had shifted toward me, a true novelty in my experience, and as I began to assert myself, I was thrilled to find that the spirits would respect my limits, even if they did so reluctantly. That fall, I made it known that I would take requests for a couple of hours late every evening, once Mama went to bed, which kept the crowd satisfied. When possible, I sent messages to loved ones via e-mail. Otherwise, I resorted to writing letters, taking careful dictation and never including a return address on the envelope.

I'd been forced to explain to Mama eventually why I needed so much stationery and so many stamps. "I have a talent that seems to be rare here," I told her as she stared at me over her morning coffee. "People are desperate, and they're *persistent*."

I hated to tell her, but then I couldn't very well steal the materials I needed. Though she kept my supplies stocked, Mama never asked me about my work with the dead, and I never brought up the subject. I was causing her enough grief in our mundane dealings as it stood.

In September, Mama invited me to come downtown and work with her in her shop, Tequila Sunrise. I was pleased to accompany her, and there was almost no labor involved beyond unpacking the occasional shipping box. Mama sold, as she put it, odds and ends—novelty dishtowels, gaudy drinking glasses, a few items of clothing, elaborately decorated cowboy boots, and a little jewelry, along with pieces of folk art, wooden plaques with funny sayings, and ceramics proclaiming the owner's support of the University of Oklahoma or Oklahoma State University. I modeled my wardrobe to echo hers and began behind the jewelry case, where I was out of the way and could observe. Often, Mama greeted her customers by name, and once they'd exchanged pleasantries about the cooler weather and the weekend football games, Mama would beam, beckon to me, and say, "Baby, come over here. This is my daughter, Hope," she'd continue to her surprised customers while I lingered awkwardly behind Mama's shoulder. "She's moved out here to help me. Isn't that sweet?"

A few of the customers just gaped, but most were civil enough to shake my hand and bid me welcome to Pauline. If they stayed long in the store after that, they gave me appraising glances when they thought I wasn't looking, quickly turning away if I caught them in the act.

I began joining Mama at the Methodist church on Sunday mornings because it made her happy. While I knew nothing of the religion, I could sit on the padded pew and keep my mouth shut for an hour a week, and with the crowd focused on the service, I could easily peek at the minds around me.

Cynaeli do not naturally excel at physical and combat magic—the tennuwaya have the advantage there, and we learn through hard practice. Instead, our strengths are in mental enchantment: glamours, illusions, and telepathy. While I couldn't yet open gates or even create passable stamps from the ether, I could listen to another's unprotected thoughts as easily as blinking. And what I heard in that church was troubling.

Everyone knew about poor Hayleigh Lozano, the late mayor's daughter, the pretty little cheerleader who was abducted one day after school and disappeared for seven years. When she surfaced again, she was in Florida, and she'd had a mental breakdown, as she kept insisting that she'd been kidnapped by purple people—and that they'd kept her baby. *Something* had happened to Hayleigh, that much was clear, and word had gotten around that she'd apparently given birth during her absence from Pauline. But no one believed her story, and whatever baby she might have had was surely dead in a landfill.

And then I'd appeared from nowhere. To say that people regarded me with suspicion would be a gross understatement. Most thought I was nothing more than a grifter, a parasite who'd heard of Hayleigh's story and was passing myself off as her long-lost child in order to take advantage of a mentally frail woman. True, my features resembled Hayleigh's, but the likeness wasn't so extreme as to make our relationship an unassailable fact—and Mama had refused to have a DNA test done. A match would have put the matter to rest in the community's mind, but Mama publicly insisted that she knew her own child and didn't need any test to confirm it. Of course, she and I both knew that we couldn't let me get too close to anyone with a medical background. Neither of us knew what a cynaeli–human cross would look like on the genetic level, and we feared that testing would lead to more questions.

Yolanda Ford had been adamant about avoiding genetic tests. Though Mama wasn't ready to get involved with the Fringe, the Irojan support organization for those with minimal magical talent, Yolanda had remained in touch with me since Glastonbury, sending messages to my phone once a week or so to ask about my recovery and my progress in Oklahoma. She'd even made a few house calls when Mama was at work. The lone Fringe coordinator left in the realm, Yolanda cut a striking figure. Tall, taut, and poised, she had the most beautiful complexion I'd ever seen, darker than my natural skin and smooth as polished obsidian, and she tended to wear her hair in complicated styles composed of many tiny braids. But though she carried herself with quiet confidence, Yolanda's eyes were kind, and she treated me more like a younger sister than an ignorant child. When I told her that Mama intended to present me in the open, she brought me the forged documents I'd need: a birth certificate from Florida, a fingerprint card to match, and incomplete transcripts from three schools. "You were mostly homeschooled," she explained as she walked me through my cover story, "and no one taught you much. This is just a paper trail to establish your presence at a few points—and since you never stayed more than a few months at any school, it's natural that no one remembers you." She added a few medical records to the pile, more proof that I'd come from rural Florida. As for my impossible accent, we worked out that I'd grown up in a little-known cult with an international membership, and many of my caretakers hadn't been natives to the region. It wasn't a great excuse, but we had no better ideas.

Even though I had documents detailing my fabricated childhood, however, the people of Pauline didn't believe me, nor did they look with favor upon my continued presence in town.

And then Max Grady disappeared.

On September 20, Max, age seven, was sent out to play in his backyard, which abutted a stretch of woods. He knew he wasn't supposed to leave the yard—his tearful parents repeated that often when they appeared on television—but when his mother stepped outside to call him in for lunch, Max was gone. People were frantic, not only for the little boy, but also because the story sounded eerily familiar to Mama's.

October came and went without any trace of Max. The Gradys appeared on television less frequently, but I saw them at church, hunched into each other and sitting silently through the singing. I never spoke to them, nor did Mama, which seemed to be the attitude that most of Pauline took. No one knew what to say to offer comfort to people who'd lost their only child. By then, the common thought was that the boy was dead, though I never heard anyone utter such sentiments around his parents.

In early November, seven weeks after Max's disappearance, I woke before dawn to find Flora standing by my bed. "You're needed," she said, and stepped aside, giving me a glimpse of the spirit hiding behind her in the glow of my nightlight.

I knew him instantly from the posters around town. "Howdy, Max," I whispered, hoping not to wake Mama. The springs squealed as I sat up and threw off the blankets, and he ducked behind Flora again. Even if his face hadn't betrayed him, the way that he clung to her hand told me all I needed to know about his fear. "It's okay," I said, showing him my empty palms. "I look a little funny, don't I?"

He nodded, his brown eyes wide and staring.

"Don't be scared. I'm Hope. What can I do for you?"

Max looked up at Flora for help. Though she couldn't have understood my question, it didn't seem to matter. "He wants his parents to find him," Flora told me. "If he led us to his body, could you show them the way?"

Of course, I replied. I rose, slipped on a jacket and shoes, and put my phone in my pocket. Carefully avoiding the creaking center of the staircase, I sneaked out of the house and into the cold darkness. "Take me there," I said to Max. "Is it far?"

"Kind of." He nibbled his lip, then mumbled, "I'm sorry."

I dropped to one knee in the frosty grass, the better to see him. "You don't have to apologize," I murmured. "I'll do what I can for you, I promise."

Ever so faintly, Max smiled, then pointed toward the trees.

Mama's house sat at the center of what had once been a large ranch, now subdivided into smaller farms and residential plots. Properties were separated by stands of trees that cropped up along the banks of a meandering stream, which flowed into a larger creek about a mile away from the house. The area around the creek was more heavily wooded, the sort of place in which a small child might get lost. As I tramped across the winter-brown fields, my hands tucked into my armpits for warmth, Max admitted that the lure of the woods was partly the cause of his disappearance. "There was a deer," he explained, easily keeping pace with me and my soaked-through shoes. "A little one. It was at the creek behind my house. And I *almost* touched it, but it ran off, and I followed it."

"All the way out here?" I asked through chattering teeth. Mama had pointed out the Grady home when we'd driven to the grocery store, and it was several miles from us—a long trek for a little boy.

"No. I got a few houses down from mine, and I climbed on some rocks in the creek to follow the deer—it was on the other side, see? And I fell off the rocks and hit my head hard, and I..."

His voice faltered, and I wished I could have put a reassuring arm around his thin shoulders. "You fell in the water?" I prompted.

He nodded. "Except I landed facedown, and I drowned before I woke up."

"So why are we going this way? The creek's current isn't that strong."

Max seemed to shrink into himself, and I looked to Flora, who'd walked along in silence as Max and I chatted. When I repeated the question for her, she grimaced in reply. "Scavengers," she said softly. "They ate part. What's left was carried here for storage, I suppose." Glancing down, she patted Max's back and pulled him closer to her.

"I'm sorry," he said again.

"It's not your fault," I replied. "Accidents happen."

"Not about that. Um..." He studied me through his reddish-brown bangs. "Do you get, like, queasy with gross stuff?"

What little was left of the corpse definitely qualified as "gross." Careful not to touch Max's picked-over remains, I quickly concocted a story that would take me from my bed to the cold November woods, and then, at Max's suggestion, I called the police.

Fifteen minutes later, I stood by the creek in little more than my nightclothes, answering questions from a green-faced young officer. By the time the body parts were photographed and collected into a black bag, the officer's older partner had been considerate enough to offer me a foil blanket from the trunk of their car. I rode back to town with them and gave a statement inside the police station, sipping bitter coffee from a white cup while I shivered in the interview room. Insomnia, I told them. I'd gone for a walk in the fields so as to avoid the narrow roads and any careless drivers out at that hour. I was looking for a path by the light of my phone when I saw Max's red tennis shoe and what remained of his lower left leg jutting from beneath a rock.

The officers let me call Mama, who, having woken to an empty house, was already in a panic, and she sped downtown to fetch me. A female officer escorted me into the lobby, then pulled Mama aside and murmured, "She saw something awful. May be a little shell-shocked. If you need recommendations for a counselor, let me know, okay?"

"Girl must be new in town," Mama muttered once we were safely in her car. "I know every therapist within fifty miles of here." She clutched the steering wheel and closed her eyes as she took several long, slow breaths, then said, "*Why*, baby?"

"Because Max asked me for help," I replied. "Would you have turned him away? He's just a child."

"And what if something had happened to you?" Mama countered. "What if they think you're involved? If they look too closely, if your papers don't check out—"

I clamped my hand on her shoulder as her words accelerated. "*Mama*. I'm fine. Let's go home, yes?"

We did so, though she barely let me out of her sight for the rest of the day, and she slept on the couch that night. I didn't know whether she was blocking my escape route or guarding me against intruders, but I gave her no cause for grief.

I was quickly dismissed as a person of interest in Max's death. There wasn't enough of him remaining intact for the coroner to reach a decision—it was plain that the body had been scavenged—but no one could find obvious signs of foul play. A tragic accident, people said, which was a simple version of the truth.

Still, in locating Max, I'd done nothing to endear myself to Pauline. I heard their minds in church and in town when they thought my attention was elsewhere: *Funny that she would find him. What isn't she saying?* While I didn't appreciate being silently accused of murder, I offered nothing to clear my name—nothing to draw further attention to myself. The only bright spot that fall was that I had a new partner at church: Max, who often sat beside me on the pew and chattered throughout the service. There was so much he couldn't tell me about his current existence, he explained, apologizing each time, but for now, he didn't want to be far from his grieving parents. Late that month, just after the Thanksgiving holiday, Max asked me if I'd be willing to talk to his mother. I told him I was in a delicate position, but if she ever wanted to speak with me, I'd do so.

Three days later, as I was unpacking a late crate of Christmas-themed mugs in the shop, the doorbell jangled, and Amber Grady slunk inside. I glanced up from the mound of bubble wrap, surprised at her appearance. She'd seemed to age after Max's death, but she looked positively haggard that morning, with bloodshot, sunken eyes, messy hair several days in want of washing, and unkempt clothing. Spotting me, she hurried to the counter where I was working, then planted her palms on the glass and stared into my eyes. "Are you a medium?" she whispered.

I blinked, giving myself a moment to think, then replied, "Why would you ask me that?"

"Because I've been dreaming of my baby for the last week, and every time, he tells me to talk to you. That's got to mean something."

We were alone in the store, Mama having gone down the street to get her hair done while I managed the place, and so I nodded and escorted Amber to the back. "Max has a message for you," I said, spotting him already waiting at the curtain separating the shop from the office. "Let me get you a glass of water, and—"

"Don't do what you did in Glastonbury," Flora interrupted, appearing beside Max. "I know what you're thinking. Don't do it."

Just a moment, I told her, then left Amber in a chair and

stepped into the kitchenette. *Why not?* I asked Flora, who'd followed me. *It would give her peace—*

"She's mundane," Flora protested. "And this isn't the sort of attention you need to be drawing to yourself."

I could swear her to secrecy.

"That's no guarantee. Besides," she said, gesturing toward me as I filled a glass at the tap, "you've not yet healed. Not fully. That's dangerous, Hope, you know it is."

Even still, I wavered until Flora cupped her hands around my chin, a feeling like a cool breeze against my face. "In a few months, if you must. But *I* can feel how weak you still are. Am I mistaken?"

She wasn't. The well I'd emptied in Glastonbury remained low, a chasm within me, and so I did the sensible thing and kept my more unusual ability to myself when I returned to Amber. Giving her the glass, I sat on the edge of Mama's desk and waited until she'd drunk half and was ready to listen to me. "As an initial matter," I said softly, "I had nothing to do with Max's death. Please believe me— I'd never do anything to hurt a child."

Amber sniffed. "Police cleared you, I thought."

"They did, but that doesn't mean the suspicion's gone away. I just want you to know that I didn't hurt your son. It was a true accident." I took a deep breath, glanced around the little office, then said, "He's standing by the door."

Her head whipped toward the opening, but she was blind to him, even as he waved at her. "You're not lying to me, are you?" she said, almost begging. "You're not saying this to make me feel better? I don't want a fantasy."

I swear it by my father's tower was on the tip of my tongue, but I corrected course. "You have my word that I'll give you the truth about Max, and nothing else." Turning to him, I said, "Just tell me what you want to tell your mama."

For half an hour, I sat between them, a mouthpiece for the little boy as he apologized to his mother and tried to reassure her. Amber was weeping by the end, but her features bore a new cast of serenity as she told him again and again how much they loved him. "Don't you stay here because of Daddy and me," she insisted, reaching toward the door as if she could hold him. "There's something better waiting for you, isn't there?"

"He says he can't answer that," I repeated for Max, "but he's smiling."

"Then you go, baby," said Amber. "You go on and be happy, and we'll see you again. Okay? Promise me you won't suffer just because we get a little sad sometimes."

"He promises," I said, watching as Max threw his arms around—and through—his mother. Amber stiffened as if shocked, and I explained, "He tried to hug you. It's difficult."

As her eyes filled afresh, Max said, "Tell her I'll be back to visit. I don't want her to be sad." I relayed the message, and he added, "Thank you. Could you tell her one last thing, please?"

Once he'd disappeared, I said to Amber, "Max says he loves you, and this is just goodbye for now. He's left us. Can I get you some more water?"

She wasn't thirsty. Instead, I spent the next few minutes holding Amber as she cried in my arms, drenching the shoulder of my new sweater and shaking as she sobbed. When she quieted, she hugged me in earnest, whispered, "Thank you, honey," and slipped out of the store, still wiping her eyes on her sleeves.

I didn't tell Mama what I'd done, hoping that I could use the time before word got back to her to come up with a better excuse for exhibiting my abilities. But to my surprise, Amber seemed to tell almost no one—I got a murmured "Thank you" the next Sunday morning from her husband, Phil, but no sudden line of visitors desperate to speak with their deceased loved ones.

"You're fortunate," said Flora when I broached the topic with her one day. She'd been keeping me company in the store while Mama ran errands, for which I was grateful. "There are two sorts of mundane people, you understand," she explained, leaning against the jewelry counter while I polished the tarnish from a tray of silver necklaces. "One type witnesses an event that is, for lack of a better term, paranormal, and simply must tell everyone he knows about it. The other type experiences it but remains silent for fear of ridicule. It seems that Amber is of the latter variety."

This suited me well, and to my knowledge, Mama never learned of what I'd done for Amber. She seemed puzzled that December when the Gradys delivered a large box of cookies to the shop, but though she gave me an odd look, she didn't ask, and I certainly didn't volunteer.

By spring, I was beginning to feel more like my old self— not yet as strong as I'd been, but less hollow than I'd felt since Glastonbury. Mama and I had fallen into a comfortable rhythm, I hadn't stumbled upon any additional corpses on my morning walks, and Pauline had accepted my presence, though I was largely ignored. I'd even managed to bring my dealings with the dead under control.

But one night in late March, after I'd spent my customary two hours taking messages from my spectral visitors, Flora brought a man to visit me and shooed the hangers-on from the room. I considered him as I turned to a fresh page in my notebook: average height for a human male, with slightly shaggy blond hair, large brown eyes, and bushy eyebrows that seemed to be stretching toward each other over his nose. He wasn't terribly old, perhaps Mama's age, and he wore a long-sleeved T-shirt and denim overalls, faded at the knees.

Hello, I told him, keeping the noise down so that Mama could sleep, and launched into my usual spiel. *I'm Hope, my skin really is violet, and I'm happy to pass a message on for you if you can give me any sort of address.*

He laughed quietly. "Done this a few times, have you, hon?"

Trying to streamline the process. What can I do for you?

Flora cut in before he could answer. "He wants much of you. I've kept him away this long, but you seem to be stronger now, and...well, it's your decision, child," she continued, glaring at the man, "but I'd advise you to be careful."

I quirked an eyebrow.

The man stepped closer and shoved his hands into his pockets. "Orson Connolly," he said. "Nice to finally meet you, Hope. I was wondering if there's any way you'd let me talk to my girls."

Recognizing the family component of his name, I felt my other eyebrow join its mate. *You're Kitty's father?*

He nodded. "And Beth's. You know, they've had one hell of a time with their mother, and I never got to have so much as a conversation with Beth, and Kitty thinks I loved her only because I didn't know I wasn't her biological father, and I..." He paused, grasping for words, then managed, "Please. Please, just two minutes with them, that's all I'm asking. I just want to tell my girls I love them. What you did last July—"

"Almost killed her," Flora cut in, arms folded. "You're asking her to put herself at unnecessary risk. Surely she could convey your message without manifestation."

Flora had a point, but this situation was more complicated. Kitty and I had a bond of camaraderie, and I wanted the best for her. As for Beth, I'd seen how awkward she'd been even in our brief interactions. A few minutes with their father couldn't hurt the situation.

Still, having taken Flora's advice for months, I was reluctant to disregard it so easily. *How long would you require?* I asked Orson.

"Only a few minutes. Would that...I mean, I know it's

hard for you, but could you…"

I looked to Flora, whose lips remained pressed in a tight line of disapproval, then back at Orson's anxious face. *Not tonight*, I told him. *Give me a few weeks.*

"Anything you need—"

You, actually, I interrupted. *Last time, I was unprepared and untested. If you want me to do this for you, then help me practice.*

Needless to say, Orson was more than willing to assist me. At night, after I'd spent an hour or so taking messages, I'd send everyone away but him and Flora, who watched Orson and me for the slightest sign of overexertion and was quick to tell us to end practice for the evening. While I appreciated her concern, I soon learned to judge my own strength. In Glastonbury, I'd been desperate and terrified, throwing my all into empowering an army with hardly a thought for my safety. Working with Orson, I learned to gauge exactly how much was needed to allow him to manifest, and we practiced in short bursts until I was confident that I could give him five minutes with his daughters.

In April, I called Kitty and told her that their father wanted to speak with them. She took me out to a remote island the next day, and while Flora superintended at my shoulder, I gave Orson the opportunity he craved. When I severed the connection, he wistfully watched as Kitty sank to the grass, crying, and Beth and Artur tried to console her. *She'll be okay*, I told him as I stood and tested my balance, weary but in control of myself. *Maybe another time.*

Orson perked, but Flora insisted, "Not today. She's given you a gift already—"

"And I'm so grateful," he interjected, nodding to me. "Thank you, I mean it."

My pleasure, I replied. To the others, I said, "I can bring him forth again another day, but I need to train more first."

The sisters didn't press me, but it was several minutes before Kitty could pick herself up and take me home. She hugged me on Mama's front porch, squeezing so hard that my ribs creaked, and when she released me, her face was wet again.

I crawled beneath the blankets that night, bone-weary and craving sleep. Flora settled onto the foot of my bed, keeping the few curious spirits in the house from intruding. "That was a very decent thing you did, child," she said as I snuggled down. "How much are you hurting?"

I'll live.

"That wasn't what I asked." She stood and glared at the door until a newcomer backed off. "You haven't fully healed. Every time you do that—"

I know.

Seating herself again, she sighed. "It is not your responsibility to deliver wonders and miracles, Hope."

But I can, I replied. *And doesn't that bear with it the responsibility to do so?*

"Only to a point. You do not owe your life for others' happiness."

I pulled the comforter to my chin and asked for the hundredth time, *What can I do for you?*

"Nothing tonight," said Flora, and left me to sleep.

Spring warmed to summer, the land began to broil, and in July, I awoke one morning to the realization that I'd spent a full year in Iroja. And what had I accomplished?

Yes, granted, I'd helped end a war with Nath and sent hundreds of messages on behalf of the dead, but otherwise, I was adrift—standing in the center of a vast plain, unsure of where to go or why I might choose to do so.

I'd considered moving out of Mama's house, as many people my age seemed to live apart from their parents, but

I failed to see the point. Working for Mama, I'd never asked for payment, and so I would have been unable to afford other accommodations. Besides, Mama would certainly have balked at the idea of sending me off into the world, far from her protective grasp.

While I was pleased to help Mama in the store, the exercise was unsatisfying. In Conota, I'd happily tended to Father's chinols—working with the animals was fulfilling, if a menial task for a highborn lady, and gave me ample opportunity to be out alone with my favorite mount. But Mama had no herds, and the Irojan animals I'd seen wouldn't tolerate my presence, much less my touch. Dogs growled, cats hissed and fled, and the rider of the lone police horse had learned to avoid me after his mount saw me and bolted in terror. Obviously, then, I couldn't work with herds in that realm, but what else was I to do? And if I were to apply for a position in town, would anyone hire me? To most, I was still the weird girl living with—and possibly preying on—crazy Hayleigh, not to be trusted.

I had no friends to speak of in Pauline. Mama loved me, and that was a wonderful thing, but others avoided me. Even the Gradys kept their distance. Yolanda was kind but always busy, and Kitty, though happy to chat, was frequently in the field with her team.

More and more, my thoughts drifted back to Arik, whose absence I felt most keenly. In my idle moments, I mulled over what might have happened, had I stayed in Conota and entered Warohn's household. He was a lord—surely he had occasion to go to Triple River. Perhaps he'd have taken me along, perhaps not. But even if I'd never left High Vale again, Arik would still have been in Triple River, reachable by a hard midnight ride down the mountains and into the caverns—a reunion I could envision, if not carry out. But now he was beyond even the swiftest chinol's reach, and the truth continued to impress itself upon me: I would never see him again. He would never know my feelings for him...but then, in light of what his father had done, perhaps that was the kindest fate.

My only real friend was Flora, and she remained a cipher. Flora never wished to discuss her life or why she had decided to help me. Though I continued to ask her if there was someone I might contact on her behalf, she always refused, giving me no answer firmer than, "Maybe later." But I didn't pry—I was just grateful to have someone, *anyone*, to talk to. I didn't know what I was doing with my life, but being able to express that sentiment to someone was a slight consolation.

And then came August.

I'd retired early one Sunday evening in the middle of the month, making my apologies to that night's crowd of spirits. Mama and I had spent the day repainting the store, and my arms were sore after a day with a paint roller in my hand. Shortly after midnight, however, Flora woke me from a deep sleep. "I'm sorry," she said as I grunted and squinted at the bedside clock. "This is an emergency. You're needed."

"Mama?" I mumbled.

"No. A man. He is on the other side of town, and I believe he's near death. Go to him, now."

Got a better idea, I replied, and reached for my phone. *I could call the emergency number. Is he near any landmark?*

"Not particularly. He found the streambed, but he's in a wooded area—"

I dialed 9.

"—and he's *purple*."

The phone fell from my hand onto the blankets. *Purple? You're certain?*

"I can't guarantee that he's cynaeli, but that was my impression. A young man. He's very weak…and he's not glamoured," she added with a slight grimace.

Nothing good could come of another cynaeli in

Pauline, particularly not one who hadn't disguised himself. *Take me to him*, I said, and reached for my shoes.

Flora stepped back while I dressed. "Do you intend to tell Hayleigh about this?"

I could well imagine what Mama's reaction would be to Flora's news. *Not unless I must*, I replied, and grabbed my phone again. *Let's go.*

CHAPTER 3

The area Flora described was several miles away, so I carried a few provisions in a bag slung over my chest: a water bottle, the phone for emergencies, and a flashlight for the times I strayed too close to civilization to safely enchant orbs to light my way. On Flora's suggestion, I threw in a box of bandages and hoped the cynaeli in the woods didn't require more intensive medical attention. While I was relatively skilled at healing magic, any enchantment took more effort in Iroja, and I'd only had a few hours of sleep.

I tiptoed out of the house, enchanting my steps into silence in case Mama was restless, and gingerly shut the door. There was no chance of taking my new bicycle from the garage; I'd only begun to learn to balance two weeks before, and a wobbly ride in the dark seemed like a recipe for abrasions or worse. Stuck on foot, I made the best of it and hurried off with Flora, taking the paved roads as much as I could and ducking into the weeds every time I heard a car near. I could hide myself relatively well with glamour, but there was no sense in taking chances, and I had no desire to answer questions about why I was going for a walk at one in the morning.

It took almost an hour to reach the far side of town, and then I left the roads for the scrubby fields, staying well clear of the cattle and hoping that the farmers weren't insomniacs. Finally, Flora guided me into the woods and down toward the stream, now running low with the summer drought. Throwing a white orb high above my head, I picked my way down the shallow watercourse, keeping an eye out for rocks and logs in my path...and then, around a bend, I saw him.

If he wasn't cynaeli, then he'd been the victim of an accident involving a vat of purple dye. While I couldn't make out details from a distance, I saw dark hair tied back and falling into the dirt, a sleeveless black shirt, and long trousers. Worryingly, his feet were bare. He appeared to be sleeping, curled up against the bank in what should have been the stream.

"That's him," said Flora.

Stay back, I cautioned. *I'll take a closer look.*

"Stay back? What can he do to me? I'm *dead*," she protested, but followed a few paces behind.

He showed no motion as we neared, and I began to wonder if he'd died while we were on the way before I saw the slight rise and fall of his breathing. Walking carefully so as not to disturb him, I crept closer, then lowered my orb until it brought the contours of his face into sharp relief.

I gasped and stepped away from him, and Flora slipped to the side before I could walk through her. "What is it?" she asked.

I know him, I replied, and took a deep breath to calm my hammering heart. Steeling myself, I drew near to him again, just to make sure.

Yes. I knew that face—or how it was supposed to look, rather. He was covered with a layer of grime, his lips were cracked, and one of his eyes appeared to have been blackened in the recent past, judging by the discoloration. His hair was matted and dirty, and his clothing was in ill repair, stained and fraying in patches. His filthy, bare feet were bloody in several places, but what concerned me most was his sunburn, which made his shoulders and cheeks appear almost rosy.

And about his neck, just above his collarbones, was a thick collar of black metal. Father, it seemed, had told me the truth.

Dropping my glamour, I crouched beside him, moved the orb out of his eyes, and gently shook him awake. "Arik. *Arik*," I murmured as his eyelids fluttered. "Wake up, you're—"

He bolted awake with a cry and rolled away from me, then saw my face and froze, his panic subsiding. "Hope?" he rasped. "Is that…"

I grasped his hand, and he gave it a weak squeeze.

"What are you doing here?" I demanded, pulling what was left of my water from my bag. "And drink this."

He sat up and greedily sucked down every drop, then handed it back to me with a little belch. "Hope…"

"How did you get here? Who sent you?"

"No one sent me," he replied, and let out a sound halfway between laughter and a sob of despair. "I fled. Two days ago. I…" He tried to stand, but his legs gave way before he could find his feet. "I tried to find you."

Part of me had feared a trap as soon as I'd laid eyes on him. I'd not seen another cynaeli in more than a year, after all, and I still feared that Father would try to drag me back. But my heart told me the truth my head wasn't ready to accept: this was *Arik*, who'd helped me tend to my father's chinols when I was left alone in the strange caverns of Triple River, who'd defended me from a pack of young lords set on making the visiting likdenfi's life difficult, who'd spirited me into his father's library and sent his favorite books home in my saddlebags, and who, with much embarrassed laughter, had taught me to kiss on my fifteenth birthday. Arik wouldn't hurt me—especially seeing as he couldn't quite stand and seemed to be on the verge of tears.

"What's happened?" I asked, helping him sit up against the bank. "And how did you know to look for me here?"

He winced as he moved. "Father sent a band of Hidden Ones after Fik."

"*What?* Why?"

"To kill him. I must warn him." He grasped my hand

again. "Have you seen him? They're going to find him, Hope, they're going to eat him alive…"

Hidden Ones. The though alone was enough to make my hair stand on end. If my tutors had been properly informed when they taught me about those fiends, then the creatures were tracking Arik's brother by the smell of his blood—and *nothing* had a better nose for blood than a Hidden One. They were the living embodiment of tenacity and hunger.

"I don't know where he is," I said, and Arik's face fell. "But I *do* know people who might be able to help. First, though, we have to get you out of here. You're a disaster."

"I—"

"Don't fight me." I pulled out my phone, braced myself for the lecture to come, and called Mama. "I'm sorry, and I'll explain once you get here," I told her as she groggily answered. "I need a ride."

Even off-roading, Mama could only drive her old Volvo to a point about five hundred feet from us, and she seemed none too pleased as she tramped through the grass toward the tree line. "Let me do the talking," I told Arik, then stepped out from the shadows to meet her, using my flashlight to guide her way.

As expected, Mama was peeved. "Do you have a death wish?" was her greeting. "These are farmers. They're *armed*. If someone hears you prowling out here, they're liable to shoot first."

"It's an emergency—"

"Oh? I don't see fire."

Biting my tongue to stop myself from snapping back at Mama, I led her into the woods toward Arik, who continued his attempts to stand in my absence and had managed to get one knee on the stream bank. She stopped in her tracks when my light hit him, and I heard her sharp intake of breath before she grabbed my shoulder and pulled me back. "What the *hell?*" she hissed in my ear.

"That's Arik. He's my friend," I replied, confident that he couldn't understand us. "I don't know everything that's happened to him, but he's in trouble, and he's very weak. Surely dehydrated—"

"No. No way."

"Mama—"

"If he's that weak, something will be along to finish him off—"

"*Mama!*" I cried, horrified.

She gripped my shoulders and shook her head. "I'm not going to risk losing you again, baby. If Enogi got wind of this—"

"He's of Triple River," I retorted. "Father isn't going to give a damn about him. And I am *not* leaving him out here. If you won't help me, I'll call someone who will, and I'll go with him."

Mama started to protest, but then she took a second look at Arik, and a strange, knowing expression crossed her face when she turned her eyes back to mine. "A friend, you say?"

"Yes."

"A *male* friend? From another settlement?"

I glared at her, impatient to be away. "Must I explain this further?"

"Oh, yes, little missy, you *will.* But I guess one night wouldn't hurt." Sighing, she pointed to Arik, who was trying to push himself upright with the aid of a stump. "We're going to have to drag him, aren't we?"

"Unfortunately," I replied, and marched off to help Arik.

As I'd moved into Mama's former guestroom, we helped Arik into my bed, which seemed a safer option than leaving him on the downstairs couch. In the light of the ceiling fan, Mama and I got a good look at Arik's injuries, and her mouth tightened as his dirty, bloodied feet shifted against the sheets. Before either of us could suggest scrubbing him clean, Arik groaned and closed his eyes. I pulled the blankets over him, and within two minutes, his face had relaxed into sleep.

Mama stood beside me at the edge of the bed, considering him with her arms folded, her sleep shirt muddied by our exertions. "Who is he?"

I flipped off the overhead light and turned on the dimmer bedside lamp in its place, but if Arik noticed, he gave no sign. "You know of Ketulm?"

She squinted in thought. "Yeah, he's over Triple River, right?"

"Exactly. Arik is one of his likdenfi."

Mama studied his bruised face for a brief moment. "Not one of his favorites, I take it."

"He's like me," I said quietly.

"*Ah.*" Her expression slightly softened. "His mother was sent home?"

"No. And I wouldn't ask him about her, if I were you."

"Something…happened?"

I said nothing at first, thinking over the things I'd seen and heard in Triple River, then murmured, "Ketulm likes inflicting pain."

Mama didn't press for details, for which I was grateful.

"We've been friends since I was ten," I continued. "He used to keep me company when Father and Ketulm met, and we were close, I suppose…"

My voice trailed off as Mama pulled the covers higher over Arik, then paused to trace her fingertips over his collar. "Is that what I think it is?" she murmured.

"Yes."

When she looked my way again, there was pity in her eyes, but whether it was for me or for Arik, I couldn't tell. "If he's a naffidar, we can't trust him," she said. "You know that."

"He told me he fled."

"Yeah, and maybe his master told him to say that. Funny that he'd find his way to you, huh? The gate I went through has been closed for decades."

The cautious, logical part of me knew that she was speaking the truth, but I refused to believe it. "Does he *look* like he was sent here to hurt me?" I countered. "He can barely stand."

"Could be an act."

My gaze lingered on his bruised face. "I'm not worth that much to Father. And Arik told me he's come to find his brother."

Her brow wrinkled. "There's another—"

"Not in town—I know Fikwed, and I haven't seen him. Arik said that their father's sent Hidden Ones after him."

Mama's jaw dropped. "*Here?*"

"I don't know. Arik's trying to find his brother before they do."

"Jesus," she whispered, then shook her head and turned to go. "I'm going to put coffee on. You want some eggs and toast?"

"Sure," I replied, and followed her into the hallway. While Mama went downstairs to cook, I wet a cloth from the linen closet, then returned to Arik and began to wash his exposed skin. He twitched at my touch, but a bit of enchantment deepened his sleep, and I cleaned his wounds until the cloth turned brown and red.

I did my best to keep Arik unconscious for much of the day, allowing him to wake enough to drink water every few hours before prodding him back into deep sleep. While I could numb some of his wounds, there was no substitute for rest in the healing process, and he desperately needed healing.

The black eye wasn't fresh—maybe a few days old, perhaps a week, but discolored enough to show that it wasn't a new injury. Many of the bruises on his limbs were similarly aged, though others seemed to have been acquired in the last days. More concerning to me were Arik's battered feet. Why he'd left Conota without shoes was as yet a mystery, but his feet weren't hardened enough to walk through the woods unshod. I washed and wrapped his cuts using a roll of gauze instead of adhesive bandages. And then there was his sunburn. The last two days in Pauline had been typical for August—hot, humid, and cloudless—and I'd suffered enough just stepping outside to get in the car and retrieve the mail. Arik had grown up not only beneath Conota's perpetually cloudy sky but also underground, and his tender skin had blistered in the merciless summer sun. I treated it with a combination of healing enchantment and my favorite aloe gel, which packed a heavy dose of lidocaine. While I couldn't put so much as a fingertip beneath his collar, I took care to apply gel thoroughly around the area. I could only imagine how uncomfortable the heavy, dark metal had to have been in the heat.

I kept Arik unconscious until eight that evening, then brought a plate of food upstairs and slowly woke him. When he first opened his eyes, he flailed at the blankets, disoriented and struggling to escape, but I pressed his shoulders into the mattress and called his name until he focused on me. "You're safe," I soothed. "This is my mother's house. You're in Oklahoma, and you've slept all day. Feeling better?"

Arik sighed and stopped fighting. "Hope."

"Seriously, how are you feeling? I can try to strengthen the numbing enchantment, but everything's more difficult here."

He shifted in bed, winced, but nodded. "I'm all right. Thank you."

I helped him sit up against the wooden headboard, then handed him an oversized plastic cup of water and a straw. "Drink it all. You're probably still dehydrated," I said. "The weather of late has been unforgiving."

He took a long swig. "Is this typical?"

"For summer. You could have chosen a better time to visit."

Arik didn't even smile at my weak attempt at humor. "I had no choice. Fik's in danger. I...I've got to go—"

I stopped him before he could try to climb out of bed. "Go where, exactly? You're going to drink that and eat some dinner, and then you're going back to sleep."

He glared at me, flabbergasted. "My brother—"

"You can't help him if you can't stand on your own. Be reasonable. I'm trying to help *you*."

"And why does it matter how I feel if the Hidden Ones find Fik before I'm up and about?" he retorted.

"You can't save him tonight," I insisted, "and we'll deal with it in the morning. For now, build your strength."

Reluctantly, he finished drinking his water, and I helped him stumble to the bathroom down the hall. When he emerged and leaned on me for the return trip, he seemed resigned to his state. "Useless," he muttered, flopping back into bed. "The one time I'm needed, and I'm *useless*."

"Stop that. Eat." I sat him up again and presented him with a plate of Mama's baked chicken and mashed potatoes. He took a tentative taste, which was apparently sufficient to wake his hunger, as he shoveled the rest down without protestation. "Now," I said, pulling up my desk chair and handing Arik a napkin as he licked the last of the gravy off his fingers, "tell me what the hell is going on. Why is your father so desperate to kill Fik? What's Fik ever done to him besides leave?"

"It's not just Father. This is about Pimati."

"*Pimati*?" I frowned. "What does he have to do with Fik?"

"Everything," Arik muttered, then leaned against the headboard and closed his eyes. "You've heard no news from home in some time, I trust."

"None. What have I missed?"

"Quite a lot." When his blue eyes opened again, I saw

the weariness in his gaze. "There's a war coming. Father intends to win it."

"A war with whom? And why hasn't the new king—or queen?" I asked, cocking my head. "Who is it now?"

"That's the problem," said Arik with a mirthless smile. "No one knows."

To one with a firm understanding of Conotan politics, the oversight of Faerie seems unnecessarily complicated. Three courts coexisting through a pact with the consciousness of the realm, each with its own sovereign, none subject to the others, sounds like a disaster in the making. When one sovereign dies, his or her eldest surviving child takes the throne, which sets up another incentive for discord, at least among the highborn. The entire structure seems messy and fraught with the potential for war.

In Conota, the mechanics of power are simplified. While the various cynaeli and tennuwaya settlements have their ruling lords (and occasionally ladies, albeit almost always among the tennuwaya), ultimate authority is vested in a king or queen chosen by the realm, usually from among his children. While few ever witness the consciousness of Conota, an unknown number of women across the realm have, perhaps unwittingly, borne his sons and daughters. Those few who come to realize their child's paternity have stated that they had no knowledge of it at the time they became pregnant. In other words, the realm selects those he desires to bear his children, and the mothers have no say in the matter.

Of course, it's likely that many women so impregnated never learn that their children are anything but the presumed father's. It's unknown how many children Conota has sired, though most who consider the question assume that at least a few are of age at any time, just in case an heir is needed. Those who aren't elevated go through life unacknowledged by their true father—which, at least in the cynaeli context, is best all around, particularly for any of Conota's children born to highborn presumed fathers. Titles and lands almost always pass in a patrilineal fashion, and a father who learned that his son was actually the realm's would surely disown him, if not worse. Anyone who suspected that he was one of Conota's line wisely kept silent, though the question of paternity offered perennial food for gossips.

Typically, when the king or queen dies, the realm immediately bestows additional power on the successor, giving him or her the strength necessary to rule the land and control the highborn. The one great exception to this was Mab, known in some accounts simply as "the Invader." More than a thousand years before my birth, one of Faerie's three sovereigns somehow forged an alliance with Conota, and when she and her court were cast out of her realm, Conota welcomed them into ours. The reason for their alliance remained unknown to cynaeli chroniclers, though speculation abounded. Mab was attractive by faerie standards, and some postulated that Conota was taken with her beauty. Others hypothesized that the two had plotted to overthrow Conota's counterpart in Faerie and somehow consolidate the realms. Whatever the cause, Mab was in our realm for a mere three days before the then-king was murdered in his bed, and Conota made Mab queen in his place. While she was technically powerless, faeries being unable to use our sort of magic, Conota made one of his rare manifestations to the highborn who had come to oust her and swore instant death to any who failed to give Mab the honor and respect due to their queen. The threat worked, and Mab ruled the realm for a millennium. During that time, she gave birth to the only child Conota ever acknowledged prior to elevation: Geheret, who was made king upon his mother's death. The succession had come as a surprise to no one. But Geheret's father seemed less concerned with him than he was with Mab, and Geheret's reign lasted only a few months before his half sister, Nath, came to power and ousted all faeries from the realm.

Nath died in Glastonbury after a forty-five-year reign, presumably killed by her own scintol. That was the last news I'd heard from my homeland, though I'd assumed a successor would have been chosen once the queen's body was returned to the realm. But as Arik made clear, the realm had been uncharacteristically silent in the wake of Nath's death.

"People think that one of three things has happened," he explained, rubbing more aloe into his burned arms. "The realm has no qualified children available, the heir has chosen not to make himself known for some reason—"

"Understandable," I muttered.

"True. Or else, the heir is outside the realm. Maybe he doesn't want the throne, or maybe he's unaware of his elevation. Then again, perhaps he's making plans to return with an army."

I saw where Arik's logic was leading. "You think Fik…"

"He doesn't even look cynaeli. And he's been away for five years. The pieces fit, don't they?"

The supposition made sense to me. Of all the half-human likdenfi I'd met, Fikwed looked the least like his father. Most of us took after our cynaeli side in terms of coloration—purplish skin, black hair, blue eyes—and had some skill with magic. Other characteristics varied. Some of us were tall by cynaeli standards, and it wasn't uncommon to find half-breeds with five digits instead of the usual four. And then there was Fik, whose mother had been as dark-skinned as Yolanda, to hear the rumors. If Fik had any purple in his complexion, it was hidden in the nearly pure black. His hair was different, too, thick and kinky instead of the common straight to wavy, and it puffed around his head unless he wore it tied tightly back. He had five-fingered hands, broader than average facial features, and stood taller even than Arik. Indeed, the only obvious sign of his cynaeli blood was his eyes, large and blue-green as the glacial lakes I'd seen on television. It was a rare hue by cynaeli standards, and when combined with his other exotic traits...well, let's just say that when Fik fled the realm, I overheard more than one young woman lament the loss.

"It's...possible," I conceded. "But does your father have any firm proof?"

Arik shook his head. "This has nothing to do with proof and everything to do with Pimati."

"I'm sorry, I don't follow..."

He squirted another palmful of gel from the bottle and carefully rubbed his shoulder. "There's been talk that perhaps the realm will never choose another king—maybe Conota has simply tired of us all. No one knows anything with certainty. But word from the south is that the tennuwaya are restless, skirmishing among themselves for primacy. Our people are on the verge of following their lead."

I cringed. "The Three-Clan War."

"All over again," he agreed. "High Vale will rally around Enogi—he's held power for nearly two hundred years, after all, and everything I've heard suggests that he has the lords' support."

"As far as I know."

"Then of the three prominent subterranean settlements, the lords of the Fangs will band together."

I nodded. The Fangs was a system of smallish caverns connected by narrow passages. Between them and the larger Triple River settlement were several caves filled with glittering quartz crystals larger than a man—and those that nature hadn't grown to points had been filed that way as a defense mechanism. The people who lived beyond the quartz caves were clannish on a good day.

"Triple River will also stand alone, naturally," Arik continued. "Which leaves Old Mother. Considering the trade between them and us, it's likely that they'd join with Triple River in the event of another war. There's too much common blood between us to expect anything less."

I'd only seen Old Mother twice, so named for the massive rock formation at its border that resembled a woman with a hundred smaller "children" at its feet. Nothing spectacular had come from Old Mother in my lifetime, either in terms of magical talent or martial prowess. Indeed, Father seldom bothered to visit its paramount lord, a young man of barely sixty years.

"Ketulm may conquer the Fangs with Old Mother's help," I said, "but if he thinks he has a chance at High Vale, he's a fool."

"Not if he can lure High Vale to the plain, but that's not Father's first concern," Arik replied. "He wants to position himself as the paramount lord within all of Heluweya, and he doesn't have the bloodline. Some of the other highborn have become more vocal about that of late."

I frowned, bemused. "Your father…"

"The lordship passed through Lady Mirink—Father's *wife*," he explained. "Her father was the last paramount lord, and she was his only child. He accepted Father as his heir when Father married Mirink. And two years later, once the other lords had grown accustomed to Father, Mirink's father died during a rather suspicious cave-in. I can't begin to imagine how that happened," he added, his voice dripping with sarcasm. "Father took over for him, ruling in Mirink's right. Now, he's taken numerous concubines—if I've counted correctly, I'm his forty-third likdenfi. But Mirink's only child in all that time has been Pimati."

I nodded in understanding. "So Pimati's the proper heir to Triple River. But what's the problem? It's not as if your father would have given the title to one of his likdenfi…right?"

Arik shrugged. "Father can be unpredictable when he's

crossed. Pimati hasn't always been as pliant as he'd prefer—they have too much in common. And he's only two years older than me, you know," he added. "The eldest of our siblings could easily have sired or birthed him. But Mirink still has the support of many of the lower lords who followed her father, and Father would be *very* unwise to upset them. She wants to be certain that her son will inherit, should something happen to Father." He switched the gel to his other hand and grunted as he touched his burned shoulder. "Which means taking precautions where his other sons are concerned. There were only four older than Pimati—Father has overwhelmingly sired daughters."

The question on my mind seemed crass, but it slipped out before I could stop it. "Naffidars?"

To my relief, Arik didn't seem insulted. "No. The eldest three were married off to ladies in Old Mother decades ago, and Fik escaped. I think he saw it coming," he murmured. "Fik's four years older than Pimati, bigger, stronger, better liked. He could have been a threat." Touching his collar self-consciously, he muttered, "I should have been so wise."

I tried to change the subject. "Fik's been gone for five years, yes? Why would he go back? He probably doesn't even know that Nath is dead."

"Unless he does, he has a king's power, and he's building an army."

"If he were," I countered, "the Fringe would surely know about it."

Arik frowned. "The what?"

"Oh, uh…low-level adepts here, I'll explain later. They would have told me *something*."

"Perhaps. But regardless of whether there's proof, paranoia is a powerful thing, is it not? Particularly when you consider how Father advanced in the first place." He put the aloe on the bedside table and shifted to better face me. "Father wants to be the paramount lord of all of us, not just Triple River. If Conota refuses to name a king, then Father will go to war and take power by force. Naturally, he has Pimati's full support."

"Well, if Pimati stands to inherit…"

"Exactly. Neither of them wants any surprises from heirs in the wings, so that's why Father's trying to kill Fik."

"But what if he's not Conota's son?" I asked. "What if his mother got pregnant in Iroja before she was taken?"

Arik shook his head. "Fik's mother was fourteen when she was taken, and she didn't give birth to him for four years. He's either Father's son or the realm's. And since he can only be a threat, Father struck a bargain with the Hidden Ones."

The thought of dealing with them made my skin crawl. "Are you *certain*? That seems drastic."

"Positive," he said bitterly. "Pimati told me all about it. I'm his naffidar, you see. Father gave me to him. Pimati knows how close Fik and I were."

"*Asshole*," I muttered.

Arik might not have known the term, but he seemed to divine my sentiment. "Pimati almost laughed when he told me, he was so giddy. Father sought out a band of Hidden Ones in the far north, and he promised them territory and tribute when he seizes all of Heluweya." Grimacing, he added, "And as a token of his faith, he gave them his newest concubine. She was younger than we are."

I knew damn well why he spoke of her in the past tense. If Ketulm had given a concubine to the Hidden Ones, it wasn't as a bed warmer, but rather as a meal.

Even with my discomfort over *that* fact, however, another disturbing notion came to mind. "So…Pimati sent you, then?" I asked, trying to sound casual in the enquiry.

He vigorously shook his head. "No, I swear it. Pimati didn't give me leave, and with any luck, he has no idea where I've gone." My disbelief must have manifested in my expression, as Arik grabbed my hand. "You *cannot* think that I would hurt Fik, Hope. Please tell me that your opinion of me is higher than that."

I didn't want to, but I heard myself say, "You just told me you're Pimati's naffidar."

He ripped back the blankets, revealing his scabbed-over feet. "If I were here on Pimati's business, I'd at least have shoes. I spent two days walking through this wasteland barefoot because the only shoes he allows me are covered in little bells, and it's difficult to sneak out if your steps jingle." His grip on my hand tightened almost to the point of pain. "I crossed the debris field around Father's hall after the lanterns were dimmed and went to my sister Kurane. She's High Mother of the Mysteries now."

Few in my home settlement kept to the old faith, which offered prayers and rites to the unseen forces of the deep darkness. Asking the silent divinity to still the mountains and prevent cave-ins was a much more practical concern for those who dwelt within Heluweya instead of between its peaks. But even we heathens knew that the senior acolytes of the Mysteries were chosen less for their piety and more for their talent with magic, and a high mother or father was not an enemy to be sought.

"She helped you escape?" I asked.

"Made a gate for me within the temple and erased my bloody footprints leading to their door," he replied. "She would have given me shoes had the High Father's insomnia not flared. I barely got across in time. That's why I didn't come directly to you—she targeted you as well as she could, but I had to go before she could perfect the direction."

"How did she find me? There hasn't been a natural gate here in years."

Arik smiled, then reached beneath his shirt and pulled out a small cloth bag tied with string. When he opened it, I found a molar in the middle of his palm, the roots reddish-brown with old blood. "Your father had come to treat with mine," he said, "and you bit into one of the sticky balls we stole from the kitchen—"

"You kept my *tooth*?" I interrupted, incredulous.

"I kept it safe. You left it in my bathroom while you rinsed out the blood. I didn't want it to fall into the wrong hands, so I hid it for you." His face, burned as it was, still evidenced the discoloration of a blush. "You know what a powerful piece of you a tooth is. I mean, Kurane used it to track you—I didn't want any harm to come to you."

"Your father has a sample of Fik's blood, I take it."

Arik nodded. "But only a trace. When he fled, he went out his window in the night. The rock around the outside of his room is jagged, and he must have cut himself in the climb down. Father found the dried blood and preserved it. Only a few drops, but I suppose that's enough for the Hidden Ones." He glanced over my shoulder at Flora, who leaned against the wall, watching us with her arms folded. *Thank you*, he told her. *If you hadn't found me, I don't know how long it would have taken to reach Hope.*

Her head bobbed in acknowledgement.

Do you know where I might find my brother? He looks rather Irojan…

Flora cut her eyes to me for assistance. *Human*, I explained. *Like Yolanda, you know?*

"Ah," she replied, and turned back to Arik. "No, I have no idea where he might be. But speaking of Yolanda, that wouldn't be a bad beginning point."

She's a leader in the Fringe, I told Arik, shifting our conversation so that Flora could understand. *They know all the strange happenings in this realm. If Fik has surfaced, they might know where to find him.*

"Or there's the Arcanum," Flora offered.

I made a face. *It would probably be simpler to go through Yolanda. My sense of the Arcanum is that they're likely to be difficult if they learned of more cynaeli hiding in this realm.*

"You're probably correct, but what resources do they possess that the Fringe lacks? What about blood magic? Could someone find Arik's brother using him as a guide?" I gave her an odd look, and Flora held out her empty hands. "I'm no wizard. This is only a guess."

Noticing the readout on Mama's old clock radio, I said, *We can work on this in the morning. I'm tired, and Arik...do you want to bathe?*

He accepted the offer, and I helped him to the bathroom and explained the tap. I changed the soiled sheets, then led him back to bed once he was cleaner and damp. He collapsed into the fresh bedding, still wearing his dirty clothes, and I dimmed the lights. "I'll be downstairs," I told him, and took my leave.

As I made up a bed on the couch, Flora said, "If I were you, I would call on Kitty. Of all the Arcanum, surely her people would be least likely to panic at an occurrence out of the ordinary."

You're probably right. I checked the time and slid beneath the borrowed quilt. *But it's rather early in Glastonbury. I'll call her in the morning.*

"And I'll watch *him* tonight," she offered as I closed my eyes. "Sleep, child. Tomorrow may be a long day."

In retrospect, I wonder if Flora, mundane as she had been in life, developed a touch of prescience in death.

CHAPTER 4

I woke at six to the clattering of pans. Unwinding myself from my cocoon, I shuffled next door to the kitchen to find Mama pulling eggs and a package of shredded cheese from the refrigerator. From the sound and smell of it, the coffeemaker was already well into its brew cycle. "Hi," I said, rubbing my face. "You're up early."

"Didn't get much sleep." She took a mug from the cabinet and glanced my way, revealing puffy eyes. "You want some?"

I nodded, and Mama prepared my mug with extra sweetener. "I see he's still upstairs," she said, pouring milk into her coffee.

"We had a long talk last night."

"Yeah, I heard bits through the wall when I came up to bed." She passed me my mug, then turned her attention to the hot frying pan. "Weird to hear that language again."

A flash of guilt sent heat up the back of my neck. "I'm sorry, he doesn't speak any English, as far as I know…"

"Mm." She cracked four eggs into the pan and stepped back as they began to spit and sizzle. "You planning to stay purple all day?"

My flush intensified. "Sorry," I repeated, "I was trying not to scare him—"

"It's all right, baby, just, uh…stay away from the windows until you get your glamour back on, okay?"

Her tone held a forced lightness that told me all too well how Mama was feeling that morning. "I won't let anyone else see me," I assured her. "If it's fine by you, I'm going to stay home again today. I need to make some calls, see if we can't find Arik's brother—"

"There's no 'we' in this," Mama interrupted, her back tightening. She turned from the stove and leaned against the sink, regarding me with her arms tightly crossed. "He's leaving today. *Ah*," she snapped as I started to protest, "stop right there. No buts. This is dangerous, and we're not getting involved."

I struggled momentarily with a surge of anger and frustration, then managed to say, "He's my *friend*, Mama. More than that. And Fik was always kind to me. I can't sit back and do nothing."

"And *I* can't get involved in another war with Conota. You saw what happened the last time—"

"That was Nath's doing!"

"Nath and Enogi. This Arik of yours is from Triple River, right? You want to drag Ketulm into this, too? Lead him right to our front door?"

"They don't know where I am," I replied through gritted teeth.

"If *he* could do it," she countered, pointing to the ceiling, "then so could the rest of them. And I'm not taking that chance. He's out of here today."

I turned away from her for a few seconds, breathing deeply to control my temper, then said, "If I don't help him, his brother will die. The Hidden Ones are hunting him. We have to move quickly."

"And this is going to sound cold," said Mama, "but if it comes down to saving him or you, there's no question in my mind." She flipped the eggs while I stewed behind her. "Let's get some breakfast," she said too calmly, "and then you can wake your friend and send him on his way. I wish him luck, but we're not getting dragged into another mess with that goddamned place." She glanced back, saw my expression, and shook her head. "*No*, Hope. That's final. Bring me a plate."

I did as she bid, though I wanted nothing more than to

smash it on the tile floor.

Mama took the eggs off the stove and dropped bread into the toaster. "I'm going to go to work. You're welcome to stay home today. I'll check in on you at lunch—we can have that chicken salad you like from the café, okay? On the good croissants. How about that?"

"Fine," I muttered.

"Okay. I'll pick us up some platters to go. And when I get home for lunch, I want him gone. Is that clear?"

"Yes, Mama."

She dropped the pan into the sink, then turned and hugged me, even though I stiffened in her embrace. "I love you, baby," she murmured, holding me tightly. "I'd do anything for you. And I *will* keep you safe, if it's the last thing I do." Releasing me, she cocked her head toward the fridge. "Get out the butter and jelly, will you?"

As Mama's car pulled away down the private drive, I checked the clock. Nine a.m.—I had three hours, and time was running.

My breakfast sat in my gut like ballast as I found Kitty in my phone, dialed, and sent a prayer into the universe that she wasn't busy. Fate was with me, however, and she picked up on the second ring. "Hi, Hope!" she said, almost shouting. "How's it going?"

"Not well," I replied, leaning against the kitchen counter while Flora looked on with concern.

"Ooh. *How* not well?"

"Life and death."

"Shit," she muttered, then yelled away from the mouthpiece, "Hey, guys, shut up, I'm on the phone! Sorry," she said to me, "I'm up in the Alps with most of the Away Team, we just got in with a cache of books, and now every man in this fucking chalet has decided that the only logical next step is to have a yodeling contest off the balcony. *Boys*," she added with a sigh. A door closed behind her, and the background noise diminished. "Okay, sorry about that. Now, what the heck is going on?"

"In brief," I said, massaging my forehead, "my home realm is on the verge of a civil war, the man who might actually be king fled to this realm five years ago, his father has sent a pack of Hidden Ones to kill him before he decides to take the throne, his brother's come to me to save him, and Mama's given him three hours to get out of the house. I need your help."

"Whoa, slow down. Who's hidden?"

"Hidden Ones," I repeated. "That's how the translation sounds to me, anyway. They, uh..." I racked my brain, recalling snippets of nature documentaries and looking for an apt comparison. "Right. Do you know what locusts are?"

"Sure..."

"Well, imagine locusts, but bigger and carnivorous, and tracking one particular scent. Um...like bloodhounds, maybe? But smarter. Smaller. Look, it's hard to explain, but if they find this guy, they'll eat him alive."

"And he may be the next king of the Gray Lands?" said Kitty.

"That's our thought."

She whistled low.

"He's not like Nath," I added. "I knew Fik when I was a child, and he was nice enough. He's half human, anyway. Please, I don't know how to find him, I don't have that sort of skill with magic—"

"Okay, *breathe*," Kitty interrupted as my speech accelerated toward incomprehensibility. "I'm going to do what I can for you. Let me get these numbskulls in off the balcony, and we'll work something out. Have you called Maria?"

"No..."

"I'll handle it. And if I know the grand magus, she'll want to get involved, but she might have to do so quietly. How soon can you be ready to leave?"

Leave.

I couldn't do that to Mama, she'd be frantic…

And I couldn't let Arik go off to face the Hidden Ones alone. I mean, he didn't even speak English, and…

And it was *Arik*. Bruised, bloodied, and badly sunburned, but Arik all the same, and *oh*, I'd missed him.

"Half an hour," I told Kitty. "Let me wake the patient and put on real pants."

"The patient?"

"My friend Arik, the potential king's brother. He had a difficult time finding me."

"Okay. Keep your phone close—I'll update you as soon as I know something," she replied, and hung up.

I looked at Flora, who raised her eyebrows in query. *Kitty's going to find help*, I told her. *I need to pack.*

"I trust that your mother isn't to know about this," she said, following me toward the stairs.

You think she'd allow me to leave?

"No. I'll stand guard in case she returns early."

Arik was somewhat better after a night's rest, but he wasn't healing as quickly as I'd hoped, which I attributed to my imperfect skills and the inadequate magic of Iroja. Still, he didn't complain, and when I conveyed to him the situation, he rose on shaky legs and asked what he could do to assist me. I put him in the kitchen with a cup of coffee and toast, then tidied up after myself, stripping my bed and dumping my towels and linens in the laundry room before dressing and tossing a handful of shirts and shorts into one of Mama's old weekend bags. Arik regarded me with surprise when I joined him a few minutes later. "Don't be so scandalized—this is the fashion here," I said, gesturing toward my bare legs. "More comfortable in the heat, at least."

"And as for *that*?" he asked, pointing toward the kitchen window and the bright morning sunlight beyond the glass.

I threw a light cotton wrap over my bare shoulders. "Sunscreen, dark glasses, a hat as necessary, and occasional sleeves. You'll adjust." I hated to let him leave in his dirty clothes, but there was nothing in the house that would fit him, and I doubted we'd have time to wash what he had before departing. Instead, I gave him two pairs of the oversized fuzzy socks Mama had bought me for Christmas to keep my toes warm on cold nights. "Layer those," I said. "Let's keep your cuts padded."

An hour after I last spoke with Kitty, I'd begun to pace the kitchen, holding my phone and hoping she'd call. Suddenly, I heard the sound of tires on the old farm road that ran by our house, then the soft grinding of brakes. I ran to the front window, afraid that Mama had come home ahead of schedule. Instead, I saw a silvery vehicle slowly making the turn onto our driveway. An RV, I realized, having seen hundreds of advertisements for the local dealer—and from the size of it, an expensive model.

"Someone you know?" asked Flora, appearing beside me.

Not a clue.

I watched as the RV parked, and then the front passenger door opened, disgorging a slender blonde in short denim shorts and a bright pink T-shirt. She pushed her sunglasses atop her head and squinted at the house, and as I registered her face, relief surged through me. "Beth!" I cried, throwing open the front door. "Hello! Over here!"

Kitty's younger sister was only a teenager, but a wizard was a wizard, and I was in no mood to turn away help.

She spotted me and waved. "Hey! You know you're purple again?"

"I'll explain in a minute. Where's Kitty?"

"Switzerland," said a much deeper voice, and I looked back at the RV to see the driver, Frank, coming around the vehicle. "With almost everyone else. I stayed behind to write, and Artur stayed home to look after this little terror," he said, patting the top of Beth's head. She stuck her tongue out at him, but he paid no mind. Even transformed into human guise, Frank was massive, two heads taller than Beth, muscular, and albino pale. Having met the dragon in his true form, I found his altered appearance only mildly disconcerting.

Another woman climbed out of the RV behind Frank. Slightly shorter than Beth, with Kitty's pale blonde hair but arms taut and toned from long years of martial practice, Artur seemed almost normal in the others' company…if one overlooked the long scabbard belted over her leggings.

"I'm afraid the B-string is the best we can do in a hurry," Frank continued, coming up the front path. "But we have double-secret Arcanum permission to borrow the land yacht, so let's get on the road. You're packed?"

"Yeah. Let me get Arik," I said, and slipped back into the house. "We're leaving," I told him as I hurried into the kitchen, and then I pulled out the notepad Mama used for grocery lists and scribbled a brief note:

I'm sorry, but there are some fights I can't sit out. Forgive me for not saying goodbye in person. I'll call when I can, and I love you, Mama.

Arik made it to the RV on his own, shuffling down the walkway in my green socks, and Frank helped him aboard. I climbed in behind him, my heart racing, and waited while Frank took the wheel and started the engine. "Where are we heading?" I asked.

"Don't know yet," he replied. "I thought north would be as good a direction as any. And turn your phone off," he added, buckling his seatbelt. "Don't want to be tracked, eh?"

I powered down the phone and put it in my bag, hoping Mama wouldn't cry.

The RV was fitted with tinted windows, which blocked the worst of the morning glare and gave those of us inside a modicum of privacy from the other drivers. Still, once we were on the road, I restored my glamour. Sitting at the dinette across from me, Arik goggled at the change, but I just shrugged. "It's safer this way," I told him. "Iroja doesn't know what to do with purple people. You might want to create a glamour now and not worry about it when there are more important matters at hand."

"I can't," he said, and touched his collar. "This damned torture device prevents me from doing almost everything."

"Will you allow me, then?"

He nodded, and with critique from Artur, I quickly worked out a passable glamour for him. Arik stared at his newly beige hands with their extra digits, wiggling them as if making sure they were attached to his body. I found the experience strange—the Arik I knew wasn't supposed to be that odd color—but Artur deemed my work satisfactory. "Can he understand us?" she asked in English, her accent far different from Mama's but comprehensible after a few minutes' aural acclimatization. To be fair, the hours of BBC programming I'd watched over the last year helped me along.

"No," I replied as Arik looked on, puzzled and waiting for a translation. "Lord Valerius gave me Fae, and Kitty gave me English, but I've never attempted to pass a language to another..."

Artur considered the front of the RV—Frank at the wheel, Beth riding shotgun and playing with the music— and made a face. "I could do it, but it might not be elegant."

"That works." Turning to Arik, I explained, "Artur's going to give you the common tongue for this area. I've had it done to me twice, and it doesn't hurt."

Though he looked troubled, he braced himself, and Artur worked the quick enchantment. "How does that feel?" she asked as she stepped away.

"Strange," he began, then frowned. "Wait…"

"Give it a moment, let your brain catch up," I suggested. "And where should I put my things?" I asked Artur, pointing to the bag I'd dropped.

"There's storage in the rear," she replied. "Come with me, I'll give you the tour." She glanced at Arik, who was still scowling to himself as he tried to process the unfamiliar words, and smirked. "Maybe you should show him around later, hmm?"

Having never seen an RV from the inside, I was surprised and impressed by the accommodations. At the rear of the cabin was the master bedroom, nearly filled by a king-sized bed and lined with storage compartments for clothing and luggage. A pair of doors opened off the short hallway as one walked back toward the front. One revealed a bathroom, complete with modest shower. The other door wasn't supposed to be there, but as the vehicle was an Arcanum purchase, someone had magically retrofit it to include a second bedroom that existed in a sort of pocket space, seemingly nonexistent from the outside of the RV. "Same technique as our flat in Glastonbury," Artur explained, opening the door to reveal a pair of bunkbeds. "Albeit on a smaller scale."

"Why *does* the Arcanum have this?" I asked, running my fingertips over the wooden dresser.

"Toula was unclear on that point. From what I gather, someone with clout at Arc 1 enjoys the occasional road trip and managed to pull together reasons sufficient to have one purchased with organizational funds. But it's ours for the duration on Toula's orders. Come," she said, ushering me back into the corridor, "I'll show you the rest."

The next part of the cabin was a kitchenette, a tight space of chrome and white tile with a small sink, countertop hotplates, a microwave, a coffeemaker, a pressure cooker, and a tiny refrigerator. Across the aisle was the dinette, where Arik still sat, looking out the window at the rushing trees, and ahead, filling the rest of the cabin, were a couch and a pair of captain's chairs, which could swivel for a better view of the television mounted behind Beth's seat. "That's a futon," Artur explained, pointing to the couch. "A third bed, apparently. I've not tried it, but Frank says they're simple to assemble."

"I'll show you when we stop tonight," said Frank from the driver's seat.

"Since he's doing the most work, I think it's fair that he take first pick of the beds," Artur murmured. "I would assist him, but—"

"But Antony's been teaching her on a compact Ford," Frank interjected, "and she's not ready for something this large. Hell, *I'm* barely ready for something this large, so if you're of a spiritual bent, pray for good traffic and solid brakes."

"You know," said Beth, leaning toward him and smiling, "this would be a *great* opportunity for me to—"

"Absolutely *not*," he snapped. "If you didn't kill us all, Kitty would kill me."

"But I'm fifteen now," she wheedled. "That's, like, old enough for a learner's permit in the States."

"First, you don't have a learner's permit. Second, even if you did, you're not driving the bus. Artur's a responsible adult, and she's still on the baby sedan. You're ready for a bicycle."

"Jerk," she muttered.

"How am I a jerk for not wanting to die a fiery death when you drive us off a cliff?"

"You're not licensed, either!"

Frank pushed his sunglasses down his nose and gave her a brief red-eyed glare over the top. "I've been driving since I was seven. Longer than you've been alive. My record is spotless."

"But no license."

"The forgery in my wallet is excellent, *thank you*."

Artur rolled her eyes and led me back to the dinette, where I took a seat on the booth beside Arik. She pulled out a chair opposite us and steepled her fingers on the tabletop. "Right, then. Kitty gave us the quick version after Toula authorized this little jaunt. Officially, the Away Team has need of this vehicle, and the little fact that every member of the Team who's actually Arcanum is in the Alps hasn't made it into the report. Unofficially, Toula wants to help you, Frank and I aren't Arcanum—"

"And I'm still on summer break!" called Beth.

"And incorrigible," Frank added.

"The others will come in case of emergency, including Maria," Artur continued. "But for now, let's see what we can do about finding…who, exactly?"

Arik cleared his throat. "My brother. Who may be our next king."

"He might not know," I explained. "Or he might be in hiding to avoid it."

Artur made a face. "That's…understandable, really. And I was told that there are assassins hunting him?"

"Hidden Ones," I said quietly. Arik shuddered beside me.

"Hidden Ones?" she repeated. "Is that one of your organizations? A military group?"

"No, no," said Arik, "they're not cynaeli, they're Hidden Ones."

"A different race," I offered. "Like the jinoda or the kadalin…yes?"

She frowned, then leaned back to see the front of the cabin. "Beth, have you got your computer?"

"Yup."

"Fringe database. Look up these Hidden Ones."

After shuffling through her bag, Beth opened her computer, tapped her way into the Fringe's archives, then muttered to herself for a moment. "I got nada," she called back.

"Just call Kip," said Frank. "Sam's saved in my phone. He'll have the number."

Beth did as he requested, setting the phone to broadcast over the vehicle's sound system, and after a moment, I heard an unfamiliar male voice answer in Fae. "Hey, bud," said the speaker. "You need Ros?"

"Kip, actually," Frank replied in kind. "What's the number?"

"Sounds like you're driving. Why don't I just transfer you?"

"Appreciated."

A minute later, a different male voice—one that still left me feeling more than a little anxious—came on the line. "Frank?" he said bemusedly. "What can I do for you?"

"You're on speaker," said Frank, segueing back into English. "I'm here with Artur and Beth—"

"Oh, hey, folks."

"—and Hope, and a friend of hers," Frank finished.

Kip sounded stiffer that time. "Hi."

"We've got a little problem, and the database is useless," Frank continued, ignoring the sudden chill in Kip's voice. "Hope, get up here. Tell him what's going on."

I did as he asked, holding on to his chair for balance. "A pack of Hidden Ones is on the hunt in Iro—in the mortal realm. It seems they're unknown to the Fringe, and I'd presume the Arcanum."

"Hidden Ones?" Kip asked. "That's a translation, I take it."

"I mean, seeing how many people in this realm speak Cynaeli…"

He snorted. "What are we talking about? Describe them."

That gave me pause. "I, uh…look, the less they're spoken of, the better. I don't know if their hearing is as good as their sense of smell, but in case it's close—"

"About a foot tall? Look sort of like overgrown piq without the wings?"

"I've never seen a piq, but the size is right."

"*Fuck.*" He sighed, then said, "We call them the Little People. If they're hunting in that realm, that's bad. Very bad."

"What *are* they?" Artur asked, joining us at the front.

"Intelligent, carnivorous, and ravenous when traveling. Let me see if I can give you an idea...okay, uh, they're humanoid, but they top out around a foot tall. Larger than piq, but not by much. I think their coloration is mottled brown or gray, but I could be wrong—the only ones I've seen up close had been dead for a while. Could have been decomp. Relatively large eyes, relatively *enormous* teeth. When they bite down, the only way to get them off is to kill them. You know how you can use army ants as emergency staples? They've got a bite like that."

"Oh, joy," Frank muttered.

"I was taught—and correct me if I'm mistaken, Hope," said Kip—"that they're primarily subterranean. They can spend *seasons* in a cave."

"Hibernation," I explained. "They eat their fill on the surface, go back beneath the mountains, mate, and then sleep until the young are born. There's usually enough in their hibernation cavern to sustain the newborns until they're strong enough to run, but I remember hearing about a bad year when they ran out of food, then wiped out six homes in a steading on the edge of the Fangs."

"The which?" Kip asked.

"One of our settlements."

"Ah. Well, when they come up again, they're *hungry*," he continued. "My father told me about the time they ravaged one of our villages. They ate people, food stores, even buildings, leaving nothing but the ashes of the fires and some bones. Great bedtime story, that. I used to see them at a distance, but we'd abandon our home and run for higher ground if they got close."

"Seriously?" said Frank.

"You know, some of us can't just fly away from ground attacks. And before you get too smug, I stood on a hill and watched them eat an injured dragon. *Alive.* They were swarming, and he couldn't shake them off."

Frank shuddered and stared out at the road.

"Now, if you're looking for detailed biological information, I'm not your guy," said Kip. "But I *do* know that they can run long distances without stopping, and when they find food, they eat it all. Maybe even several times their body weight. Something has to fuel them."

"They can track a particular blood scent over great distances," I added. "There are stories of them being used in the past on targeted missions—"

"Foothold."

I turned to find Arik making his slow way to the front of the RV, clinging to the seats for balance. "Foothold," he repeated. "High Vale destroyed its competition, remember?"

The others gave me curious glances, and I nodded. "Far before my time, when my great-grandfather was paramount lord. A splinter group surfaced and established a settlement on the north side of Heluweya, where the mountains flatten again. Wide open prairie, ample space to farm and raise livestock. If they'd flourished, they would have overtaken High Vale—their resources were simply better."

"So why didn't you just move?" Beth asked.

"Because High Vale is defensible. Foothold was trickier. And so, my great-grandfather sought out and bargained with the Hidden Ones to destroy it. There are still stone ruins on the site," I said. "I rode down there many times, and we use some of their former territory as overflow farmland. But there were no survivors when Foothold was attacked. They came in the night." Thinking of walking the streets of the ruin, long overgrown with wild grasses, left me feeling slightly ill. "In High Vale, we received reports from below about the Hidden Ones' movement, whether they were still sleeping or were on the move, just in case. Foothold was too remote, since all the major caverns are in the south."

"Kip, how did you fight them off?" Artur asked.

"We didn't—we ran, then waited them out. There are hills to the northeast of the Kint Porda—nothing like the mountains where the cynaeli live, but more easily defended than the plains. We kept at least one hilltop ready at all times: stores of food cached underground, material to assemble shelters, water barrels, and plenty of wood. We'd take shelter inside a fire ditch, see," he explained. "A big ring dug out around the campsite. When we knew the Little People were coming, we'd go up, fill the ring with wood, soak it with fat and oil, and light it. It might take a few days, but they'd get hungry and go elsewhere eventually." He grunted. "And with that happy trip through my memories, may I ask how the hell the Little People got into your realm? Is there a new gate near their breeding caves?"

"No," said Arik, who steadied himself with one hand on my shoulder and the other on Artur's. "One of my brothers fled to this realm several years ago. He may be our missing king. My father wants him dead, and he bargained with a pack of...*them*. I believe they're tracking my brother here."

A noise of disgust came from the telephone. "What is the *matter* with you people?" Kip exclaimed. "He sent them against his own *son*?"

"The problem is that he might be Conota's son instead of Father's."

"Conota..."

"The realm," I offered. "Like Ros. He chooses our next king or queen."

"Not *ours*," Kip muttered. "Look, I'm sorry about your brother, uh..."

"Arik."

"Arik. Really, I am. That's one hell of a problem to be running toward him. If you can contact him, I'd suggest telling him to evacuate to Faerie. Ros would probably understand. If he won't go...I mean, he should know better than to try to hide underground, and I have it on good knowledge that the little demons can swim, so an island's no protection."

"And then there's the other problem," said Artur. "Assuming we find and evacuate the target, how do we drive these things back to the Gray Lands?"

"You don't," he said. "Maybe one of the cynaeli with you knows how to talk to them—maybe you can bargain them back. But given my druthers, you'd eradicate them. They're a plague."

With that sobering information, I helped Arik to a chair as Frank ended the call. "Who was that?" Arik asked me, wincing as he settled in.

"He's called Kip. Lives in Faerie."

"Huh. Tennuwaya?"

"Nikot."

"*Nikot?*" His eyes practically bulged, and his jaw hung slack for a few seconds. "*That* was a nikot?"

"They call themselves kadalin," I said quietly.

"They have actual language?"

"You sound surprised," said Artur, rejoining us. She sat and gave Arik an appraising look. "Ah, but that's right—your people hunt them, do you not?"

He started to flush as he sputtered. "I...I didn't know..."

"I've learned a lot in the last year," I said, cutting off his protestations. "They don't have any talent with magic, but they're as intelligent as we are. Kip's not exactly fond of me, but that call was a great improvement over our first meeting."

As Arik continued to search for a rejoinder, Artur took her computer from the side table and began to read.

"Perhaps you should rest," she said, glancing at him over the screen. "You look awful. And what did you do, run naked in the sun for a week?"

"Come on," I said, and hoisted Arik to his feet. "I put the aloe in my bag."

"Bunkroom," Artur ordered as we headed for the back. "Save the bed for Frank. And wait, Arik, do you intend to go about in socks all day, or have you got shoes?"

As it turned out, Frank declined the offer of the largest bed, opting instead for the futon. Beth and Artur agreed to share the bed instead, leaving Arik and me with the bunkroom. We worked out the arrangements once we stopped for the evening at a dilapidated RV park in central Kansas, having made a westerly turn midday and pushed aimlessly across the prairie. The park was, to be generous, grungy, but we didn't need much in the way of services. The vehicle's magical enhancements weren't limited to its second bedroom: the fuel and water tanks remained full, the chemical toilet remained clean, and the electricity never sputtered, though Frank pointed out the backup solar panels on the roof in case of disaster. The RV's champion, it so happened, was one of the Arcanum's few so-called technomages, wizards with the patience to force spellcraft and electronics to work in tandem. In truth, we could have parked on the side of the road and been quite comfortable, but Frank insisted that we find a proper site and at least go through the motions of hooking the vehicle up for the evening. "No sense in drawing suspicion, is there?" he said, connecting the water line as I held a laminated sheet of instructions for him.

There was also nothing to be gained by all of us going down the road to the little hamburger restaurant together. Considering our variety of accents, Beth's relative youth, and Frank's striking physique, we made an odd assortment, memorable for all the wrong reasons. Claiming that he was in desperate need of a walk, Frank offered to make the dinner run, leaving the rest of us to take turns stretching our legs in the dark parking lot.

Still weak even after sleeping for most of the day, Arik did his best to stay out of the way as Beth and I set the table with the surprisingly nice china we'd found in the kitchen cupboard, while Artur examined the beers on offer in the refrigerator. I caught Beth giving Arik worried looks as we worked. His reticence was unsurprising—it was his brother in danger, after all, and the only thing we'd managed that day was to put distance between ourselves and Pauline—but his continued fatigue worried me more than I let on. True, my healing work wasn't perfect in Iroja, but it should have done more for him, especially with the amount of sleep he'd had. I patted Beth's shoulder and gave her my best impression of a reassuring smile, and she, in turn, tried to reach out to Arik. Bringing him a glass of water, she said, "By the way, I like your necklace. *Neat* metalwork."

She turned away before she could see him cringe.

Beth soon stepped outside, and as Artur was busy hunting for glassware, I sat beside Arik and murmured in Cynaeli, "She doesn't understand. That was a legitimate attempt at a compliment." His eyes were doubtful, and I insisted, "I helped augment the Fringe's notes on us. There's nothing in there about *that*. Really, she was trying to be nice."

"She seems young," he mumbled.

"Fifteen, she said. Her older sister, Kitty, got me out of Conota," I explained, "and the other woman, Artur—you've heard of the Sleeper?"

"That's *her*?"

"Yeah. Also Kitty's sister. Beth is Arcanum, but she's underage, and something tells me she really shouldn't be on this jaunt. Artur is partly fae, I believe, but Kitty says that she's been staying with them and assisting with their group. They call themselves the Away Team."

He frowned. "Meaning?"

"From what I gather, they retrieve hidden magical objects, but they also seem to be called in for unusual assignments. Like this one, I suppose," I added with a slight smile.

"And the man? Irojan?"

"Who, Frank? No, he's a dragon. Ensorcelled, I mean, but—"

"What *have* you been doing in this realm?" Arik interrupted, staring at me in disbelief.

"Getting myself in trouble, more or less, but that's nothing new." I rose and offered him a hand. "Come outside with me. Fresh air will do you good."

I'd been too optimistic—if the evening air made a difference, I couldn't tell. Frank devoured six hamburgers and a small lake of ketchup, but Arik picked at his meal, claiming that he had little appetite. After dinner, I helped him down the short steps to a folding chair, where he sat with a beer on Frank's orders and stared spellbound at the sunset. Night still fell late in mid-August, and there were just enough scattered clouds to make the western sky glow pink and orange as the sun sank below the RV park's office. Arik remained outside late into the evening, watching the stars come out, and I left him in peace. It had been a long week for us both, and it was only Tuesday.

Inside the RV, the mood was quiet. Artur read on her computer, Beth retired to the bathroom for a long shower—and an offkey concert, for those of us outside—and Frank passed the evening sprawled on the folded-out futon, tapping at his phone. I assumed he was sending messages to someone, but he looked serious enough that I decided not to interrupt him with enquiries. As Beth emerged in a cloud of steam, Artur glanced up and motioned me away. "Take your turn and go to bed," she said. "I'll see that Arik comes inside eventually."

I brushed my teeth and climbed onto the top bunk, which was far more comfortable than it had any right to be. But sleep arrived reluctantly that night and lingered only for short periods. In fairness, I had much on my mind: Arik and Fik, but also the potential disaster Ketulm had precipitated by sending Hidden Ones into Iroja. And then there was the matter of Mama. My phone remained in my bag, powered down and silent, and I'd resisted the urge to check it. As much as I wanted to call her and try to put her mind at ease, I knew that doing so would be a mistake. I told myself that if she were truly worried, she could call Yolanda, who would know how to track me down. But that self-reassurance did nothing to quiet my mind, and I tossed and turned long after Artur had helped Arik into bed.

Around two the following morning, I gave up and crept out of the RV, hoping the cooler air would make me sleepy. I was leaning against the vehicle, considering the dark eastern sky above and the cracked asphalt beneath the security light, when I heard the door open and saw Artur descend, fully dressed and carrying a bottle of beer. "You, too, eh?" she murmured, closing the door behind her.

I nodded. "Is Beth that bad?"

"No, she's not a terrible bedmate. Sleeps like the dead," she replied, joining me. "But being in an unfamiliar place, with an enemy we don't fully understand that could be anywhere…" She swigged from the bottle. "Old habits. Old feelings. My instincts tell me to stand watch, even if this place is perfectly safe. Hence the beer."

"I'm sorry," I began, but she brushed off the apology.

"Not your fault. Ask Frank—I get like this every time we go into the field. The first night or two is the worst, and then I usually begin to relax." She drank again, then sighed. "My therapist says I may be like this for the rest of my life. Habits learned young and deeply engrained, you know…I can tell myself I'm safe, but I don't believe it."

"Would it help if we posted a watch? I'm awake—I

could go first, let you sleep."

But Artur shook her head. "Tried that, no difference, and besides, it's stupid to ask others to inconvenience themselves over my hang-ups. It's…" She paused, frowning at the night as she chose her words. "Command is a difficult thing to relinquish, you understand. This expedition of ours doesn't have a clear leader, and so part of me insists that it's my responsibility to keep everyone safe. I've seen what happens when I fail." She shrugged. "It's illogical, but it is what it is. And it's better for everyone that I be awake outside rather than screaming through another nightmare."

"You dream of Warohn's tower?" I asked.

"No. I don't remember anything about that tower—I was unconscious all the while I was in your realm." Artur drank deeply and stared at the sky for a long moment, then said, "I went into battle for the first time at twelve, and I spent most of the next thirteen years at war, either with Saxons or with things coming out of the Gray Lands. Thirteen years without peace, with the fate of *your* kingdom, *your* people on your shoulders…it shapes you, Hope, and not always for the best. I know on a factual level how long I was enchanted, but in *here*"—she tapped the neck of the bottle against her chest—"you know, it's been little more than a year. It's all still rather fresh. And when I last failed, a great many men died screaming. I hear them some nights in my sleep."

We stood in silence for a time, listening to the chirping insects in the field adjoining the RV park.

"Your friend," Artur began.

"Yes?"

"I saw how he reacted when Beth mentioned his necklace."

I hesitated, unsure of how much I should tell her, but I decided that as long as she and the others were putting themselves at risk for Arik and me, I owed them the truth. "That's because it's a collar."

"Symbolizing what?"

I sighed and stepped closer to her to keep my voice low. "Arik is a naffidar. Best not to discuss this around him."

"Very well. What's a naffidar?"

"It's…" I thought briefly, then said, "I don't have a direct translation, but I'll do my best. Among our people, a father has great authority over his children. For daughters, it largely means that he'll arrange their marriages or concubinages, unless they decide to become acolytes of the Mysteries…priestesses, you might say," I explained as her brow furrowed. "Even in High Vale, no father would attempt to force a daughter away from the temple. But sons can be more complicated. It's not so bad for the lowborn, but a highborn man, particularly someone like my father or Arik's, probably has many concubines, which in turn often means many sons. They're all highborn, naturally, but only one can inherit their father's lands and clout."

"The territory isn't split among them?"

"Seldom. A father might parcel off a small piece on his son's marriage or use land to secure a promising marriage for his daughter, but the main territories are kept intact. Anyway, considering how many sons a lord might sire, you see where there could be competition among them."

Artur nodded and drank her beer.

"Typically," I continued, "the sons born to a man's wife will inherit before the sons born to his concubines, but that's not guaranteed, especially if the likdenfi—the concubines' children—are older than the wife's. In that situation, if a lord wants to ensure that his favored son inherits without a challenge from his brothers or half brothers, he really only has two options. First, he can marry off his less favored sons and make a small inheritance part of the marriage agreement, which binds both families. If a son like that tried to seize more after his father's death, his wife's father would be honor-bound to stop him. A man whose word can't be trusted is no fit leader, you see."

"Agreed," said Artur.

"That's what my father has done thus far. I have three half brothers, and he favors the middle of them to be the next paramount lord. Both of the others have been given good marriages, and everyone seems satisfied. Or they were the last time I saw them," I amended. "To hear Arik speak of the situation now, I'm left to wonder."

"What is the other option?"

"Far less pleasant. Father doesn't like the practice, but others employ it." I folded my arms and raked my teeth over my lip as I tried to choose the most delicate phrasing. "You must understand that among my people, *sons* inherit. A daughter inherits only if she has no brothers, and then the lands are governed by her husband in her name."

"Yes…"

"So, if a lord has too many sons, particularly likdenfi sons…he can make naffidars of them." Artur regarded me blankly, and I muttered, "I think the term here is 'emasculation.'"

Her eyes widened, and she threw a quick gulp of beer down. "Are you serious?" she asked, wiping her mouth on the back of her hand. "*Everything?*"

I nodded. "Naffidars aren't considered male, so that's the son problem solved."

"And these fathers have no fear of angry eunuchs murdering them in their sleep?"

"I'm sure they would rise up against their fathers if not for the collars. Those etchings on Arik's aren't decorative. A collar like that dampens a naffidar's power to almost nothing, so he can't use magic to fight back. It's also marked with the name of the naffidar's master—"

"Wait—your fathers *enslave* their own sons?" she demanded.

"Occasionally. The common practice is for a man to bind his naffidars to him, but Arik's father gave him to his half brother, Pimati. That's part of the etching—it's the Cynaeli script. The other markings are power channels in the metal to hold the enchantment together. I think the collar gives the master power to really hurt his naffidars if they don't do as he says, so..." I glanced at the nearly empty bottle in Artur's hand and wished I had a beer, too. "Arik's brother ran to this realm about five years ago because he feared their father was about to go the naffidar route. Arik stayed, and...you see what happened. Please don't mention this to him," I said, looking her in the eye. "I don't want to shame him. But you see now why he was upset by Beth's comment."

"Of course, and you have my silence," said Artur. "But if you would, make clear to him that Beth meant no insult. It would wound her to know she'd hurt him." She finished the beer and rolled the bottle between her palms. "Beth has made much progress in the last year, but she's not whole. Her mother left scars that have yet to heal, and Beth is...brittle. Does that make sense?"

"Yes," I said, thinking of Mama.

"She's not even supposed to be with us out here—in the Arcanum's eyes, she's as yet a child. But I didn't want to leave her alone. Kitty and Marcus are together almost all the time these days, and Beth...well, she's felt somewhat left out, I believe. She's insecure. I'm attempting to change that, but it isn't a quick process."

I recalled Kitty's boyfriend, a dark-haired man, perhaps handsome to Irojan eyes, who had gently guided me through much of my first hours in Faerie while I camped at his father's house. Marcus and Kitty had been making up after an argument when I met him, and from my subsequent conversations with Kitty, I'd gathered that they'd only grown closer since I'd last seen them. If Beth needed time away from the couple, then I wasn't going to object.

"I'll make Arik aware," I assured Artur, and nodded toward the door. "Why don't you try to sleep? The beer should help, right?"

"We'll see." She hoisted her bottle in a brief salute, then returned to the RV and closed the door.

I waited until I was certain that she'd gone toward her bedroom, then thought, *I know you're there.*

A spirit passed through the wall of the RV and joined me outside. I remembered him from Glastonbury: a pale-faced man with deep wrinkles across his brow, shoulder-length gray hair, and a trim gray beard. He sported a beaten gold circlet—a crown of sorts, I supposed—but whereas I'd last seen him in armor, he came that night in a rough-spun white tunic, dark trousers, leather boots, and a blood-colored cloak. "Perceptive," he said.

You're Artur's father, are you not? I asked, but immediately regretted it, as I feared the question would be taken poorly. The man who'd sired Artur had also sired Kitty before attempting to kill them both. This man had raised Artur— I recalled that much from my conversations with Kitty— but he was no more blood to her than I was.

But the man just nodded. "Uther."

Hope, I replied. *Do you have a message for her?*

"Nothing in particular—"

"*Don't,*" said Flora, appearing in front of me in time to shake her finger at Uther. "The girl's in a crisis situation as it is, and she needs her strength. She does not need to waste it."

He lifted his hands as if warding her off. "I wasn't going to ask. All I was saying," he continued, glancing around Flora, "was that I stay near Artur sometimes. That is all. She doesn't know, and I would prefer to keep it that way."

I won't say anything, I replied, and caught myself in a yawn.

"Go to bed," Flora urged. "Arik isn't the only one who needs rest."

I couldn't argue with that. Bidding them both goodnight, I slipped back into the RV, stepped around the futon—and Frank, who appeared to be running in his sleep—and climbed into my bunk.

Sleep did come, then, but not nearly enough. About two hours later, I woke to find Flora standing beside me—a convenient trick for the incorporeal, as my bed was several feet off the floor. "Something is very wrong," she said as I blearily blinked in the near-darkness of the bedroom. "To the west."

What happened?

"I'm not certain," she said, "but the men feel it, too. Rouse the others."

I sat up as she descended. *Men?*

"Orson's returned." Flora sighed and shook her head. "Impeccable timing," she muttered, and waited by the door, tapping one foot, as I climbed down and shook Arik awake.

CHAPTER 5

"Let me get this straight." Frank stood at the end of the futon, shirtless and rubbing his forehead. "You've got…what, a spirit guide? Is that what they're called?"

"I suppose," I replied, self-consciously hugging myself. The only living person on the RV who wasn't staring at me with a mixture of surprise and concern was Arik, who was silently talking to Orson and Uther at the dinette. "It's nothing formal. Flora's been helping me adjust, and she led me to Arik. I trust her. If she says something's wrong, I'm inclined to believe her."

"And where is this Flora now?" Artur asked.

"She's here," Arik offered. "Down the corridor."

As the others turned to look at what must have seemed like empty space to them, I shot a quick thought to Arik: *Don't mention the men. It's not the time.*

His head barely dipped in understanding.

"I say we investigate," said Artur, glancing at Frank, then Beth, who yawned and leaned against the wall. "We have no way of finding the missing cynaeli—"

"Fik," I said.

"Right, Fik. We have no trail on him now. If this—"

"You're thinking what I'm thinking?" Frank interjected.

"That there's a band of tiny, ravenous creatures on the move in this realm, something so bad as to upset the dead has happened, and the two are possibly related? Yes."

At that, Arik lifted two fingers for her attention. "About Fik. I was wondering if you couldn't do a blood trace. That would lead us to him, would it not?"

To my surprise, Beth stepped in. "Blood traces run vertically," she said, wiping a bit of grit from one eye. "You need the subject's ancestor or descendant to set one up. Or that's what I've been taught, I mean. I can't do them yet."

"Your sister sent you to me with a tooth," I said to Arik. "Do you have something like that we could use for Fik?"

But he shook his head. "Fik was careful. When he fled, he took everything, even his brushes. All he left behind was a tiny bit of blood, and Father has that."

Frank and Artur traded looks again, and Artur shrugged. "Well, I haven't got a better idea as to finding him, and neither has anyone else, from what I'm hearing. Hope, can this Flora of yours guide us to the trouble?"

I turned to Flora, who regarded us gravely, and repeated the question. "I feel it, but as a direction," she explained. "I cannot accurately choose the roads. Go west, and I will tell you as you near it."

"She says she can give us a direction, but not a route," I told the others.

Beth shuffled into the kitchenette and turned on the electric kettle. "Hot and Cold. I *love* that game," she grumped. "Who wants tea?"

As Frank unhooked the RV and Artur pulled up a map on her computer, Orson sidled up to me and cleared his throat. "Sorry to crash the camper. I'm just worried about Beth."

Artur is watching out for her, I told him, heading back to the bunkroom to find my clothes.

"That may be, but Artur's also invited her along on this magical mystery tour, and I'd rather Beth not be anywhere near whatever the hell has just come creeping out of the Gray Lands. No offense, but when things from your realm pop over here, it ain't for sightseeing."

I'm aware. Turn your back, I ordered, pulling a rumpled shirt from my bag.

Orson did as I asked, and I quickly changed. "Beth takes after me," he said as I slipped into my shorts. "I was never the talent that Eva was, and I know Beth's been working her butt off, but she's not ready for full-on combat. The Games is one thing, but these…Hidden Ones? Is that it?"

Yes.

"They give you two the willies, don't they? You and that boy out there."

Absolutely. I ran a brush through my hair, feeling for snarls. *I'll do what I can to keep Beth out of danger…unless you'd like to tell her to go home?*

He grimaced. "Your lady friend wouldn't like that at all. She's a bit *protective*, shall we say."

I'm still offering.

"And I appreciate that, hon. Maybe later. Just, uh…if you could keep Beth from going full berserker if y'all are confronted by an army of evil leprechauns or whatever the hell these friends of yours are, I'd be grateful."

We drove west, then northwest, all morning, largely following I-70 across Kansas and into Colorado. Flora lingered near the front of the RV, staring out the windshield and recalibrating her internal compass. Orson and Uther felt it, too, though they remained in the rear of the vehicle, keeping a cautious eye on their daughters as Beth and Artur compared maps on their computers and plotted trajectories. The two of them had at least five routes worked out at all times, depending on shifts in direction, but Flora was satisfied with the easy Interstate drive until lunchtime, when Frank called a brief halt to rest and eat. Flora wandered back to join me and looked over my shoulder at the marked-up maps as I silently explained where we were and what our options might be. "That one," she said, pointing to a red squiggle on Beth's screen. "We need to go further north."

I conveyed the message to the navigators, who took the news well. "I-70 will lead us into Denver," said Beth, adjusting the screen view. "After that, it depends on how far away we still are. The Interstate turns south again, but there seem to be a few secondary roads through the mountains. Does Flora have any sense of how much farther we have to go?"

I glanced at her and silently repeated Beth's question, but she spread her hands and replied, "We are closer. More than that, I can't say."

When Frank was ready to push on, he guided us into Denver, then stayed on the Interstate as it passed through the mountainous terrain and dipped south. By the time that Beth was pointing out signs for ski resorts, the sun was heading for the horizon, and Flora was growing anxious. "We need to turn to the north," she said, frowning at Artur's computer. "This line—that's a road?"

I nodded. *A smaller road, but that's our last major northerly route for a while. Do we take it?*

She looked toward the front again, then nodded. "Yes. Tell Frank."

For a man taking driving directions from someone he could neither see nor hear, Frank was remarkably patient. He adjusted our heading, and Flora again stood behind his shoulder, considering the two-lane road ahead of us, its surface marked with the repairs of winters past. I was beginning to think we'd drive through dinner when we came to a four-way stop.

"Left," Flora instructed, and Frank obeyed. But half a mile down the road, we found an unexpected impediment: a pair of sheriff's department cars blocking both lanes with their lights flashing. Frank slowed, and a deputy marched to the window as he lowered the glass.

"Afternoon, sir," said Frank in a passable American accent, keeping his hands on the wheel. "Looking for a gas station. Is there one around here?"

The deputy shook his head. "Not this way. Turn

around, go back to the four-way, and you'll find one about five miles north of here."

"Thanks. What's with the roadblock?"

I couldn't see the deputy's face well, but I heard the strain in his voice. "It's ugly."

"Could you use a hand?"

"Thanks, but I've seen three ten-year vets puke in the street so far today. This is no place for civilians." He gave the door a pat and stepped back. "You drive safely, now. Go easy once it gets dark, eh?"

"Of course. Thank you," said Frank, and carefully turned the RV around. As we returned to the four-way stop, he said, "So...what's the plan, Flora?"

"She says we're close. Park a little up the road," I replied.

Not wanting to attract the deputies' attention, Frank came to a stop two miles away and cut the ignition on the side of the highway. "What now?" he asked.

"Now," I said, noting the crowd of shell-shocked dead coming out of the trees to meet us, "you wait in here and let me handle this."

With Flora by my side—and, to my surprise, Arik trailing us—I stepped out of the vehicle and approached the spirits. "Howdy," I said aloud, showing my empty hands. "I'm Hope, and I know I look weird. That's Arik," I continued, nodding toward him, "and this is Flora. What happened?"

They traded uncertain glances, no one eager to make the first move.

"I brought them here to help," Flora said gently. "We felt the shock a great distance from here..."

"Kansas," I offered. "We came as soon as we could. I, uh...I'm sorry. I trust that whatever happened was...unexpected."

A young woman with a frightened toddler in her arms stepped from the crowd. "It was *horrible.*"

"Can you tell us about it?"

She stroked the little girl's hair as she held the child to her shoulder. "They came in the night. Hundreds of them. Little...*things*...with teeth."

"God," a man muttered, "those *teeth*..."

My heart sank into my stomach. "About this high?" I asked, holding my hand around my knee. "Fast, look a bit like tiny people?"

The dead nodded. More than a few of them clung to each other, which was understandable. Being devoured alive in one's own bed, hearing the rest of one's family screaming down the hall, had to be traumatizing.

"Is there anyone left alive?" Arik asked.

"Sarah Roche," said a woman wearing spectral scrubs. "They didn't so much as nibble her."

He frowned. "What's special about Sarah?"

"Stage four breast cancer. She just finished her last round of chemo in Denver and came home—she didn't want to die in a hospital. I work for an in-home care company, I look after her at night..." She paused, and her shoulders slumped. "Or I did, I guess."

I wanted to comfort her, but I didn't have the words. "Your town...is this everyone but Sarah?"

A man near the front stood on a rock and did a quick head count. "Seems to be," he told us. "Only two hundred and seven of us after April and Corey had the twins...got you," he said, pointing to a sad-eyed young couple with a pair of infants in their arms. "I can't speak for everyone else, but I thought for sure that Sarah would be the next to go." He laughed then, a sound like a brief, hysterical hiccup, and slapped his hand over his mouth.

"I'm so very sorry," I said, cringing inside at how useless that sounded. "The little people...did you see where they went?"

Many in the crowd shook their heads, but not all. "East," said an elderly woman on the edge of the pack. "God help us all if they find Denver."

"Not to be coarse," Arik replied, "but they've eaten

their fill. It should be at least a day or two before they feed again...and we must have passed them," he added, turning to me. "We have to go back and—"

"Tell the others," I interrupted, nudging him around the RV.

As Arik left, the man on the rock asked, "What the hell *were* those?"

"Nothing that's meant to be in this realm," I said. "We're trying to stop them."

"What *realm*? And, uh...you going to tell us why you're purple?"

To my relief, Flora intervened. "Hope, go inside. I need to speak with them, and this conversation isn't for your ears."

The look she gave me forbade argument, and so I climbed into the vehicle and watched through a tinted window as Flora addressed the assembled. I couldn't hear her, but as I watched, the crowd began to thin as spirits vanished. When she rejoined us, she seemed drained but satisfied. "Most are where they should be. A few have business yet in this place, but I've offered them direction."

I repeated that for the others, adding, "The Hidden Ones are on the move, but they'll be slow for a time, this soon after eating. Frank, how are you feeling?"

He pushed his sunglasses onto his head and rubbed his eyes. "Honestly? Wiped. We've been on the road for the better part of twelve hours, and I'd rather not push through the night if we can avoid it."

"Beth," said Artur, "you know where we are. Check the maps and find a campsite." When Arik started to protest, she held up a hand to stop him. "Frank is the only one of us qualified to pilot the vehicle. If he's exhausted, we stop. End of discussion."

"But—"

"*Enough*," she snapped, and Arik wisely dropped the matter.

There would be no hooking up the RV that night. With little of civilization around us, Frank found an abandoned gas station and parked beneath the rotting overhang where the pumps had once been. Artur pulled dinner from the ether, apologizing for the quality as it appeared on the table. True, the chicken tasted far gamier than any I'd theretofore eaten, but Frank cleaned his plate without a word of complaint, folded out the futon, and flopped down as we washed the dishes. No one was in a talkative mood, and the others retired early, Beth and Artur taking their computers with them to bed. I got a glass of water and bade Frank goodnight, and he looked up from his texting as I cut the lamps, his face bathed in the pale white glow of the screen.

Sleep found me more quickly that evening—reasonable, considering how long it had eluded me the night before—but still, I was roused by a voice in my head shortly before midnight. Arik was talking, I realized, lying still beneath my blankets, and though I didn't open my eyes for fear of giving myself away, I deduced that the other voices I was hearing belonged to Uther and Orson. Eavesdropping may be rude, but I was too weary to care about propriety—and in any case, it was Arik who'd woken *me*. Feigning sleep, I listened in.

What if I'm already too late? Arik asked, his thought tinged with despair. *What if they found Fik before they attacked that town, and now they're just searching for more food?*

"You don't know that," said Orson. "And it would be a damn lucky thing for your dad to find a gate that close to him, yeah?"

Who's to say he didn't? Maybe he still has something of Fik's, a lock of hair, a tooth, fingernails... He trailed off for a moment, then added, *Father is strong, and I don't know what sort of tracking magic he's capable of working. Fik's probably dead because I was too slow. Too useless.* Arik sighed, and the mattress squeaked as he shifted position. *That's all I am, a useless failure.*

"You're trying," Orson replied, "and that's what counts. No one can ask more of you than that. Don't give up yet, son, you're not—"

"Stop coddling him," Uther snapped. "Sit up, boy, and look me in the eye."

The bottom bunk creaked again, and I assumed Arik was following orders.

"Now, I want you to hear me. Every word." Uther hadn't raised his voice, but the edge to it was more effective than mere volume could ever be. "The four people sleeping around you are risking their safety, if not their lives, for your brother. Because *you* asked for help. Until you have proof otherwise, assume he's alive and do the right thing. He doesn't know what's coming for him, does he?"

No.

"Then it's up to you to protect him. Stop feeling sorry for yourself, focus, and do what you must to take care of him *and* everyone else here. You must..." He paused, then huffed in frustration. "What is the phrase I want, Orson?"

"Man up?" he offered.

"Yes, *that*. Man up, Arik."

And how would you like me to do that? Arik retorted. *I'm not even a man anymore—*

"My *daughter* is one of the finest soldiers I've ever known," Uther interrupted, "and she was never a man. Your problem isn't what was taken from you—it's your mentality of failure. *Weakness*," he said, drawing out the word. "You act as if your father stole from you what truly mattered. For now, tell yourself that he did you a favor. You have one less target to protect."

"Uh...sorry, guys, I think I'm out of the loop, here," Orson cut in. "What am I missing?"

Arik quickly explained what a naffidar was, his thoughts colored by shame. When he finished, Orson sat in silence for a few seconds before muttering, "*Shit*, kid. What sort of man would hurt his own child?"

Uther cleared his throat. "You do recall that time that Myrddin tried to kill the girls, don't you?"

"*Ooh.* Yeah, good point, but he's fae—"

"As are the girls."

"Touché," Orson muttered.

It was Arik's turn to be confused. *Wait, who tried to kill whom?*

"Our daughters' asshole sperm donor," said Orson, and snorted. "I'm Beth's father biologically, but I didn't get to raise her. I raised her sister Kitty, who was actually fathered by a guy named Myrddin, but Kitty didn't know we weren't blood until she was grown, and I didn't know *what* Myrddin was until after I died. He also fathered Artur—"

"By which you mean he repeatedly raped my wife," Uther interrupted. "I didn't know the details. He made it seem as though Artur were my son, and I was too ignorant of the ways of magic to discern the truth."

"And then once the girls started asking pointed questions, Myrddin tried to kill them," Orson continued. "*Nice* guy. I heard he offed himself in Faerie, but if I ever catch him in this realm, I'll beat his fucking face in."

"I'll help," said Uther.

Arik sounded befuddled. *So...you're watching over daughters who aren't yours?*

"Who said they aren't ours?" Orson retorted. "I'd do anything for Kitty, and I'm sure Uther feels the same about his kid. We're the ones who raised them, yeah?"

"I would die a thousand times for Artur," Uther said softly. "Whoever sired her, she will always be mine. Why does this surprise you? Are most fathers in that realm like yours?"

I can't adequately answer that, thought Arik, *but what my father did to me isn't uncommon.*

He sounded depressed, and I fought the urge to reveal myself, slip down to his bunk, and hug him. But Arik needed what was left of his pride, and prudence counseled me to let him think I'd slept through it all. As the men conversed, I felt the sound wash over me until sleep took me once more.

I rose early the next morning, peeked into the quiet main room, then stepped outside the RV to see Frank tending a small grill. "Found this in a closet," he said, his morning bass almost a rumble, and waved me over. "And a tank of propane. I thought it'd be better to cook out here than to risk smoking up the cabin."

Atop the grill were ten hot dogs, well on their way to charred. "For breakfast?" I asked.

"There were no real sausages in the fridge, and Artur's cooking leaves something to be desired. Oscar Meyer it is."

I had to agree with his assessment. Artur may have been skilled in many disciplines, but the culinary arts wasn't chief among them. "Did I smell coffee?"

Frank pointed to the steel kettle on the edge of the grill. "Camp-style. Grab another mug."

He didn't have to tell me twice.

As I drank and watched him turn the blackening hot dogs, Frank murmured, "You want to tell me how many more dead hitchhikers we should expect?"

I coughed, almost inhaling my last sip, and Frank pounded me between the shoulder blades until the fit subsided. "Sorry," I croaked, "what was that?"

"There are more ghosts than just Flora in the RV, aren't there?"

"Why would you think—"

"Natural telepath. I woke in the night and overheard Arik's side of a conversation."

"Oh," I mumbled. "So, um...you didn't hear—"

"I can't hear these friends of yours, no," he replied, "but from what Arik was saying, I've got a decent idea of who's around." A pale eyebrow rose. "We're keeping mum about this?"

"For now."

"Good. This trip doesn't need more complications." He speared a hot dog with the meat fork, twirled it to check the coloration, then took a bite. "Not terrible. Want one?"

"I saw a box of granola bars in the cabinet. You enjoy," I said, wrapping my hands around the warm mug. "But while we're on the subject of hitchhikers…"

"Yes?"

"Should I be expecting someone to show up for you?"

Frank chuckled. "*No*. And seeing as there are already…what, seven of us?"

I nodded.

"Mm. RV's getting full as it stands. I'd hate to try to fit a spectral dragon in there." He plucked the still-sizzling remains of the hot dog off the fork and ate it in two bites, then turned as the side door unlatched. "Morning," he called as Beth slowly blinked at the lightening day. "Get a mug. Caffeine's out here, kid."

She grunted—perhaps all the communication at her disposal, considering the hour and her age—then shuffled to the grill, armed and ready. "It's strong," Frank cautioned.

Beth took a test sip, shuddered, and mumbled, "Thanks," then returned to the vehicle to let the magic work.

Beth might have required chemical assistance, but Artur was dressed, alert, and working when Frank and I came inside. "Granola is on the counter, tea's on the hotplate," she said, barely looking up from her computer. "I heard something about hot dogs?"

"If you wanted one, sorry." Frank sipped his coffee and leaned against the kitchen sink. "Grill's cooling, but we should be set in half an hour. Any word on *where* we're to go?" he asked, glancing toward Arik, who'd settled into a chair with a mug of tea.

"Nothing yet," Arik replied. He and I looked to Flora, who shrugged.

Artur sighed and rubbed her forehead. "I have thoughts, but they aren't pleasant."

"How so?" asked Frank.

Her expression turned grim. "We have no indication where this brother of yours might be, correct?" she said to Arik.

He shook his head. "Not as of yet."

"And these Hidden Ones are tracking him. Can we presume that they are not following the roads?"

Arik and I silently consulted with each other before he nodded. "They regularly traverse the plains, and those are barely marked with trails. No, I wouldn't think that they would need to follow a road."

"They're probably pointing themselves toward his smell and running," I offered.

"Incredible senses," Artur muttered. "Any idea of their range? How far can they be from their target and still smell him?"

"I don't know," I admitted. "Most of my education as to the Hidden Ones concerned how and why they should be avoided."

"Likewise," Arik mumbled.

Artur made a face. "I suppose that's practical. Right. Beth, did you find a gate around here?"

She looked up from her own computer, which was logged on to the Fringe network. "There's no record of one. We could ask Amy for a detector..."

"Which would only be useful if the gate's still open. Whoever sent the little bastards into this realm might have made a gate and resealed it." She scowled at her computer for a moment, taking long sips of tea as she pondered the variables. "Very well. Let's assume that the recently dead were correct and the horde is heading east. There's a fair bit of land between here and the ocean in that direction, and that's assuming Fik is somewhere on this continent. You don't think they could smell him from across an ocean, do you?" she asked me.

I could only grimace and shrug.

"Fine. Here's hoping not," she continued. "They're moving east at an unknown speed. We don't know what, if any, resources they have—"

"Probably nothing," I said. "Their usual pattern is to gorge themselves, then run until they need to feed again."

"And how long will that be?"

I'm sure Artur was tiring of my lack of answers, but I could barely speculate. "It depends on the size of the band. They just ate a town, but whether there were ten of them or ten thousand makes a difference…wait, I'll ask…"

I spoke silently to Flora, who offered, "I was told about three hundred."

"Flora says three hundred," I relayed to the others, "but that's also an estimate taken in the dark, in the middle of an attack. It doesn't really matter, anyway—I don't know how long a meal will sustain one of them, especially not if they're on the move."

"They're probably traveling quickly, though," said Arik, "so I would think they'd stop again in a day or two. No longer than that, even if it's not a feeding on the scale of yesterday's. They'll tire. I don't know if they have young with them, or if there's anything in this realm capable of preying on them—"

"If they can eat a live dragon, then probably not," Artur interrupted. "Beth, did you find any reports last night?"

"Nope," she said. "But there's also nothing yet on the massacre yesterday, so if there *was* another incident, maybe the powers that be are covering it up."

Artur drank her tea in silence for a brief time, then said, "If they're following his scent, they will probably move in a straight line. When we find a second incident, we'll know where they're going and how quickly."

Frank and I started to protest at once. "We're trying to *avoid* more deaths," he said. "If we backtrack, head them off—"

"We can't just sit here and let people get *eaten!*" I cried.

Artur's eyes were weary but cold. "And what better counsel can you offer? By all means, let's go east, but we can't predict their route, nor can we follow it if we're bound to the roads. Once we know their trajectory, we can find a way to drive toward them, yes?" She glanced at Beth, who looked aghast, then sighed. "I wish I had a better plan, but unless someone in here has a way to track the horde, this is the best I can suggest."

It was a bad plan, and it hinged on innocent people dying in a horrific manner so that we could put a dot on a map. But Artur was correct, and there was nothing for us to do but head toward Denver.

For the rest of the morning, Beth and Artur worked together in the sitting room with their computers, plotting out possible target cities and the best routes to them. Arik, who seemed more listless by the day, nibbled on half a granola bar and stared out the window, unable to assist. As for me, I took Beth's vacated seat up front beside Frank, who kept a steady stream of coffee going down as we retraced the previous day's miles.

I examined the dashboard, comparing it to that of Mama's car, and noticed an odd piece of black plastic mounted to the front, attached to a coiled cord. "What's that?"

"CB."

"Beg your pardon?"

"CB radio system. Old tech, but when you consider how much magic is at work on the RV, it probably has a better chance of surviving a trip unfried than anything else in this vehicle." He slightly cocked his head toward the cabin. "The computers in there are shielded, and all of the phones onboard are either shielded or enchantment-made. We can't risk breakdowns in the field, see. Quite honestly, I wouldn't trust any mundane electronics within five meters of this thing. Speaking of which, is your phone—"

"Kitty gave it to me."

"Then it's probably safe."

"It's still off," I added.

"Good." Frank's mouth twisted in thought, and then he snapped on the CB radio and flipped through the band. "Right…basic primer. Anyone with a unit in their vehicle can talk over the radio. Mostly truckers. Do me a favor and monitor this channel."

I heard a smattering of staticky comments from the radio. "What am I listening for?"

"Anything odd. Reports of a swarm of little people, unusual police activity, things like that. Here, get the notebook out of my bag. There's a dog-eared page near the beginning." He pointed to the stained canvas tote leaning against his seat, and I did as he asked, opening it to find a two-columned series of words and explanations. "Basic CB slang," he explained as I glanced over the page. "Most of it archaic, though we've made some additions at the bottom of the page. Don't try to start a conversation— it's best to just lurk. That might give you some idea as to what's being said, though, and if you start to hear of Smokeys or bears, tell me."

While I made myself comfortable, he pulled a set of small earphones from his bag and played with his phone. "Something better to listen to?" I asked.

Frank grunted. "Long night. If I don't get something with a beat in my ear, I'm going to fall asleep. But seriously, if you hear of anything bear-related, poke me in the arm."

Though I'd initially feared a preponderance of large carnivores on the road east, the only bears we passed were of the law enforcement variety, and none gave chase to the RV. No one on the road mentioned anything out of the ordinary, though I did pick up a few restaurant recommendations and the name of a particularly well-built prostitute outside of Topeka. All in all, my time with the CB was interesting, if not overly useful.

Frank called a halt for the night on the western side of Kansas City—the part actually in Kansas, not Missouri, which confused me until Beth explained the situation with a map. Our RV park that evening was adjacent to a family-owned joint serving burgers and barbeque, which suited our carnivorous driver quite nicely. Beth and I made the food run, returning with several slabs of ribs for Frank and more modest dinner platters for the rest of us. While Frank, Beth and Artur took their meals outside into the balmy night, I remained in the cool RV with Arik, who listlessly picked at his food. I offered him some of my chicken tenders, fearing that he didn't like the thick barbeque sauce on his plate, but he declined with a wan smile, claiming he wasn't hungry. This made no sense to me—Arik hadn't eaten when we stopped for lunch, and I didn't think he'd been raiding the pantry during the day. Then again, I reasoned, perhaps his worry over Fik had knotted his stomach. That seemed to be a reasonable assumption, but it didn't stop me from trying to temp him with baked beans and fries.

After dinner, Arik dragged himself to bed, while Beth and Artur retreated to their room with their computers. A few minutes later, I heard a muffled cinematic score coming through the wall and assumed they'd settled in with a movie. Bored, I took the remains of my pop outside to watch the sunset, a view of which I'd yet to tire after a year in Iroja. Orson joined me as the first stars appeared, stretching out in the mown weeds with his hands linked behind his head. A few dandelions poked through his insubstantial torso, and an anthill rose through his thigh, but if he noticed, he didn't mind.

As the other guests of the RV park had the common sense to sit indoors in the warm August night, I was free to speak aloud to Orson without giving the impression that I'd lost my mind. "Is Arik asleep?"

"Yep." He tilted his head backward to see me. "I'm going to be honest, hon—he doesn't look so hot."

"I know."

"Think he's sick? Maybe something like mono?"

At that, I could only shrug. "We don't get sick. I mean, *cynaeli* don't get sick," I amended, "and I've never been ill. It's possible that Arik takes after his mother, but surely he'd have said something if he were feeling odd." I sipped my flat pop and kicked a chunk of asphalt into the grass. "Would you do something for me?"

"Depends, but probably yes. What'd you have in mind?"

"I'm worried that something's wrong with Arik, but he's trying to do the manly thing and suffer in silence. If you could pry the truth from him…"

Orson chuckled and pushed himself to his feet. "I'll do my best. Come inside before the skeeters get you."

He had a point. I slapped one of the annoying insects dead on my arm and climbed back into the RV. As Frank had folded out the futon in my absence, I maneuvered around him and headed for the kitchenette. "Can I bring you anything?" I asked, exchanging the remnants of my pop for tap water.

Frank, who was lying on his stomach and texting, jerked as if surprised to find me inside. "Oh, uh…no, thanks. Thought you'd gone to bed."

"On my way. How are the Alps?" He frowned bemusedly, and I pointed to the phone in his hand. "Figured you were checking in with the rest of your team. No?"

The light inside the RV was dim, but I could have sworn I saw a flush of color in his face. "I wrote to them earlier. They're fine."

He offered nothing further, and prudence counseled me not to pry. "Well…goodnight, then," I said, and left him to his conversation. As I closed the bunkroom door, I heard him softly laughing.

I finished my drink, stowed the glass on the fold-down table, and checked on Arik. He'd curled in on himself, and his collar glinted in the nightlight's glow. I pulled the blankets up to his chin, but he didn't stir at my tuck-in efforts, and so I climbed the ladder to my bunk and rolled over, concentrating on my breathing until my mind drifted off.

But it seemed as though my eyes had barely closed before I heard Flora calling my name. Disoriented, I made out her shape hovering next to my bunk, then groaned. "Time?" I mumbled.

"You need to wake up, Hope."

There wasn't even the faintest light of sunrise from behind the shaded window, and my head felt fuzzy, still heavy with sleep. *What's wrong?* I managed to ask.

As my eyes focused, I realized that Flora's face looked drawn. "I believe there's been another incident," she murmured. "To the west. We need to move."

CHAPTER 6

Beth made the coffee per Frank's instructions while he unhooked the RV. The resulting liquid was thick, bitter, and the color of tar, but he drank two big tumblers of the noxious brew within his first hour behind the wheel and said little to anyone beyond periodic requests for heading checks. I kept him company, and Flora lingered near his seat, watching the strobing white lane divider in our headlights. The road was open as the clock ticked toward midnight, empty but for the occasional trucker, and the prairie rolled away from us on either side, blackness pocked with the occasional light of a distant security lamp.

After several wrong turns, we drove into a quiet town shortly after three-thirty. On first impression, there was nothing to cause alarm: a deserted downtown like a smaller version of Pauline's, a pair of streetlights blinking yellow and red at the intersection of Main and Independence, a gas station three blocks away, incongruously modern and brightly lit beside the old brick storefronts. We rolled slowly down the street, seeing the darkened front windows of a café and a pair of antiques stores. Vinyl banners hung from the streetlights, bidding us welcome and reminding us that Hazelwood had been an All-American City twenty years before. There was no sign of life, but then why would there have been? It was the middle of the night in small-town Kansas, and anyone who wasn't tending to sick livestock was surely in bed.

But then we passed the old patrol car parked in front of City Hall, a rust-flecked Ford sedan with its blue lights flashing and the driver's door open. Frank slowed to a crawl, giving me a good view of the skeletonized remains in the front seat, a pile of bones, ripped cloth, and fragments of meat. The body's former occupant stared down at it, shaking his head in evident disbelief. Suddenly, perhaps hearing our tires on the pavement, he turned and looked at the RV, his face pale and panic-stricken. Even with the windows up, I could hear him in my mind: *Help. Help me.*

Then they came.

They stepped through locked doorways, having come down from renovated second- and third-floor apartments. They sprinted downtown from side streets and alleys, from across the little park up ahead. They simply appeared in the middle of the road, the dead of Hazelwood, men and women, old and young, all wearing a look of mingled confusion and horror.

"Stop," I told Frank, then climbed out and faced the crowd. "Let me guess," I said to the assembled, "a swarm of creatures about knee-high with big teeth?"

The police officer grabbed the gun at his hip and took aim at me. "Not another step," he ordered. "Get on the ground, *now.* Hands where I can see them."

I heard a soft sigh behind me, and then Orson strolled forward. "Buddy, I hate to tell you this," he said, showing the officer his empty hands, "but that's not going to do you any good."

The officer's gun shook. "You, too. Get down."

Orson stopped, then spread his arms. "Go on and try, if it'll make you feel better."

"I'm warning you—"

"*Shoot,* damn it!"

The gun fired, and a spectral bullet passed cleanly through Orson, then my right arm—cold but painless. Orson shrugged as the officer gaped at him. "I'm sorry. Guessing the last few hours are kind of a blur, huh?"

The poor man seemed to be on the brink of tears.

"How…how are you…" he babbled, trying and failing to make a coherent sentence.

"How am I not lying in the street in a pool of blood?" Orson finished. "I'm already dead, man. Have been for fifteen years. You'll get used to it." He looked around at the shaken crowd, then hoisted himself onto the hood of the officer's car and called, "Can everyone hear me?"

The townsfolk nodded.

"Great. I regret to inform you all that you were probably just eaten alive. The good news is that the worst is over, and if you'll stick around for a few minutes, we can help you on your way. But while I've got your attention, Hope here is trying to stop the little monsters." He pointed to me, and the crowd's gaze shifted in my direction. "Yeah, she's purple. It's really not a big deal right now. What the hell happened?"

At that, at least ten people tried to talk at once, shoving their way toward me and gesticulating, and I backed into the RV as they closed around. Before I could make sense of their stories, a teenage girl pushed through the ring and started pointing to the gas station. "Mrs. Hartley is still alive! You've got to help her!" she pleaded.

By then, the rest of our party had disembarked, and Arik repeated the message for the others. "*Shit!*" Beth cried, and took off running toward the convenience store, sprinting through several dozen shocked spirits.

Artur's eyes widened in alarm. "Beth, wait!" she called as she ran to catch up. I followed in her wake, leaving Frank to help Arik hobble along.

When I reached the fluorescent lights of the little shop, I understood what had troubled Artur. Hazelwood's lone survivor was barely clinging to life, but considering what the Hidden Ones had done to her, it was miraculous that the old woman had yet to succumb to her injuries. Both of her legs were gone below the knee, the bones picked almost clean, and her left hand was missing. She'd lost a great volume of blood already—the white tile floor was slick with it—and her breathing was well beyond labored. But her right hand held a worn wooden wand, and I could just make out the faint shadows of spellcraft around her broken body.

A wizard, then, living among mundanes. Perhaps she was a member of the Minor Arcanum. I didn't know, and she was in no position to tell me.

Beth knelt in Mrs. Hartley's blood, desperately trying to shore up the spells keeping her alive. She mumbled in a shaking voice, but her wand moved with practiced strokes that belied her fear. I began to step in, ready to assist, but Artur grabbed my arm and shook her head. I met Mrs. Hartley's eyes, weary behind her blood-spotted glasses, and saw the resignation there.

"Thank you, honey," she whispered to Beth, and then, with a flick of her wand, the spells around her disintegrated. She started to cry out, but the sound died as a gurgle, and her head slumped to the floor, her eyes open and unseeing.

Beth whimpered and cast more rapidly, attempting to force life back into the corpse until Artur pulled her up and away. "You tried," Artur insisted, holding Beth against her as the girl struggled to break free. "There was nothing to be done."

When the others arrived, Frank helped Artur drag Beth back to the RV, while Arik and I stood in the wrecked store beside Mrs. Hartley's newly freed spirit. "Well, now," she said, giving us a long, hard look, "this isn't what I expected."

"Cynaeli. Gray Landers," I explained, and her white eyebrows rose in simultaneous comprehension and query. "Half. We're trying to stop those things."

"What *were* they?"

"We call them Hidden Ones," said Arik, resting against the window. "Your people don't seem to have a term for them…" His voice drifted off as he considered her corpse. "I, um…I'm terribly sorry."

The deceased snorted. "*I'm* not. I'm a hundred and five—spellcraft only does so much against arthritis, you know. Winters around here are brutal on the joints." She cracked her back and grimaced at the mess on the floor. "Hell of a way to die, mind you, but at least it doesn't hurt anymore. You're going after those bastards?" Arik and I nodded, and she folded her arms. "Good. I was keeping myself alive, hoping to tell someone what's out there, but it seems you already know. Do me a favor, won't you?"

"What's that?" I replied.

"Call 911. My phone's in the office. Be vague about it, but, uh…you know, I think we'd all feel better if we weren't left out to rot."

I could hardly refuse her last request. Once Orson had gathered as much useful information as he could from the townsfolk, and Flora and Uther had helped most of them on, we piled back into the RV and headed out of Hazelwood. Five miles down the road, I placed a quick call to the emergency dispatcher, saying only that I'd been on the phone with a friend and heard screams before the call abruptly ended. As soon as the dispatcher promised to send help, I hung up, and Frank did the honors of incinerating Mrs. Hartley's phone in the middle of the road. When the little device was nothing more than a pool of bubbling plastic and asphalt, we drove away, backtracking toward the Interstate.

"Where are we going?" I asked, looking between Frank and Orson. "Did they give us a direction?"

"We're getting the heck out of Dodge at the moment," Frank replied, "and after that, we'll plan something. Tell Artur that I need a route."

I glanced behind me, but Artur was sitting at the dinette with Beth, whose clothes were still soaked with the old wizard's blood. A glass tumbler with an inch of amber liquid sat in front of Beth, and Artur seemed to be coaxing it down her in small sips.

Orson's brows lowered in consternation. "She doesn't need *whiskey*. She's fifteen, for God's sake."

"It's a steadying drink," Uther protested from the kitchen. "Look at her, she's shaking."

"And *fifteen*!"

"It may be a while," I told Frank, and left him to join Beth and Artur.

As I neared them, I could make out Artur's murmuring over their bickering fathers' voices. "Her wounds were fatal. Nothing you could have done would have saved her life," she said while Beth drank. "You tried, and you fought valiantly, and I applaud you for that. But you weren't going to win that fight."

"She said she was only holding on to pass the message about what killed them," I added. "And she was rather old for a human. She was at peace when we left her. Said to thank you again for making the effort."

But Beth remained slumped in her chair. She stared into her glass for a long, quiet moment, then muttered, "Mom was right."

"*No*, Beth," Artur began, but the girl ignored her. Mouth tight and eyes brimming, Beth pushed back from the table, retreated to the bedroom, and slammed the door.

Artur mumbled—I couldn't make out the words, but her tone suggested they were profane—then sighed and rose. "Unless you feel like navigating, tell Frank to pull over. I've got to see to this first," she told me, and followed Beth to the rear.

I relayed the message to our driver, who announced that we'd stop once we found the Interstate and twenty-four-hour services again, and then I headed for the sitting area, where Frank's unmade futon bed still lay open. Arik had taken one of the chairs, and I sat beside him, hearing muffled shouts and sobs from behind the closed bedroom door. "She's taking the woman's death poorly," Arik murmured, swiveling his chair to better face me. "Tender, is she?"

"Not like you're thinking," Orson interjected, lowering himself to the edge of the rumpled futon. "I mean, it'd be hard on any kid to have someone die in your arms like that, but Beth's got other issues."

Arik frowned. "She's…unstable?"

If Orson was offended by the question, he didn't let on. "Stable enough—by teenager standards, yeah?" he added with a weak chuckle. "But her mother ground on her for *years*. Eva raised her alone, see. Say what you will about Eva—and believe me, she's earned it," he muttered—"but she's got an impressive talent. She was a magus before they locked her up."

Seeing Arik's confusion, I explained, "Magi run the Arcanum. They're powerful Irojan adepts."

"But what *is* this Arcanum?" he replied, frustrated. "You speak of it as if I should know—"

"There's two kinds of people in this realm," said Orson, "the magically gifted and the mundane. The mundanes run the world, and almost none of them know that the rest of us exist. The magically talented have separate governing bodies to keep it that way. The Arcanum is supposed to be the worldwide oversight organization for wizards—that's one sort of talented people. Most of them go along with it, though some wizards are of a more separatist bent. But politics aside, with all of the groups, the goal is to stay hidden."

That explanation left Arik even more perplexed. "Why would the adepts hide? What's the point of secrecy?"

"The point is that there are billions of people in this realm, but fewer than thirty thousand or so have any magical ability. If the Arcanum were to come forward and announce that a tiny fraction of the population has the power to warp reality with a snap of their fingers, what do you think the majority would do? Welcome a new upper caste of adepts or find a way to eradicate the freaks? And before you answer, consider that many of the major religions are at best wary of the concept of magic, and there's a well-documented history of persecution of those thought to be talented. Hundreds of thousands of people tortured or killed, most of whom couldn't have cast a spell if their lives had depended on it. Does that make things clearer?"

Arik swallowed hard and nodded.

"As I was saying, Beth's mother is very talented, and she played the political game well, to a point. I was never her equal on either front. Kitty's witch-blooded, so Eva knew she would probably never show talent, but Beth's a full wizard, and Eva...I guess she got it in her head that Beth would take after her. Unfortunately, Beth's my kid, and she shows it. Don't get me wrong," Orson insisted, "she's talented, and she works her butt off to do well. But that was never good enough for Eva, and she spent years making sure that Beth knew just how disappointed she was." He sighed softly and glanced toward the bedroom. "Every time she's less than perfect at casting, she beats herself up. No surprise that she's internalized her mother's criticism, but it breaks my heart to see her like this. I don't know how to make it any better. Wish I did."

Even with the door closed, I could hear the faint sound of crying coming from the bedroom.

"Do you want to talk to her?" I asked Orson. "Artur's doing her best, I'm sure, but the message might be better received from you."

He sat up, surprised, and looked at the door again with undisguised longing before shaking his head. "That's sweet of you, hon, but no."

"It might make a difference—"

"And I saw what it did to you last time." He pointed to Flora, who scowled at the kitchen sink with her arms crossed. "Besides, we don't want to upset Mama Bear, do we?"

"It's *my* decision," I protested.

Flora might not have understood my words, but I

suppose my face said enough. "Don't do it. Don't be foolish, girl," she chided. "You need your strength."

Orson laid his insubstantial hand over my bare knee like a cold blanket. "Thanks anyway. One crisis is enough for now, right?"

By the time Frank found a rest stop, Artur had emerged alone from the bedroom. Her expression discouraged questions, and I was too weary to fight her for an update. She opened her computer at the dinette, produced a cup of tea from the ether, and studied her maps while Frank stretched his legs in the dark parking lot.

When he returned, droopy-eyed, she called him over to see her findings. "This is the first town," she said, pointing to one of two red dots on the screen, "and this is the one we found tonight. Assuming the Hidden Ones are taking the most direct route…"

At her tap, a thick line appeared to connect the two dots, then continued toward the east with a slight southerly dip.

"Missouri," muttered Frank, "Illinois, Kentucky, Virginia…"

"It's a broad area," Artur concurred, "but we have an idea now of where they're going. Possibly how quickly." She drew another set of dots along the trajectory line. "If they keep their current speed…"

The two of them looked to Arik and me, but we had no facts to offer them. "They've been running hard for several days, I'd think," I said. "Even with stops to hunt and feed, they're going to tire eventually."

"Yeah, but how soon is 'eventually'?" Frank asked. "And what if they find their target before they wear out?"

Arik looked sick at the notion—well, sicker than usual—but Frank pushed himself from the table and winced as he unkinked his shoulders. "Artur, see if you can plot a route along that line. I'm going to get us back on the road."

"Going where?" she asked.

"We've got maybe another four hours to Kansas City on I-70," he replied, heading for the driver's seat. "I'm taking us back to the place we parked last night. Should be there by midmorning at the latest."

"I'll have routes by then…"

"Take your time," he mumbled through a yawn. "I've got to sleep for a while when we get there."

Arik stiffened and began to get up. "But—"

"But nothing," said Frank, glancing toward him before sliding into his chair. "If I fall asleep behind the wheel, we die. Unless Arc 1 has been holding out on us, the RV won't pilot itself. Ergo, I get a nap."

He started the vehicle and pulled onto the quiet Interstate as Arik sat behind him, frustrated and fuming.

"Just a suggestion," Artur murmured to Arik once we were rolling again, "but leave him be. We're doing the best we can. Besides," she said, turning her attention to the computer, "it's seldom wise to antagonize a dragon."

"Personal experience?" I asked.

She snorted. "There are life lessons that one learns only through experience, and then there's common sense. This would be the latter."

Arik, however, wasn't convinced to let the matter lie. "Is there no one else we could ask for help?" he demanded of Artur. "Another driver? You said you have people elsewhere, did you not? Could they not assist us?"

Her eyes remained fixed on her map. "Yes, we have people," she said calmly. "Most of them are competent drivers. All but one are working in Switzerland, and the last is in Glastonbury to assist them." She paused, then added, "There's Maria as well, I suppose, but she's the contact for emergencies."

"And this isn't?"

"Not yet."

"The people of two settlements have been eaten in

their beds! The Hidden Ones are on their way to kill my brother! How is this not an emergency?" he cried.

Artur took a deep breath, but she never raised her voice. "I assure you that the Arcanum leadership has been apprised of the situation," she said, and shifted herself just enough to pull her phone from her pocket. "Officially, the Grand Magus regrets the loss of life and wishes us well in our endeavor. Unofficially, Toula's on the brink of calling out whatever army she can muster, politics be damned. Her position is more precarious than she publicly acknowledges, and it was only a year ago that the Arcanum stood on the edge of war with Nath. They lost people fighting her. The courts, too. And though Toula, the Three, and anyone with the barest comprehension of the situation understands that Hope's 'abduction' was nothing more than a convenient excuse for Nath to call her army, many in the Arcanum refuse to look beyond a gross simplification of the incident like, 'We involved ourselves in a Gray Lands matter, and our people died.'" She snorted her disdain. "Now, Toula is not a queen. She rules with the support of a council of magi, and if I've been correctly informed, the majority of them are reluctant to touch anything that isn't purely an Arcanum matter. So yes," she said, cutting her eyes to Arik, "we have people. If the situation worsens, then perhaps Toula will have what she needs to convince the magi that assisting us is the only wise course of action. But we haven't reached that point, and we're doing our utmost in the meantime. I would suggest that both of you rest. It sounds like Beth's fallen asleep, and I would hate for your shouting to wake her," she added, giving Arik a long, steady stare.

He locked eyes with Artur for a few seconds, his mouth beginning to open as if a rebuttal were on his tongue, but something in her expression made him blink first. Without another word, he rose and limped to the bunkroom, and I murmured my thanks to her and followed him to bed.

Though I was weary—weary with the hour, with the interrupted night, with all of the death I'd witnessed—sleep eluded me. Guilt had finally found me, and it refused to allow me to escape.

Mama had to be frantic. I ran away on Tuesday morning, it was now Friday—officially Friday, judging by the faint eastern glow—and I hadn't sent her word to reassure her that I wasn't dead in a pit. Yes, Mama had been somewhat smothering, but there was a foundation to her fears. She'd been barely older than Beth when a slave trader had opened a gate into the woods near her home, snatched her into Conota, and sold her to Father as a concubine. He'd used her as he desired, got me on her, and five years later, he'd ripped her away from me and sent her back to Iroja. Of course the mundanes of Pauline had thought her crazy. Poor, crazy Hayleigh, who'd had so much promise. Her mother was the mayor, her father a doctor. She could have done anything she'd wanted, *been* anything. But she'd run off and lost her mind, and when she finally slunk home to Pauline, having been medicated and therapied back to sanity, she was a shell of herself. Nice enough, sure, and competent to manage her finances without a guardian, but the vibrant, bubbly cheerleader that her former classmates sometimes remembered when they looked at her had been reduced to a fragile thing who never spoke of her missing years.

She didn't have to take me in. Perhaps I should have left her alone—all I'd done was complicate her life. The good folk of Pauline still didn't trust me, and they pitied my crazy mother for letting a con artist use her. And that's the way it would always be in Pauline: side glances, muttered comments, and me unable to fix the situation for Mama or myself.

I'd once broached the idea of moving. Mama could open her shop in another town, somewhere that her name wouldn't carry such baggage. Maybe I could make a friend besides Flora. Maybe Mama could, too, someone who wouldn't listen for hints of insanity whenever she spoke. But Mama had killed the notion. Pauline was home, the place she'd grown up, the place where her parents were buried, the place to which she'd dreamed of returning every time that my father raped her. "It'll get better, baby," she'd assured me. "You'll see. And even if it takes a while, we have each other."

We had...and then I'd sneaked away.

I didn't feel guilty for calling Kitty and accompanying Arik out of town. He needed a friend more than I did, and the events of the last days had made it clear that there were lives on the line. In my shaded bunk, however, as I stared at the ceiling and the occasional strobing light of a passing vehicle, I pictured Mama holding the note I'd left behind, sitting sleepless at the kitchen table and checking her phone, hoping I'd call.

I lay still when Arik's bunk began to creak. When he rose and let himself out of the room, I slipped down and rummaged in my bag until I found my cell phone. Steeling myself, I powered it on, muffling its welcome chime with my pile of shirts. After a few seconds, I felt the phone vibrate with messages waiting for me, and I sneaked a peek.

Twenty-three missed calls, all of them from Mama.

Eight voice messages.

My finger tapped open the text messages first, a long string of fear and pain:

WHERE ARE YOU?!?
Hope you're scaring me where are you?
Please baby I'm sorry, just tell me where you are.
Are you ok??? Tell me you're ok.
HOPE TALK TO ME.
I'm sorry. Whatever I did, I'm sorry.
Are you ok?
I love you honey please call me. Please please please.

Feeling eyes on me, I glanced up to see Flora standing near the door. *I've got to tell Mama* <u>*something*</u>, I thought.

"The truth?" she suggested. "Your mother loves you, child. She's certainly worried. Give her something real."

I sighed, mulled it over, then tapped out a brief message:

I'm okay. Safe. I'm with Arcanum people. Don't worry about me. I'm so sorry for hurting you, but I did what needed to be done. I'll be home as soon as I can.

I turned the phone off again before Mama could respond and shoved it deep into my bag.

"Better?" Flora asked.

Maybe. I shrugged and sat on Arik's bunk. *I've done nothing but make Mama's life worse ever since I found her. She'd be better off if I never went back to Pauline.*

An unfamiliar sharp note entered her voice. "Oh? And you've asked her opinion of this, have you?"

Well, no—

"Then don't presume to know what would be best for your mother. Imagine how she would feel if you vanished."

Things would be easier for her in town if I weren't there to draw attention.

"This has nothing to do with *easy*," Flora retorted. "Motherhood isn't about finding the easiest path. Don't you think she agonized about you for all the years you were apart? Even if she doubted her sanity, something in her surely knew the truth and worried for you. *Mourned* for you. And it always will. Until the day she dies—and far beyond that, believe me," she said, holding my stare in the nightlight's dim glow—"Hayleigh will fret over you, and she will want you with her. I'm sure it would be simpler for her to have pretended not to know you and gone on with her life, but that's not the choice she made. Respect her choice. Respect *her*."

You think I shouldn't have gone with Arik?

"I think you made the correct decision, but that doesn't invalidate your mother's anguish."

I sat in silence for a time, Flora watching from a few paces away. Her face betrayed nothing, and yet...

You were a mother once, weren't you? I asked.

Her expression didn't change, but rather crystallized, a mask hiding whatever lay beneath. "Not as good a mother as I would have preferred," she murmured, then took a seat beside me on Arik's bed. "I'd rather not discuss it."

My offer still stands. If there's someone you'd like to contact...

"Now is not the time to think of such matters," she replied, rubbing her arm. "What do you know of Arik's mother?"

Her attempt to change the subject was unsubtle, but I acquiesced. *Human.*

"Did she return to this realm?"

No. I flopped backward and stared up at the springs of my mattress. *Most concubines never leave Conota. My father's an exception among lords—he sent several concubines back to their fathers when he tired of them, and he did the next-best thing for Mama, I guess.*

"What do other men do, then?"

Dispose of them. Raising myself onto my elbows just enough to catch Flora's horrified expression, I thought, *They seldom last long, in my experience.*

"Your men simply execute them?"

Highborn men do as they like, I replied, and laid back down. *If a lord tires of his concubines, no one will stop him from killing them. Nath never bothered with us, and there was no law against the practice in High Vale.* I paused to listen for Arik's return, but he seemed to have abandoned the bunkroom, and all I could hear was the rumble of the tires on the Interstate. *Arik's father killed his mother when Arik was ten,* I explained to Flora, *or so my sister told me. Ketulm made him watch and learn. Word travels among the highborn, even between settlements.*

"That's horrible," she whispered. "Inhumane."

Harsh even by cynaeli standards, I concurred. *My understanding is that she asked him one too many times to send her away with Arik, and he lost patience. Killing her in front of Arik must have taught him the importance of obeying his father, right?*

"Poor boy." She hugged herself and stared toward the nightlight. "And his brother? Does *his* mother yet live?"

Fik? No. She killed herself when he was two. Couldn't take the abuse, I suppose. Some concubines are stronger than others. I clutched a wrinkle of sheet in each hand and gently tugged at the blankets, giving my anxious mind a small physical outlet. *Mama and I don't always agree, you know, but I'm grateful to have her.*

"Mm. Then perhaps you should turn your phone on again."

My stomach knotted, but I did as Flora suggested, preparing myself for a fresh string of missed calls. There was only one, however, and a single text message: *I love you so much. Please come home.*

I held the phone close, wishing I had Mama with me instead of the little machine, then tapped a brief reply: *I'll be there as soon as I can. Love you.* With that, I turned the phone off once more, stowed it in my bag, and climbed into bed.

"Trying again?" Flora asked, levitating until she could look me in the face in the top bunk.

I grunted and closed my eyes, mulling over clever responses until sleep came and erased them all.

CHAPTER 7

A bad pothole bumped me awake. I flailed at the blankets until I recalled where I was, then caught my breath and took stock of my surroundings. The bunkroom, yes. We were still moving, so I hadn't been out long, and the glow around the shade showed that dawn had finally come in earnest.

"Arik?" I whispered, and rolled over to check beneath my bed.

His bunk was empty, untouched since I'd left it, but before I could climb down and investigate his whereabouts, Flora appeared beside the door. "Main room," she said softly. "Listen."

Curious, I slipped to the floor, padded across the tiny bedroom, then lifted on the door handle as I turned it, taking the weight off the hinges. The door cracked open without a sound, and I shared a brief conspiratorial look with Flora before peeking out.

The rumble of the road would have made ordinary conversations difficult to spy upon, particularly if the speakers kept their voices low. But Orson and Uther had no reason to be quiet, and Arik's thoughts were open to me. Considering his dampening collar, I doubted that he could have shielded them, had he tried.

He looked terrible. Exhausted, unwashed, and road-weary were to be expected, but Arik's eyes were sunken, and his glamour, designed to mask as little as possible, didn't disguise how pale he'd become. Frankly, it baffled me. I'd seen illness in Mama, but cynaeli didn't get sick—

was this a quirk of his mixed blood, then? Had Arik, protected all his life from the pathogens of Iroja, accidentally exposed himself to all manner of disease? He wasn't coughing, and of course I couldn't tell from that distance whether he was feverish or chilling, but even my limited experience counseled that whatever the symptoms were, he needed to be put to bed.

"I know you are frustrated," Uther was telling him. "I hear you, boy. But the...*creature*...steering this vehicle is correct. He grows weary, and that endangers all of you."

"And this isn't the time to put Beth behind the wheel," Orson continued. "That's a recipe for disaster. Hell, Artur's barely handled more than a compact car. You could park that little thing in here," he said, sweeping one arm around the room. "Asking her to drive *this* through whatever sort of rush hour KC gets is asking for a wreck. So hold your horses, let Frank get a power nap, and you'll be on your way soon. Look, I've seen him in the field," he added. "The guy's an endurance champ. They're doing their best, Arik."

I know, he replied, and let out a short sigh.

"Why don't you try to sleep?" Orson suggested. "I'm not going to lie, kid, you're worrying me. There's no point in pushing yourself until you pass out."

Uther nodded. "He's right, you seem ill. Sleep should help that, yes?"

But Arik shook his head. *It's the collar. I'm running out of time.*

Orson frowned. "What about the collar?"

Cursed, you might say. He shifted position in his chair, wincing as he did. *There's no point in making naffidars if they only run away, you see? The collar prevents that.*

"But you're here now—"

And growing weaker by the day. Arik hesitated, then asked, *You'll keep this between us? Hope doesn't need to know.*

The other men nodded.

If I don't return to my brother—my master, he added, the

thought red and jagged with suppressed anger—*within ten days of running away, then the collar will kill me.*

Uther stiffened, but Orson leaned toward Arik, tried to grab his arm, and grunted as he failed. "Then what are you doing here?" he demanded. "Tell the others—someone in the Arcanum has to know where a Gray Lands gate is, or maybe Artur can make one. Let's get you home. These folks can find a way to stop the horde without you."

Arik laughed, but there was bitterness in the sound. *Go home? Why? So Pimati can torture me to death? He's fond of torture, as it so happens. I could tell you stories, but I think you'd prefer that I not. And if he deigns to let me live, all I have to look forward to is centuries of servitude. No.*

"You don't know what you're saying."

I do, and I've made my choice. My life is ruined—my father saw to that. At least I can do something worthwhile with what's left of it.

"But this is suicide!" Orson protested. "You're just a kid!"

I came here to save my brother, Arik thought, staring Orson full in the face. *I'd like to see him once more before the end, if my strength lasts that long. Regardless, until the damn collar stops me, I'll do anything I can to save him. He's got a future to live for. So yes, I knew that coming here was suicidal, but if I can protect Fik, then maybe there can still be meaning in my life.*

Orson and Uther traded looks.

"You have had a difficult time," said Uther. "I appreciate that fact. But you're young, Arik. Surely this isn't what you want."

"And before you argue," Orson added, "ask yourself why you're keeping this from everyone else. You know it's a terrible idea. Hope—"

I love her. Why would I make her suffer like that?

"You know she'd tell you to go home," said Orson.

Which I won't do.

"So…you're just going to spring this on her, then? Try to explain yourself once you've joined us? Because son, I've got to say that I can't see that ending well for *anyone* in this RV."

Maybe not, Arik replied, *but better than paining her prematurely.* He started to rub his neck and winced. *A question, if I may.*

"Ask away," said Orson with a shrug. "I'm sure you know there's certain things we can't answer, but you can always try."

He hesitated, and I held my breath until I heard his thought: *What does it feel like to die? Not the injury before, but the actual moment—does it hurt?*

I couldn't take it any longer. "You're not about to find out!" I shouted, resorting to Cynaeli out of long habit, and slammed the door open as I stormed from the bunkroom. The three men whipped around as I marched toward them, and Arik, unable to hide the guilt on his face, opened his mouth. "*No.* Hear me," I snapped, cutting him off before he could begin. "I will *not* sit here and watch you die. We're going to fix this."

"Don't waste time—"

"It's not *wasted!* Why is Fik's life worth any more than yours?"

"Because I have to believe that *his* isn't a waking nightmare," Arik said quietly. "Let me have what little remains of my dignity."

I stood over him, effectively pinning him to his chair. "How could you think this wouldn't hurt me, huh? You weren't even going to warn me?"

"I thought it would be less painful—"

"*Why?* I love you, Arikol!"

He stared up at me, shocked, and his mouth opened and closed for a few seconds before he recovered his voice. "How could you possibly love me? I'm weak, I'm…mutilated…"

"That doesn't matter. Hasn't changed my feelings," I said, blinking back angry tears.

Uther pointedly cleared his throat. "What were you saying, Hope?"

"She's chewing his ass out, that's what she's saying," Orson retorted. "Hell, that doesn't need a translation."

More or less, I replied, stepping back and folding my arms. *We're getting that collar off.*

"Hey, guys?" Frank called from the front of the vehicle. "Is everything okay back there?"

"No. Pull over," I said in English, and dared Arik with a glower to argue. Wisely, he kept his mouth shut.

Arik and I gave the others a brief synopsis of his situation, omitting the most humiliating details. Though groggy, they listened without interruption, until Beth finally said to Arik, "So, just to make sure I understand: your dad *enslaved* you?"

"Essentially," he replied.

"I mean, not to be rude or culturally insensitive or anything, but your family's fucked up."

"Oh, believe me, no offense taken." He tugged at his shirt until the black metal was on full display. "While I appreciate the concern, we're wasting time. No one here can remove this."

Artur's brow furrowed. "Is it a solid piece, or is there a lock?"

"I assume it opened once, but I was unconscious when it was fitted. Less struggling that way," he muttered.

"What sort of key would it require?"

"Nothing physical." His fingertips traced the etchings on the collar until they found what they sought. "Pimati's name is here," he said, tapping the spot. "That marks him as my master. He could remove the collar—and I'm certain that our father could, since he made it—but no one else."

"Forget keys," said Frank. "What if we broke it off? Artur, Beth...I could always melt it, but that's the risky option."

At that, Arik wrapped his hands around his neck and

shook his head in alarm. "No, *no.* You mustn't. The collar is enchanted in several ways, and one of them is to prevent tampering. A trap against escape, you see. If anyone but Pimati or Father broke it, the trap would kill me instantly."

We pondered that wrinkle in silence for a moment, and then Artur, who'd been frowning at the wall in thought, murmured, "Faerie."

"Come again?" I said.

She pointed to Arik's collar. "That thing is powered by dark magic, correct? It seems there's a sufficient amount of the stuff here to sustain it. But if we took him across the border…"

Recalling the unsettling ether of that realm, I suppressed a shudder. "Without magic to sustain it, the enchantments *should* fall apart."

"They will," she insisted. "Morgen's work on me broke down as soon as I arrived. All we need to do is make a gate and slip Arik across, and then we can remove the collar—"

"Unless one of the enchantments in it kills me when the system begins to fail," Arik pointed out.

Which would leave him dead in Faerie, I realized, limited to visiting a realm in which no one could so much as hear him. Unless we could convince Fik to make the journey—assuming that Fik hadn't already died in Iroja—Arik would never see his brother again. I huffed in frustration. "Do you have a better idea?"

"Yes," he said, and whether the serenity in his voice was simply calm or resignation, I couldn't tell. "The important thing is to find Fik. I can't waste time on hypotheticals concerning the collar while he's in danger. Once he's safe, I'll think about my own problems."

"If you're not dead by then," I retorted. "We could reach out to some people in Faerie—"

"Anything less than removing the collar properly is flirting with suicide. Father has made that *abundantly* clear."

"He could have lied to you."

But Arik shook his head. "I wondered about that until

three years ago. Father hosted several lords and their entourages, and two of their naffidars decided to help each other escape while their fathers were distracted. I was the lookout, fortunately. When the first collar started to break, it exploded, killing them both. I was outside the blast radius, but the one who'd been helping was left in ribbons. As for the naffidar with the broken collar…" He looked sick. "What was left of the head was splashed on the walls."

As the rest of us stared at him, aghast, Arik shrugged weakly. "Ten days. I still have time."

"How much?" Frank asked, crossing his arms.

He began to count on his fingers. "Today is…"

"Friday."

"Yesterday was…the first town we found?"

"No, that was Wednesday," said Beth. "We drove all day yesterday."

Arik tapped his true three fingers against his thumb, one at a time, then ignored the glamour-created fourth and restarted the sequence. "And the day before that, you picked us up…"

"Tuesday," Beth offered. "That's four."

"Flora took you to me early on Monday," I added. "Day five. How long had you been here when I found you?"

He grimaced. "I remember two nights…"

"Say he arrived on Saturday, then," said Frank, who was keeping his own count. "Today is day seven."

"Monday," I murmured, my stomach twisting.

"Three days," said Arik, gripping my wrist. "That's time. We have a direction now, so surely we can find Fik in three days."

I thought of the long, uncertain path ahead of us and tried to smile for Arik. "We have a direction, you're right—"

"Screw it," Frank muttered, pulling out his phone. "If Toula needs to blame someone," he said, looking to Beth and Artur, "this was my decision, understood?"

"Who are you calling?" Artur asked. "What time is it in Glastonbury?"

"Not calling Glastonbury." He waited, and I heard the muffled sound of a voice on the other end of his phone. "Hi, Sam. Sorry if I woke you. Could you put me through to Badger Parsons, please? *Now*?"

I recognized only one of the three people who strode through the rapidly opening gate on the side of the road half an hour later. My acquaintance with Carey Jones had been brief—and, to be frank, I'd spent much of our time together focused on finding a way to keep Nath from invading that didn't involve my return to Father—but she'd been kind. She was a little woman, shorter than me and somewhat stooped with age, but her arms remained sinewy, and her dark eyes were bright in her brown, sun-weathered face. Her snow-white hair fell to her chin in a bob that might have been flattering if washed and styled, but it hung limp around her cheeks that morning. She sported a stained plaid shirt, rolled to the elbows, over a similarly worn T-shirt and jeans.

"Well, if this isn't a weird bunch," she said, giving us a once-over, and frowned.

While the last of her party closed the gate, Frank shook her hand. "Dr. Jones, good morning. I'm sorry for the early wakeup, but—"

"Early?" the gray-haired man with her interrupted, chuckling. "Never done a morning feed, have you?"

Frank cocked his head, and Carey explained, "Ranchers. My brother's kids do most of the heavy lifting these days, but I'm still up predawn, and that's when I *don't* have an overnight patient. Old habits," she said with a shrug, then gestured toward her companions. "My husband, Zeb, and this is our colleague, Hua."

Zeb was apparently of an age with Carey, though much

taller, and he kept his hair long and tied back with an elastic. Hua was a different matter: younger than the others but still of mature years, her hair dark black but her face bearing the lines of age. Like Carey, she was on the short side for a human woman, but she was softer and pudgy—and unlike the others, she was neatly dressed and coiffed.

"Hua is another sleepwalker," said Carey as the other woman nodded in acknowledgement. "One of our best, and since it's somewhat late in Beijing, she shouldn't have any trouble drifting off."

"And I'm along for moral support and coffee duties," Zeb offered.

Carey gave him an indulgent smile. "You do far more than that, dear. Now," she said, turning back to us, "we can get better acquainted later. You need us to find a Gray Lander?"

"I've heard from Badger that they're visible in dreams," Frank began. "Please tell me I'm not confused."

"Some are," she replied. "Those with talent. The blue ones, sure, and the purple ones should be, assuming they're all magically gifted—"

"Tennuwaya and cynaeli," I said under my breath.

Carey paused, gave me a closer inspection, and said, "*Ah.* I thought you looked familiar, hon, but I couldn't place you. But, uh…yes. Tennuwaya and…"

"Cynaeli," I finished, and pointed to Arik. "We're looking for his brother. Talented, but half human. Will that matter?"

Hua shook her head. "Probably not," she replied, her accent unfamiliar to my ear. "Your people—both kinds—glow blue in the dream space. Maybe he won't be as bright, but he should appear. Do you have his picture?"

"No," said Arik, who was trying to brace himself against the RV as subtly as he could. "I can show you…" Carey and Hua nodded, and their faces twitched as they received the transmitted thought. "Will that suffice?" he asked.

"Good enough," said Carey. "Badger said you have a search area?"

"More like a path," Artur muttered. "Come inside, see the map."

When they were occupied with the computer, Arik quietly asked me in Cynaeli, "Who are these people? Adepts?"

"Of a particular sort," I explained. "There's a strange form of Irojan magic that allows them to trance and find people. Or so I understand—I certainly haven't attempted to learn how."

"Friends of yours?"

"Friends of friends." I drew close to him and tried to be subtle with my gestures. "Frank, Beth, and Artur are affiliated with the Arcanum. These three are Minor Arcanum. A splinter group, one that the Arcanum tolerates. Last year, when Nath invaded, the Minor Arcanum sent people to help in the defense. I trust her not to harm us," I said, pointing to Carey, "and if she trusts the people with her, then that's good enough for me."

Arik considered that, then nodded. "Irojan politics are complicated, aren't they?"

"You have no idea."

After a quick perusal of the target area, the two women retreated to the bunkroom, while the rest of us stood around the RV's living quarters in awkward silence. Finally, Zeb cracked his back and headed for the coffeemaker. "You guys don't mind if I get this brewing—"

"*Please*," said Frank, heading for the driver's seat. "You're sharing, right?"

"How do you take it?"

"Hot and coffee-flavored."

"You got it, brother," Zeb replied with approval. "Anyone else? You all look like you've had better nights."

"I'll join you," said Artur, putting her arm around Beth. "And she will, too. Arik, take the main bedroom." He started to protest, but she spoke over him. "You're weak, you've barely slept, and there's nothing you can achieve while conscious right now. Go."

Sighing, he shuffled off, swaying dangerously as Frank pulled back into traffic, and closed the door. I waited for a time, tempted by the smell of Zeb's handiwork to stay with the others, but after a few minutes, I headed to the back to check on Arik.

He was asleep on the far side of the rumpled bed, a tightly curled ball beneath the covers, shivering even in the warmth of the room. Carefully, I slipped down beside him, trying not to disturb his sleep. In that, I failed—he jerked awake in a panic with my movement, and I wondered how bad his nights had been in recent years. Seeing me, he relaxed, then frowned and settled into the hollow of the mattress again. "What are you doing?" he whispered.

"This," I replied, and pulled him close.

He stiffened at my touch, but I tugged until he relented and let me stretch out beside him, a warm counterpoint to his cold limbs. "There," I said, tucking the blankets around his back, and rested with my forehead nearly touching his. "Is the chill better?"

He mumbled something that might have been an affirmation.

"Sorry about the intrusion," I said, "but there's no better bedwarmer than another body, and since you're still shaking…"

"It's improving."

"Good."

We lay together in awkward silence. While we were clothed, I was inescapably conscious of our proximity— my first time to be so close to a man, though there was nothing erotic about the experience. My older sisters had assured me that my first night as a wife or concubine would be unlike any other, terrifying with the unfamiliarity and with the expectation of sexual touch. This was nothing like that…but still, I had chosen it.

Chosen him.

I'd almost fallen asleep with the gentle swaying of the RV when Arik whispered, "Don't waste your time on me, Hope."

"I'm not."

"But—"

"If you've made up your mind to kill yourself," I interrupted, opening my eyes, "then at least you're not dying alone."

He sighed, then snaked one cold hand from beneath the blankets to cup my cheek. "I have nothing to offer you."

"And I'm not asking anything of you but to live."

We fell quiet again, but I couldn't maintain it for long. "I just want you to know that I...I asked my father to make an arrangement with yours. For you and me. It was, um...I was too late. But I wanted that very much."

Arik's eyes were difficult to read, especially in the dimly lit room, and I feared I'd gone too far before he replied, "I'm so sorry. I would have liked that, too."

I felt a small smile crease my face. "Can you imagine? You, me, maybe a little place of our own on the edge of High Vale...children, someday, though who knows what they'd be like? Both of us half Irojan..."

My voice faded as he gently stroked my face. "Even if I survive to find Fik," he murmured, "even if your friends think of a way to remove the collar...I could never be a husband to you. You know that."

"Says who? This is Iroja—no one here need know what came before for us."

"You do know what it means to be a naffidar, yes? They—"

"I *know*," I insisted before he was forced to explain. "And I would still have you. Children aren't everything, and here especially..."

He paused, gnawing on his lip as he thought, then tried again. "I...I'm not certain of what you've been told, but it's not merely a matter of, uh...of fertility. They took *everything*," he said, drawing out the word. "I have nothing to offer you. Not even that."

Despite the shade in the room, I could make out his expression that time, a blend of sorrow and shame. My eyes pricked, but I smiled again as if I could force the tears back into hiding. "Maybe no one explained it to you, but there are other ways to physically please a woman," I murmured.

He squinted in bemusement. "Such as?"

"There is so much one can learn," I replied, lowering my voice to the barest of whispers, "when one has a computer and nothing but time. Irojans are more, uh...*open*...when it comes to discussing the things one can do in a bedroom. They give actual *instructions*," I said, thinking of how scandalized my sisters would be by the how-to articles I'd read, much less the images I'd seen. "Techniques that don't require what your father stole. Once we save Fik and get the collar off...I might be available to further your education. If you're interested, I mean."

The offer was nothing but a fantasy, and I suspected that we both knew it. Arik was practically fading in front of me, and the odds of him surviving to freedom grew slimmer by the hour. But fantasy has its place in dark times, as even the pretense of hope is better than nothing.

Arik smiled back at me. "These Irojan exercises, you've practiced them?"

"Some, but not all. I've been waiting for the right partner."

"Mm. I suppose that once Fik is safe, I might be available to assist you."

"Yeah? You promise?"

His thumb, stroking my face once more, wiped away one of my escaped tears.

I woke to stillness and muffled voices. We'd stopped, I

realized, and recognized one of the voices as Carey's. Gingerly extricating myself from the bed so as not to disturb Arik, I slipped back into the main room and found the two sleepwalkers sitting on the folded-up futon, wrapped in afghans and drinking coffee. Spying me, Carey lifted her mug in greeting. "Morning," she croaked. "How's the patient?"

"Unconscious," I replied, and accepted a mug from Zeb. "I'm sorry, how long have you been awake?"

"Oh, half an hour or so. Long enough to readjust to a body," she said with a slight chuckle, then pointed to Artur and Beth, who'd taken the chairs opposite. "Those two have been filling us in. Frank was on the floor of the bunkroom, last I checked. He parked and sneaked in while we were out."

"I covered him," Hua added, "but he did not move, and I did not investigate. Shuì lóng," she muttered with a quick grimace.

I frowned, but Zeb came to the rescue. "In other words, no one's too eager to poke the sleeping dragon."

"He's really not that grumpy," Beth protested. "You guys act like he's going to bite your head off if you nudge him."

"You're probably right," said Carey, "but bear in mind that there are no disguises in the dream space. No glamours, no transformed looks, none of that. Frank...well, he's a lot to take in, especially when you consider the constriction on him. Seeing him behind the wheel, but also simultaneously seeing him in his true form..." She briskly shook her head. "The human mind isn't wired to witness that sort of contradiction. Like trying to navigate an Escher staircase. And it's odd," she continued through a yawn. "He actually glows a little, very faintly. Maybe that's indicative of his body's reaction to dark magic, but who knows? I've worked with large animals all my life, but he's *way* out of my practice area."

"In other words," Beth told me, "we're back in the RV

park on the Missouri border, and we'll be here until Frank's feeling perky again."

Zeb cleared his throat. "I've certainly hauled horse trailers. In a pinch—"

"*No*, dear," Carey cut in. "Let's not break the Arcanum's toys." She leaned into the futon and sighed. "Good news and bad for you, Hope."

"Oh?" I asked, taking a spot against the wall with my steaming coffee.

"The bad is that we've got nothing firm, and no sign of anyone of your Fik's description. We searched all the way to the Atlantic—a high-altitude search, mind you, but those are still useful. Not even a hint of him."

"What about the Hidden Ones?" I asked.

"If they're out there, they're behind us. I didn't see a massive glowing mob to the west, so I assume they're not talented—right?"

"A blessing," I muttered. "Was that the good news, then?"

"Not exactly," said Hua, adjusting her blanket. "I think I saw something. A flash of blue, not anything certain, but it *was* blue."

"I didn't see it, but Hua's a pro," Carey added. "She showed me where it happened. It's west of the Appalachians, but I don't have a town or anything...maybe Kentucky."

"That's more than we had yesterday," I replied, and nodded to them both. "Thank you. What do we do now?" I asked, turning to Artur.

But Carey beat her to the opening. "Now we rest for a little bit and get a meal down us, and then Hua and I will give it another shot." Seeing my surprise, she smiled and sipped her drink. "You didn't think we were giving up that quickly, did you? Give us time—we'll figure it out."

"And since time is in short supply," said Hua, tapping Carey's knee, "we shouldn't waste it."

The microwave chimed, and Zeb extracted a bowl of

rubbery scrambled eggs. "Best I can do in a pinch," he said, and partitioned them onto two plates of toast. "Honestly, you'd think that with so many wizards at their disposal, someone in the silo would have worked up a real kitchen in this land yacht."

Carey took her breakfast and dug in. "No complaints here, dear, but is there any hot sauce? It covers many sins."

Frank woke around two that afternoon, bleary-eyed and ravenous, and Beth was sent next door for provisions. She returned laden with heavy plastic bags, their handles digging into her arms as she jostled them inside, and we spread the bounty on the dinette as a makeshift buffet—all but the ribs, which were by silent understanding Frank's alone. The sleepwalkers were grateful for the late lunch when they emerged shortly thereafter, and while they brought Frank up to speed, I checked on Arik in the back. He remained where I had left him, curled up beneath the blankets with the shades drawn, and I sneaked close to the bed to reassure myself that he was still breathing.

The second long sleepwalk had been less fruitful than the first. "Not even a flicker of blue," Carey reported with frustration. "And we weren't even sure if we were staking out the right area. The dream space could do with signage." Still, she and Hua were confident that the hunt would be successful, albeit in time. They announced a third sleepwalk after lunch, asking us to stay parked for a few hours more. "It's easier to keep a heading if your body isn't constantly moving," Carey explained. "One more shot, and then we can move east and try again."

Our driver was unopposed to the proposition, and I couldn't blame him. As could be anticipated, however, Arik was a different story when I woke him for dinner. "They're our best hope," I told him, helping him out of bed. "If this makes the search easier, we can't deny them."

He wasn't mollified—I could see it in the set of his

jaw—but he didn't argue when we rejoined the others around the warmed-over leavings of lunch. I put Arik in a chair and piled a plate with food, trying to tempt him, but his appetite was nonexistent, and he ate a few bites only with my cajoling.

Hua and Carey emerged at twilight, both looking exhausted despite having spent the better part of the day unconscious. Zeb put food and more strong coffee in front of them, and the rest of us waited for a report. Hua nibbled on a chicken tender, braced herself with a few sips of coffee, then turned to us and shook her head. "Nothing," she said with a sigh.

"I don't know how," Carey muttered beside her, "but we've lost him."

Arik groaned across the room.

"Your people can make gates, yes?" Hua asked me.

I nodded. "Some can, but the skill is more common among the tennuwaya. I'm not strong enough. Arik..."

"I've never managed it," he said dully. "If Fik has learned how, I'd be surprised."

"So maybe he is not alone," said Hua. "Maybe he has a friend. Someone who makes gates."

We had no answers for her. "Fik ran alone," Arik said. "I don't know what sort of people he's met in this realm."

"Assume it's someone with gate capabilities, then," said Carey, wiping barbeque sauce from her fingers. "They find out about these Hidden Ones of yours and split for parts unknown. Probably not into Faerie," she mused, "or else I'm sure someone would have called to complain."

Frank nodded and held up his silent phone.

"But let's say they put, oh, an ocean between them and the Hidden Ones. Let's say they made a gate to Europe or Africa."

"We can make a higher search next time," Hua suggested. "But it is...what's the phrase?"

"Needle in a haystack," said Carey, then looked at me. "Frank said you had a spirit guide—can she not sense Fik?

He'd be a natural medium like you and Arik, right?"

I repeated the question to Flora, though I already suspected the answer before she gave it. "No, she can't," I replied. "They're sensitive to people with abilities like ours, but they can't just locate them. They can easily hone in on people they know and places they've been, and they can sense mass death, even at a distance"—Orson nodded emphatically—"but Fik doesn't fit any of those categories."

Artur spoke softly. "If we wait long enough, the creatures will need to feed. We can compare their heading at that time and see if it's shifted."

Hua, who'd been reaching for her chicken, stilled her hand. "That's a horrible thought."

"Pragmatic," Artur countered, glancing at Arik, "but also too slow. I propose that we continue on the planned trajectory until we have reason to do otherwise."

"And Hua and I are happy to keep searching," said Carey, "but we're going to need some real sleep first. At least a few hours, just to keep up our strength."

"Do what you need," said Frank, heading for the leftover burgers. "Let's overnight here, and we'll push on at first light. Less chance of an accident if we drive by day," he said to Arik, who stared miserably at his cooling dinner.

I didn't need magic to know Arik's thoughts. The look on his face was edging ever closer to full-blown despair.

While the sleepwalkers returned to the bunkroom for true rest, the rest of us milled around the RV, making the best of the situation. Zeb and Beth walked next door for milkshakes, Artur brooded over her computer, and Frank unfolded the futon, giving us a place to sprawl in front of the modest television. Wrapped in a blanket but still shivering, Arik settled against a pillow to watch a movie, and Frank plopped down beside him, sitting shoulder to shoulder. I wondered briefly about Frank's disregard for the norms of personal space until Artur, noting the direction of my stare, murmured, "He's the warmest thing in this vehicle. Should you find yourself making camp in the snow, you could do far worse than to share a tent with a dragon."

If Arik minded the contact, he didn't show it. By the time I stepped out to stargaze, his grip on the blanket had begun to loosen, and Frank winked at me as I opened the door.

At least the RV came equipped with reclining camping chairs. I set one up near the vehicle, out of the way of the security lamp, and leaned back to watch the sky. It wasn't the worst bed I'd ever made—the night was warm, the stars bright, and the breeze felt good after a day spent on the road. I remember waving to Beth and Zeb when they returned, but I must have dozed after that, as the next thing of which I was aware was Arik's hand on my shoulder.

"Hope," he murmured, giving me a little shake. "Were you planning to sleep outdoors?"

I sat up, yawning. "What time—"

"I don't know, but Artur has gone to bed, Zeb's asleep in a chair, and Frank and Beth are watching that, uh…"

"Television?"

"Yes. Something comedic, I think, but the jokes…" He made a face.

"It takes time before they become funny. Here, sit," I ordered, rising from my chair, and pulled another from the storage bay while he made himself comfortable. "Are you warm enough?"

He smiled wanly. "Don't worry so much."

"Too late," I replied, but sat beside him and leaned back to resume my sleep-interrupted vigil.

After a time, Arik said, "It's a stunning view, isn't it? The way they move…"

"That one's an airplane, I think."

"A what?"

"Dragon-sized vehicles that fly. I haven't yet been in one, but maybe someday."

"Powered by enchantment?"

"No, that's what so remarkable about them. Humans are resourceful, I'll grant them that," I said, tucking one arm behind my head. "But the ones that don't move, those are stars. Except for the ones that are planets. I still can't tell them all apart," I confessed. "But I do love the night sky here. That's the first thing I saw in Iroja—the moon and stars. We flew in by night, over the sea, Frank and Kitty and me. I looked around, saw *this* above us, and that's when I knew I'd escaped."

"No wonder you love it."

I reached across our armrests and took his hand. "We'll learn the stars together, you'll see. All their names."

"I'd like that."

"Then that's what we'll do," I said with far more confidence than I felt. "Find Fik, get the collar off, and go back to Pauline. Mama lives out in the country, and the stars are even better there."

Arik chuckled softly. "Do you really think your mother would let me back on her lands? After this?"

"I'll talk to her. I, uh…I sent her a message, just to let her know I'm okay. The phone's off, she can't track us—"

"I'm glad you did," he said, squeezing my hand. "You're fortunate to still have her. I'm sorry for all the trouble, I never meant to come between you—"

"My choice. Don't worry about it."

He sighed and kept his hand in mine. "I miss my mother so much," he said, his voice barely audible over the rustling of the nearby field.

I chose my words carefully, not wanting to reveal just how much gossip I'd heard about her death. "Does she not visit you? The spirits of my father's family won't leave me alone."

"Not since this," he said, tapping the collar with his

free hand. "I suppose she's too disappointed in me to come around."

"That's ridiculous," I protested.

"Is it? What mother wants a weakling?" He scowled at the heavens, his face twitching. "Father made me watch her die, did you know that?"

"I...heard something to that effect, yes," I admitted.

"He had two of his sons pin her to a wall, then flung a bolt through her. She stared at me as she died. And I did *nothing* to save her. I didn't move, didn't cry. I just...watched," he said with disgust. "Father incinerated what was left of her, and I stood there until she was ashes. My own mother."

I squeezed his hand so hard that he flinched. "It's not your fault. You couldn't have stopped him."

"I could have *tried*. She used to say she didn't blame me, but I haven't seen her in years. Maybe she's found peace. Found her way to her ancestors, I don't know. But I miss her." He shifted in his chair and adjusted his blanket. "I should have run away as soon as Father killed her. I knew there was something wrong with him, with the *family*, but—"

"You were a child."

"I wasn't quick enough." Finally, he turned to look me in the eye. "Fik offered to take me with him when he ran. I almost went."

"What stopped you?"

He started to speak, then shook his head and glanced back at the sky. "It doesn't matter."

A cold hand wrapped itself around my heart and began to tighten its grip. "Tell me," I said, though I feared I already knew.

"Really, it's of no consequence now—"

"*Tell me*, damn it!"

He said nothing, but he couldn't keep me out of his thoughts, and the horrible truth was waiting there for my prying mind.

He'd been preparing to ask his father to make an arrangement with mine.

Arik looked back at me in time to see my face crumble. "No, *don't*," he insisted, rolling over to meet my watery stare. "It's my fault."

"I'm sorry—"

"*No*, Hope. I made that choice, not you." His smile was forced, but there was a sad tenderness in it. "And I'm so grateful to have been able to see you again. When you fled, I thought...oh, please don't do that," he murmured as my tears spilled. "Please, I don't want you to cry. Not for me. The last thing I want is to cause you pain, and...well, that hasn't worked, has it? But you're going to be fine," he assured me. "You're going to go home to your mother, and you'll be happy again, and *safe*, and—"

"Hope?"

I looked up at the interruption to find Orson standing beside Arik's chair. "What's wrong?" he asked, looking back and forth between Arik and me until the answer seemed to come to him. "*Shit*, Arik, I thought you weren't going to say anything," he muttered.

Arik threw up his hands and responded in English. "I didn't! I can't keep her out of my head!"

Orson grunted but turned his attention to me. "This is not your fault," he said. "So don't go blaming yourself for something you didn't do. Don't you try to carry that, kiddo."

I released Arik's hand and swiped at my face. "I know, but—"

"But nothing. *This isn't your fault.*" He sighed and folded his arms. "Don't try to tell me that I'm imagining things, either, because Beth does this all the time."

I sniffed, willing myself back to composure. "Her mother?"

"Bingo. Kid keeps telling herself that she could have prevented Eva from going off the deep end—if she'd been a better wizard, better student, better daughter, all that nonsense. She still carries that, and I *hate* it, because Eva made her own choices. *Eva's* the one who hurt Beth, not the other way around." He glared into space and shook his head. "I want you to listen to me, okay? You didn't do *that* to him," he said, jabbing one finger toward Arik. "You love that boy. And you love that girl," he said to Arik, pointing to me in turn. "And seeing as the clock is running, don't waste the time you've got left on self-blame. You're together now for at least another day or two, right? Don't take that for granted."

While Orson was speaking, I was faintly aware of the sound of the RV door opening. "Hey," said Beth, wandering up in her nightshirt and shorts, "what are you two doing out here? No one has to sleep outside—Zeb's offered to make a blow-up mattress. We can all fit."

I glanced from Beth to her father, who at that moment had eyes only for his little girl—a girl lanky, rumpled, and seemingly older than her years. I looked around, saw no sign of Flora, then reached a snap decision.

Orson jerked when I sent power flowing through him and wheeled on me in surprise. "What are you—"

"*Dad?*" Beth cried, jumping back in shock. "What...how..."

"Flora's going to skin us both," Orson warned me.

"I'm fine," I said through gritted teeth. "Talk to her."

He turned back to Beth and held up his hands, as if afraid—and not unreasonably so—that she would bolt. "Hi, sweetie, it's okay. Sorry, I didn't know that she was going to—"

"What are you doing here?" Beth asked, brow furrowing. "How'd you find me?"

"It's not hard. And, uh...well, I mean, you're riding around the Midwest, chasing after a horde of man-eating monsters, so...I was worried," he said, sounding almost apologetic.

"He's been with us for days," I added.

"But...*why?*" Beth pressed, flabbergasted. "Why would

you—"

"Because you need someone there," said Orson, floundering. "And I'm lousy for this gig—believe me, I know it—but if I can't help you, really, then…all I can do is be here. Bear witnesses. I…I do it all the time, honey, and I'm sorry it can't be more—"

"You…" she began, then stopped, shook her head briskly, and looked back at her father as if trying to see through an illusion. "You hang around *me?*"

"I don't mean to be creepy—"

"Why me?"

The question took him aback. "You're my baby girl," he said. "I worry about you, Beth." As her eyes filled, Orson hurriedly added, "I'm so sorry, I didn't mean to upset you—"

She sniffled and blinked back tears, and when she spoke again, her jaw trembled. "I just…I thought you'd only look in on Kitty…"

"Sweetie, *no*. I know we didn't get to spend any time together, but…but I was so excited to have you, and I was going to move you down to the farm with Kitty and me, and we were going to be a family, the three of us, and…" He fumbled briefly, then managed, "I'm really sorry that I never got to be your dad. I love you, baby."

Perhaps forgetting for a moment that Orson, though visible, was still incorporeal, Beth ran to hug him, ran *through* him, and almost fell into a trash can. She caught her balance and turned back to her father, laughing even as she cried, and Orson ever so carefully cupped his hand against her cheek. "Beth, honey, that's so sweet, but please don't break an arm on my account," he said, which sent her into another fit of slightly hysterical giggles.

I would have given them hours together—the joy in Beth's countenance was enough to override my good sense—but before long, Flora appeared at my side. "You are tiring," she warned me. "Save your strength."

Orson noticed her, and guilt flashed across his face.

"We should cut this short, Hope. Beth…" His smile for her was tinged with sadness. "You're not alone, sweetheart. You are loved. You're doing your best, and I am *so* proud of you."

It took Beth, Arik, and me a few minutes to return to the RV after that. Beth needed a break to cry, Arik needed assistance in maneuvering out of his chair, and I needed time to catch my breath and focus. I hadn't overdone it, but the exercise had been tiring nonetheless, and as I shepherded the others inside, I could hear Flora, protective as usual, chastising Orson in the parking lot.

CHAPTER 8

Zeb's air mattress wasn't going to win any accolades, but I could have slept on stone that night. Exhausted physically and emotionally, I helped Arik to bed, then lay beside him and knew nothing further until sunrise, when the smell of fresh coffee lured me back to consciousness.

"Morning," said Zeb, passing me a mug as I shuffled to the kitchenette. "So, I understand this RV is actually haunted by *multiple* spirits."

I glanced around the room and spotted only Flora, who was peering out through the half-open blinds. "You're sensitive?" I asked Zeb. "I'd heard it was rare in humans."

"Oh, I'm not sensitive in the slightest," he said, doctoring his own coffee with powdered creamer. "Beth told me about her dad when I got up. Kid's in high spirits—seemed almost giddy. I sent her out to get breakfast. The place next door looks closed, but there's a Waffle House just up the road."

Noticing me, Flora said, "Ah, Hope, you're awake. How do you feel?"

Just a moment, I told her, then said to Zeb, "They find me. Beth is in no danger, and neither are you."

"Didn't think I was," he replied. "Just one more reason not to walk around in my skivvies in here, huh?"

I chuckled and leaned against the wall. While Zeb hunted for clean mugs in the cabinets, I cut my eyes to Flora and thought, *I'm fine.*

"Good. That was a risk you took last night. Keep yourself in top form, girl—you cannot afford to be weakened if you intend to fight those...*things*," she said with a shudder of distaste.

It was just for a few minutes, I protested.

"Yes, because I intruded. I know you," she said, though not unkindly. "You have a great gift, and you want to make people happy—that's a commendation, dear, not criticism. But you *cannot* sacrifice your own safety to do so. Not now." She rose and joined me by the dinette, staying out of Zeb's way. "There is a veil between life and death, child. It's understood. That you can see through it, even part it, is an incredible thing, but you are not *obligated* to do so. Passing a message from Orson would have been more than enough. What you did goes far beyond what anyone should ask of you."

I don't mind, I replied. *And it meant more coming from him than it would have filtered through me. You saw how hard she took that woman's death yesterday—she needed <u>something</u>.*

"The child is wounded in ways you cannot repair, Hope."

But Orson can help her, I countered.

"Perhaps," she allowed. "But while he looks out for her, *I* am here to look out for you, understood?"

I sighed into my coffee. *Are you ever going to tell me why?*

"Because someone needs to do so. Is that not reason enough?"

Is there no one you want to speak with? No one at all? It doesn't have to be today, I assured her. *Later. You know I would do it for you.*

She flashed a brief smile. "Don't trouble yourself about that."

Before I could press her, the back bedroom door opened, and Artur emerged, clean and dressed. "Hope, Zeb," she began, then caught sight of Arik still sleeping on the floor and lowered her voice. "Beth told me," she said as she threaded her way between the furniture toward the coffee.

A flicker of motion caught my eye, and I saw Uther

appear near one of the chairs across the RV. I cocked an eyebrow, but he shook his head.

"Don't even think about it," Flora chided.

Unaware of the conversation going on around her, Artur helped herself to the pot and sat at the dinette. "She's in a better mood than I've seen from her in weeks. However you managed that…thank you."

While Zeb retreated to the bunkroom to check on the sleepwalkers and Frank, I joined Artur at the table. "Pleased to do so. She needed it."

"Indeed." She sipped her coffee, wrapping her fingers around the mug, and stared into space. "I'm happy for her."

I had to force myself not to glance toward Uther. "She never knew her father," I said. "A few minutes together is the best I can offer right now, but I suppose it's better than nothing."

She gave no response, and I was beginning to wonder if she'd heard me at all when she murmured, "My father came when you raised that army in Glastonbury."

"Did he?" I replied, playing dumb.

She nodded. "I saw him only briefly—long enough to watch him disappear. Never had a chance to explain myself."

Uther frowned in consternation. "What is she saying?"

That she wishes she could have explained her situation when she last saw you, I replied, sipping my coffee to stall.

"But there's nothing to explain," he protested. "There are few secrets on this side. I've known the truth about Artur since she was ten."

"I'm sure he would have understood," I told Artur. "You didn't put a transformation bind on yourself."

She offered a one-shouldered shrug. "Perhaps. But he raised me as his son, and he was deceived in all ways. He has a right to an explanation. I would have liked to apologize."

"Tell me what she said," Uther demanded.

She wants to apologize for deceiving you, I thought, trying to remain patient with two conversations.

"She did nothing wrong! Remind her of that."

I drank deeply, covering my silence with coffee. *Why don't I let you tell her yourself? I feel fine*, I added before Flora could jump in with an objection. *A few minutes won't hurt me, and it would give Artur peace of mind.*

Flora scowled a warning, but it was unnecessary. "No," said Uther. "Thank you, but no. This is not the time."

"You know," I said to Artur, "if your father came to your aid in Glastonbury, then he's probably not upset with you."

"Perhaps," she said again, and looked up as Zeb emerged from the bunkroom. "Are they still asleep?" she asked as he neared.

"Stirring," said Zeb. "Going to get more coffee going, and…ah, good, she didn't get lost," he said, peeking out the window. "You two make room, we've got food incoming."

As Zeb helped Beth inside with her bags of breakfast, I woke Arik and shooed him toward the bath, then turned around to find Uther at my side, his face drawn. "I don't want to be cruel," he said. "Artur doesn't need a distraction now."

Oh? I think it would do her good.

"*I* think she doesn't need to feel as if I'm second-guessing every decision she makes," he retorted. "Beth may be in need of a father's guidance, but Artur is not, and I would not insult her by insinuating that I think her anything less than capable of the task at hand. Do you understand?"

Don't worry, I'll respect your wishes, I replied, folding a blanket. *I disagree with them, but she's not my daughter.*

"I know her far better than you do," he said, then leaned closer to me. "Another time, and I would be grateful. But now is not that time."

I cut my eyes to Artur, who lingered near the

kitchenette with her mug, considering the assembled with a distant stare.

I'll hold you to it, I told Uther, and deflated the mattress.

The sleepwalkers' brief early-morning attempt had been fruitless, but Artur was undeterred. "Here's the plan," she announced, guarding the coffeepot as the rest of us picked through Beth's breakfast offerings. "Hope, your, ehm...*sources* haven't reported activity from the Hidden Ones?"

Flora shook her head.

"Nothing," I replied.

"Good. Then we trust the original trajectory and head east. Frank, you're fit to drive?"

He flashed one thumb, his mouth full of greasy sausage.

"Excellent. I needn't remind anyone that we're on a schedule, correct?" she added, looking around the room.

I cut my eyes to the Minor Arcanum group, but judging by their somber expressions, someone had already explained Arik's predicament.

If anyone took offense at Artur's quiet power grab, no one voiced a complaint. After the long previous day, it was a relief to be on the road again with a direction in mind. Frank took the wheel with Artur navigating, Carey and Hua returned to their bunks to sleepwalk, and Beth turned on a movie for something to do. I was useless once breakfast was cleared away, but Zeb, seeing Arik's deterioration, revealed his talents beyond the kitchen.

"Where does it hurt?" he asked, studying Arik, who huddled in a chair with a blanket wrapped around him.

Arik lifted his listless eyes. "Honestly? Everywhere."

"Mm. Let's see what we can do without touching that collar, eh?" he said, and pulled a wand from the back of his waistband.

His spell manifested around Arik like a fine mesh made

of shadow, but relief flashed across Arik's face almost immediately. "There, now," said Zeb, smiling tautly. "Put a bit of warming in that, too, so let's see if we can get you feeling hu—well, I guess not *human*, but better." He chuckled at his own slip-up. "Are you sure you don't want to try to get the collar off? We know plenty of folks in Faerie, and I'm sure that someone could get the attention of the powers that be."

But Arik shook his head. "Thank you, but from what I've seen, the risk is so great..."

"You're going to have to risk it eventually, son."

"I know," he said, and clasped Zeb's gnarled hand. "Once my brother is safe."

"Come Monday, whether he's safe or not, you'd better try something before it's too late." Zeb gave Arik's shoulder a light squeeze. "Hang in there, kid. And here." With a flick of his wand, Arik's blanket shifted, growing fuzzy and thinner. "Electric," he said, adjusting the new dial, and returned to his coffee duties, keeping vigil for the sleepwalkers.

We didn't have to wait long.

Beth's movie was barely halfway over when Hua slammed open the bunkroom door and ran out. "We have blue!" she announced, pumping her fist.

"*Where?*" Artur called from the front as she scrambled to unbuckle and join us.

"Don't know the place name, but we saw it. We *both* saw it," Hua replied, then beckoned for Carey to join us as she staggered out. "An adult man, yes?"

Carey murmured her thanks as Zeb helped her to the futon. "Male, yes. Late teens to early thirties, I'd guess. He was driving a pickup truck."

Arik leaned toward her, clutching his blanket. "Was it Fik?"

"Can't say," she began, but held up a hand as his face

fell. "I can't say that it *wasn't* your brother. The problem is that we didn't get a good close-up look before he disappeared."

Beth and Artur traded bemused glances. "A gate?" Artur asked. "As you thought?"

"No," said Hua, "or if it was, it was unlike any gate I have seen."

"Then what—"

"Hold that thought, dear," said Carey, taking a fresh coffee from her doting husband, and closed her eyes in seeming relief at the first sip. "I'm sorry, kids, but this doesn't get any easier as you get older. Thank you, sweetie. Now, I don't believe it was a gate, and I'll tell you why. Gates always show outflow—even intra-realm gates have a sort of current to them. It's faint in the dream space, but if you know what you're looking for, you can pick up on them. There was none of that with our blue friend."

A look of comprehension, followed quickly by concern, creased Zeb's brow. "You think it's a Fringe-type situation?"

"Signs point to yes," she replied. "The question is who's running the system."

"Wait, *stop*," Artur interrupted. "What has the Fringe got to do with this? Their people can't make gates—"

"It's not about what the Fringe has *done*, but about what was done *to* them," Carey explained. "You've heard about the Mulligan years?"

"In detail."

"Then you'll recall that Badger and a few of us in the Minor Arcanum spent more than a decade looking for the Fringers that good old Grand Magus Psycho hid away. We never found a trace of them, and Badger picked the silo *apart*. As it turns out, the original Grand Magus Psycho—"

"Otherwise known as Simon Magus," Zeb offered.

"Precisely," said Carey with a look of distaste. "Genius, but twisted. He worked out a method of hiding people in the dream space and scribbled it down in that nasty little diary of his, and the regime did their homework. They were under our noses all along, and we couldn't see them because of the spells around them."

"Bonus feature," Frank called from the driver's seat.

"Come again?"

"Mulligan just wanted to hide his hostages. He didn't know anything about sleepwalking, right? He got lucky and picked the spell he didn't know he needed."

She sipped her coffee. "I suppose I give him too much credit. Anyway, there's a complicated spellcraft construction that can hide people from sleepwalkers. I think we may have found one in use."

"I've never heard of such among our people," I said. "Maybe Fik's made friends with a wizard. One of yours?"

"Not ours," said Hua, "and probably not Arcanum. But highly talented."

The thought was sobering.

"Where, exactly, are we going?" Frank asked.

Carey rubbed a spot in her neck. "My best guess is eastern Kentucky, this side of the Appalachians. I think the edge of the protected field was near a valley—guess you'd call it a holler, eh?"

"Oh, great," Beth muttered. "*Deliverance* with wands."

"Maybe, but what choice do we have? We don't have time to scout—and if there's a pack of bloodthirsty beasts headed their way, then maybe the locals won't be upset if we warn them." She drained the rest of her coffee, then passed the mug back to Zeb and pushed herself to her feet. "Give us a minute to rest, and we'll get back to it. And one of you pull up some topographical maps," she added, pointing to Artur and Beth. "We're going to need to do some guesswork."

Beth kept the television on throughout the day, but if she meant it to be a distraction, her plan was an abject failure. No one sitting in the living quarters of the RV could focus long enough on the screen to follow the stories of the movies she selected, and after lunch, she switched the program to a documentary on sea life, which at least had soothing background music. Most of the time, we sat staring out the windows, watching summer roll past at seventy miles an hour and waiting for a word from the sleepwalkers.

They emerged with greater frequency that day, coming out every hour or so to offer their findings and check the details they'd gleaned against the maps left open on Beth's computer. Having dropped almost to ground level and narrowed their focus, they were catching more and more glimpses of blue, all of which disappeared once they crossed an invisible barrier. "It's a circle, as far as we can tell," Carey explained on one such coffee break. "Maybe a mile in diameter. The inside of it is nondescript in the dream space—it looks like trees. If there's anything down there, it's probably hidden from us."

"Can we get there by gate?" Frank asked from the front.

Hua and Carey exchanged a look. "If we could pinpoint this place, then a gate would be possible," Hua replied. "But the dream space can be difficult to plot against a map, especially if there are no striking features. If, for example, this circle were on the outskirts of Beijing, then I could narrow the field and make a reasonably close gate. But in this case…"

"I don't know Appalachia well," said Carey. "This place isn't near a major city, which doesn't help us. So I can either waste time poring over topographical maps or try to find more information sleepwalking."

Frank sighed but didn't complain.

Late that morning, they told us of their odder sightings around the barrier. "I saw a gold flash," Hua reported, "the driver of a car. In the back was a child—*greenish.*"

"Green?" Zeb's forehead wrinkled in query. "What looks green in there?"

"Nothing that we know of," said Carey, "but…"

"You have a theory?" he prompted.

She nodded. "And it's just that, bear in mind. So, witch-bloods look weird in the dream space, right? Faeries show up in white, wizards and witches in gold, but witch-bloods are kind of an in-between shade. It's almost creamy. You two, now," she said, pointing to Arik and me, "show up as true blue. No wizards in your families, I take it."

"That would be news to me," I replied.

"Uh-huh. So what do you think would happen, color-wise, if you stumbled onto a Gray Lander with a wizard parent?"

"Blue and gold," Arik murmured. "Blended would be green—"

"*Bingo*," she said.

"Multiple blue people, some gold, at least one green," said Hua. "All coming in and out of a protected area. How does one interpret that?"

"A settlement?" Arik suggested.

"Maybe," said Carey. "Some sort of community. Bottom line, we've got sightings of multiple Gray Landers. I don't know if we've spotted your brother yet, but if he's anywhere along this route—"

"The odds are good," he finished.

And for the first time that day, Arik smiled.

Frank pushed hard, keeping the RV on the upper end of its safe speed while Beth and Artur took turns beside him for the all-important tasks of navigating, bringing snacks, and monitoring the CB for speed traps. We stopped only once all day, and then for a mere half hour, just long enough for our driver to stretch his legs and order an obscene number of fast-food burgers, which he ate while he drove. Finally, after a grueling ten hours, and with the sun dipping well below the trees, Beth directed Frank off the Kentucky state route he'd been following into the wilderness and onto a poorly maintained strip of asphalt— a tertiary road at best. The RV slowed to a crawl and bumped across the ruts and potholes, while the woods rose up thick and tangled on both sides of the street.

"Is this a private road?" I asked, clinging to the back of Beth's chair to steady myself.

"Not as far as I can tell, but it's a dead end," she replied. "I'm just following orders from the sleepwalkers…"

"Watch for deer," Frank interrupted, and Beth turned her attention back to her copilot duties. "Wouldn't be a bad place to hide a magically protected homestead," he said. "A piece of forested land in the middle of nowhere, a shitty road to deter snoops…" He paused, sniffed deeply, then frowned and pulled the vehicle to a stop.

"What's wrong?" Beth asked.

"A moment." He opened his window, unbuckled his seatbelt, then leaned his head and shoulders outside. I saw the tip of his tongue flick in and out of his mouth a few times and waited, perplexed, until he returned to his seat and turned to face us. "Dark magic. The concentration's rising. I *thought* I smelled it."

Beth frowned and peered out at the scenery. "Could be, but with the shadows out here…"

"He's right."

I looked over my shoulder and found Arik wobbling up the aisle. "You think?"

"Look how much brighter it is," he said, gesturing to the swirls of color in the RV's headlights. "It's not like home, but I haven't seen this much of it since I arrived."

"So we're probably on the right track, then," said Frank, rubbing his chin, "but we've got a new complication. Brace yourselves, I'm going to start us up again."

He didn't drive far. A few hundred feet ahead, the road widened to the left, a turnaround spot of sorts. Frank pulled off and cut the engine, and we rejoined the others in the main room.

Zeb, who'd been tending to Hua and Carey, watched us with concern. "Where are we?" he asked, tapping one knuckle against the window. "Tree in the road?"

"No, and we're close," Frank replied, "which is why I'm getting off now. Someone else will need to finish the drive."

"Well, uh...sure," said Zeb, cocking his head, "but I don't understand why—"

"*This* is held together with magic." Frank swept one hand up and down his body. "The concentration of dark magic ahead is higher, and presumably climbing. I'm certainly no expert, but if the magic concentration drops too low…"

Beth whistled. "Puff, the Magic Dragon."

"And bits of RV *everywhere*," he replied, giving her ponytail a sharp tug. "Let's not take unnecessary risks."

Artur cleared her throat. "If the concentration drops that low, then perhaps we shouldn't be driving a magically enhanced vehicle into the area, either. What happens if the spells on this thing fall apart?"

"Goodbye, bunkroom," Beth muttered.

"For starters. The RV remains here, then. We'll finish the journey on foot." She picked up her sword, which had been propped in a corner of the room, and considered the assembled as she belted it on. "Perhaps the two of you could stay with Frank," she suggested, nodding to Zeb and Carey. "In case of emergency, you can drive this thing, can you not?"

It was a polite out because of their age, and we all knew it, but they agreed without a fight. Hua insisted that she could accompany us, but as Arik headed for the door to follow her out, Artur stopped him. "This could be some distance, and you're in no condition to march. Stay here."

Arik shook his head and tried to shoulder past her. "I've come this far, and if Fik is down the road—"

"We'll bring him to you."

"*No*." His shove was more forceful that time, but Artur didn't flinch. "Let me out."

"It's unwise—"

"Artur," I interrupted, drawing her attention, and shook my head.

She glared at Arik for a long moment, then sighed and stepped back. "I'm not carrying you."

"I can manage," he muttered, bracing himself against the opening as he descended to the road.

Carey hurried after him. "Just a second, kid," she said, catching his arm, then pulled her wand from her waistband and made a few adjustments to the spell around him. "There, that should shore it up a bit. I can't guarantee it'll hold together if the magic drops too low, but maybe it'll get you there."

He thanked her, and we started off, Artur on point, Beth and Hua in the middle, and Arik and me bringing up the rear. When the others weren't looking, I wrapped my arm around his waist and murmured in Cynaeli, "Lean on me. I can take your weight."

"I'm fine," he said through a grimace.

"And I'm the next queen of Conota. Don't be stubborn, Arikol." Noticing movement from the corner of my eye, I saw that Flora had appeared beside me and thought, *Stay with the RV. If there's a problem, would you let me know?*

She seemed troubled by the request. "You don't know what lies ahead."

If we find cynaeli, I'd rather not explain why I have a spirit escort. One complication at a time.

"I won't be seen," she replied, and walked on with us. "Believe me, child, I am more than familiar with my capabilities. Besides, the only reason the men stayed behind is because I promised to keep an eye on you lot. Would you rather have Orson and Uther here as well?"

This works. I shifted my grip on Arik as we traversed a

pothole, and though he said nothing, his arm snaked over my neck.

"All right?" I asked.

"Thanks," he whispered.

Even as the shadows lengthened toward sunset, the day remained stiflingly warm and humid, and the undulation of the road didn't help matters. I was soon sweating, and though Arik didn't complain, his breathing was labored and wheezy. When we'd hiked for perhaps twenty minutes in silence, Flora vanished, only to reappear a moment later with an update. "This is the final climb. The road levels and falls after this hill."

Good, Arik replied.

"It descends into a little valley. The perimeter is heavily wooded. Within the valley is a settlement of some kind—a village, perhaps, or some sort of family collective. About twenty houses and larger buildings. Barns, I think, though I saw no livestock."

People? I asked.

"Yes, a fair number. No guard, as far as I can tell, but the valley is definitely inhabited."

I passed on her impressions to the others, and Artur called a brief halt. "The important thing is not to frighten them," she told us as we leaned against the trees. "Walk slowly, keep your hands visible, and pray that whoever is living at the end of the road prefers to shoot only as a last resort."

Hua patted the slim wand bulge beneath her shirt. "I am not the greatest wizard, but I am competent."

"Likewise," Beth mumbled.

"Which is well and good," said Artur, "unless we're faced with fifty angry cynaeli." She cracked her back and stepped onto the pavement again. "Come, we're wasting daylight."

Flora's report proved accurate: the hill we'd been climbing was the last. What stretched before us appeared—or would have appeared, I suppose, to the human eye—to be nothing but trees, a forest stretching away and ahead with nothing to recommend it. When *I* looked out, however, I saw the brilliant lattice of a camouflage ward in the distance, a dome rising from the ground and arcing well above the canopy. "Ward," I said, pointing toward the valley.

"That's not just shadow?" asked Beth.

"No, it most certainly is not. It's *huge.*"

"There is a gate into your home realm nearby," Flora told me. "Beyond the valley."

I relayed that tidbit, which gave Artur pause. "How close?" she asked.

"Not far, I understand. But much of the outflow must be powering that ward—it's massive," I replied. "Purely camouflage, from the look of it. I don't believe it's a barrier ward."

"Still, we use caution," she murmured, and slowed until our pack bunched up.

We were within fifty feet of the ward when a soccer ball bounced toward us, seemingly having manifested from thin air. Beth intercepted it and scooped it into her arms just as a little girl ran out onto the road in pursuit. Spotting us in the middle of the street, she froze, her dark pigtails bouncing as she came to a terrified stop.

Beth dropped to one knee and extended the ball. "Hi, sweetie," she said, her voice surprisingly gentle. "Is this yours?"

The child managed to nod.

"Good thing we caught it before it went into the woods, then. Here you go." When the girl didn't budge, Beth said, "That's okay, I can pass it to you." She stood and put the ball on the ground, then barely kicked it with the side of her foot. It rolled down the street, and the girl caught it with both hands, almost hugging it. "I'm Beth," she offered when the girl didn't immediately flee. "What's your name?"

"Emmaline," she mumbled.

"Emmaline? That is *so* pretty!" Beth cried in the exaggerated tones of one addressing the young and uncertain. "I love it. Do you like soccer? I play it sometimes in school, but I'm not very good at it."

Emmaline nodded.

"What grade are you in? Tenth, at least," she teased.

At that, the child giggled. "Second."

"Second, huh? Maybe I need glasses." She mimed a deep squint, earning another smile from the girl. "Listen, Emmaline, I'm looking for someone," said Beth. "His name is Fik, and he's a grownup. Do you know anyone like that around here?"

Emmaline sobered immediately, her arms tightening around the soccer ball as she regarded Beth warily. Before she could bolt, I stepped close to Beth, caught the child's eye, and dropped my glamour. "If Fik is in there, we need to talk to him," I said in Cynaeli. "He's in danger. We've come to warn him. Could you find him, please?"

She stared at me for a moment, then turned and ran through the ward, vanishing before our eyes.

"So, uh...what was that about?" asked Beth, folding her arms.

"Yes," said Artur, giving me a pointed look, "do you think *that* is wise?"

"Did you notice her hands?" I replied.

"What about them?"

"Four fingers. Either she has a birth defect or she's partly cynaeli." I glanced at the ward, but if there was motion on the other side, I couldn't detect it. "What do we do now?"

Artur shrugged. "I suggest we wait. Cynaeli or not, surely the child will alert someone to our presence."

Fifteen minutes later, as we were quietly discussing alternative plans, a crowd of people came marching out from behind the ward, several with rifles in hand. We jumped into a rough formation—to no one's surprise, Artur took the lead, sword drawn and ready—but as the wizards reached for their wands, I spotted a familiar face in the pack. He wore his hair differently than he once had, now in a thick ponytail comprised of tiny braids, but his blue-green eyes were undisguised, so striking against his dark skin.

"Fik!" I called, waving. "It's Hope! From High Vale, remember me?"

He jerked at the sound of my voice, then raised a hand and laughed aloud. "What are *you* doing here, girl? And…" He stopped in his tracks, his eyes widening. "Is that…"

I dropped Arik's glamour, and Fik, grinning like a madman, began to push his fellows aside. "It's okay," he said in English, "stand down! That's my brother!"

The others made way, and Fik ran to meet us. "Arik," he said, beaming, and wrapped him in a tight hug. "This is wonderful! Be welcome. How did you find me? I thought I would never see you again, little brother."

When Fik released him, Arik smiled sadly, then tugged at his shirt until his collar was revealed. "Not your brother any longer, I'm afraid."

"*My brother,*" Fik insisted, holding his stare, then turned to me and chuckled. "Well, now, if it isn't Lady Imaranta. Grabbed one of those stubborn chinols of yours and fled, did you?"

"It was a little more complicated than that," I replied. "And you're in trouble, Fik. Arik came to warn you, and our friends have been helping us get here."

Fik glanced at Hua, Beth, and Artur, who had at least put their weapons away, then looked back at Arik. His eyes fell to Arik's collar again, and as he got a closer look at Arik's haggard condition, a look of dawning horror crossed his face. "You escaped," he murmured.

"I had to find you," said Arik.

"How long do you have?"

"We think until sometime Monday," I said quietly.

"The wizards with us have been trying to help, but unless the collar comes off…"

I didn't need to finish the sentence.

Fik's joy had quickly morphed into anguish. "Why would you do that, Arik?" he demanded. "You must go back, there's a gate nearby—"

"Father's sent Hidden Ones to kill you," Arik interrupted. "Honestly, though, I prefer my odds facing them to returning to Pimati, don't you?"

He retreated a pace. "Father did *what?*"

"Hidden Ones," I said. "They've wiped out two towns already, and they're headed this way. We don't have long."

Fik swore, then wrapped his arm beneath Arik's shoulders, almost lifting him off the ground. "Come with me. You look terrible."

Arik laughed weakly. "It's nice to see you again, too."

Behind the camouflage ward system was a second set, a smaller bubble nested within the larger one. To my eyes, it appeared to be a smoky network, but those in our party sensitive to the other magic stopped and stared. "*Whoa,*" Beth finally managed. "That is *tight.*"

"Impressive," Hua concurred. "A camouflage ward of magic within one of dark magic. And this system…unique," she murmured, pressing her palm against the lattice. "This must be the border we saw in the dream space."

"Spellcraft later, predatory horde now," Artur reminded them, dragging Beth away from her inspection.

We followed after Fik, who half-carried Arik down a gravel lane toward a modest house, a one-story brick construction that wouldn't have been out of place in Pauline. There was no mailbox, but the yard was green and neat, and a young dogwood was in full leaf beside the blue pickup truck in the driveway. Fik helped Arik up the three steps to the porch, then pushed open the screen door and hurried inside. By the time I'd made it in, a young woman had appeared from down the hall, wearing a T-shirt, shorts, and a bright green wrap crisscrossed over her chest. She seemed human at first blush, an attractive brunette, but when she stepped into the bright light of the den, I noticed a slight purplish undertone to her otherwise beige skin—and a distinct lack of fifth digits on both hands.

"Is everything okay?" she asked in drawled English, putting her arms around the bulge beneath her wrap. "What's going on out there?"

Fik helped Arik to the couch and deposited him with a soft grunt. "Janice, honey, this is Arik. Arik, this is my wife—"

"*Arik!*" she exclaimed, her concern replaced in an instant by excitement. "Oh, my goodness, you made it out! Hi!" She hurried across the room to give him an awkward, if enthusiastic, hug. "Sorry, the princess gets cranky if I put her down," she said, peeling back the wrap to reveal a little purple face. "I've heard so much about you! Did you just come through the gate?"

Arik seemed overwhelmed by the sudden attention, and Fik stepped in to assist. "We've been married for two years," he murmured to his brother, "and that's our Lilian. She's only six months old."

He floundered briefly, then gave Fik a genuine smile. "You're married and a father. Congratulations. My very best to you all."

"Thank you," said Fik, folding his arms, "but we'll have to show you the photo albums another time. What the hell is going on?"

Arik began to speak but doubled over in a coughing fit that left him panting. Janice watched with concern, then hurried to the kitchen, returning a moment later with a glass of water. "Rough trip?" she asked.

While he drank, I took the lead. "Did you know that Nath is dead?"

Fik was taken aback. "No. *How?*"

"She attacked Glastonbury last year," I replied, skimping on the details. "Anyway, the next king or queen has yet to be discovered. Arik says that your father's about to go to war to seize power in the vacuum, and now he's sent Hidden Ones to kill you."

Janice gasped, but Fik's brow wrinkled. "Why would he do that? I've been gone five years, I'm no great loss to him—"

"He thinks you're the missing king," Arik interrupted.

"*Me?*" Fik laughed in disbelief. "What would give him such a stupid idea? I'm no king!"

"Are you certain?"

"Absolutely. You remember our history tutor, yes? When one king dies, the next immediately receives a surge of power. Or did you sleep through that lesson, too?" He put an arm around his wife and pulled her close. "Trust me, whatever Father thinks I might be, he's mistaken. I'm his son, nothing more."

"That's good to know," I said, "but there's still a pack of Hidden Ones on the way."

"You left a trace of blood when you sneaked out," Arik explained. "They're tracking you."

"Can we reason with them?" Janice asked. "Tell them it's all been a mistake?"

I stared at her, surprised by the absurdity of the question, and Arik slowly blinked before saying, "You're not native to Conota, are you?"

"My grandmother was half-blooded," she mumbled, "but no, I was born here. Why?"

"You don't argue with Hidden Ones," Fik said, rubbing her arm as he tightened his hold on her. "You run. If you're sure about this, Arik—"

"On my life," he said.

Fik nodded sharply. "Then we're in deep trouble."

"We should get Papa," said Janice.

"Absolutely. Go," said Fik, releasing her, and Janice jogged out of the house, cradling the baby against her.

As the door slammed, I took a seat beside Arik. "Who's Papa?"

"Her grandfather," said Fik, frowning at the wall above our heads. "His family settled this place, and he keeps the inner ward going."

"A wizard?" Artur asked.

Fik jumped, then seemed to remember the rest of his company. "Yes. Are you?"

She smirked. "Not at all. What's a cynaeli doing in a ward-protected settlement with a wizard, pray tell?"

Before he could respond, Arik had another violent coughing fit, and Fik waited for it to subside with concern. "Has this been happening long?" he asked.

"Just now," Arik wheezed. "The walk here...I'm out of breath, that's all..."

"Bullshit," Beth muttered, and took out her wand. "I'm probably not as good at this as the Joneses, but I'll try to help," she offered.

Hua pitched in as well, and by the time they'd finished strengthening the healing wards around him, Janice had returned with a white-haired old man, who walked behind her with a carved wooden cane. His dark eyes, narrow behind his thick glasses, squeezed almost to slits as he gave us a quick perusal, then settled on the three with us who weren't visibly cynaeli. "Wizards?" he asked.

"You must be Papa," said Artur.

"I am. You're Arcanum?"

Beth raised her hand, while Artur lifted one slightly and wiggled it.

"Minor Arcanum," said Hua, stepping forward. "We mean no harm. He is in danger," she said, gesturing toward Fik, "and we came to help."

The old man's head tilted. "*Minor* Arcanum? What's that?"

Her mouth curved into a slight smile. "An inconvenience for the other Arcanum."

"Are *you* Arcanum?" Artur demanded. "You're

obviously a wizard of some degree, if you're the one maintaining the ward."

"I was," he replied. "My aunt was a magus."

"Was?" she echoed.

Papa nodded. "Tell me, is James Mulligan still kidnapping witches?"

"No, no," said Hua, emphatically shaking her head. "He's been dead for more than thirty years. The Fringe was freed. You didn't know?"

He let out a long, slow breath, and a strange emotion crossed his face, one that looked suspiciously like relief. "Hidden Ones, you say?"

"I swear it," said Arik.

"Well, damn, son." He took out his phone and punched a short code, then turned and started for the door. "Y'all come on to the main barn. We're going to have ourselves a town meeting."

CHAPTER 9

Having spent most of my childhood on chinol duty, I knew barns.

The building into which Papa led us was barn-shaped, but I doubted that it had ever housed an animal larger than a rat. The wooden floor was polished to a glossy sheen, the windows were large and clean, and instead of stalls or troughs or any sort of equipment, the room held a low stage and several rows of metal folding chairs. Papa seemed to have sent out a summons, as the seats were rapidly filling—and many of the people I recognized from our welcome party were still carrying guns. Our group took seats in the front row—Artur casually replaced her chair with a wooden model—and as the doors closed, Papa hobbled up the stage steps, leaning on his stick and grimacing when his knees bent. Reaching the top, he rapped the rubber butt of his cane on the floor for quiet, then gestured to Arik and me. "We've got guests, and they've got bad news," he announced. "You two come up here and tell us what's going on."

Arik stood on his own, but he looked miserable, and the tension in his face and body spoke of pain. "It's all right," I whispered, putting my arm around his waist, and he wrapped his in turn over my shoulders for support as we took the stage. By the time we'd made it up the short flight of steps, Fik had followed us up with a spare chair, and Arik, though blushing, put aside his pride and took a seat. I looked down at him, waiting to see how he wanted to proceed, and he squeezed my hand and nodded.

"Uh…hello," I said, turning to the crowd. "I'm Hope Lozano. To anyone who knows Conota, I'm also Lady Imaranta of High Vale."

A low murmur went around the room, though I couldn't tell which of the assembled might have ever laid eyes on my home. Everyone in the room appeared human enough but for the youngest children. Even Janice had glamoured for the occasion—I'd caught her asking Fik to help her on our way over.

"The queen is dead," I continued when the buzz subsided. "She attempted to invade Glastonbury last year, and the combined forces of this realm and Faerie drove her back. Or her army, I mean. She was trampled. Anyway, that doesn't matter," I said, conscious that I was rambling from nerves. "The problem is that her successor hasn't been identified. Either Conota hasn't selected one or else the successor is in hiding." I paused to glance back at Arik, who nodded encouragement. "Meanwhile, there's about to be a civil war among our people. The tennuwaya have already begun. If Conota won't choose a king, then the strongest among us will fight for the throne."

"And this war is coming here?" one of the men near the front asked.

"No. Not yet, at least. The problem is that *his* father," I said, pointing to Fik, "would very much like to be king, but he's worried that Fik is the real king in hiding."

"Which is nonsense," Fik insisted, half-rising from his chair.

"Be that as it may, Arik here says that their father has contracted with the Hidden Ones to kill him," I continued, gesturing to my companion. "We haven't seen them, but we've seen what they've done. Two towns have been eaten in the last week, one in Colorado and the other in Kansas. We found your settlement in part because it's along their projected path. They're tracking Fik by his blood. And depending on whether and how long they stop to rest, they should be here within a day or two."

The murmuring started up again, and a woman near the back yelled, "Why the heck would anyone think *Fik* is a king?"

"Paranoia?" said Arik, raising his voice to be heard over the crowd. "That, and the fact that he looks nothing like our father. If you've seen cynaeli with human parents, you know how infrequently we favor them. Fik is an exception."

Another woman closer to the front spoke up. "Less of an exception than you might think. And it's not just cynaeli—I look mostly human, too," she said, going to her feet. "See?"

When her glamour fell away, Arik and I were taken aback. The woman's head of blonde curls had vanished in a blink, laying bare her pale scalp, which had a bluish undertone. A pair of small pits had appeared on either side of her face, stretching between her eyes and slightly pointed ears. Vestigial eyes, I realized, which meant...

"You're *tennuwaya*?" Arik asked, leaning forward for a better look.

She nodded. "Half. I was sired by one of the bed servants of a pleasure house."

"We don't discriminate here," said Papa. "Cynaeli, tennuwaya...if it comes out of Conota and needs a place to go, we're open."

"And I know these 'Hidden Ones' of which you speak," she said, crossing her arms. "Ykoro, we call them. They attacked my village when I was seven."

"How do you fight them?" a man near her asked.

She snorted. "You don't. My mother put me up a tree, and anyone still alive built fires for hours until the creatures tired and moved on."

"Fire," I murmured, turning to Arik. "Remember what Kip said? They built defensive fires, too."

Before he could respond, Fik went to his feet, then stood on his chair to see over the room. "Obviously, I am the problem," he said. "If they're tracking me, then I need to go. They should leave the rest of you in peace."

"Go *where*, exactly?" Janice demanded, standing in turn. "You can't run forever, and how do you plan to defend yourself?"

He looked down at her, his face softening. "I have to protect you and Lily—"

"Not by getting yourself killed."

"And there's another concern," said Artur, jogging up the steps to join Arik and me. "As long as those things are in this realm, they will keep feeding. What would stop them from leaving a group here? Splitting the pack, starting over with fresh hunting grounds—"

"I'm sorry," Papa cut in, "you're…"

"My name is Artur," she said, scanning the crowd. "And I've fought all manner of things that have come out of the Gray Lands. Never these creatures, but quite a bit else."

A man with a shotgun across his lap gave her a hard look. "Like *what*, girlie?"

The stare Artur returned was cold and uncomfortably long, and he fidgeted beneath it. "Scintol," she murmured, "for starters. Can you say as much?"

He shook his head.

"Then hold your tongue, *boy*." Turning her attention back to the suddenly quieter room, she said, "Practically speaking, we have two choices. Either we surrender Fik to the Hidden Ones and hope they go home in peace, or we make a stand and attempt to slaughter them. In neither scenario is this settlement's safety guaranteed."

"Or we could fight somewhere else," a woman in the crowd suggested. "Lead them away from here."

"Do you know of a location nearby that's easily defensible and *far* from unsuspecting humans?" Artur asked. "If we lure these things near a larger town, then that's merely more lives at risk."

She winced and shook her head.

"Very well. Having seen what we've seen in the last

week, I suggest we fight them here. As we cannot treat with them, our best option is to kill them."

"How?" Arik murmured.

"Fire," said Artur, "is a useful tool if employed correctly. I propose building a fire ring around this place—say, at the edge of your wards. The Hidden Ones will come in search of Fik, they'll find themselves faced with a wall of flames, and we can pick them off."

"Maybe we could try that in April," Papa protested, "but this is August, and we're under burn restrictions as it is. We're in drought conditions, you know, the trees are dry. If we try to start a controlled burn, it'll probably turn into a wildfire."

"What about Magus Corelli?" Beth blurted.

As the focus of the room swiveled her way, she hunched lower in her chair, but she didn't lose her nerve. "She's supposed to be good with fire, right?" she said, looking to Artur for confirmation. "Think she could control it?"

Artur mulled that over. "Perhaps. We could ask her—"

"And we'd still be setting up a siege situation," Papa interjected.

She sighed and closed her eyes. "Are you or are you not a *wizard*?"

"Well, yes—"

"And how difficult is it for you to cast food and water into existence?"

"Significantly," he retorted. "I'm not a *great* wizard."

The tennuwaya woman raised her hand. "I can manage, but the result isn't particularly palatable."

"You and I should compare notes," said Artur. "But that's at least two of us, then. And since the most pressing threat of a siege is starvation, we should have the upper hand."

"Unless the little bastards get hungry in the meantime," said Papa. "There's towns all over the county. What if they just keep eating our neighbors?"

She smiled grimly. "They won't be able to do such if we pin them."

"With *what?*"

Ignoring him, she turned instead to Arik and me. "We keep Frank and the Joneses outside the fire ring, probably with a smaller ring around the RV to protect them. As soon as the horde passes, Frank can block their retreat. He's rather skilled with fire, that one. Presumably, the wizards can mitigate any unintentional burning."

"That could still lead to a wildfire," I cautioned. "Carey and Zeb have healing talents, and Carey sleepwalks, of course, but can they manage fire?"

We turned to Hua, who seemed uncertain. "Fire can be difficult," she said. "The Joneses are strong, but…maybe, maybe not."

"A question for Maria, then," said Artur, pulling her phone from her pocket, then raised her voice and addressed the room again. "If no one has a better plan, I'm calling a magus. Objections?"

We looked at Papa, who silently shook his head and grimaced at the floor.

The Away Team, as I understood it, largely looked after itself. Its membership was sufficiently diverse—five wizards, three people who were functionally half fae, one dragon, and a shifter with a touch of magical talent—that they could settle their own problems most of the time. But the Arcanum was nothing if not a bureaucracy, and so the group had a supervisory magus in case of emergency. Maria Corelli wasn't a wizard in the strictest sense— confusingly enough to me, she was more or less fae—but I wasn't going to question her credentials too carefully if Artur and Beth thought she was our best hope.

If nothing else, Maria was gracious about the midnight summons out to rural Kentucky. "Eh, time zones are fun," she said, closing her gate behind her, and paused in the road to take in the outer ward system. "That's…different."

"Camouflage," I explained. "You'll like the one inside."

She did, by which I mean she stopped in her tracks two feet inside the bubble and gaped at the inner ward. "*Wow*," she finally managed. "Who the hell built that? And *when?*"

"Not this Papa of theirs, apparently," said Artur. "I gather that he's skilled enough to do maintenance, but he wasn't the architect."

"Huh. And exactly *what* are we dealing with, here?"

She folded her arms and stared through the inner ward at the restless settlement. "Cynaeli and tennuwaya, but something tells me that most have at least a little human in the mix. We haven't asked for demographics, to be honest."

"Something to sort through later," Maria agreed. A tiny cup of espresso appeared in her hand. "Toula's kept me informed, but what's the latest? Why do you need me now?"

She'd knocked back a second espresso by the time Artur and I brought her up to speed, and while she looked more awake, she didn't seem convinced. "You want me to manage one fire ring and supervise a second? With a pack of man-eating things in between?"

"Basically," said Artur.

She drummed her nails against her cup for a few seconds, then sent it back into the ether from whence it had come. "Probably doable, but I'm not in love with the idea."

"Have you got a better one? I'm listening."

"No. This whole situation is problematic." Maria pointed to the nearest houses and said, "To be safe, this place needs to be evacuated. In case something happens to me or the fire gets out of hand, I don't want casualties."

"Where would you send them?" I asked. "And Fik can't leave, can he? He's meant to be the bait."

She rubbed her bare arm—a T-shirt seemed to suit her as well as the formal trappings of a magus—and frowned in thought. "Let me make some calls. They're still meeting?" she asked, glancing toward the well-lit main barn.

"That's where we left them," I replied.

"Keep them there. I won't be long." Taking her phone out, she started down the road toward the houses.

"You have a favor with someone?" Artur called after her.

Maria turned and grinned. "Better. I have a grandfather who's amenable to persuasion."

She soon rejoined us with good news: the people of the settlement could stay in the Fringe town in Faerie for a few days. "Ros is on board," she announced, "which is a relief." She glanced around the barn, then asked, "Where's Frank?"

"A couple of miles back up the road. He was worried about dark magic," Beth explained. "Why?"

"Val told me that Ros wanted him to check his phone. Oh, well," she said with a shrug. "I'll pass the word when I see him. Bigger problems at hand, right?"

On that, she was absolutely correct. If it was difficult for a group of wizards to gain the locals' trust, it was nearly impossible to convince them that evacuating to Faerie was the wisest course of action. Maria kept calm and answered their questions—they were expected, guest accommodations were being prepared, they would be free to return as soon as the danger had passed—and after a time, with the others looking to him for guidance, Papa straightened on his cane and announced that they would be evacuating. "Pack quickly," he told them.

"Only what you absolutely need," Maria added as the people hurried for the doors. "Anything else can be provided over there."

Naturally, there were holdouts. A few of the younger settlers were ready to fight and offered to stay, but Papa sent them on to grab their things. Their older neighbors—the ones native to Conota, as Papa quietly pointed out to us—put up no protest about leaving. "The kids have no idea what's coming," he said. "*I* hardly know what to expect. But if the Conotans know it's time to run, then I'm not going to second-guess them."

The one who raised the greatest fuss was Janice, who refused to leave Fik to face the Hidden Ones alone. "I'll be fine," he said, trying to reassure her as her eyes welled. "Arik won't let anything happen to me."

"Arik can barely *walk*," she retorted. "You need me here."

He cupped his hands around her face and wiped her stray tears away. "Lily needs her mother," he murmured. "If something happens to me, Lily will need you even more. I'll fight better knowing that the two of you are safe."

"I don't want you to fight at all."

"That's not my choice." He kissed her, then pulled the wrap aside and bent to kiss the baby. "I'm going to make this right," he promised. "One way or another, I'll keep you safe. But you need to go."

Half an hour later, with the barn full of nervous people and their luggage, Maria checked her phone, then opened a gate into a sunny park. I spotted a fountain and recognized the Fringe town. Before the evacuees could cross the border, however, three people stepped into the opening—a redheaded woman in a pale lilac twinset and gray trousers, a dark-haired man in a button-down shirt and jeans, and a shorter man in a looser-cut yellow tunic belted over brown pants. The last I recognized as Valerius, who'd sheltered me on my exodus from Conota—Maria's grandfather, I recalled. The others, though backlit, could only be Lady Eleanor and Lord Coileán. Apparently, the kings and queen of Faerie wanted to oversee the matter personally.

Artur raised a hand in greeting. "Apologies for the

short notice," she said in Fae. "We just found them."

"It's no trouble," Valerius began, and Eleanor nodded.

But Coileán, who'd been looking around the room, stepped through the gate and pointed at Papa. "*You*," he barked in English. "Are you—"

Papa, who'd blanched on seeing him, hobbled backward. "I can explain, hear me out," he babbled.

With a smirk, Coileán folded his arms and watched Papa squirm. "Well, I'll be damned. Drago, Dark Lord of the fucking Storm. Or is it something else these days?"

"I was a little shit back then, all right?" said Papa. "I admit it. I'm sorry. Don't take it out on everyone else, *please*."

"This had better be one damn good explanation."

Eleanor frowned and joined Coileán in the barn. "You know this man?"

He kept his eyes locked on Papa's. "Steve Brownfield. A no-account little wizard who broke down Meggy's front door, then came after me a few days later with...what was it, Stevie, knuckledusters? *Steel* knuckledusters? This was just before we got Faerie open again," he added to Eleanor, "so there was no magic available for defense. You can probably imagine why we didn't part on the best of terms."

"You broke my wrist and three ribs," Papa protested.

"Steel. Knuckledusters. I'm waiting for that explanation."

As the crowd stared, their patriarch put up his free hand as if trying to keep Coileán at bay. "You know about Magus Mulligan?"

"Intimately," said Coileán. "Worked for him, did you?"

"*No*. My aunt Cora was a magus."

He nodded. "Yeah, I seem to remember that. What about it?"

"She was based in the silo, right? Mom and Dad and I were back in Virginia. A few weeks after Mulligan took over, Aunt Cora showed up on our doorstep in the middle of the night and said we had to get out of town. She'd heard about what he did to those witches, you know? That wasn't right. And Mulligan had ordered everyone to move into the installations, and my parents didn't want to go, so Aunt Cora was worried that he'd come after us next. Dad had this place as a hunting property. He just had a cabin, but it was a start, and Aunt Cora built the ward to hide us."

"How did she build it so well?" Maria interrupted. "I've not seen its like."

"It is the same sort of ward that Mulligan built around the kidnapped Fringers," said Hua. "Or so I believe—I never saw the one in Montana. But it hides everything in here from sleepwalkers."

Papa—or Steve, rather—frowned. "Sleepwalkers?"

"It looks like your aunt made a lucky guess," Hua explained. "The ward system she built was very special. *Very* good. Mulligan used something similar to hide his hostages."

"It was bound to be good," he replied. "She got it from Simon Magus's diary."

Coileán's eyebrows rose. "She did what?"

"Aunt Cora had access to the diary," said Steve. "All of the magi did. She studied it and memorized some of his techniques, just in case. Served us well. Anyway," he said, shifting his grip on his cane, "we'd only been here two months when a small gate opened from Conota. Aunt Cora stabilized it instead of closing it, explaining that if anyone came to repair it, that would be our signal to run. Fortunately, no one ever did."

"The Arcanum gave up on that during the Mulligan era. Anything that was closed was thanks to the Minor Arcanum," said Coileán, and nodded to Hua.

"Lucky for us," Steve muttered. "A few months after the gate opened, the first escapee came through. Abila. She was half cynaeli, half human, and she'd been one of Nath's servants. Her father had tried to recall her to marry her off, and she'd found the gate instead. It opens onto the plain between the cynaeli and tennuwaya territories, or so I've been told. So Abila ran through and found us, and because she'd been with Nath, she spoke Fae. Aunt Cora knew enough of the language to get by until she could cast English into her mind. Abila told us what she was running from—her intended was an abusive asshole—and we let her stay. She just glamoured herself when she was off the property. And then more people wandered through over time, and most of them were running from something or someone, and we built ourselves a community here. *They* built the outer camouflaging ward system," he said, gesturing to a few of the older people on the edge of the crowd. "Aunt Cora died of a heart attack about ten years after we got here, but she taught me enough to patch up the inner ward and keep it going. The nice thing is that the outer ward siphons off so much dark magic from the gate that it doesn't wear down the inner ward."

Coileán swept one hand over the crowd. "And this is the result?"

Steve nodded. "Abila was crazy enough to marry me. We've got six kids and twenty-three grandkids here—hell, I'm related by blood or marriage to almost everyone in the room."

"And this Abila of yours?"

His mouth tightened. "Car crash with a cement mixer seven years ago out on the highway. She didn't suffer."

"I'm sorry," said Coileán. To my surprise, the sentiment sounded genuine.

"Yeah, me, too," Steve mumbled. "Today's the first that I've heard that Mulligan's no longer in control. We cut all ties with the Arcanum—I mean, it's not as if they'd have approved of my wife, and I'm not that much of a wizard. But we're not hurting anyone," he insisted. "These folks just want to make lives for themselves, and I'm here to help keep things going as long as I can."

"They took me in," Fik interjected. "I came through

that gate, and they gave me food and shelter. And the tongue, obviously," he added with a weak chuckle. "Papa is my wife's grandfather, and he's good to us all—"

"It's okay, son," said Steve, then turned back to Coileán. "Look, I'll stay here, but the rest of them haven't done anything wrong. If you've got a beef with me, that's...understandable. I was an angry kid without a proper Arcanum education who just wanted to be something I'm not, and, uh...in retrospect, those knuckledusters were kind of a shitty thing to pull. I just...you know, I had something to prove, and—"

"And I did almost make you piss yourself," said Coileán.

Steve grunted. "No almost about it. Of course, I did blast Bellamy's door down," he added with a grimace. "Funny how things work out, though, isn't it? I didn't get the damn diary, but Aunt Cora made it work for us all the same. Not like I could have done jack with it."

Coileán considered him for a long moment, then stepped back and motioned toward the gate. "Come on, Drago. I'm not going to leave a gimpy old man here to get eaten."

"Thanks." He shouldered a small duffel and started for the gate. "And really, it's Steve now. I got rid of that stupid necklace a long time ago."

"Why 'Drago'?" one of the Brownfield sons quietly asked.

His father blushed furiously and tightened his mouth as Coileán snickered to himself. "Another time, eh?"

The evacuation went smoothly thereafter, though some of the settlers seemed nervous about leaving the realm. I couldn't blame them—it was disconcerting at best to find oneself without any useable magic, not to mention suddenly unglamoured. Recalling my last trip over the border, I had a sudden, unpleasant thought, and I pulled Valerius aside to quietly ask, "Has Kip been told about this?"

"Ros informed him," he replied, and patted my shoulder. "I doubt that he joins the welcoming committee, but he shouldn't take up arms and start a one-man execution squad, if that's what you feared."

"I really don't mean to make his life difficult."

"He's a grown man who understands what it means to end up in an unfamiliar realm," the king replied. "And should he forget, his wife is there to remind him. I wouldn't worry, were I you."

Last to leave were Janice and Lily, who lingered on the edge of the gate with Fik. "I'll be careful," he promised Janice. "Nothing too risky. As soon as the danger has passed, I'll send word, yes?"

Her tears had ceased, but there was a deep sadness in her eyes. "You don't think a man-eating horde is too risky?"

"You haven't met my father," he replied, and kissed her. "I hope you never have the chance. I swear to you, I'll make this better."

She rested one palm against his face. "Just don't get yourself killed, okay? Please? For us?"

He covered her hand with his, then gently pulled it away and kissed her fingers before nudging her toward the gate. "Be safe, dearest. And, uh…"

Janice paused, one foot in Faerie. "And?"

"Should something go wrong—"

"Lily will know that her father loved her," she murmured, and hurriedly crossed.

Fik watched the gate until it sealed, saying nothing, and I touched his arm to break his reverie. "Not to be morbid," I said, "but you *have* seen the dead here, yes? I'm visited constantly. If the worst happens, you can tell Lily yourself."

"Yeah, I know," he muttered. "It's not the same." He turned and began walking away from the place where the gate had been, then paused and glanced down at me. "*Constantly*, you say?"

"I'd probably be mobbed now if I didn't have a gatekeeper. A kind woman who's looked out for me. She's around somewhere," I added, waving one arm toward the walls of the barn. "You mean you don't have a steady stream of visitors here? With this many cynaeli?"

"No." He seemed surprised by the enquiry. "Janice's grandmother visits, but aside from the occasional stray, we rarely see any. I mean, there are a few with ties to the land," he admitted, "but that's all. We don't bother each other." His eyes narrowed. "Why would they seek *you* out?"

"I can energize them," I explained. "Perhaps that makes me more attractive."

"You've *attempted* it? At your age?"

I lowered my voice. "You heard Artur say that she's fought scintol, didn't you?"

"Yes…"

"How do you suppose she defeated them?"

Fik stopped and stared at me. "Are you serious?"

"Not like it's going to do us any good against Hidden Ones, but yes."

I could have been mistaken, but I thought I saw a new glimmer of respect in his eyes. "That's a rare gift, Hope," he said.

"So I've been led to understand."

Before I could walk on, Fik pulled me to an empty corner of the room and slumped until we could comfortably whisper. "Tell me the truth. How long does Arik have?"

"We think Monday, but that's as accurate as we can be. I don't have a countdown clock for you," I replied.

His jaw tightened. "Tonight and tomorrow, and after that…"

"I don't know. He won't let us work on the collar until you're safe."

Fik laughed, but it sounded more like disbelief than mirth. "Only the maker can remove a collar like that without taking the naffidar's head with it, and if it explodes around other people—"

"Arik gave us the visual," I muttered.

"It's like a bomb. The only hope for Arik is for him to return to Father."

"Pimati." Fik frowned, and I explained, "Your father gave him to Pimati."

He looked across the room, where Artur was helping Arik limp toward the door, then turned back to me. "Should I ever see Pimati again," he said, "I'll kill the whoreson myself. I owe Arik that much."

Before I could say more, Artur noticed us and called, "Were you two planning on participating in this, or should I let you know when it's safe to come out?"

I gave Fik a weak smile, then jogged away to rejoin the group.

CHAPTER 10

What we had to work with wasn't exactly encouraging.

The elderly Joneses were better than decent wizards, per Hua, but they remained at the RV with Frank, who still didn't trust the integrity of his bind around the open gate. Hua was also talented—Beth noted her pine wand and explained to me that the tool was the mark of a skilled wizard. Unfortunately, Beth's skill at spellcraft was lower, given the girl's age and incomplete education. Maria was skilled at enchantment, and while Artur lacked her technical finesse, she more than made up for it with sheer power. As for those still present of the cynaeli persuasion, the eldest among us was Fik, who wasn't yet twenty-seven. I was six years younger and adept for my age, but that didn't make me useful where it counted—physical magic. We were going to war, after all, not playing with glamours. I couldn't help but think that we'd have been better served if a few of the tennuwaya of the settlement had stayed, but they'd fled with the rest of their friends and family. And then there was Arik, who couldn't even glamour himself with the collar in place. He was little better than dead weight, but Fik and I had silently agreed not to send him away, and even Artur, pragmatist though she was, understood the reason for his continued presence. The man was on his deathbed. If he wanted to spend his final hours in battle, we wouldn't deny him.

Maria didn't disguise her frustration as we sat around Fik's kitchen, planning out the night's chores. "I told Toula that we could use more people," she said, pacing by the sink. "Faerie is offering shelter, which is more than the Arcanum has provided."

"They did loan us the RV," I pointed out. "And Artur, Frank, and Beth—"

"Who are here in an unofficial capacity," Artur reminded me. "Have you talked to the Team, Maria?"

"They're willing," she replied, "but Toula wants them to hold back for now. A second wave, if needed. Besides, you know how Val would feel if I dragged Marcus out here." Catching Fik's blank look, she said, "His son. Val is *slightly* protective."

"But he permits you to be here?" he asked, bemused. "You said he was your grandfather, correct?"

Maria smirked. "He knows what it means to be a magus. If he doesn't like what I'm doing, he's learned to keep his thoughts to himself." She folded her arms and leaned against the counter. "And he's on standby. I don't want to go running to him every time there's a hiccup in this realm, but he's made the offer—which, again, is more than the Arcanum has done. You would think that the people of this realm would see the importance of coming to its defense, wouldn't you?"

"Arcanum," said Hua, and shrugged. "I'm not surprised."

"Which says a lot about us," Maria continued. "If we just had a few more magi—"

"But we don't," Artur interjected, cutting short her complaint, "and so we make do. Come to the table," she said as she finished taping several sheets of printer paper into a large rectangle. "We can't complain our defenses into existence."

Pencil in hand, Artur made a rough sketch of the settlement, filling in details with Fik's assistance. She considered the structures and the terrain, then drew a circle around the buildings and through the woods. "This is the ring for the fire," she said, tapping it with her eraser. "We need a decently deep ditch around the perimeter, and anything resembling tinder should be cleared away. Dry leaves, grass, overhanging limbs—*everything*. The fewer accidental fires we start, the easier this will be on everyone, especially Maria."

"Let's be safe about this," Maria added. "Say we clear the brush about three meters on both sides of the ditch. It'll be a swath through the woods, but I'd *really* prefer not to wrestle a wildfire."

"Your decision," said Artur. "I'm going out to mark the ditch ring. Beth, help Hua. You two start in the other direction," she said, pointing to Fik and me. "Let's meet in the middle. Maria, stay here and rest—"

"I could make snacks," she offered.

"What about me?" asked Arik, struggling to rise from his chair. "I can help."

Artur had an answer at the ready. "Stay with Maria. If Hope's *friend* needs to convey a message, then you'll be here to pass it along."

Arik wasn't thrilled at being relegated to moral support duty, but when Fik and I came inside for a break, he was watching over Maria, who had fallen asleep with her head on the kitchen table. Several bowls of chips, a vegetable tray, and a surprisingly well-decorated chocolate cake waited on the counter, all courtesy of the sleeping magus. While we ate, Beth and Hua joined us, and finally, Artur stomped in around ten that evening. "I can finish marking overnight," she said, lopping off a hunk of the cake, "but the rest of you should sleep in shifts. Have you got guestrooms, Fik?"

He pointed to a back bedroom. "It's nothing fancy. I've got an air mattress…"

"That will do." She nudged Maria awake and guided her onto the couch in the next room. "Take first rest," she told the wizards, "and you, Arik, you need it. Hope, give Fik your phone number. You're coming with me."

We did as ordered, and I marched off through the night with Artur, each of us creating a floating orb to light our steps. "What am I to do?" I asked, lengthening my stride to keep pace with her.

"Watch for ghosts, I suppose. Other than that, nothing. I thought that Arik and Fik could use a moment of privacy."

She had a point. We continued the walk in silence—the uphill trek was even less fun in the darkness than it would have been by daylight—and soon found the RV where we'd left it, a warm glow emanating from behind the shades. When we opened the door, a steamy, mouth-watering cloud of spice washed over us. "Oh, hi!" said Zeb, who was busy at the hotplates with a stockpot and spoon. "Checking the chili. I thought it might be good to have food on hand." Seeing the look on our faces, he grinned. "Give it a few hours, let it simmer. You don't want to rush this."

We knocked the debris off our shoes and came inside to find Carey asleep on the futon and Frank sitting at the dinette with a computer. "Trouble?" he asked.

"Not yet." Artur sank into a chair beside him and rubbed at a knot in her shoulder. "We're working on the fire ring. You have yet to begin here, I take it?"

"Carey's going to do the heavy casting, but only after a nap. In the meantime, I've got a line open to Toula." He patted the computer for emphasis. "She's making headway with a few magi, but—"

The beeping of his phone cut Frank short, and he glanced at the message. "Excuse me," he muttered, tapping a reply.

"Everyone understands the plan?" Artur asked as he put the phone aside.

"Yeah," said Frank. "Make a ring and light it when the little bastards come close. The Joneses will manage that. Once the pack has passed, they'll break my bind, and I'll cut off the exit."

She pulled back the shade with one finger, studying the narrow road outside. "Do you want to practice now? I'm concerned about maneuverability."

"As are we," said Zeb, bringing a pair of plates to the table. "Here, leftover hamburgers from dinner. You two look like you could use them." We tucked in gratefully, and he said, "When Carey makes the ring, she's going to take down the trees nearest the road for a good ways. Give Frank a little wiggle room."

Her mouth full, Artur resorted to nodding. Once she could speak again, she said, "Let's have Carey clear the area, and then, unless the Hidden Ones are already upon us, Frank can try it at full size and see what else needs to be done."

Frank snorted at that, and Zeb made a face. "Well, see," said Zeb, "the thing is, Carey and I don't create binds, and I know Hua would prefer not to."

"Whenever the Joneses break mine, that's it," Frank added. "Hence at least one string of messages to Toula. I'm going to need a way out of here eventually, and unless she pops in, I won't be going by RV."

Artur lowered her burger before she could take another bite. "Oh...that *is* a complication. My apologies, Zeb, I thought you or your wife would be capable of the spell. Beth is too young to make the attempt—"

"Moon and stars, *no*," Frank muttered.

"—and I have no experience with it." She eyed Frank cautiously. "I don't suppose you would prefer that I practice on you, correct?"

"If it can be at all avoided."

Zeb returned to his chili. "It's not a matter of ability. We could probably pull it off. But Carey really hates binds, and she won't do them, period. Out of respect for her wishes, I haven't worked a bind in decades."

"Even if the subject wants it?" Frank asked, not hiding his irritation.

"Talk to Kip."

Frank started to respond, but once again, his phone beeped. He replied to the message and looked at his computer for a moment, only to be interrupted yet again.

"Is Toula upset?" I asked while he wrote his next message.

He jerked—I suppose I'd broken his concentration—and glanced up to find Artur and me watching him. "Oh, uh…no, this isn't her," he mumbled, and returned to his work.

The phone was barely out of his hands before it beeped again. "Another magus?" I pressed.

He said nothing until he'd sent a reply, though his neck began to color. "No. Sam."

"*Ah*," said Artur between bites.

I frowned, trying to make sense of this sparse information. "Sam?"

"Ros's…boyfriend, I suppose. She can't use a phone without frying it, so Sam does it for her."

The picture became clearer. I remembered Ros from my brief stay in Faerie, a glowing blonde who appeared at will and seemed to be on familiar terms with everyone. She was, I came to learn, the consciousness of Faerie—the female counterpart to the male consciousness of Conota. Through circumstances that were still somewhat muddled to me, she had raised Frank from a hatchling and still felt rather maternal toward him. I thought it only reasonable, then, that she should want to talk to him before the Hidden Ones attacked.

To my surprise, however, Frank shook his head. "Not Ros. We've already talked it over, and she understands what we're doing here. She says hello, by the way," he told me. "You're still in her good graces."

Artur's brow furrowed. "Then what does Sam have to…*oh*." Her mouth curved into a knowing smile. "Passing messages for someone else, is he?"

Frank's flush continued to rise. "She's distressed. I've kept her apprised all week, but she's not happy with the plan, and I'm trying to convince her that I'm not making a huge mistake. She knows what these things can do."

"Who?" I asked.

He sighed and picked up his phone again as a new message appeared. "Ione."

"Frank has a lady in his life," said Artur, leaning toward me and dropping her voice to a conspiratorial tone, "but he refuses to admit it."

He shot her a red-eyed glare at her over the top of his dark glasses. "Okay, *first*, dragons don't form pair bonds, and you know that. Second, she's living in the barn with both of my brothers, so when she wants to mate, she'll choose one of them. Third, she's probably just bored—"

"Which is why your phone hasn't stopped dinging for the last two hours?" Zeb asked. "Because correct me if I'm wrong, but I didn't think dragons were ordinarily big on texting."

"You're not helping," he said testily.

"What? There's nothing wrong with having a girlfriend."

Frank sent off a reply. "She's not my girlfriend. We are friendly, and she happens to be female. That's all."

Zeb patted him on the shoulder. "Keep telling yourself that, kid." The phone beeped yet again, and Zeb chuckled as Frank, now fully red in the face, took it into the bunkroom and slammed the door.

Zeb promised that they would send word if Carey couldn't make the ditch in time, and so, with matters under control, Artur and I started back to Fik's house. Once we were on the road, however, she announced that she was going straight into the woods. "Much of the perimeter still needs to be marked," she explained. "Return to the house and rest. You'll be of more use at first light."

"Unless the horde descends before then."

"Have your sources mentioned impending doom?"

"No," I admitted, "but just in case, maybe I should go with you. The woods are dark."

An orb manifested in the air before her. "I'm not afraid. Go to bed, Hope."

With that, she set off alone, the orb lighting her way through the dry grass and scraggly pines. I watched her go until the orb was nothing more than a pinprick in the trees, and then I heard a voice beside me: "She has always done this. Leave her be."

I turned to find Uther at my right shoulder, staring into the trees after his daughter. *She prefers to take her walks in the dark?*

"No. She used to walk alone before battle. Clearing her head, you see. Come, you shouldn't stand in the road all night."

I called forth a pale bluish orb of my own, and he kept pace with me as I headed for the camouflage ward, its channels of magic brilliant in the darkness. *She hasn't been quite so alone on those walks as she believes, I take it.*

"Not always," he admitted. "Many a time I've wished I could offer her counsel—not that she's ever been in desperate need of my advice. But so much was thrust upon her at such a young age, and I should have been there to shield her from it. She grew up far too quickly."

Kitty had told me a little of Artur's past, but I hadn't wanted to pry; in my limited experience, I hadn't found Artur to be one who was quick to talk about herself. *You died when she was young?*

"Ten," he replied, his spectral cloak hanging almost motionless even with the night breeze. "A prodigy at arms and touched by magic even then, but still a child...and suddenly, a king. I did not have the time I would have liked to prepare her. And then high king five years later. Our people, our lands, *all* of that fell upon her. So yes, I walked with her. I don't believe she ever felt my presence, but perhaps she did. Perhaps it gave her comfort." He peered into the trees, but Artur's orb was almost too faint to see. "Here, even now, she knows she will be called upon to lead. She is readying herself."

I'm sure that Maria could take over, I replied. *She's the Away Team's magus, after all.*

"I grant you that," said Uther, "but she has made no attempt to take command, has she? She sleeps yet. I mean no insult to her," he quickly added, "she's a talented woman, but this is not her strength. Toula, now, from what I've seen, would assume control of the situation, were she here. But even if there is no clear leader, in a situation such as this, someone *must* lead. And whether it is by nature or force of habit, Artur will do so."

There was a note of sadness in his voice, but also a strong undercurrent of pride.

She hasn't let us down yet, I thought. *Her plan is solid, no matter what Frank's non-girlfriend thinks about it.*

Uther laughed softly. "She is a clever one, my daughter. Brave to a fault." He tried to kick at a pinecone in the road, but his foot went through it. "I watched her become a warrior. Take on responsibilities that should never have been hers."

Because she was too young?

"That, yes, but more so because she wasn't my son." His eyes met mine as we walked. "You have been told that there are few secrets on this side of death, I trust."

Many times.

"Well, I knew the truth about Artur long before she did. She didn't learn that she had been born female until she was thirteen. She grew up under a glamour, and the truth horrified her. That was her greatest secret. She forced herself to be a better swordsman, a better rider, a better leader, as if she were trying to make up for her deficiency. Or so *she* thought," he muttered. "There was nothing deficient about her. And then there was the *other* truth that she only learned on returning from your realm."

She's not yours.

"Not my blood," he corrected. "She *is* mine. The faithless bastard who got her on my wife kept her alive by sending her with the cynaeli woman, and for that, I am grateful. Not so grateful that I'd overlook what he tried to do to her last year, mind you."

Though I'd been warned that there are some questions the dead simply cannot answer, I pressed my luck. *He died, didn't he? Have you…met him?*

Uther shook his head. "The coward took his own life in Faerie. You know we cannot go between the realms. If he lingers in this…this *plane*, I have heard it called, then he does so within Faerie's borders. Fortunate for him, I suppose."

You couldn't kill him a second time, I pointed out.

"Maybe not, but I would do my best."

I rubbed my bare arms, wishing I'd snagged a warmer shirt from my bag on the RV. *Would you like to speak with her now?*

"Thank you, but no. Not yet. Besides," he added with a snort, "Flora would be furious if I wasted your strength."

It's not a waste, I began, then nearly tripped on a pothole in the darkness and caught myself from a stumbling fall. *Sorry. But I'm serious, I don't mind. Just because Flora never wants to talk to anyone doesn't mean that it's always a waste for others to do so.*

"What's your connection to her, if I may ask?"

I frowned at him. *Shouldn't you know?*

"I know the answers to secrets that concern me," he explained. "Things about my wife, Artur, my greater family. But Flora is a mystery to me, and Orson and I have not been able to pry answers from her. Is she kin to you?"

Not that I know. I've met my mother's parents, but no one else from her family—I suppose they don't want to visit. Flora just appeared one night and started helping me manage, I replied, and smiled to myself. *I spent so many years without a mother, and now it's as if I have two. Maybe she's trying to give Mama a hand.*

"Curious," said Uther. "I do wonder why she lingers here."

She's never told me about her family.

"I would be surprised if she had any yet alive. Flora is

old. How old, I cannot say, but she's not among the recent dead." I felt a coolness over my shoulder and saw that he was trying to pat it. "You have an extraordinary gift, girl. Who knows? Perhaps Flora did not come to you on her own initiative. Perhaps she was *sent.*"

That's a possibility?

He started to answer, then shut his mouth and shook his head. "I've said too much already."

I grunted but let it go. *Whenever you're ready to talk to Artur, find me. I promise I'll give you time with her. And I can make it back alone,* I thought, pointing to the wards. *Be with her tonight. She needs you more than I do.*

He vanished, and, shivering, I walked onward toward Fik's house and the rest of our waiting forces.

The house was quiet when I let myself in. Maria slept on the couch, covered with a blanket, one hand trailing on the thin rug. I saw no sign of Fik or Arik, but I found Beth in the kitchen with a bowl of chips and her phone. "Hi!" she whispered, beckoning me closer. "Look, I found salsa in the fridge. Hungry?"

I wasn't, but I'd become something of a sucker for salsa since moving to Pauline, and chips were a mindless food. I sat beside her and helped myself—and once Beth was absorbed in her phone again, I looked up and barely nodded to Orson, who stood near her with his arms folded. *Something wrong?* I asked him.

"Other than the fact that my kid is playing with fire and a ravenous pack of monsters, you mean?"

I licked a stray blob of salsa from my finger and tried to be sneaky, but I find it difficult to carry on a conversation in the same room with someone and not look at him. *There are three trained wizards nearby, plus Maria, plus Artur, plus Fik and me, and let's not forget Frank. It's not as though she's here alone.*

That did nothing to soften Orson's expression. "Beth

talks a big game, but she's not ready for this. For crying out loud, she's *fifteen*," he protested. "You know what I did at fifteen? Screwed up a spell and set my own head on fire. I had a bald patch for a month."

We can't just send her away.

"Yes, you can! Have Maria or someone open a gate and send her back to England!"

She wants to be here, and if Maria is so concerned, then she'll make that decision.

"We've seen what those monsters can do. It was one thing for y'all to be out ahead of them, but *this*?" He spread his arms to encompass the tiny kitchen. "This isn't a fortress. You're talking about defending yourselves with a friggin' forest fire, and Beth does *not* need to be on the front lines."

"Who are you talking to?" Beth asked.

I jumped at the interruption and turned to her, wearing what I'm sure was a guilty expression. "Sorry, uh…what did you say?" I managed, trying to cover.

Beth's face told me she wasn't buying it. "You're staring at the wall, and your expression keeps changing. Either you're having a conversation or there's something weird going on in your head. I mean, I've talked to myself, but you were zoned out."

At least Orson had the decency to look mildly panicked at being caught.

The hour was too late for me to work up a passable lie. "Your father is worried about your well-being here," I told her. "He'd feel much better if you returned to Glastonbury."

She huffed, then glared at the area where Orson was standing. "I'm *fine*," she insisted. "I know what I'm doing, I've studied wards and shields, and I'm not going to try anything stupid. Artur won't let me."

Orson started to answer her directly, then remembered she couldn't hear him. "Pass this on, would you?" he said to me. "There is something incredibly nasty coming this way. Right now. Could be here in the morning, could be here in a few days. Y'all don't know exactly where they are, and neither do I. You've got nothing in the way of defense right now besides camouflage wards, which are about as effective as wet tissue. And as for Artur, she's never faced these things. She doesn't *know* what she's up against." Though he was, technically, speaking to me, Orson had eyes only for his daughter. "We've seen what they can do. Beth didn't see the dead left behind. That wizard she met with the legs picked down to the bone? That was nothing special. I don't want that to happen to her."

I relayed the message, and Beth's expression turned sullen. "I'm not a little kid, you know," she told her father. "I can do this."

"Sweetie," he replied, "I can't make you do anything, but if I had my druthers, you'd be on another continent right now. You're smart, and you're being very brave, but I don't want you to get hurt." He paused while I repeated that, then said, "You're getting to be so grown-up, but you're my baby girl, and if something happened to you…"

When I finished, Beth mumbled, "Mom wouldn't care."

"But I do," said Orson. "Please, honey, just think about it, won't you?"

She was silent for a long moment after I passed the last message, her face working as she thought. After a time, she said, "What if I stay close to Arik and Fik? They're going to be at the center of this place, way back from the ring of fire."

"What about the RV?" he countered. "At least one of the Joneses can make gates, right? You've got an exit in case of disaster."

She considered his proposal, then heaved an overly dramatic sigh and rolled her eyes. "*Fine.* If it'll make you happy."

"Much happier," he said.

"But only after we finish the ditch," she said once I'd

conveyed his satisfaction. "I've got to help Hua."

"Hua can handle that herself," Orson began, but I shot him a look to silence him.

"He understands," I told Beth, and slid the salsa container out of her reach. "Bed, you. Go crash somewhere."

"I guess," she said, and rose. "Night, Hope. *Goodnight*, Dad."

I gave her ponytail a tug in passing, and Orson shook his head as she wandered toward a bedroom. "Teenagers," he muttered. "I tell you, Hope, it's a wonder that the species survives."

The sleeping arrangements were haphazard that night. Fik and Arik took the master bedroom, Beth and I shared the guest bed, and at some point, Artur inflated the air mattress and passed out on the floor beside us. I heard her come in, though I couldn't say when. Honestly, I heard every sound that night, each creak of the settling house like a shout of danger to my subconscious. When I gave up and groaned at the light filtering through the blinds, I found Flora standing over me. "You will feel better after you bathe," she said as I pushed back the covers, then followed me toward the little bathroom down the hall. "And eat something, child. Something more nutritious than chips and salsa," she amended. "You need your strength."

I pulled a towel from the linen closet and peered at the bags beneath my eyes. Unmasked by my customary glamour, the dark circles looked like black bruises with my violet complexion.

"Bathe, Hope," said Flora. "You are wasting time."

I turned away from her to slough off my shirt. *You're good at the whole "mom" thing.*

When I glanced over my shoulder, Flora seemed slightly pained, but she smiled anyway. "Tell Hayleigh you are alive, won't you? It's been almost two days."

My phone is back on the RV.

"Surely you will pass that way at some point this morning, hmm?"

Fine. Yes. Out, I said, turning on the water to bring it up to temperature.

Flora slipped through the closed door. "I think I saw eggs in the refrigerator. Eat those," she said, and left me to shower in relative peace.

An hour later, clean, dry, and having downed a sub-par frittata made with the last of Fik's salsa, I let Beth and Hua take the first shift of ditch-digging and hiked back to the RV to check in. On arrival, I found Zeb and Carey outside, just finishing the last of the ring around the vehicle. The trees on either side of the road had been uprooted and disintegrated, leaving a space wide enough for perhaps a six-lane highway. "You've been busy," I remarked, taking in the clearing work.

Carey popped her back, then gave her wand a twirl. "Up before the sun. We decided there was no sense in waiting, especially if we're going to be on the front end of this. How are thing going down your way? We'll come help."

"Hua's working now. Artur was out most of the night," I replied. "Beth will be joining you later today. I assume you don't need any assistance, but—"

"*Good,*" Zeb interrupted, nodding fervently. "That's wise. Let's keep the kid out of the way."

"How's Frank?" I asked. "Did he and Ione straighten matters out?"

The Joneses shared a look. "Judging by the texting…not exactly," said Zeb. "She let him go for a while last night, but they've been back at it since four."

"And we're letting them work through it," Carey added. "Want some coffee, Hope? We were about to put a fresh pot on."

I grinned. "If you're offering. I just need to get my

phone from the bunkroom."

I only made it to the second step of the RV before the woods echoed with the crack of an opening gate. Wheeling around and jumping off the staircase, I spotted the gate perhaps an eighth of a mile back up the road, widening at a rapid pace. Within seconds, it had stretched to cover almost all of the cleared space between the trees, a bright spot in the dark woods...and something *big* was coming through. I recognized the bluish-green bulk as a dragon just before I heard its telepathic cry. While the thought was far too layered to translate as pure speech, I gathered that the newcomer was frantically seeking Frank.

A tall, redheaded man stood on the edge of the gate behind the dragon, his hands cupped around his mouth for amplification. "She wouldn't take no for an answer!" he yelled down the road as her footsteps shook the ground. "Ros just opened the hole! I'd have warned you—"

Ros, glowing as always, manifested beside him and waved to me. "Hi! I thought this would be far back enough so as not to crush anything. Tell Frank no heroics, okay?"

Before I could answer them, the RV door slammed open. Frank, clad in sweatpants, jumped to the road and gaped at the dragon. I heard his answering thought—like hers, it was too complex for my mind to untangle it into words, but I did make out *Ione*.

The dragon's massive head swung around until one red eye spotted him, a tall, broad figure with mussed white hair sticking out in all directions. She stopped where she stood, her wings settling against her back, and spoke to him, the thought colored by what sounded to me like incredulity.

Frank hurried closer to meet her, barefoot and shirtless, and pushed his dark glasses onto his head. The Joneses quickly slid out of the way, but Zeb asked him, "Are you going to introduce us?"

He glanced at them, then at the dragon, and held up a hand for patience. "This is Ione," he told them in English.

"Do you speak any Fae?"

"Little more than profanity. Why?"

"I do," I said, jogging over to join them.

"Translate," Frank told me, then narrowed his communication into words. *They can't understand pure thought,* he told Ione in what sounded like Fae to my mind. *What are you doing here? This isn't safe, it's not a good place for you—*

She followed his lead. *How is it any safer for you? And why do you look like that?*

Frank's shoulders hunched. *Disguise. Also, it's the only way to fit inside the RV,* he explained, pointing to the vehicle.

But how do you plan to fight these things if you're tiny?

I won't be. It's to be a surprise. Once they pass, bind comes off, poof. It would be something of a giveaway if they came down the road and found a full-sized dragon waiting for them, yes?

Ione seemed to deflate and sank to her belly. *Sorry.*

Frank hesitated for a few seconds, then moved closer and stroked the side of her head. *You didn't understand.*

I didn't mean to mess it up, she thought, sounding more dejected by the second. *I just wanted to help. Stupid runt can't do anything right...*

"*That* is a runt?" Carey muttered as I translated.

You haven't messed anything up, Frank reassured her. *But I'd feel better if you went back to Faerie.*

I want to help, she insisted. *No one else in the barn wanted to come with me, but Ros said I could go. She's worried about you.*

"Sounds like she's not the only one," Zeb whispered.

Maybe I could be small for now, too, and we could surprise them together, Ione suggested.

Frank cut his eyes to the Joneses, then turned his attention back to the dragon. *There's no one here who could safely replicate this bind, and anyway, you wouldn't be able to walk. It takes practice. But...* He squinted into the distance, toward the settlement. "Hope, what's been cleared down there?"

"Partial ring," I replied. "What do we need to do?"

I have an idea, if you insist on helping, he thought to Ione. *I'll stay here. Go with Hope and wait for them to clear a place for you on the other side of the houses. You can stay there and cut off the Hidden Ones' escape if they come your way. Would that work?*

Ione perked immediately. *Yes. Which one is Hope?*

Purple. He pointed to me, though it was hardly necessary. "Is there a place around the houses where she'll fit for now?" he asked.

"There's a big vegetable garden…"

"We'll replace their carrots." To Ione, he continued, *The way there is narrow. Best if you fly over—it's a short distance. Hope can show you where to go.*

Her answer had a cast of uncertainty. *You want me to carry her?*

She's not large.

It's not that. I've never done it before.

Trust me, thought Frank, *if anyone can stay on without a saddle, Hope can. I've taken her on far worse flights.*

I ducked into the RV for my bag while Frank continued to convince her. When I emerged, though Ione still seemed wary, she lay still and let me scramble up to the base of her long neck. *Can you hear me?* I thought.

She looked back at me and slowly blinked. *Yes. Are you secure?*

As long as you don't go upside-down, I replied, which earned a faint burst of mirth from the dragon. *It's a very short flight. Stay as close to the trees as you can, and you'll see the clearing.*

I leaned forward and held on as she leapt, and after a quick circle of the area, she made the tight landing, trampling the settlers' crops. As I slid down, Artur and Fik ran outside, and I waved. "It's okay!" I called. "This is Frank's girlfriend! She's here to help!"

What did you tell them?

I repeated myself in thought, and Ione's head tilted. *Girlfriend?*

Fearing that I'd caused offense to a creature large enough to eat me like a pretzel stick, I tried to backtrack. *Sorry, we thought that the two of you were…mates.*

Oh, I'm not ready to mate, she replied. *I lost a clutch only last year. But I would like for him to sire my next clutch. He's quite handsome…at full size, of course. Is that what you meant?*

More or less, I told her, trying to keep anything extraneous from my thought. *Does Frank know?*

I haven't told him as much. No need to bring that up before I'm ready to mate, is there?

As Fik and Artur hurried down the path to meet us, I thought, *We should talk about this later, but…yes. I believe that Frank would be very interested to know your plans.*

If you say so. Her tongue flicked from between her teeth as she sniffed the air. *Smells more like home here.*

There's a gate to Conota nearby, I explained. *You're smelling proper magic.*

I know—my fire is back. I feel it burning. The plan is to roast the creatures, I gather?

If it's no trouble.

There was amusement in her thought. *None at all. I prefer my meals charred.*

CHAPTER 11

That Sunday was both one of the longest and shortest days of my life.

Without knowing exactly where the Hidden Ones were, we had no time to waste, especially with the additional clearing necessary for Ione. The Joneses helped us make good headway, and by lunch—Zeb's chili, to general approval, plus half a dozen sheep imported from Faerie for Ione—the ditch had been dug, the trees cleared, and our plans rehashed until Artur was satisfied that everyone knew what to do. I'd taken a break midmorning to send a message to Mama, and her reply was almost enough to make me call home: *I love you, baby. If I can take your place, I'll do it.* For the rest of the day, while Maria, Artur, and Hua walked the fire ditch to check for impediments and talk strategy, Beth, the Joneses, and Frank kept watch in shifts back at the RV, searching for any sign of movement in the distance and listening for the pounding of running feet. The work was either taxing or tedious, and the hours slowly ticked by.

Simultaneously, they rushed past me, especially once I joined Fik in looking after Arik. He wanted to be useful, but it took all of his energy just to swallow a few bites of food at lunch, and we soon put him to bed. That afternoon, as Arik shivered with his chills, Fik and I piled on blankets in a vain effort to keep him warm. I climbed in with him for a few hours, holding him as he shook in his fitful sleep, and eventually dozed myself. When I woke, we were alone in the bedroom, and Arik's eyes were wet. "I'm sorry," he whispered.

I pulled him closer. "You have nothing to be sorry about. Stay with me," I pleaded. "We'll fight off the Hidden Ones, and once Fik is safe—"

"I'm so cold, Hope." His eyes continued to leak onto the pillow. "I'm sorry for everything."

"Arik, no," I said, brushing his sweat-damp hair from his face. "You did beautifully. Your brother will be safe, and your niece. We'll make sure of it."

But he shook his head and took my hand beneath the blankets. "I should have run. I should have gone to High Vale and taken you from your father's tower, and we could have come here together. You and me." He squeezed his eyes to blink back the tears. "I wanted to be your husband so badly. I thought I might be worthy of you once."

"Arik," I murmured, "it's all right."

"No, it's not. We could have been happy together."

Though my heart clenched in my chest, I swallowed to release the tightness in my throat and slid closer to him. "Hold on," I whispered. "You have to hold on. We'll get the collar off, and I'll be right here."

"I'm sorry for being so weak."

"Then let me help you be strong."

I held him until he fell asleep again, cursing the passing minutes that stole more and more of him from me.

But for Ione, who had saved back a sheep from lunch that had somehow multiplied several times in the intervening hours, no one was hungry at dinnertime—even the leftover chili tasted like sand to me. At nine, with no sign of the Hidden Ones, Artur ordered us all to bed. "The RV has the watch," she said, shooing us away. "I'll see about Ione and join you presently."

Surprisingly enough, I heard her collapse onto the air mattress a few minutes after Maria and I took the guest bed. "Thought you'd be walking the perimeter," I whispered as she settled in—which, for Artur, seemed to mean only unbuckling her sword and kicking off her shoes.

"Perimeter is as secure as we can make it for now," she mumbled into her pillow. "Ione has the rear. Sleep, Hope."

I'd curled up again when she asked, "How is he?"

"He's trying," I replied, unable to bring myself to utter the truth of the matter. Arik was dying in the next room, trembling in his brother's bed, and my last thought as I drifted off was a prayer to anyone listening that he saw the sunrise.

To be clear, I have certain telepathic abilities in an area with sufficient magic. By manipulating magic in one way, I can communicate with the dead. Tweaking that enchantment, I can speak to the living as well. In other words, unless I find myself in Faerie, I can reach out to the minds around me. I've never measured the extent of my range, but it's safe to say that anyone within a hundred feet is fair game.

Dragons, by contrast, are natural telepaths—magic has nothing to do with their communication. And as I discovered that night, their range is far, *far* greater than mine.

INCOMING, was my alarm at three a.m., a mental shout from Frank. Ione picked up the cry and repeated it, and within seconds, the house was awake. Artur didn't even bother with her shoes—a pair of leather boots simply manifested around her feet as she ran, sword swinging at her side. Less gifted with physical magic, I stopped long enough to shove my tennis shoes on before following her to the porch in my T-shirt and pajama pants, and Maria and Hua arrived on my heels. "Light the ring," Artur ordered. "It's time."

Fik shouldered the door open behind us, practically

carrying Arik. I spotted the nylon straps of a pair of shotguns crisscrossed over our host's chest. "Going to the main barn," he said, struggling beneath his brother's weight.

"Be safe," I told them, then ran after the others toward the perimeter.

Combat magic not being my specialty, I struggled to focus on my few childhood lessons and keep up with the others. The better-trained had no trouble—Maria had the ditch alight almost as soon as she reached a safe position, and a shield bubbled forth from Hua's wand, its contours translucent in the fire's glow. Artur had produced a shield that seemed to wrap around her left arm, while her right hand held a yellow fireball the size of a child's head, poised to be lobbed. I heard a deep roar coming from the direction of the RV—Frank, I realized, freed from his bind, which meant that the Hidden Ones must have passed them by.

"You have the fire, Maria?" Artur asked.

The magus's hands were extended, and thin tendrils of smoke extended from her fingers toward the flames, my perception of her enchantment. "Under control," she said, staring toward the road.

"Good. Hua, Hope, with me."

The house nearest the perimeter was, like most of its neighbors, a single-story dwelling. Artur took a running leap and propelled herself onto the mostly flat roof—assisted by magic, I had to assume—then helped Hua and me quickly climb the porch railings and join her. Our heightened vantage wasn't great, but it was sufficient to see beyond the flames.

When I did, I wished I'd still been on the ground.

The road appeared to be undulating as the horde neared, firelight glinting off skin and metal buckles. Beside me, Hua whispered a spell, and a magnified projection of the front of the pack appeared in the air before us. "As you expected?" she murmured to me.

The Hidden Ones were much as I'd been taught: some pale as snow, some dark as night, some mottled like stones beneath a running river, none taller than my knee. Their hair was wild and wispy, flowing behind them as they ran, and their great eyes, twice the size of mine, gleamed reddish in the fire's glow. Their mouths, though...

No illustration, no description, could have adequately prepared me for the horror of those mouths. I'd ridden dragon-back—I knew what it was to look upon a cavernous maw lined with teeth longer than my arm—but dragons were a fact of life in Conota, creatures usually viewed from a distance and respected as powerful predators. The Hidden Ones were tiny, almost childlike in their proportions, but for their mouths, which opened nearly from ear to ear. As they ran, panting, it looked as if the bottom halves of their faces were poised to fall off at any moment. Lining those unnatural mouths were jagged teeth—scaled for size, perhaps twice as long as mine, and ending in razor points.

Adding to my rising desire to break into a complete panic and run was their emaciation. The Hidden Ones I'd seen in books were well-formed, of average bulk if not plump. These, however, were practically skeletal, their faces pinched, their swinging arms like sinewy twigs. Their odd assortment of clothes—bits of stolen cloth and fur and leather made from previous meals—hung from their thin frames and flapped as they ran.

"They're starving," I muttered, staring at Hua's projection.

"They do look sickly," Artur concurred.

"See how thin they are? They've been running hard. Perhaps they rested, but they must not have eaten since Kansas."

"Good."

"*Good?*" I echoed, aghast. "If they get through the fire, there won't be enough of us left to identify!"

"They are hungry," she replied calmly. "Hungry men

think with their stomachs, not their heads. And if those monsters are as desperate as you suggest..." She looked out at the perimeter fire, then back at the projection. "They're slowing. On your guard, now."

The Hidden Ones might have been famished, but they weren't entirely suicidal. The pack stopped at the six-foot wall of flame, tiny chests heaving and thin tongues lolling, and considered their circumstances.

"Maybe they will turn back," said Hua. "They have no talent, do they?"

"For magic? No," I said, watching the little things puzzle out the impediment. "But I wouldn't anticipate a retreat..."

There was no need for me to finish that sentence. As I was speaking, two of the Hidden Ones at the front linked their hands, and a third climbed into the makeshift catapult. With an impressive display of acrobatics, he was flung over the fire, flipped twice, and landed on his feet—

—and was instantly fried by lightning, courtesy of Artur.

His fellows on the other side of the fire ring might not have known exactly what befell their comrade, but his death shriek seemed to give them pause. They frowned and huddled together in clumps, their voices little more than squeaks to my ears.

"What are they saying?" asked Artur.

"No idea. How quickly can you fry them?"

She drummed the fingers of her shield arm against her leg as she calculated. "If they launch one by one, it shouldn't be a problem. If they rush the fire..."

"Electricity can jump between bodies," Hua pointed out. "If they come through in a tight press, then perhaps we can stop them with fewer shots. My lightning is not so good, but I can shoot fire. Hope?"

My mind whirled as I watched the Hidden Ones plotting. Sure, Artur and Hua could try to pick them off from the roof—or at least shoot any that came too close to Maria, who was expending all her energy in keeping the fire under control—but I was no sniper. While I could work a healing enchantment, the single greatest act of physical magic I'd ever managed was slowing our descent when Kitty and I leapt from Warohn's tower with unconscious Artur, and even then, I hadn't been able to stop our fall. Combat magic would never be my strength.

But the magic pouring in from Conota, fueling the brilliant outer ward beyond the fire line, gave me power the like of which I hadn't theretofore known in Iroja.

I couldn't fling bolts of lightning...but maybe I didn't *have* to.

It was the work of a few seconds to formulate the illusion in my mind, and then, forcing my will outward like a blast, I plunged the Hidden Ones into total darkness.

"What's happening?" Artur demanded as the projection showed the creatures squealing in confusion, then groping for each other and bumping about as if suddenly blinded.

"Fog," I said, concentrating on the illusion. "I've created a dense fog around them, at least to their eyes. They can't see their hands in front of their faces. That should buy us a little time—"

"That's *brilliant*," she interjected, and let fly a volley of lightning bolts with both hands. They soared over the flames like arrows and fell upon the pack with devastating effect, and the survivors, perhaps smelling the burning flesh in their ranks, began to panic. Some ran straight for the fire; one even made it through alive, albeit alight, and Hua finished her before she could reach Maria. Others trampled their neighbors, feeling about in the darkness for an exit, while a few near the front seemed to be squeaking orders. Surely, I thought, the heat of the wall of fire should eventually serve to orient them.

And within a minute, unfortunately, it did. Though blind and falling with Artur's continued onslaught of bolts, they managed to regroup near the fire, and then, with a high-pitched war cry, they charged—some toward the flames, and some into the earth, tunneling beneath them.

"A little help!" Maria called as the first of the vanguard surfaced and ran at her.

Artur had leapt from the roof in seconds and landed in a crouch, training her shots at the ones advancing on Maria. She killed the first round, but as a fresh wave made it through, she took up a stance at Maria's side, shooting at the Hidden Ones as they sped toward her—and, more worryingly, *past* her.

Having made it to the ground, Hua took up the interior defense, standing in the path to the barn and shooting flames at any of the invaders who made it that far. "They smell Arik," I said, running to join her. "They're going to funnel in this direction—"

"Help Artur," she said, aiming her wand with deadly accuracy. "Stop them at the source."

There wasn't much I could do to kill the Hidden Ones, but I did my best to confuse them. Taking a position out of Artur's way, I closed my eyes and focused, forming a second illusion to add to the first. If I crafted it correctly, I reasoned, I could reverse their sense of direction, sending them running back toward the fire when their eyes said they were heading for the barn.

Looking away from the Hidden Ones was, admittedly, a mistake.

I'd almost finished designing the illusion when I felt a pain like fifty knives stabbing at my right calf. As I screamed, my eyes flew open, and I spotted a Hidden One with its teeth buried in my leg, gnawing at the muscle. My kicks did nothing to loosen its grip, and I could barely hold the existing illusion together for the agony.

"Be still!" Artur yelled, and reached for my assailant's scrawny body. Clutching it in both hands, she ripped it— and part of my leg—away from me, then slammed the thing's head into a young tree until its skull cracked. Snarling, she dropped it, and it quivered in its death throes, then lay unmoving in the grass.

Reeling from the shock, and with a new sort of pain throbbing in my leg, I ripped off my T-shirt and bound it around the wound, trying to stop the bleeding. Artur electrocuted a clump of smoking Hidden Ones, fresh from the fire, then knelt beside me and wrapped her hands around my maimed calf before I could begin the task of healing myself. I could feel the enchantment take effect— or, more properly, I could feel the pain ebb as the numbing began—but while the enchantment began to clot the hole, it wasn't fast enough. The next group of Hidden Ones to emerge from the tunnels paused inside the border, sniffing the air, then turned their faces toward me and charged. Artur fried them and looked back at me, uncertainty etched across her face.

"Like sharks, you know?" I said, hoping I wasn't mixing up my aquatic documentaries. "Blood in the water. They're starving, remember?"

She muttered something—I sensed that it was profane—then said, "Stand with Maria, but stay out of her way."

"I thought the point was to keep them *away* from Maria," I protested.

She zapped a runner from several yards, and it died with a squeal. "I can't defend you both if you're in two places. Here." She pulled her sword free of its sheath, and the long blade glittered in the firelight. "Can you wield one?"

"I…uh…well…" I stammered.

With an impatient huff, she pressed the hilt into my hands. "If they come close, skewer them. Behead them. Whatever it takes. I don't care about style," she added, then sent a blast through three Hidden Ones at once. "Are they still seeing fog?"

"Should be," I replied, remembering what I'd meant to do. "Hold on, I'm trying to add to it…"

"I'll give you what time I can," she said, and calmly picked up a Hidden One in an invisible grip, then tossed it back into the fire ring.

Our attackers were relentless. Even after I managed to confuse their sense of direction, I couldn't confound their sense of smell, and more kept braving the fire and the tunnels. For more than two long hours, Artur methodically shot them singly and in groups, and Hua picked off most of the few who escaped her bolts. I only heard Fik's shotguns sound a handful of times, though each blast sent a wave of fear through my guts like ice water.

But even with their target so close, the Hidden Ones eventually began to weigh their losses. For every ten who attempted to run through the fire, only one or two survived, and the tunneling group fared little better against Artur. My illusions held firm, and by the time the sky lightened from black to dark blue, the survivors were scattering in a haphazard retreat. A red burst of light and a roar from the direction of the RV told me when some of the fleeing creatures reached Frank, while an echoing roar behind me alerted us to Ione's kill.

As Artur caught her breath, Flora, Orson, and Uther appeared before me. "They're in the woods," Orson reported. "Some of them have taken shelter. Want to finish the little bastards off?"

Flora's brow puckered. "Hope, your leg…"

I can manage, I told her, leaning on my borrowed—and awkwardly used—sword. *Lead the way*.

Artur glanced up as I limped toward the fire. "Going somewhere?"

"My spies have offered to take us to the hiding stragglers," I said. "Want to come, or should I try to whack them?"

She marched up behind me and took her sword back. "This should be more useful to you," she said, and replaced it with a proper wooden crutch. "Right, tell them I'm in."

"They can hear you," I replied, and waited while Maria created a gap in the flames to allow us passage into the trees.

She grunted, then gave me a longer glance. "Probably a good thing for modesty's sake that you slept in a bra. What *would* people think?"

I looked down, remembered that my shirt was being used elsewhere, and started to flush, only to hear Artur's low chuckle beside me. "You act as if anyone should care," she said, but a twitch of her finger produced a fresh T-shirt, which immediately stuck to my sweaty back.

We worked together until full sunrise, me relaying locations and Artur dispatching the Hidden Ones. There was no talk of mercy, no suggestion that we send a survivor back to Ketulm as a warning. Artur was quiet and efficient, and highly thorough.

When we tromped back to the settlement, Artur with her bloodstained sword in hand and me propped up with my crutch, Beth met us at the cooling fire ring. "Ione's going to join Frank," she said as the blue dragon passed overhead. "They're guarding the road in case any of the little beasts escaped and try to circle back. Hua and Carey and Zeb are out looking for hot spots in the woods—Ione got a little sloppy at the end, but Hua thinks she put out all the fires."

"Are you hurt?" Artur asked.

She shook her head. "Wired. Thought I'd go help them." Giving my leg a second look, her face contorted into a grimace. "Uh...Hope?"

"I know," I muttered, leaning on my crutch.

"Your pants are, like, *soaked*."

Artur glanced behind me at the damage, then looked at me, aghast. "Why didn't you say something? I failed at the enchantment—"

"Really, this is an improvement," I told her, and turned back to Beth. "How are Fik and Arik?"

"Alive," she reported. "I mean, Arik's not doing so hot,

but Fik said that only five of the Hidden Ones made it to them, and he blasted them with buckshot."

I sighed as the vise in my chest began to slightly loosen. "Good. Go help the others, okay?"

Once she'd run off, Artur led me to a nearby porch, and I gratefully sank onto a wooden swing. "Up here," she said, sliding a short table beneath my foot, and I hoisted my bad leg for inspection. She untied my makeshift bandage, but when her fingers reached around to the wound, they came away tacky with blood. "Still open," she muttered. "I'm sorry. I'll make you new trousers."

Before I could object, she ripped the cloth at the knee and gently peeled it away from the leaking scab. I cried out, and she murmured apologies as she inspected the place where my missing muscle had been. A warm, wet rag appeared in her hand, and she gingerly cleaned the excess blood away as I turned my eyes to the porch rafters, trying not to scream. The numbing enchantment had helped while terror had suppressed every other sensation, but as I calmed, my body reminded me that I was missing a significant chunk of that limb. Soon enough, however, the pain started to fade, and I glanced down to see Artur weaving a tighter enchantment around me. After several minutes of work, she produced clean bandages and wrapped the area, which by then had ceased to ooze. "There," she said, wiping her bloody hands on the stained cloth that had once been my pantleg. "I'm sorry it wasn't better to begin with. Sloppy."

"You worked that more quickly than I could have," I told her, slowly lowering my leg from the table. "I can heal injuries, but under pressure—"

"I let you down," she said, balling the rags in her fists. "I'm sorry."

She looked miserable, but I couldn't stop my incredulous laughter. "What are you *talking* about? You saved my leg! My *life*!"

"You're injured. Perhaps maimed," she muttered. "I

should have been quicker—"

"I'm the one who wasn't watching my surroundings. This is my fault," I insisted, patting my knee. "Why would you blame—"

"One of my people was hurt. *Again*. And I allowed it to happen." Ignoring my sputtered protestations, she stepped off the porch and began to walk away.

Spotting a flash of movement out of the corner of my eye, I turned to find Uther beside me, watching Artur with a stricken expression. "Please," he said, "I know you are weary, but please…"

I was more than weary. With the immediate danger past, my body was recalling both its lack of sleep and loss of blood—and my thoughts were with Arik, who could barely stand the last time I saw him. But there was anguish in Uther's eyes, and I'd given him my word. Nodding, I gripped the edge of the porch swing, centered myself, and sent power flowing through him. As soon as the connection was established, he ran to the edge of the steps and bellowed Artur's name.

She froze for a split-second, then whirled around, saw him, and gasped. I couldn't tell whether she intentionally fell to her knees or whether her legs gave way, but Uther was off the porch in an instant, hurrying to her side. "Child, why do you punish yourself?" he asked as she stared up at him. "You won the night. Your enemy is destroyed, and the girl will heal," he said, pointing back at me. "You fought well!"

She stammered out a response, but the words were unintelligible to me. Vaguely, I understood that Uther must be speaking to her in kind, but as he and I were bound, I was privy to his half of the conversation.

"Yes, she was injured," he said with faint impatience. "This is the nature of battle. Casualties are to be expected. But she has her life, and not because you *failed*." He knelt in front of her, tried to take her hands, then sighed at the futility of the attempt. "They do not blame you, my dearest. None of them do, least of all Kei."

Her voice rose and began to strain.

"You went out to die with your men. You asked nothing more of them than you were willing to give. Their deaths were brutal, yes, but brief. None of them suffered long. And you would have been among them had Myrddin not intervened. Artur, hear me: *they do not blame you.*"

The two of them were just close enough to my perch on the porch that I could see her face redden and twitch in warning of imminent tears, but more telling still was the hitch in her voice as she answered him.

"Have you not thought of how many lives you saved?" said Uther. "The men who went out to face those monsters made time for the women and children, for the sick and elderly. They served as a distraction until Morgen could act. Their sacrifice was not in vain, child." He tried again to touch her, then settled for holding his palms against the sides of her splotchy face. "I suspect that Myrddin didn't tell you the full truth. Afallon endured after that coward fled. *Our people* endured. One of my cousins was made king—Menw, do you recall him? He restored order, and people returned to their lives. Do you know how Afallon met its end? A *marriage*. Not a war, not a great calamity—two little kingdoms uniting beneath one banner. Now, I grant you," he continued with a slight chuckle, "Menw was not nearly the warrior you are, but he protected our people from the Saxons. He was a decent king."

Artur's head bowed, and she was still murmuring a response when Uther cut her short.

"My dearest, you did not deceive me. Myrddin betrayed me, not you. You were a child—and more importantly, you were *my* child. You always will be."

She raised her watery eyes and asked a question.

"How could I *not* claim you? I raised you as well as I could, I watched you grow into a marvel...you were the one thing I desired above all else," he said gently. "A child.

I told Myrddin that I did not care whether I could be father to a son or a daughter—*he* made that decision. Trying to protect his own interests, I'm certain."

She spoke again.

"I cared nothing about that. Menw would have made a fine heir all along. I just wanted *you*, whoever and whatever you were."

As Artur's tears brimmed over, Uther pressed on. "I knew what Myrddin had done from the time I died. I could see through that illusion he put on you, you know. For fifteen years, I watched you grow and fight and struggle against yourself for no reason. I cannot count how many times I tried to find a way to tell you how proud I am of the person you have become."

By then, she was crying in earnest, her face in her hands, her body shaking with exhausted sobs.

"You have done nothing but bring me pride," he said. "And I'm so sorry for last year, I would have stayed to speak with you, but Hope was fading, and..." As if remembering my presence, Uther turned around, frowned as he studied me, then returned to Artur. "She's weakening, we haven't got long. Look at me, daughter."

After a brief moment, Artur composed herself enough to wipe her eyes and raise her head.

"I am so grateful that you have your sister and her sister," said Uther. "If you find satisfaction with your associates, then do so with my blessing. All I want is for you to be happy and at least reasonably safe."

She frowned in query and spoke.

Her father laughed softly. "You didn't think that Orson was the only one to look after his daughters, did you?"

Though I couldn't understand her, the tone of her voice suggested disbelief.

Uther nodded. "I came with Orson. Hope has graciously offered to allow us this opportunity for days, but I did not want to be a...*distraction*...for you. You did well," he said, leaning toward her. "Here, and in

Glastonbury, and in Afallon that was. You were a remarkable king, my dearest. For whatever part I played in that, I am forever grateful."

Artur murmured a question.

"All the time. She loves you dearly. She would have come, too, but we decided that one parent fretting over you while you tried to strategize would be more than sufficient."

Her response was nearly inaudible to me, but it earned a slight chuckle from Uther.

"That's long been forgiven. Your mother knows you only had half the truth—she does not blame you for thinking her unfaithful. We love you, dearest. We always will. Swear one thing to me."

She looked at him expectantly.

"It is Orson's understanding that you have a counselor of sorts in Faerie. Is this correct?"

Though most of her answer was incomprehensible to me, I made out the word *therapist*.

"Good. She seems to have a positive effect on your mind."

Artur nodded.

"The swear to me that you will continue to seek her counsel. I would rather you have more good nights of sleep than screaming nightmares."

When Artur answered him, Uther turned back to me and nodded. "Thank you. Rest, Hope."

I withdrew my power, but as I did, the world began to go gray around the edges of my vision. "Happy to help," I mumbled, smiling at them, and then I knew no more.

CHAPTER 12

When I opened my eyes again, I was in Fik's guestroom, tucked into bed, with Artur sitting in a kitchen chair by the nightstand. Beside her stood Flora, who watched me come to with her arms tightly crossed. "What am I to do with you, child?" she demanded. "I leave you briefly, and I return to find you pushing yourself beyond all reasonable limits—"

"I apologize, truly, I didn't realize how tired you were," Uther began from the doorway, but Flora silenced him with a sharp glare.

"You overexerted yourself," she chided me, "you were injured already, and—"

"Hope? Can you hear me?" Artur asked, talking over Flora without realizing that we had irate company. She gingerly shook my shoulder until my eyes focused on her face. "Hope? You fainted. Do you understand? I put you to bed…"

I reached one hand from beneath the blankets and squeezed her wrist. "I'm okay," I mumbled. "Tired. Waking."

She let out a sigh of relief. "*Good.* I was worried. You shouldn't have done that, you must be exhausted—"

"Your father needed to speak to you. I promised him."

"And I am beyond grateful, but it could have waited until you were stronger."

"I owed you. The leg is nice and numb." Yawning, I looked to the window and noticed bright light around the edges of the shade. "How long was I out?"

"About an hour. Do you see why I was concerned?"

"Long night," I said, and started to sit up, trying to put the fragments of the previous hours back together. The Hidden Ones, yes, we drove them back…but my guts were still twisting…

When Fik ran into the room, the pieces fell together. "Is she awake yet?" he asked Artur, then saw me moving. "Hope, quickly. He's on the couch."

Arik.

"How is he?" I asked, scrambling to untangle the blankets.

Fik didn't soften the blow. "Fading. I think he's holding on to say goodbye. He's asking for you."

I slid to my feet, took staggering steps until the room stopped spinning, then hurriedly limped after Fik down the hallway and into the den, where the Joneses, Hua, Beth, and Maria were already waiting. Arik's face had paled to a soft lilac, his eyes were sunken, and he seemed to gasp for each breath, but he reached for me as I took a seat on the cleared coffee table beside him. "You're all right," he whispered, smiling up at me. "I heard that your leg was injured."

"I'll heal," I told him, gripping his hand. "Hold on, Arik."

He glanced over my shoulder, and I turned to find Orson lingering in the corner of the room, watching us with a drawn face. *I'll know shortly whether you were lying about how much this is going to hurt*, he thought, a late attempt at levity.

"Little pain," Orson replied. "I promise you, son. But it's not too late, the gate's in walking distance…"

"Forget that gate," I said aloud, drawing odd looks from the non-cynaeli in the room. "The collar is coming off. *Now.*"

"Hope—"

"Fik is safe." I jabbed my finger toward his brother, who stood behind the couch, nodding fervently. "You did more than your duty. Now we work on you."

He smiled again, though it was strained. "You don't have to worry about me. I got to see him again, and I got to see you. That's really the best I could have hoped for. Don't put yourself in danger trying to break the collar. If you were killed on my behalf—"

"I'll take the risk," I insisted, and turned to Maria. "The collar is powered by dark magic. If we take him into Faerie, maybe it will fall apart. Can you get permission?"

"Hope," Arik began, but I turned back to him and shook my head to stop his protestation.

"What do you have to lose? *Stay with me*," I said, squeezing his hand so hard that he winced.

"On it," said Maria, pulling out her phone. She stepped into the kitchen for a moment, and I heard the low, rapid murmuring of conversation before she returned, raising her thumbs. "Permission granted. Val's waiting—he's an excellent healer," she told Arik. "Someone help him up, and I'll handle the gate…"

By the time that Fik and I had hoisted Arik to his feet, the promised gate had opened in the middle of the den, a portal into a room I recognized from my last stay as the king's office. The windows were still dark with night in that realm, and lit sconces lined the walls. The king himself stood by, beckoning us on, but before we could cross, Ros appeared at the lightning-wrapped edge of the gate, a glowing woman in jeans and a green tunic.

"He's dying," Maria told her in a rush, "this is an emergency, he's no danger—"

"Oh, I'm not worried about *that*," Ros interrupted. "Bring him to me."

Arik shook—whether from the effects of the collar or from the fear of what it would do to him on breaking, I couldn't say—but he tried to help Fik and me maneuver him across the room.

As we started to cross, Ros reached out and wrapped both hands around the collar. The black metal began to glow, first red, then orange, brightening with incredible speed. Ros closed her eyes and held on, though she grimaced with the evident effort.

"What's happening?" the king asked from behind her. "Can I—"

"*Stand back,*" she snapped through gritted teeth. "The damn thing is trying to explode…"

Suddenly, she cried aloud, and a brilliant burst of white flared from her hands and shot up her arms before dissipating into the ether. "Ow," she groaned, "*shit,* that thing was nasty."

My heart raced. "Was?"

Glancing at me, she nodded, then smiled at Arik and pulled the halves of the broken collar away. The metal crumbled to dust in her hands and fell harmlessly to the floor.

The three of us stood there just inside the gate as Arik reached up with trembling fingers to feel his bared neck. "Is it…" he managed, then slumped down.

I almost fell with the shock of his dead weight, and as Fik lowered him to the rug, I feared the worst. But Fik pressed his fingers to Arik's neck, then held his hand just over Arik's slack mouth. "Breathing, and there's a pulse," he announced. "Both weak. I…" He reached out over Arik as if he were intending to create a healing enchantment, but he stopped short, frowning as he realized our sudden limitations. "Right," he muttered, "there's no magic here."

"Allow me," said Valerius, and floated Arik onto a couch with a slight gesture. He bent over the patient in examination, then looked up with a scowl. "You couldn't have brought him sooner? The boy looks to be on the edge of death."

"He insisted that we take care of Fik's problem first," I explained.

Valerius gave Fik a once-over. "You seem healthy enough," he said, then muttered in Fae, "*Children.*"

"I heard that," said Maria in kind, stepping through the gate. "We *did* just spend hours frying little monstrosities out of the Gray Lands. It was a busy weekend."

"And this one should have evacuated with the others," he retorted. "What's the point of unnecessary heroic sacrifices?"

"He was concerned for his brother!"

"Who is obviously in far better condition." He rolled his eyes as she huffed. "No matter. The danger is over?"

"We think we got them all. I'm going to do a last sweep with Artur and try to clean up the fire damage, but yes. The evacuees—"

"Are comfortable for now. Do what needs to be done, and don't trouble yourself about them—they're hurting no one."

"What are they saying?" Fik muttered in my ear.

Valerius glanced our way, then seemed to perceive the problem. "Ah, yes. You do not have the local tongue, do you?" he said, reverting to his oddly accented English. "One problem at a time. First, your brother. Maria—"

"I've got matters under control in Kentucky," she said, stepping back across the border.

"I was going to tell you to be careful and call. *Yes?*"

"Love you, too," she said, and closed the gate.

A few seconds later, a short, brown-haired woman in a white bathrobe appeared at the door—Bonnie, I recalled, the king's chief of staff. "You wanted me, my lord?" she asked in Fae, then recognized me. "Oh, no," she drawled, switching to a familiar twang. "Ms. Lozano, what *have* you been up to now?"

"They will be staying here for the time being. If you would please spread the word..." Valerius began, then noticed the missing half of my pajama leg and Artur's wrapping. "You're injured?" he asked me. "Maria said nothing about—"

"Artur saw to it," I replied. "I'm just stiff."

"I'll review her work. Come with me," he said as Arik

levitated off the couch and drifted ahead of us out of the room. "There are certainly enough beds in this building."

Artur was more skilled than I with healing magic, but Valerius put us both to shame. Once Arik was wrapped in a thick, smoky mesh of enchantment and Fik had pulled a chair close to his bed to keep watch, Valerius led me into the adjoining room and undid the bandages around my leg. He hissed at the sight beneath, while I kept my eyes firmly averted. "What happened?" he asked.

"One of them bit me."

"And chewed, it seems. The wound is clean enough, but ragged. Be still." He dressed it again, then redid Artur's work. When he'd finished, the magic around my leg was so thick and active that it looked as if he'd wrapped a black bandage over the white one, and I felt no pain. "More effective in this realm, you understand," he said as the bottom half of my pantleg reappeared. "And I've learned a few techniques beyond Artur's knowledge, though her work was passably done. Her strength is combat, not its aftermath," he added with a wry smile.

"Why am I not surprised?" I replied, but as I tried to slide off the bed, he stopped me.

"Rest and let that work," the king insisted. "Arik will not wake for hours—Ros has seen to that. You need to sleep as well."

"I've already had a nap this morning," I protested. "I let Artur and her father talk, and then I passed out for an hour. I'm fine."

He regarded me with deep incredulity. "That...*no*, Hope. Bed."

"But—"

"Don't make me call Bonnie in here."

I surrendered, but while I was stripping pillows from the bed and trying not to dirty the nice blankets, Bonnie took it upon herself to look in on me. "Oh, for heaven's sake," she said, getting a good look at my condition. "You're a mess, girl. And…" She sniffed deeply, then grimaced. "Smoke, blood, and what else?"

"Honestly, I don't think I want to know," I mumbled.

"*Bath*," she ordered, marching me into the next room with two fingers between my shoulder blades.

"But my bandages—"

"I'll waterproof them. Go on, hon, you stink."

She wasn't exaggerating. I'd barely entered the bathroom and dared to take a good whiff of myself when the soaking tub was full and bubbly, a stack of fluffy towels had appeared on the ledge beside it, and Bonnie was arranging a dozen bottles of soaps and shampoos. "There, now," she said. "Take your time. Let me see these bandages." I rolled up my pants, and she added a bit to the healing enchantment. "Swim at will. Get in, I'll be back in a minute."

Once I was submerged to my chin, Bonnie returned and gestured my dirty clothes off the floor. "Should I wash these or burn them?" she asked.

"I'm not in love with them," I replied.

"Oh, good. We can do better."

When I finally dragged myself out of the bath, I found clean pajamas waiting for me, and I dressed and slid into bed. The last thing I remember was a vague sense of peace overriding even the disquieting sensation of being in a realm without useable magic. Fik was alive. Arik was alive.

For the first time in a week, I allowed myself to truly rest.

When I saw daylight again, I had a flash of panic, as the sunlight was nearly golden with approaching twilight. "It's okay, you're safe. You've been down for hours," said Ros, appearing at my side before I could rise.

"How long…"

"Eh, hard to say exactly. It was still a few hours to

dawn here when you zonked, so…fifteen, maybe? If I've got my days straight, we're about six hours behind the time zone you left—or maybe it's eighteen hours ahead, I lose track. Really, that gets kind of fluid around here."

I caught my breath and flopped back into the thick pillow. "Is Arik—"

"Still sleeping. Give the enchantment time to work—he was in bad shape." She hoisted herself onto the foot of my bed, her radiance throwing odd shadows onto the walls. "You were wise not to attempt to break the collar yourselves. It *was* booby-trapped."

"Crossing broke it?"

"Yes and no. There was a last trap in the system as it failed. I absorbed it before it could take his head off," she added with a grunt. "*Nasty* piece of work. Technically complex, but what a waste of potential." She nibbled at her lip and regarded me closely. "You *are* aware of what was done to him beyond the collar, yeah?"

I frowned. "Shouldn't you know that answer?"

"Well, yes, but I find that I can put folks more at ease if I at least pretend to not be nearly omniscient. Can't do much about the glow, but I can try to have a conversation."

"That's fair," I replied, and sat up in bed. "And yes, I know what making a naffidar entails."

"I can't heal *that*," she said, her voice low. "If he were even a little fae, then maybe, but not in his case. My power works best on the natives, especially when they can help me help themselves," she explained with a shrug. "I can somewhat augment what Val's done and speed it along, but I can't…you know…put him back together. Wish I could."

"I'm just grateful that he's alive," I said, stretching to take her hand. "Thank you."

"You're more than welcome."

I didn't want to annoy the realm with questions, but then she *was* sitting in my room. "Have you heard any word from the others? Was there much damage from the fires? Frank and Ione—"

"Everyone's okay," she assured me. "Maria and Artur patched up the ditches your group made and threw in some new trees. The land will recover in time. Maria said they found no sign of Hidden Ones, so put your mind at ease."

The tension in my shoulders loosened at the news.

"Ione went back to the barn here several hours ago," she continued, "and *apparently*, it didn't take much persuasion to make Frank go with her instead of waiting for Toula to get out of a Council meeting. I'm sure she'll be over eventually to fix his bind again, but for now…" Her mouth slowly spread into a lopsided smile. "Ione took your suggestion, I believe."

"Did she?"

"Had a little talk with him."

"And how did he take the news?" I asked.

Ros's smile widened. "Let's just say that someone, and I'm not naming names, is rather badly smitten with a female someone, and he's finally accepting that it's reciprocated."

"Oh, *really*?"

"Mm-hmm. And another someone who might or might not be Sam did me a favor and called Toula and asked her not to come for a few days."

"Ione told me she's not ready to mate," I pointed out.

"No, but they could do with a little time together without poor Sam having to play transcriptionist at all hours. Anyway, Carey took her people home, and Maria took the RV back to Montana by gate. I know Beth was gunning for a chance to drive it, but Artur doesn't need that heart attack."

"They returned to Glastonbury?"

"No, those three are here. Maria's room is down the corridor, and Val put the others a little further along. The night finally caught up with Beth, and Artur barely got her boots off before she collapsed. I took her sword off and put it on her dresser. She didn't *budge*. But if you're trying to get your bearings, it's about eleven p.m. in Kentucky, I think." She paused and gave me a long, searching look. "That's ten-ish in Oklahoma."

"I should call Mama, shouldn't I?"

"Yeah, you should."

"I mean, it's late..."

"Trust me, if your parents are anything like mine, she won't give a damn about the hour. Need a phone?"

A little black model appeared on the blanket beside me, unlike any phone I'd seen but, I suspected, able to contact Iroja. "Wish me luck," I said, dialing Mama's number.

When I glanced up, Ros had vanished, and the phone was ringing on the other end. The second ring had just sounded when Mama's voice came on the line. "Hello?" she said, her voice slightly groggy but touched with fear.

I braced myself. "Hi, Mama. It's me."

"*Hope!*" she cried. "Hang on, baby, I'm turning the TV off..."

Listening to the noise on the other end, I could well envision where she was: her worn leather recliner in the den, probably wrapped in the old plaid throw she kept for naps. The televised mumbling on the other side ceased, and the chair's hinges squeaked as she kicked in the footrest and sat upright. "Oh, my God, Hope," she said, nearly in tears. "Are you okay? Where are you? I'll come get you, I don't care where you are, just tell me where to go."

"I'm, uh...actually, I'm back in Faerie," I mumbled.

"*Faerie?*"

"Resting. Healing. I got a little leg injury, nothing too bad, I'll live—"

"*What is going on?*" she demanded.

I cast my mind back over the week. On the previous Monday, Flora had me out of bed and hiking through the woods to find Arik. The few intervening days felt like a year, and it was only just Monday again…almost Tuesday, I realized, trying to count the hours I'd lost to sleep. "Right," I said, collecting my thoughts. "So…you know how I kind of ran off with Arik last Tuesday?"

"There's no 'kind of' about it, young lady."

"He needed help," I continued, inwardly cringing at Mama's tone. "And the Arcanum sent some."

As plainly as I could, omitting some of the more graphic details of the last week, I told my mother where I had been, with whom, and why I was currently limping. "The enchantment works best here," I concluded, "and since Arik is still asleep, I…well…"

"You want to be there when he wakes," she finished.

"I do." I hesitated, then said, "You understand, don't you, Mama? I didn't want to hurt you or scare you, but Arik needed me, and—"

"And you love him." It wasn't a question.

"Please don't be angry. I was trying to do the right thing."

"Hope, baby," she said, and sighed deeply, a long, low exhalation. "You could have been killed."

"But I wasn't. I'll be okay."

"If something had happened to you…something *more* than a bite out of your leg…"

"I know, Mama."

"You don't." She began to choke up. "I thought I was going to lose you again, honey. And I can't do that, I *cannot* lose you."

"I'm going to be careful," I promised. "And assuming that Ros lets me keep this phone, I won't turn it off. You have the number?"

"Yes…"

"I'll call you tomorrow and every day thereafter until I'm back in Pauline. At a more normal hour. But I need to be here now. My leg is feeling better, I'm resting, and Lord Valerius is allowing me to stay at his place, just like last time. Nothing's going to happen to me." When she remained silent, I added, "I'm so sorry, Mama, I know I scared you."

"I've been sick to my stomach for *days*," she replied. "Barely eaten, barely slept—"

"And Arik and Fik and a bunch of other innocent people are alive right now because we went on the run," I countered. "I don't just sit by—that's not who I am. I hope you can understand. But I swear to you, I'll call."

She hesitated for a few seconds, then murmured, "Okay, baby. Okay."

Mama didn't sound happy, but there was nothing I could do about that from Faerie. "Talk to you tomorrow. I love you."

"I love you more than anything. Please be careful," said Mama.

We said our goodbyes, and as I ended the call, Ros reappeared. "Sure, you can keep the phone," she said. "Put it on the nightstand."

I did as she bid. "Is that how it charges?"

"No, that's just to get it out of the way. You're going back to sleep."

"Already? I'm fine," I began, but Ros just shook her head.

"Really?" she asked, crossing her arms. "You *really* want to argue with me? Here?"

That, I knew, wasn't a winnable fight, and so I lay down again and pulled the blankets up. "I'm going to get my days and nights confused," I muttered as she tucked me in.

"It's called jetlag, you'll live. See you in the morning."

Ros wasn't kidding. I opened my eyes again to full sunlight, and I might have slept longer had she not awakened me. "You're wanted at the breakfast table. Feeling up to it?"

It being difficult to turn down an invitation from my

host, I washed my face, tidied myself, and dressed in the long teal shirt and leggings that Bonnie had left for me. Even my tennis shoes were clean, for which I was grateful; judging by the stains I'd noticed on them the day before, I'd stepped in more than just mud. When Ros showed me to one of the smaller dining rooms, I found the king there, plus the other two of the Three, all watching with concern as I limped to the table. "How's the leg?" Valerius asked as I pulled out a chair.

"Only stiff. No pain, thank you," I replied.

"Well, of course it's stiff," said Eleanor. "Given your injury, I wouldn't expect overnight healing."

"At least it isn't still bleeding," I offered, then quickly wished I hadn't, glancing at the food spread around the table.

To my relief, no one seemed offended by the gaffe. "Moon and stars, kid," said Coileán, "you're lucky to still have a leg, based on what I've heard."

"We'd like the full details, if you are amenable to the telling," Valerius added as a large cup of coffee appeared beside my plate. "Artur said there's a threat of civil war in the Gray Lands. I trust her recollection, but I'd prefer to hear a native's interpretation."

For the next hour, as I satisfied my ravenous appetite and downed far too much excellent coffee, I related what had transpired over the previous days and what Arik had told me of the situation in Conota, answering the questions that I could. "The good news," I concluded, "is that Ketulm is unlikely to attempt war with the mortal realm or Faerie to reclaim Arik, at least not yet. He has bigger issues."

"The missing king," said Eleanor, sipping her tea. "Or queen, I suppose. Mab *did* hold that post for a time."

"Could be either. The realm hasn't made his choice known…but having seen Fik," I said, turning to Valerius, "surely you agree that he doesn't look cynaeli."

"Perhaps in the eyes, but nowhere else," he concurred.

"There is a simple way to narrow the field, if everyone is willing."

Coileán reached for another roll. "*Ooh*, we don't want to bother her today."

I wasn't sure whether I could decipher the look that Eleanor and Valerius exchanged. "Oh?" my host asked.

"Yeah. She has a long day planned with Arc 7. The installation head is throwing himself a birthday party—"

"How old is he, *ten*?" Eleanor interrupted.

Coileán gestured the butter toward his plate with a little smirk. "No, I think we've reached the big four-one. Truly, a milestone. I asked whether she was anticipating a clown or pony rides, and she told me to behave myself, so I suppose it's a surprise. Anyway, since she's going to be in Australia for the festivities, she's lined up a schedule of committee meetings. But maybe we could get her over here tomorrow. Couldn't hurt to ask."

"Aural analysis," said Eleanor, reading the confusion on my face. "Toula is an expert."

"She could compare Fik and Arik," Valerius explained. "If they share half their aural lattice, then they share a parent. If not…"

"That could work," I said, nodding. "If we prove that Fik *isn't* the new king and send word to Ketulm, then maybe he won't make any further attempts on his son's life. It's worth a try."

"Even still," said Coileán, "that would only take care of one problem. If the Gray Lands falls into all-out war, then what's to stop it from spilling over into the mortal realm?"

"We can't seal all the gates," Eleanor replied, refilling her tea. "Even if we knew the location of every gate into that realm, it would require a massive undertaking to patch the holes—"

"And they could punch new ones," he finished. "Which means the Arcanum needs to go on high alert. The Fringe can detect new gates, but they won't be much use if an army marches over the border."

Valerius considered that, then turned to me and asked, "This Fik...how well do you know him?"

"We're friendly," I replied. "I've always been closer to Arik, but Fik's never been cruel to me. Why?"

"Were he to be king, do you think he would respect the borders? Nath did little to stop incursions, and Mab likewise."

"Let's not forget Geheret," Coileán muttered.

I had to laugh at that. "The Three-Season King? He wasn't on the throne long enough to do anything of consequence, was he?"

Coileán didn't share my mirth. "More than you might imagine."

"My mother made many unfortunate choices," said Valerius before I could press for details. "Having a child by your realm is certainly among them."

Fortunately, my mind moved more quickly than my mouth and gripped my tongue before I could say something unwise. Mab the Invader was my host's mother, making Geheret, the laughable blip between her long reign and Nath's, his brother. Knowing nothing of *those* familial politics, I kept further commentary to myself.

"The first step is to bring Toula here," Valerius continued. "Until then, there's little to be gained by speculation...though I do have one question. Fik's wife is mostly human, is she not?"

I couldn't offer an actual percentage, but I knew it had to be high. "One of her grandfathers is a wizard, and his wife was half human. Other than that, I can't say."

"But she's native to the mortal realm?" When I nodded, he grew pensive. "Surely his wife could convince him to do no harm to that realm. If Fik is indeed the missing king..."

He let the thought hang as I sipped my coffee.

"I'll talk to Toula once she's done her duty at Arc 7," said Coileán. "Until then, where *is* this Fik?"

"I sent him to the settlement late last night," Valerius

replied. "His wife and daughter are there, and he wanted to put their minds at ease."

"So no one's with Arik?" I interrupted.

"He's deeply asleep. I doubt he'd wake if an army marched by his door."

"Still," I said, folding my napkin, "someone should be waiting. If you'll excuse me…"

My coffee cup refilled, and Valerius waved me on my way as I snatched it up.

My Ros-made phone told me that it just after eleven Wednesday morning in Kentucky—dawn in Faerie—when Arik stirred and opened his eyes.

"Hi, you," I murmured, rising from my chair by his bed to take his hand. "Feeling better?"

He blinked groggily, but his fingers found mine and intertwined themselves. "Hope?" he croaked.

"You're going to be all right," I soothed. "Looking better already."

That was the truth—he'd regained some of his color, and his eyes seemed far less sunken. The chills and fever that had plagued him for days had calmed, and Arik wasn't sweating. He shifted his legs beneath the blankets, groaned softly, then tried to sit up on his elbows.

"Slow, now," I said, helping him upright. "Take it slowly. How do you feel?"

He considered the question for the space of a few long breaths. "Like I've been tossed off a cliff," he finally replied, "but that's an improvement." When he turned to me, I saw tears in his eyes. "I'm alive?"

"Yes, Arik."

He stared into space, his face twitching with emotions I couldn't count—and neither, in that magical desert, could I pry. "Arik?" I asked after a moment. "Are you in pain?"

"I didn't plan for this outcome," he mumbled, still gazing into the distance.

"I know." Tightening my grip on him, I said, "I think I prefer this one to the outcome you had in mind, don't you? Personally, I'm glad you're alive."

That seemed to snap him back to himself, and as he turned to me again, he reached his free arm toward me. I completed the hug, saying nothing as I felt Arik shake.

Once his quiet sobs subsided, he pulled away, wiped his face on the sheet, and glanced at the ceiling until he'd brought himself under control. "How long did I—"

"About two days. The realm has kept you unconscious to speed the healing."

"Two—" He frowned in consternation. "Fik, is he—"

"Perfectly fine. He's with Janice and the baby. He calls me every few hours," I added, lifting my new phone from the nightstand as proof. "They're staying in the settlement—it's a nice place. Toula from the Arcanum is supposed to come by this afternoon to compare your aura and Fik's, so he'll certainly be back by then."

"My aura?"

"There's an Irojan spell that shows bloodlines. If you and Fik have a matching half, then we'll know that Fik isn't the king, and maybe we can send word to your father."

"Father," he muttered, and the hand not locked with mine went to his bare neck. "I..."

"You're free," I said gently. "He can't touch you here."

Arik embraced me again, but there were no tears that time, and when we parted, he was smiling. "Feels good, doesn't it?" I said.

His smile widened, and a hysterical giggle slipped out before he clapped his hand over his mouth.

"Arik? Are you okay?"

"I have no idea what I'm doing," he said. "This is the first time in five years that I've not been bound to Pimati's will, and I...I don't..."

A quick rap at the door interrupted us, and Valerius poked his head inside. "Ah, good, you're awake," he said in English, letting himself in. He cut his eyes to the dim lamps around the room, which brightened until Arik and I were squinting. "You seem healthier," he declared, studying Arik. "Any pain?"

"No, thank you," said Arik. "Um…"

"Somewhat disoriented," I offered. "And at a loss as to what he's meant to be doing."

The king seemed bemused for a second, and then comprehension dawned on his face. "Well," he said, leaning against the dresser, "at the moment, nothing. You are convalescing. The more you can rest, the more quickly the enchantment will work. The same applies to you, my lady," he added, giving me a stern look.

"I've been in that chair for hours!" I said, gesturing toward my padded seat and afghan.

"Yes. You slept in a chair, never mind the perfectly good bed in the next room. But it's your leg, not mine. As for you," he continued, turning back to Arik, "there are options, none of which need to be decided today. Especially not at this hour," he muttered, glancing out the glass door at the long shadows of dawn over the garden. "I assume you have no immediate plans to return to your home realm."

"*None*," Arik insisted.

"Then here are two options for your consideration." He held up a finger. "One, you remain here. The Fringe settlement has no lack of housing, and it's a rather peaceful place. If you'd prefer not to be quite so distinctively pigmented, shall we say, glamours are easy to arrange."

"And what would be asked of me in return?"

Valerius shrugged. "Nothing. We've hosted much of the Fringe for decades. One more won't plunge the realm into a war-torn disaster."

"There *is* Kip to consider," I said.

"And Ros informs me that he is, and I quote, putting on his big-boy pants and dealing with it. The guesthouse has been full of cynaeli and tennuwaya for four days, and he has yet to initiate a one-man murder spree," he added. "Arik, have you heretofore made a habit of hunting kadalin?"

"Nikots," I muttered.

"No," Arik replied. "No, I've never been on a hunt—"

"Then we could work through this," said the king. "In any case, the rest of the Fringe has been welcoming to the evacuees. Many of them were in a similar position not so long ago." A second finger joined the first. "Or there's another option. I understand that this realm is as uncomfortable for you as the Gray Lands is for us."

Arik smiled slightly. "I mean no disrespect, and I am indebted to you for your hospitality—"

"No explanation needed," Valerius told him with a soft chuckle. "Your brother's neighbors seem to feel the same way. We've kept them here for their safety, in case your father were to send something new to attack them, but they will go home eventually. You could go with them. Start fresh."

"At least I could glamour myself there...or I suppose I could," he said, rubbing his neck again. "With the collar off, I *should* have talent again..."

"And if you cannot, I could pull something together, though you would need to avoid the Gray Lands gate. But a house, clothing, stores of food...these are simple things. If you choose to go with your brother, I'll see to it that you're not left homeless."

"That...that's more than generous," said Arik. "You certainly owe me nothing."

"This isn't about debt," Valerius murmured. "I know what your father did to you. Ros told me, not Hope," he said as Arik's eyes flicked toward me. "I've never been fond of torture, myself, particularly when it's undeserved. Consider it a gift. No conditions, no debts. Truly, I'm, uh...I'm sorry for what's befallen you."

Arik's eyes began to mist up once again. "Thank you."

"Of course. I would do anything for my children," he

said, folding his arms. "I cannot fathom your father's mind, but—"

The sudden brightness of Ros's manifestation cut him short. "Sorry to interrupt," she told him, then turned her attention to Arik, who was staring at her from the safety of the bed. "Hello, again," she said, waving. "I'm Ros. Don't think we met properly."

"You...you're the woman who saved my life," he began, but stuttered as he tried to further the conversation.

She put him out of his awkward misery. "My pleasure, kid. So, uh..." She made a brief show of examining her glowing arms. "You may have noticed the subtle radiance."

"I...*had*, yes."

"I'm the realm's consciousness. The latest incarnation of it, I mean, it's been passed down a few times."

Arik's head dipped in understanding. "My lady."

"Eh, don't worry about that—I'm not big on ceremony."

"Or privacy," Valerius mumbled.

She gave him a good-natured jab in the ribs. "*Anyway*, Arik, I've got a message for you from the Gray Lands."

The king's brow wrinkled. "How could you—"

"I can extend myself slightly into the mortal realm, you know? Generally, it's not far enough that I can see into the Gray Lands, but if I line up one of my gates with one of theirs, then there's a degree of communication possible between us. It's sort of like standing on opposite sidewalks, calling to each other across the street. Sorry, does that make sense?" she asked Arik.

"I think so..."

"Great. So, as I was saying, there's someone who'd like to talk to you at your earliest convenience."

His shoulders tightened. "My father?"

"Ketulm? No," she replied. "Actually, Conota reached out to me. Your realm wants a word."

CHAPTER 13

Some invitations can be ignored. When the voice of your homeland wants to chat, however, you pull yourself out of bed and heed the summons.

Valerius offered to simply will Arik clean, but Bonnie, who had stopped by Arik's room to check on my dwindling coffee supply, wouldn't hear of it. "Absolutely not. I don't care who's waiting," she snapped as Valerius retreated in placation. "The boy's been through hell. He has time for a hot bath."

Soon finding ourselves kicked out of the room, the king and I looked at each other, and he sheepishly rubbed the back of his neck. "I prefer not to cross her," he said. "Bonnie helped raise Maria and Kitty, and Sam before them. She knows what she's doing."

"But…didn't she seem a little, uh…curt?"

He chuckled and gestured in the direction of the dining rooms. "Come, we'll eat while she works. And the curtness is just Bonnie. She means well, and she's excellent at what she does." Seeing my lingering doubt, he smiled. "You will learn, as you come into responsibility of your own, that one secret to leadership is knowing your weaknesses and finding people you trust who can compensate for them. Bonnie can be gruff, but I need someone at my side who will hear my plans and tell me to my face how stupid they are. Most of the court would rather flatter me and hope for favors in the future, but she doesn't seem to care about that. It's a true gift to me."

We'd long finished eating and had lingered over

coffee—I admitted to myself that I'd developed more than a mild addiction to it while living with Mama—when Bonnie finally showed Arik into the room, clean, dry, and looking a bit like he wasn't sure what had just hit him. The clothes he'd worn for days had been washed and mended, and Bonnie had replaced the shoes that Artur had made for him. "I, um," he began, standing uncertainly in the doorway, "I was told to eat?"

He was speaking Fae, I realized, and wondered what else Bonnie had done in our absence.

"She gives good advice," said Valerius, pointing to the empty chair beside me. "Help yourself."

Arik should have been hungry—whoever saw to Valerius's table was a master of cuisine—but he picked at his food and spoke little. Eventually, the king asked, "No appetite?"

He hesitated, swirling his water, then blurted, "He can't make me go back, right? Conota can't make me return to Father, not if I'm here—"

"He has no power in this realm," Valerius reassured him, "and Ros has approved your stay here indefinitely. You're beyond his reach within our borders."

Arik let out a long, soft exhalation. "Do you suppose he's looking for Fik? He must know that I left to seek Fik out...maybe he doesn't know that my brother is here, too."

"Could be. You can ask him soon enough. No need to waste your energy on speculation."

But Arik was still ill at ease. "What if he tells Father where I am? You know what happened when Hope's father wanted her back. What if my father tries to do as Nath did and invades Iroja?"

I saw a flicker of enquiry in the king's face at the term, but he seemed to puzzle it out almost immediately. "This king or queen of yours is more powerful than anyone else in the realm, yes?"

"Yes..."

"Then seeing as your father does not appear to be king, I strongly doubt that he could do any better than Nath, and we sent her home as a corpse. One step at a time," he said as Arik continued to fidget with anxiety. "Worry about the problems at hand before you plan for the ones ten steps down the road."

Arik mumbled something that might have been agreement, but he continued to push his food around his plate. After a moment, sharing a look with Valerius, I prodded Arik from his chair and escorted him into the villa's main courtyard, a tiled, open-air space dotted with trees, flowering plants, and an intricate network of fountains. Ros appeared on a bench as we emerged, and she rose and beckoned for us to follow her. "Going for a little walk, if you're up for it," she said. "I thought privacy might be a good idea."

We followed her out of the villa and into the wide mountain meadow surrounding it, a green carpet of lush grass ringed by peaks—well, with the exception of the western edge of the valley, which offered an unobstructed view of the sea. The sun was climbing but not unpleasant, and I noticed Arik sneak occasional glances at the blue sky. I stayed at his elbow, ready to catch him if his knees buckled, but he seemed firm on his feet. In truth, I had the worse time of it with my limp, and after a few minutes, it was Arik who slowed to walk at my side. "How much farther?" he asked Ros. "Hope is still injured."

She stopped, gazed at the empty valley, then nodded. "This'll do. Okay, just a second, let me get this gate aligned…"

Arik and I stood back and watched as a gate opened—a perfect circle, ringed with lightning that flowed like water, quite different than the ones I'd seen from Carey and Maria. Ros looked back at me and grinned. "There are certain perks to this job, you know. If you think that's fancy, I made a whole continent once."

I barely had time to process *that* offhand remark when

a similarly neat gate began to open perhaps a yard from Ros's. I couldn't see much around the two gates but trees—she must have chosen a remote area in Iroja for the meeting—which was fortunate, as what I witnessed when the second gate spiraled open would surely have sent any nearby humans running.

The first thing I saw as the gate widened was an outflow of magic, brilliant and colorful, which flowed freely until it ran into the smoky outflow from Faerie. The two streams seemed to reach an equilibrium point midway between the gates, a wall of light and shadow, potential and nullity, neither stronger than the other.

And then I saw *him*.

The man standing in the opening was not overly large—perhaps Arik's height, tall for a cynaeli but average by tennuwaya standards—nor was he particularly imposing. He was naked from the waist up, and his visible musculature was unremarkable. He had dark hair, which fell unbound to his shoulders, but that barely registered on first impression. Far more striking to me was the fact that he was *green*—a deep hue the color of mature pine needles—and, like Ros, he glowed with his own corona. His facial structure seemed cynaeli enough at first blush, but his teeth were sharp like a tennuwaya's, his irises dark brown…and as he studied us, a third eye opened above his slightly upturned nose.

He and Ros stared at each other for a moment, neither speaking, though the twitches in their faces suggested they were carrying on a silent conversation. Abruptly, Ros stepped aside, leaving Arik and me to face the consciousness of our homeland.

Arik cleared his throat, then stepped closer to the edge of our gate and said, "You asked to speak with me, my lord. What do you want of me?"

Conota's lips curled into a slight smile. "I would think that obvious," he replied, his voice low but melodious. "No?"

"Fikwed is nearby, within this realm. I don't know precisely where, but I'm sure that Ros could take me to him…" She nodded when he glanced her way, and he turned back to the gate with apparent relief. "If you want to speak with him, I…I'm happy to convey the message…"

He cocked his head, his expression shifting toward bemusement. "What would I want with Fikwed?"

The question took Arik aback. "Well…um…I assumed, I mean…Father believes that Fik is your chosen."

At that, Conota shook his head and laughed aloud. "Ketulm is a fool," he told Arik. "Scheming and fortunate to this point, but a fool in many respects. Wasting a perfectly good concubine on the gigora…that's what they call themselves, you know," he added. "They pass down enough of this tongue to negotiate with the cynaeli as the need arises, but they have their own. Then again, I suppose neither side has any great interest in better understanding the other," he allowed. "Their appetites *are* rather fierce—"

"Sorry," Arik said, interrupting the lecture, "but if you don't want Fik…is this about Father? I won't return to him—"

Conota lifted a finger to silence him. "You need not return to his household. Ketulm is not your father."

Arik stepped back from the gate, and I caught a glimpse of his face as the blood drained. "What are you saying—"

"*You* are my chosen." The realm snickered as Arik, lost for words, silently flapped his mouth in an effort to respond. "Come, now, why else would I want to speak with you? If I wanted Fikwed, I'd have asked for him."

He closed his eyes and held up his hands, a plea for silence, then took a long breath before looking at Conota again. "*How?* Fik is the one who doesn't even look cynaeli!"

Conota shrugged. "He favors his mother. That's hardly impossible."

"But...but *you*..." Arik jabbed one hand toward him, waving frantically in Conota's direction.

"You're curious about pigmentation? Tell me, how many of my children have looked *anything* like me?" the realm asked. "I can help you if that's a difficult question."

"My mother was Irojan. If you're my father, then how—"

"I can raise mountains on a whim, Arikol. I designed you to blend, in case I ever had need of you. Ketulm is none the wiser, is he?" While Arik struggled to form a complete sentence, Conota folded his arms and smirked. "It's simple, really. Geheret was too enamored with the notion of conquering his mother's realm to rule effectively, and Nath was...a disappointment, shall we say? I mean, I started considering replacements as soon as she allowed herself to be tricked by that Irojan woman. Foolish girl," he muttered, shaking his head. "But even since Geheret's reign, the political climate in the other realms appears to have shifted—and mine, of course, now stands on the brink of war."

"Because you haven't named a king since Nath died!" Arik protested. "This is *your* doing."

"I *did* name a king. You didn't know, but you've been my choice since Nath fell. She was decent with the tennuwaya, but she largely ignored Heluweya, and the little lordlings now think themselves kings, even as the upstarts to the south proclaim themselves Nath's heirs. I don't want this war." He walked closer to the gate, focusing on Arik. "You, technically, are of neither race. I got you on your mother as an experiment—power, strength, but a somewhat more Irojan temperament. In light of the recent upheavals—I mean," he laughed, "you're standing in *Faerie*, of all places, and as a guest. Your predecessor would never have permitted such," he said, turning to Ros.

She shrugged. "Kura and I don't agree on everything,"

she replied—to my surprise, in Cynaeli. "Are you and your predecessors in perfect lockstep?"

"What predecessors? I *am* Conota—there has never been another. But no matter." Looking back at Arik, he said, "I don't fully understand the Irojan madness, but as the Three of Faerie are afflicted with it—and, of course, the mortal adepts—I've decided that you are best suited to treat with them. You do favor your mother in many respects, so let us hope that my influence on you has tempered hers to the point that you will rule wisely."

"But…but why didn't you say—"

"Why did I not come to you a year ago?" Conota finished. "The collar."

Ros screwed up her face. "You couldn't have broken it? Hell, *I* could do that."

"It's not a matter of *ability*," he replied with a contemptuous glance. "I was curious to see whether I'd chosen well. Nath's power would have fallen on you at the time of her death," he explained to Arik, "but the dampening collar kept you weak. I wanted to see how long it would take you to remove it. Of course," he added, "had you died with it in place, then the power would have transferred to another of my children. But you managed it—congratulations. Took you long enough." With that, he stepped back from the gate and beckoned to Arik. "As soon as you're in a realm with sufficient magic—Iroja will suffice—the power will fall on you, and you can return and take the throne. Stop this silly war before it escalates."

Arik didn't move, nor did he speak. Standing beside him, I could see his face, but there was no longer confusion or fear in his expression.

What I saw there instead was quiet rage.

After a long, silent moment, Arik murmured, "You are my father."

Conota nodded, wrinkles forming around his third eye. "Yes, I said as much."

"You knew what Ketulm did to me."

"Naturally."

Arik's fists, clenched at his side, began to shake. "You let him kill my mother?"

His father stared at him blankly. "That was Ketulm's prerogative. I had no further use of her."

I had never seen Arik so calmly furious, a coiled spring on the edge of release. "And you did nothing when a pack of Hidden Ones came after my brother?"

"Gigora, remember. You should know the proper names of things—"

"Deepest darkness take you," he said, and turned away.

Arik's sister, the High Mother of the Mysteries, would surely have been appalled by the curse. As for me, I took his hand, and he gripped mine so strongly that my bones creaked. "Come on," I whispered, and limped beside him back toward the villa.

Behind us, we could hear Conota's shocked cries. "Arikol!" he bellowed between the realms. "What are you doing? Come back! Where are you going? *Arikol!*"

Arik kept his eyes on the horizon, and when my limp grew too pronounced, he released my hand and switched his grasp to my waist. Neither of us spoke until we had returned to Arik's guestroom, where he pulled a pillow from the bed, pressed it over his face, and screamed his pain.

I offered to leave him be, but Arik needed an ear more than he did his privacy.

"I watched her die," he said, pacing in front of the garden door while I sat by his bed, a largely silent witness. "Father—*Ketulm*," he corrected himself—"made me stand there and watch. I said nothing, I didn't shed a tear. He would have beaten me. And I can still see it, Hope, I see her eyes the moment the bolt hit her, the pain and shock and fear…" He scrunched up his face as if trying to block the memory. "Her eyes were so pretty. Brown, and they had little green flecks…and I watched the life leave them."

"You couldn't have stopped him," I murmured. "You know that. *She* knows that."

"But Conota could have, and he didn't."

"He does seem to take a hands-off approach to the realm…"

"If he's my father, then why did he let that happen?" Arik asked, almost pleading. "What little effort would it have cost him? Instead, he did nothing, and I still see my mother's face in the moment before it caught fire." He pressed his palms against the wall and leaned against it while his chest heaved. "I was ten. *Ten.* And she just wanted to go home."

I held my silence, letting Arik regain his control.

"Do you know what I've seen in these last days?" he asked after a time. "There was Orson, trying to look after a daughter he barely knew in life. Uther, who wanted nothing more than to talk to Artur but not before the time was right for her. Fik was ready to run to protect his wife and daughter. He could have evacuated. Wouldn't have helped us," he added, weakly laughing, "but he could have left. He stayed. Made sure they were safe, then stayed to face the damned Hidden Ones. And then there's your mother."

"What about her?"

His smile was strained. "She was ready to throw me out to protect you. Can't deny that she loves you." He sighed and faced the wall. "So what do I get? The monster who thinks he's my father mutilates and enslaves me, and gives his son full leave to torture me. The monster who *knows* he's my father witnesses everything and does nothing in my defense."

"Some parents are terrible," I said, hearing how lame that sounded even as the words left me. "It's not fair, but—"

"All he had to do was claim me! Tell Ketulm not to lay a hand on me! Maybe I'd have been cast from his household, but living off scraps in a side tunnel would have been a paradise in comparison to what I had." When he glanced my way again, his eyes were wet once more. "Maybe I could have had you. But no, he allowed Ketulm to ruin my life, to threaten Fik...and now he has the audacity to show himself? *Now?* I'm *worthy?*" he snapped. "Am I supposed to be honored?"

A knock at the door interrupted him, and Ros let herself into the room. "Hi. Mind if I come in?"

Flustered, Arik forwent politeness. "I can't keep you out, can I?"

"No," she admitted, "but we don't have to talk now, if you can't handle it."

It took three long breaths for him to regain some semblance of tranquility, and the dark purple of his flush revealed his agitation, but he nodded and fell into a chair beside me. "When did you learn our tongue?" he asked.

"Oh, about five minutes after Hope first arrived," she replied, hoisting herself onto the foot of the bed. "Got it from you," she said, glancing my way. "I trust that's not a problem."

"No, of course not," I said, and rose to leave. "I, uh...I'll give you two a moment—"

Arik caught my wrist before I could take the first step. "Stay. *Please.*"

"That's fine by me," said Ros, and waited until I sat again to continue. "So," she said to Arik, drawing the word into a long sigh. "*You've* had a morning."

"Did you know?" he asked.

"No." She tucked one foot beneath the other knee, making herself comfortable. "If you were fae, I'd have felt it, and I can accurately detect wizards, but my alarms don't differentiate when it comes to the Gray Lands. There's basically a big red light and a warning horn that goes off on all of you. Toula is still scheduled to be here this afternoon, and I've told no one yet about what happened, so if you don't believe Conota, your paternity can be tested pretty easily. Or *fraternity*, I suppose," she amended. "I sincerely doubt that you and Fik share blood."

"Fik," he mumbled, resting his face on his fingertips. "What am I going to tell him?"

"I'd suggest nothing at the moment. You're a mess," she said gently. "Anyway, to put us all on the same page, I just had a long talk with Conota."

Arik grunted. "By chance, did you tell him to fall into blackness and die?"

"Eh, I could have pulled out a few choice terms, but that seemed somewhat unhelpful. Here's the short version: he's thoroughly confused."

"Why? I thought I made myself clear enough."

Ros flopped back onto the rumpled bed, the golden threads in the coverlet twinkling in her radiance. "Your people—the tennuwaya, too—have a term, 'Irojan madness.' What does that mean to you?"

As Arik scowled into space and considered the question, I took the lead. "The human psyche is different than the cynaeli. Empathy, altruism…"

"Love," she finished. "In that regard, the cynaeli and tennuwaya are much like the fae. Tell a full-blooded faerie that you're doing a favor for a friend at cost to yourself and without any intent of being repaid, and he'll look at you like you've lost your mind. And if you're surrounded by nothing but faeries, then you have. Nothing is done without benefit, or at least compensation. Hell," she muttered, "do you know how faeries survive infancy? Adults instinctively find them interesting and worth preservation until they're old enough to avoid walking off cliffs. It's probably the only time you'll ever find a faerie acting out of anything resembling altruism, and then only because instinct demands it. After that, if the child wants anything resembling affection, he'd better be either amusing or useful."

"Sounds familiar."

"And correct me if I'm wrong, but it's probably also

why those of you with human blood tend to stick together. There's a part of you that everyone else thinks is crazy, right?" Turning to Arik, she asked, "Your sister Kurane, the one who helped you escape—another half-human likdenfi, isn't she?"

"Yes," he replied, nodding vigorously. "I would never have asked the others because I had nothing to offer them in turn."

"Exactly. So here's the problem: Conota's ancient, but his mind works much like your average cynaeli's. He doesn't understand why you're upset with him."

"Did you explain? Small words, perhaps?"

She snorted. "It's not that simple. As far as he's concerned, you're his experimental project—if you're useful, great, if not, no big loss. Remember that this is the same mind that cobbled together the kadalin instead of doing the compassionate thing and opening a gate home."

Arik and I stared at her in confused silence, and she sat up. "Didn't know about that, hmm?"

"*What* did he do to the kadalin?" I asked.

Ros smiled slightly, though it did nothing to mask her distaste. "The first of them were nothing more than humans who accidentally crossed the border. I assume you've seen a horse, Hope?"

"Only from a distance or on TV. Mama tried to take me to the rodeo last fall, and I didn't make it past the barn without sending a bull into a panic."

"Good enough. Those people who crossed had their horses with them. Their defenses weren't great, so instead of making a gate to send them back the way they came, Conota decided to give them a sporting chance by fusing them to their mounts." She paused while we digested that disturbing information, then said, "Their ancestors were human. They're as intelligent as you are, if not as well educated, and they can't enchant. But they are anything but dumb brutes," she said, locking eyes with Arik, "and you would do well to remember that."

He shifted under her gaze, discomfited. "I've never hunted them—"

"That's a start. But back to Conota. I told him that your thinking and sensibilities are closer to the human end of the spectrum, which is the result he was trying to achieve in siring you. He just didn't take all of the ramifications into consideration," she added, a touch of smugness in her tone. "I tried to explain, but you've got to realize that it's difficult to convey what you're feeling to someone who can't fully understand humanish emotions."

"What did you tell him?" asked Arik.

"I used a more transactional model. I said that with humans, there's an understood bond between a parent and a child in most instances. It's like a two-way debt that can never be cleared. Most parents don't mind entering that relationship and taking on that debt because it's driven by love. They don't *care* if their offspring never fully compensate them for the benefits they render, but most children do eventually reciprocate in one form or another. At the very least, the affection between the two encourages each to do things of benefit to the other. Parents care for children, and children try to please their parents, and maybe care for them in turn when they're old."

My thoughts flashed to Mama, who'd taken me in, fed and clothed me, and never asked for payment.

"I told him that you dearly loved your mother," Ros continued, "and that her death was deeply traumatic to you. That instinctively, you've sought to please Ketulm all these years because he's the closest thing to a father you've ever known, even though he's never shown you love in turn. Instead, Ketulm reciprocated with...well, with something horrific," she muttered. "I explained to Conota that frankly, you've been through hell of late—oh, I know all about it," she said as Arik's eyes cut to me. "Can't keep secrets from me in this realm. Hope hasn't been gossiping while you've slept."

"Oh," he mumbled, chastised. "Sorry."

I reached over and patted his shoulder.

"As I was saying," she resumed, "I told Conota that you're upset because he could have intervened at any point and spared you...everything. The way he sees it, he owes you nothing and can't quite comprehend why you should be angry that he failed to give you a favor that wasn't due. I told him that with the permanent debt model, the majority of human parents will go out of their way to protect their children, even at great cost. Saving your mother or you would have cost him almost nothing, but he didn't lift a finger." She made a face and spread her hands. "He understands it from an academic perspective, I believe. Fuzzy on the details, but he sees the general contours of the problem."

"Good for him," said Arik, folding his arms. "He can still rot."

She leaned forward and held his gaze. "Listen to me, kid. You're furious, and you're hurt, and you have every right to be. But petulance isn't going to solve anything."

"And what is there to solve?" he retorted. "I want nothing to do with him."

"That may be, but he's not done with you yet, and..." She paused. "I'm not sure whether you'd call it diplomacy or professional courtesy, but in any case, I said I'd make you available tomorrow morning."

His eyes flew open wide. "But—"

"But nothing, Arik. Sleep on it, and you can have it out with him tomorrow."

"Sleep won't change my mind," he protested.

Ros shrugged and slid off the bed. "My realm, my rules. Sorry, bud. You know, think of it this way," she said as Arik glowered at her. "Poor Kip's been dealing with a guesthouse loaded with cynaeli and tennuwaya for a few days. If he can be decently civil under those conditions, then you can talk to your father."

With that, she vanished, and Arik groaned in frustration. "Kip is the nikot, yes?" he mumbled.

"Yeah."

He was silent for a moment, then said, "Must be uncomfortable for him."

"That's the impression I got."

Arik rose, but before he could resume pacing, I hugged him. He held on tightly, his chin on my shoulder, and I rubbed his back until I felt his breathing slow. "You know," I murmured, "my father was going to give me to Warohn. His tenth concubine. Can you imagine not only having to bed him, but to happily do so while *sharing* him eleven ways?"

He laughed softly. "Such a fine man. I bet his concubines fight for the privilege."

"I bet they fight to avoid him. Loser warms his bed, winners get to hide. I've had to think about him *naked*, Arik, and I can't get those images out of my head."

Maybe my misfortunes didn't equal his, but my griping was having the intended effect. "Now I'm thinking about him naked, too," he muttered. "*Thanks.*"

"Truly, the horror never ceases."

His arms shifted, pulling me more closely against his chest. "I'm glad you escaped," he whispered into my hair.

"I'm glad you found me."

We stood together in his room for several moments, barely swaying to the rhythm of our breathing, until I pulled away and took his hand. "Come on," I said, and opened the door to the garden. "Look at the fountains with me."

He eyed the three-tiered basin in our shared garden. "What's so special about the fountains?"

I smiled and tugged him outside. "You haven't seen the fish."

I wasn't entirely surprised when Bonnie showed up unannounced with a bottle of sunscreen half an hour after I coaxed Arik into the fresh air. His burn from his time in

Oklahoma had almost healed by then, leaving his skin pleasingly darker, but she pursed her lips and pointed to the sky. "You came from one of those underground cities, right?" she said, and squirted the white goop into her hand. "Let's not take any chances. You've got enough to heal as it stands."

He endured her brusque mothering without protest, and having experienced my share of clear Irojan skies, I took my turn with the bottle. Bonnie left us with sunglasses as well, then added a wide, padded chaise to the walled garden and left with an admonition to come inside for lunch.

While Arik found the fountain mosaics—enchanted depictions of fish and aquatic plants that moved on their own—as charming as I had, he soon collapsed onto the chaise, and I joined him. As his arm snaked beneath my neck, I curled up with my head against his chest, enjoying the sunlight and the warmth of late morning.

I'd almost dozed off when he said, "You like this? Blue sky, I mean."

I opened my eyes, squinted through the dark glasses, and said, "Mm. The sunrises and sunsets are my favorite part…and the night sky is gorgeous. But yes, I like the blue. Do you?"

"Very much so. Sunburn is awful, mind you, but this view…it's pleasing. The sky feels larger." He hesitated, then quietly added, "I could acclimate to this."

I said nothing, and soon, he was asleep beside me. It was, I mused, precisely what he needed, considering the healing enchantment that was still coating him like a second skin. I resolved to just close my eyes until he was soundly asleep, then extricate myself from his one-armed embrace and give him more room on the chaise. Instead, I fell asleep with him.

If Toula ever came by that day, I couldn't prove it. When we woke, the sun had nearly set, and the still-warm flowers of the garden filled the air with their heady fragrance. Pressing lightly on my cheeks, I sensed the beginning of a sunburn, and Arik seemed similarly afflicted, his skin imbued with a dusky rose hue beneath the surface. I sat up and tested my leg—the nap hadn't hurt my healing process—while Arik blinked dazedly at the elongating shadows. "I didn't intend to do that," he said, his voice husky with sleep.

"Neither did I." I rubbed the back of his neck, which was several shades paler than the rest of him. "Feel better?"

"Better rested, perhaps. I still hate him."

"That's fair." Pushing myself from the chaise, I offered him a hand up. "Dinner? Sleeping gives me an appetite."

We were in luck—a buffet had been laid in the smallest dining room, and Maria, Artur, and Beth were already eating when we arrived. "Hey!" said Beth, waving a roll from the far end of the table. "You guys hungry? The chicken's, like, *amazing*."

Maria smiled and lifted her glass. "Val knows my favorites. Come in, join us. Load your plates before this one hoovers everything up," she said, cocking her head at Beth, who took a defiant bite and grinned at her through a mouthful of bread.

"Will he be dining with us?" I asked Maria.

"Not tonight. He's over at Eleanor's—*I* didn't say this, now, but she hosts a regular game night. Do you need a word with him?"

"No, just curious." I took a plate from the sideboard and began piling it high, salivating at the smells, and Arik fell in line behind me. "Surprised to see you three still here," I said, loading up on pasta. "I would have thought you'd return to Glastonbury by now."

"Medical leave," said Beth. "It's almost half a day behind Glastonbury time here, and school starts on Monday, but I got medical leave after that, and the grand magus said I could have the rest of the week to get back on the right time zone."

"Supervising," said Artur.

Maria shrugged. "This is breakfast. I've got my second-years for practical in three hours, but I wanted a home-cooked meal." Seeing Artur's raised eyebrow, she muttered, "Don't give me that look. I'm a freaking magus."

Arik and I sat, and Artur pushed a jug of wine down the table. "How are you feeling?" she asked.

"Still limping, but I'll live," I replied, "and Arik…"

He concentrated on pouring. "Better."

"Good. Your brother's been asking about you," she said, picking up a drumstick. "Janice has some anxiety issues, it seems, so he has stayed with her, but he asks for updates. You should visit the settlement tomorrow, reassure him that you're still breathing."

Arik took a long drink, then another one, before answering her. "Will you keep my confidence?"

The Glastonbury crew traded looks, and Artur said, "Probably. What's troubling you?"

He'd finished his glass of wine and poured a second by the time he'd recounted his meeting with Conota. When he fell silent, Artur frowned at the wall, twirling her drink as she thought. "In brief, then," she said, "you don't want to be king."

"I want *nothing* to do with him. He—"

"Is a terrible excuse for a parent, yes. I heard you." She began to wipe at the mixture of sauces left on her plate with a roll. "Have I mentioned my sire? I prefer not to think of him as my father, all things considered."

"Uther spoke of him," I replied.

Her mouth tightened. "Had he anything complimentary to say about Myrddin, then?"

"My impression was that he'd like to try to kill him again."

She popped a piece of bread into her mouth, but not before I caught her smile. "At least your father ignores you," she told Arik. "My mother's rapist tried to kill me."

"But wasn't he fae?" I asked.

"Half. He had no excuse."

"There's always my mom," said Beth. "My sister tried to send me letters for years, and Mom intercepted them because she didn't want us to have any sort of relationship. I thought Kitty was the worst until Mom went to prison."

Arik lowered his fork. "For *what?*"

"Treason," said Maria, not looking up from her plate. "And she tried to kill me. Almost managed it, too. She was horrible to Kitty," she added, and patted Beth's shoulder. "It's not just the fae ones—there are some humans who should never be parents. Hell, talk to Ros—her parents are lovely, but her mother's parents earned their execution."

"What of yours?" Arik asked her. "Valerius is your grandfather, correct? His child—"

"Slight simplification, actually. He's my seventy-second great-grandfather," she explained. "His son is Kitty's boyfriend, Kitty is my best friend, so things are...*odd*...in my family." She sipped her water, and a cup of espresso appeared beside her plate. "To answer your question, my parents died when I was a baby. Our landlady took me in, and her husband scared me so badly that I burnt him alive when I was five." Looking up, she saw the expression on Arik's face and held his stare. "Human. Not even slightly talented. And he beat up a little girl on a regular basis. Not everyone gets storybook parents. I mean, if you want poor parenting, look at Val. He lived in this realm with his mother for, oh, twelve hundred years, and she never claimed him. He had no idea he was highborn, much less hers. Oberon and Titania had a bet going for centuries about when he'd finally figure it out."

"What we are trying to say," Artur interjected, "is that your father's behavior, while despicable, is not unique in its cruelty. You deserved better—we all did. Now, it's up to you to decide how you move on...and how you plan to rule," she added, tearing off another bite of roll.

"I *don't,*" Arik protested, but Artur continued to eat,

slightly smiling to herself.

After dinner, Arik and I returned to our adjoining rooms, and he followed me back into the lamplit garden. The sky had fully darkened, and so we stretched out in the chaise again beneath a blanket I'd snatched from my bed, contemplating the twinkling stars above us.

"I don't tire of this view," I murmured, tucking my knees to keep my feet covered and warm. "Tells me I'm free." Staring up, I said, "It's better here than in Pauline—there's less light pollution, I suppose—but I can actually name some of the ones back there. I don't know these stars, but I love them, too." When Arik remained quiet, I rolled over and found him gazing heavenward. "You can't still your thoughts, can you?"

"I don't know what I'm going to tell Fik," he said.

"The truth, when you're ready. He'll understand."

"How am I supposed to tell him that we're not brothers? Growing up, he was my protector, my *friend*…"

"You love him," I finished.

Arik barely nodded. "More than any of the others."

"You went on a suicide run to save his life. That means more than mere blood, doesn't it?"

He struggled, then managed to say, "My family…they were largely either cruel or apathetic, but I knew where I came from. Where I belonged. Now…I mean, what do I have? The only true sister I can name has been dead for a year, and whatever others of this line are living, I'm sure that Conota wouldn't tell me. I'm free, too," he said, turning to me, "but I've never been so alone."

"But you're *not*," I insisted. "Surely Fik would have you in Kentucky, or…"

"Or?" he prompted when my voice faded.

"We could do what we talked about. Come back to Pauline with me. If you still want to," I said, hating how awkward I sounded. "I'll work on Mama, she'll understand. I've been checking in since we got here, and she hasn't disowned me yet. She knows—"

"About Conota?"

"No, *no*," I hastily reassured him. "About my feelings for you."

His brow furrowed. "Hope—"

"Let me say this before I lose my nerve," I interrupted, conscious of the query in his eyes. "Father tried to make an arrangement for me. I never wanted it, and he has no power over me now. Especially not here. What *I* want— what I've wanted since I became aware of the capacity for such wanting—is you. I don't care about lands or fathers or titles. Be with me. We can start over, forge a life together."

Arik stared at me in stunned silence, then whispered, "You *want* me?"

"I thought I made that clear a few days ago."

"I...uh..." Still gawking, he paused, cleared his throat, and tried again. "I thought you were just being kind to a dying man."

My resolve began to falter. "No, that was...I meant it. All of it. If that's not what you want—"

"*Hope.*" He cupped his hand against my cheek. "I want you, too. More than anything. But I can't be a husband to you, we both know that."

I reached up from beneath the blanket and covered his hand with my own. "You are enough. As you were, as you are...that's enough for me. I love you."

"I can't even get children on you—"

"Then we'll do without. We'll make it work." I stared into his eyes, which were almost black in the dim light. "You don't have to decide anything tonight. But if you still want me, I'm willing. We can make our own arrangement."

Arik didn't give me an answer, but there was longing in his kiss.

CHAPTER 14

The walk out into the meadow with Ros the next morning was easier for me than the previous day's had been. Though I'd passed the night on the chaise with Arik, I felt well rested, and my leg, still numb from the enchantment around it, took my weight without threatening collapse. Arik, too, seemed stronger—his color was better, and though he was a bit too thin for his frame, he'd had a hearty appetite at breakfast. He didn't need me for physical assistance, that much was clear, but when Ros had appeared to fetch him, he'd asked me to come along. If he wanted moral support, I was happy to help.

As before, a gate opened to face Ros's, and Conota manifested at its center. Paying me no mind, he said to Arik, "Well, now, are you thinking clearly today?"

"I was thinking clearly yesterday," Arik replied, his voice measured. "My feelings are unchanged. I want nothing of you. Find someone else to rule."

His father frowned—not angry, I thought, but rather baffled. "You want revenge on Ketulm? Take it, I won't stop you. Do as you like to him."

"This isn't about Ketulm."

He huffed, exasperated. "Your existence was a gift. I owe you nothing more, but now I am giving you power to rule the realm."

"And I'm telling you that I don't want it," said Arik. "Give it to another of your spawn. It's hardly fair to call us your children, considering how little you've bothered with our lives to this point."

"That's not an option."

Arik's eyebrows rose. "What do you intend to do about it? You can't touch me in Faerie. Bluster all you want, but this will be far less painful for us both if you go with your second choice."

Conota closed his eyes and rubbed at the corners of the pair while the third squeezed itself shut. "You don't understand. I *cannot* choose another."

"What, you're out of bastards?"

"Far from it, and should you die, I will call upon one of them. But when I established this process with my firstborn, I swore that for the sake of stability, I would give her the power she required to rule, and I wouldn't withdraw it. That way, she could act as more than my mouthpiece. I was free to turn my attention to other matters, and she established order. When she was killed, I continued the terms with my son. I have upheld these terms ever since," he said, locking eyes with Arik, "and I will *not* break them now."

Arik shrugged. "I don't want it. Make an exception."

"If I were in the business of making exceptions, then Mab would have been expelled centuries ago," he snapped. "I thought she could be equitable between the tennuwaya and cynaeli. She was interested only in bettering her own people's lot. Had I not been bound by my word, then I would have expelled them all. But the magic around my vow—that is an old magic, Arikol. A primal, fundamental thing. Ask *her* if you don't believe me," he said, gesturing toward Ros. "There are rules even on such as we."

She made a face. "He's not wrong."

"I have granted you the throne," Conota continued. "The power will come to you as soon as you leave that realm. Had you been quicker with the collar, you would have had it sooner—"

"You could have removed it at any time," Arik interrupted, his shoulders tensing.

"I wanted to see if you could do it."

"You saw what Pimati did to me," he murmured. "Every last thing. Every blow. Every petty humiliation."

"I don't deny it," Conota replied. "But cross the border, take the throne, and have your revenge."

"Keep your damn throne. I kind of like it here."

Conota was growing progressively more frustrated, but Arik had a solid point: as long as he remained in Faerie, Conota couldn't touch him. "You're not looking at the larger picture," he protested. Though he kept two of his eyes on Arik, his third rolled in annoyance. "We are on the verge of all-out war. Three tennuwaya factions, three cynaeli factions, all vying for control…that isn't what I want. You must take the throne and end the war before it begins."

Arik seemed unfazed, though whether it was real or a convincing act, I couldn't say. "Why do you care? You weren't bothered when my mother was murdered, so why are you concerned about casualties?"

"Because it's distracting! I have better things to do then watch them squabble among themselves. It's why I established your position in the first place!"

The two of them held each other's gaze for a moment, and then Arik shrugged again. "Not my problem. If they want the throne so badly, let them kill each other for it. This is your mess, not mine."

He turned and started to walk away, but he'd only taken a few steps before Conota stopped him with a question: "What about Fikwed?"

Arik paused and looked back, his eyes narrowing. "What about him?"

"He will never be safe as long as Ketulm believes him to be my chosen."

"Fik is here. *Safe*," Arik retorted. "No thanks to you."

At that, Conota's lips curved into a sly smile. "Ketulm doesn't know that. When the gigora with whom he negotiated fail to return to collect their due, his suspicions will be strengthened. Surely he'll make a second attempt.

Perhaps another band of gigora, perhaps something less subtle. He'll loose this next threat upon Iroja...but Fikwed will be missing, won't he? What do you suppose will happen then while they make the futile hunt? Gigora must eat, you know." He paused and cocked his head. "Do you want to be responsible for what they do in that realm?"

Having seen *exactly* what Hidden Ones could do, Arik recoiled a step from the gate. "Why don't you do the decent thing for once in your miserable existence? Tell Ketulm that Fik isn't king. Stop him before he tries to kill Fik again."

Conota's smile never wavered. "Tell him yourself."

Arik looked sick, but his simmering anger proved to be the stronger emotion. "Whatever deaths Ketulm causes are on your head, not mine. You never asked if I wanted to be king. Take this as my resignation," he said, and stormed off toward the villa.

"It might not be Ketulm you need to worry about," Conota called after him. "Do you know how easy it is for me to open gates into Iroja? What if I opened a thousand at once and allowed through whatever wished to cross?" He glanced at Ros, who stood by with her mouth pursed and arms folded. "The Arcanum had some difficulty when Nath used that tactic, did they not? Imagine it at a far grander scale."

"You wouldn't," she said.

"He can stop me," he replied, pointing to Arik, who continued his retreat. "Tell him I await his decision."

When Ros slammed the gate closed, she peered across the meadow at Arik, then turned to me, worry tightening her features. "Stay with him, okay? Keep him from doing anything stupid."

"What's the plan?" I asked.

"I'm working on it," was all she said before vanishing.

I expected anger. What I saw instead was pensiveness.

When I returned to the villa, I found Arik in our garden, sitting on the edge of a fountain, watching the mosaic fish investigate the shadows of his feet. He looked my way when I opened the door, but then he returned to the fish, one finger trailing through the water in a slow pattern.

"I'm going to call Mama," I told him. "I'll be in my room if you need me."

He nodded, and I let him be. When I slipped into the adjacent room, however, I drew back the sheer curtain, giving me a view of the fountain while I sat at the little table with my phone. Clearly, Arik wasn't in a talkative mood, but I fretted over what he might do if left unattended.

My watch ended late in the morning, when Bonnie stopped by. "The king would like a word with you both," she said, and tossed Arik a towel for his wet legs. "Follow me."

It wasn't a suggestion, and once he was tidy again, we did as we were bid.

When she pushed open his office door, I saw that it wasn't to be just the three of us. Valerius was waiting in an armchair, while Eleanor and Coileán watched from the couch. Even Artur was there, perched on the flanking chair and watching us with an excellent poker face.

"Come in, please," said Valerius, gesturing another pair of chairs into existence. "We need to talk."

Arik's wary eyes flicked over the assembled. "Who, um—"

"The Three," I whispered in Cynaeli, which did nothing to put him at ease.

"My colleagues, you could say," the king replied, nodding to the couch. "Coileán, Eleanor. And you know Artur, of course. Please sit."

We took our seats, Arik still tense and waiting for the trap to spring. As we settled in, Artur leaned forward, propped her elbows on her knees, and steepled her fingers.

"This is what my therapist might call an intervention," she said. "I prefer 'laying bare the facts.'"

"Ros filled us in," said Coileán. "What are you going to do, kid?"

Caught off guard, Arik stammered until Valerius spoke over him. "I told you that you could remain here, and I'm a man of my word. But if you do, then you do so accepting that innocent people will die in a war they know nothing about."

"You're young," Eleanor told him. "You're *so* young. I've taught students older than you."

"Hell, I have shoes older than you," Coileán muttered.

"We understand that this isn't what you want," she continued. "You've only just got your freedom, and you're already being ordered about again. It's not fair."

"And your father's an uncaring asshole," Coileán added. "Join the club. None of us were close to the parent from whom we inherited this gig."

Artur shifted in her seat. "Speak for yourself."

"Okay, *one* of us, but he was mundane. That doesn't count."

Valerius glanced at the ceiling, an expression that spoke of a silent prayer for patience. "What we're trying to say is that you need to take the throne. We didn't seek ours, either, but sometimes, the decision is made for you."

"I never saw myself doing this," Coileán offered. "I avoided this place for *centuries*. But then it's hard to do much other than fight back when your own mother attacks you, and when she fell, her mess became mine. No questions, no negotiations. The queen is dead, long live the king."

"My father was not yet in the ground before his men crowned me," Artur murmured. "I was a weeping, newly orphaned ten-year-old, and I was told to dry my eyes and not embarrass his memory. Do you think I wanted a kingdom?" she asked, her blue eyes boring into Arik's. "I wanted my *father*. I wanted to be a child. That wasn't an option."

"I'm sorry," he mumbled.

"Oh, it got better. The high king was like an uncle to me, a skilled mentor. He was kind and patient and firm as I needed him to be, and I cared deeply for him. He was murdered in his own hall when I was fifteen. In front of me," she said simply. "And I was given his crown the next day. You don't have the luxury of proper mourning when people's lives depend on you. I thought that would be a burden I carried until the day I died, and...well, life is strange, isn't it?"

"You were more responsible about it than I was," Eleanor interjected. "I knew for a year that I'd inherited my father's court, but I went on with life and pretended that nothing was amiss. I didn't want it. *He* hunted me down," she said, cocking her head toward Coileán.

"Aiden gets the credit for that one," he replied.

"The both of you, then. I remember looking across the restaurant, seeing you sitting there, and thinking, 'Oh, *shit.*' But I do know something of what you're going through," she told Arik. "I wanted nothing to do with my father, either. He raped my mother—I had no love for him. But I had a duty, I shirked it, and people died. My poor husband was tortured because of me...and I'll carry his death for the rest of my life." Her eyes darted toward me, then back to Arik. "Don't make my mistake."

"Your feelings are legitimate," said Valerius, drawing Arik's attention again. "Nothing about this is fair—and believe me, I know what it is to be frustrated when the realm makes decisions for you."

"It was for the best, and you know it," said Ros, appearing beside him with her arms crossed.

"Perhaps, but I distinctly recall making my feelings about taking this position clear to you *and* your predecessor. Who, as it happens," he said to Arik, "knew who my mother was and declined to tell me. Twenty-two centuries of wondering, and she never said a word. It was chance and Toula that brought the truth to light." Sliding forward in his chair, he lowered his voice and focused on Arik. "I won't pretend to understand everything you have endured. What I *can* tell you is that it hurts to discover that your mother thinks so little of you that she never acknowledges you. Some of the ache you feel is very familiar." Glancing up at Ros, he added, "If any part of Kura is aware of this conversation, tell her I still haven't forgiven her for her silence."

"That silence probably saved your life," Ros replied.

"I'm aware of that. It still would have been nice to know I was in line for a throne before I swore my life to Titania."

"Granted, but I can't change the past."

"And *that* is my point," said Valerius, turning back to Arik. "Your past cannot be altered. What's before you now is the opportunity to take everything that has come before—everything that was done to you and to your loved ones—and prevent it from happening again. Yes, you are young. No, Conota should not have thrust this burden on you without so much as a word of warning. But all of that is behind you. What happens next is up to you, and it will have grave consequences."

He fell silent, and Arik stared down at his hands as he locked and unlocked his fingers. When the stillness had stretched long past the point of discomfort, Arik, not looking up, murmured, "The last thing I want is to return to that realm. I've dreamed of escape for five years. Maybe that doesn't seem like a long time to you—"

"You're twenty-three," Ros finished. "Relatively speaking, that's a considerable time."

He nodded. "But if I don't go back, then Fik can never leave this realm. Ketulm will hunt him, or Conota will do worse from spite."

"I was there last year when Nath decided to constantly open gates," Artur told him. "People barely slept, they ate what they could grab, and their fatigue led to mistakes.

Casualties, fatalities, and that was only Nath's doing. If the realm itself went on the attack…"

"And you know better than I do what's about to happen," I quietly said. "A six-way civil war? How many people will die because Ketulm and my father and the others want to fight for a throne they can never hold?" I rubbed one hand up and down his shoulder, and Arik finally lifted his head. "You know who they'll use in the front lines, right? If someone needs volunteers for a suicide mission, don't you think they'll call upon the humans and half humans first? What else are we good for?"

Seeing his uncertainty, I pressed on. "What happened to you, and to me, and to our mothers, and Fik's mother…that doesn't have to happen to anyone else. You can stop it. I can't, *they* certainly can't," I said, sweeping my hand toward the Three, "but you would have the power. No more naffidars need be made. No girls need be given as concubines against their will. And no other child need watch his mother be killed without recourse."

At that, something subtly shifted in his expression. Clearly, Arik still hated the idea of going home, but perhaps, I thought, he was seeing the potential.

"You could send all the humans back to Iroja," I pressed. "Prevent any more from being taken, or at least kept. Our mothers deserve that much." I took his hands and held them between mine. "It's not perfect, I know. It's not even the Pauline plan. But there is so much good you could do, so much that someone like Nath never would. And you know, for whatever it's worth, I'm on your side."

He studied our hands, then gently pushed them apart and linked his fingers through mine.

"For our mothers," he said softly. "For *us*."

"You'll do it, then?" Coileán asked.

Arik nodded, his eyes on mine.

"I'll tell him," said Ros, and disappeared.

"Maybe she could open a gate for us back to Mama's

house," I said. "You haven't had any power for a while, and whatever else comes with the job—"

"If it's anything like what happened to us, it will be momentarily debilitating," Eleanor cut in. "Overwhelming, but it passes, and you'll feel...*better* isn't quite the word, but...well, *energized*, I suppose. It's difficult to describe..." She tapped her fingers together as she mulled it over. "Right. Imagine that your potential is like a full glass of water. Maybe yours feels more like an empty glass now"— I nodded fervently—"but you know what it's like when it's full. When the boost hits you, you'll still have that sense of fullness, but the glass will have become...I don't know, a barrel, a vat."

"Given his youth..." Coileán muttered.

"Maybe more than that, then. And you'll see just how small that glass was by comparison. It's an incredible feeling. Terrifying, too, if you're wise. But if you can find somewhere with a bit of privacy to go through it, you should."

"Mama would understand," I said, still holding his hands. "Let me call her and explain."

"Thank you," he murmured, then looked at Valerius. "I hate to impose on your hospitality, but may I have one more night here?"

The king faintly smiled. "Of course. Build your strength—you will have work to do soon enough."

With the world on Arik's mind, Artur and I agreed that a distraction was in order.

The dragon barn was immense, a stone and wood construction rising like a minor mountain from the green field around it. Its clean lines were marred only by the lovely gray house on one end, which, while comfortably large, seemed more akin to an aberrant outgrowth than to a building in its own right. As Artur closed the gate behind us, a woman stepped out onto the wraparound porch and waved. "He's in there," she said. "Getting close to lunchtime, though, so try to stay away from the sheep."

Artur thanked her and led us on toward the open doors to the cavernous barn. "That would be Ros's mother," she informed us. "Good advice about the sheep."

"What's a sheep?" Arik asked.

She pointed to a fenced pasture pocked with a fluffy white flock. "Frank says he was raised on a steady diet of them. If visits here have taught me nothing else, I've learned that standing between a hungry dragon and the sheep pen is a *painful* mistake. Clumsy dragonets," she explained when we looked at her in alarm. "One of Frank's sisters had a clutch last summer. The young ones don't always think before they start running…"

Her voice trailed off as a roar sounded from the west, and we looked up to see a trio of dragons coming in for a landing. "The boys," said Artur, pointing to the formation. "Gareth is the larger purple one, Benedict is the darker purple on his left flank, and the spotted one is Milo."

The third dragon bore coloration I'd read of in old books but never seen: white with black splotches all over his body.

"A word of warning," Artur quietly told us as the yearlings ran toward the waiting sheep. "Frank is fond of his nieces and nephews. Don't make cow jokes about Milo or Jane."

"Who?" I asked.

She pointed to the barn door, where another two yearlings were hurrying forth toward their lunch, one black, the other white with purple spots. "Those are Katarina and Jane. Just a friendly caution."

Though there were plenty of sheep—and if my eyes didn't deceive me, they were multiplying—the dragonets still snapped and snarled at each other as they selected their lunches. I could only hope that they did so for fun.

"Come," said Artur, waving us on. "They're distracted."

Arik and I followed her into the barn, a straw-packed room whose eaves rose several stories above us. As my eyes adjusted to the shade inside, I picked out the enormous lumps of resting dragons, some curled in on themselves, others stretched out and sleeping. The straw had been pushed and dragged into gigantic nest piles, bedding on a colossal scale. I scanned the room, then spotted Frank just as he raised his head, his white scales almost iridescent in the patches of sunlight pouring through the high windows.

Hi! he thought, going to his feet. *If you've come for lunch, I suggest standing at the back of the line. The hatchlings are a menace.*

"I'm sure you were a perfect delight," said Artur as she picked a path through the straw.

I wouldn't go that far. Wait, don't come back here—the boys tussled over a sheep in here last night, and there's still bits lying around. I'll come out.

We retreated into the grass, and Frank lumbered outside behind us, followed closely by Ione, whose attention was drawn to the activity in the sheep pen. Frank nudged her with his head, and she, with a playful snap at his neck, walked off to eat.

I couldn't help but notice how he watched her leave.

"Having a nice holiday?" Artur asked.

Frank jerked—and truly, a draconic startle reflex is something to behold, wing flaps and all—then wrapped his long neck back to find her waiting with a knowing smile. *Sure, it's been fun, but I'm rested and ready to get back to work.*

"Mm. And Ione?"

What of her?

"Does she know of your plan?"

She understands. It's not as if I'm cutting off all communication—Sam is generous with his time and his thumbs. I told her she could come visit, but she seems uneasy about the idea of transformation. Can't blame her.

"So…that's it, then? You're off, goodbye, see you eventually?"

He snorted, then turned to us fully and lay down in the grass. *My life is in Glastonbury, and this is an interlude. I can't sit here and wait for the day when Ione decides she's ready to mate.*

"You're a real romantic," I said.

His red eyes rolled. *Again, we don't pair bond. I enjoy her company, and she seems to enjoy mine. We're friends, I guess.*

"Friends," Artur repeated, her voice laden with disbelief.

Yes, friends. I'm allowed to have female friends, aren't I?

"Certainly, but I've never known a man to stare at a friend's back end quite as you were just then."

Frank couldn't blush in his true form, but his flustered thoughts betrayed him. *I wasn't staring! I was looking toward the hatchlings, that's all. Supervising.*

"Sure."

I swear!

"There's no reason to be embarrassed. She has a nice back end."

His head landed a few feet away from her, giving Artur an excellent view of teeth and little else. *If you tell the rest of the Team, I'll lightly blacken your office.*

"Your secret's safe," she replied—far more calmly than I would have, given her proximity to reptilian death. "Go on, don't let us keep you. We'll brave the pen without an escort."

Your funeral, he thought, but rose and glared at Arik and me. *I mean it, this stays here,* he warned, then hurried off to join Ione.

Laughing to herself, Artur started after him and motioned for us to follow. "Lunch is mutton," she called over her shoulder. "I can kill and cook it, but only if we beat the dragonets to it. Pick up the pace, now."

Artur did her best, but mutton will never go down as one of my favorite meals. Nonetheless, the outing had its intended effect. As Artur worked on dismembering her chosen victim just outside the pen, the satiated dragonets abandoned their wrestling and investigated Arik and me, the oddly tinted newcomers in their midst. They peppered us with questions, a rapid stream of overlapping thoughts that mentally manifested as words about three-quarters of the time, and Frank, who was enjoying a more leisurely lunch with Ione across the pen, made his amusement known.

In terms of maturity, a yearling dragon is roughly of an age with a ten-year-old cynaeli or human. One might have been manageable, but the five over-excited younglings were a handful, especially once two of the boys broke away to play with a sheep that had strayed too close to them. The other three showed off their aerial acrobatics as we ate, competing with each other and almost knocking poor Milo from the sky, and we might have been sitting in the field until sundown had their mother not finally emerged from the barn to claim them and coax them in for a nap. "Neve appreciates the occasional bit of child minding," Artur explained as she opened a gate back to the villa. "And seeing as Frank is useless with his lady around…"

I heard that.

"Enjoy," she called, and sealed the gate behind us before he could resume his denials.

When Artur left us, Arik was in better spirits, if still frazzled by the dragonets. Once again, we napped in the garden, letting the enchantments on us work as much as they could before their inevitable dissolution. We woke late in the afternoon, warm and comfortable, but I rolled over to find Arik regarding me with a troubled expression. "Just to be clear," he said, "I *did* agree to rule Conota, didn't I? That wasn't a nightmare?"

I slid closer and kissed his puckered brow. "You'll be magnificent."

"Damn." He sighed and sat up, rubbing a kink from his shoulder. "I suppose it's time I give Fik the news."

We freshened up and sought Bonnie, who was happy

to make the gate to the settlement. "The guesthouse is off the main park," she said. "Past the bandstand, across the street, and it's the brick building on your left with the big oaks in the front. Call me when you're ready to come back," she instructed, producing a scrap of paper and a pen from the ether to scribble her number.

With the arrangements set, we soon found ourselves on the sidewalk outside the guesthouse, a spacious building with blue shutters and crisp white trim. Straightening his shirt, Arik scanned the windows two floors above the street as if searching for Fik behind the glass. "I'll wait out here, if you like," I said, spotting a wooden bench beneath one of the leafy trees. "Don't suppose you're in any danger of collapse anymore."

I'd intended it as a joke, but Arik *did* seem queasy. "Would you think less of me if I asked for backup?" he mumbled.

"No."

"Oh, good. Let's get this over with."

A young blonde—a teenager, I estimated, and surely one of the Fringers—staffed the reception desk in the quiet guesthouse lobby. She was cheery and helpful to a fault, even offering to escort us up the flight of stairs to Fik's family's room, but we assured her that we could find our way, and she settled back in her chair, disappointed. "It's a good sign," I murmured to Arik on our way up. "People are behaving themselves, and their babysitter is bored."

He nodded but kept silent, gripping the banister a little too firmly and tugging at his clothes as if the cloth were shrinking.

Arik took a deep breath before knocking twice on Fik's door, then stepped back and waited in the peephole's view while the latch turned. The door flew open wide, and Fik, looking decently rested for a man sharing a room with an infant, hurried into the corridor, beaming. "Arik!" he cried, gripping him by the shoulders, then pulled him into a tight hug. "So good to see you up and walking. You're well?"

"Better," Arik gasped, and Fik released his hold. "You see the healing enchantment all over me…"

"Difficult to miss it, but then I expect it was necessary. How do you feel? I'm sorry for not staying," he hastily added, "but Janice was alone with the baby, and she was a little freaked being here, and I thought I could do more good for them here than I could watching you sleep it off."

"Wise man," Arik replied, but the smile he cracked faded almost immediately. "Fik, I…there's something I need to tell you."

"Sure," he said, his relief shifting toward concern. "Come in, no need to stand in the hall. Get you a drink? Janice, dear, look who made it!" he said as he reentered the room.

Their accommodations, though more modest than ours, were generous and clean. A large bed had been placed against one wall with a bassinet beside it, within reach of an end table and the rocking chair where Janice sat, nursing Lily. Fik showed us to a four-person table on the other side of the room and pulled a jug of water and glasses from the tiny kitchenette, which made the RV's seem spacious.

"Hi!" Janice called, waving her free arm. "I'd get up, but *someone* is hungry."

"Oh, don't bother," I insisted, pulling out a chair. "You're busy."

"Always." She made a face and chuckled. "Are you moving in? There are plenty of empty rooms upstairs."

"Any word on when we can go home?" Fik asked, handing Arik a glass of water. "The town's been great to us, but it would be nice to be back in a place with useable magic, know what I mean?"

"Nothing firm yet," said Arik, and took a long gulp while Fik gave me a drink and took his chair. "Probably a few more days, to be safe."

"They haven't found signs of Hidden Ones, have they?"

"No, they're gone," he assured Fik. "It's, uh…more a matter of making sure that nothing else comes for you." His hand clenched around the glass before he put it aside. "I have good news: you're definitely not the missing king."

Fik spread his arms and grinned. "Truly, a shock to us all. How do we convey the message to Father?"

"Well, uh, you see…" Arik cut his eyes toward me, and I nodded reassurance. "I'm going back there tomorrow."

"Are you *insane?*" Fik cried, eyes bulging. "You can't—"

"There's about to be a war," Arik quietly interrupted. "I have to stop it. I…" He smiled weakly. "It's me, not you, Fik. I'm the heir."

For a few seconds, the only sound in the room was from Lily, who cared nothing for politics, and then Fik whispered, "Are you serious?"

Arik's head bobbed. "Father went after the wrong likdenfi—"

"How do you know?"

"I've spoken with Conota. *Twice.* He's adamant that I do this."

Eventually, Fik managed to stop gaping. "You…you spoke—"

"To the realm, yes. He's an asshole, if you were wondering, and, uh…my father, as it happens."

Something unspoken passed between them in the silence that followed, and then Fik rose and motioned for Arik to do likewise. Once Arik found his feet, Fik embraced him again and said, "As far as I'm concerned, you will always be my little brother. Nothing can change that."

When they parted, I saw relief in Arik's face. "Anyway, that's why you need to stay here for a few more days," he said. "Let me see what I can do in—"

"*Wait*, now," Janice interjected from the rocking chair,

"hold it. *You're* the new king?"

Arik's discomfort revealed itself only as a twitch in his cheek. "The heir, at least, if not a king. Valerius has been generous with his talent, but the, uh…the naffidar conditions remain."

"Forget that. Did you just say you were going to go try to stop a war?"

"Yes…"

"*Alone?*"

"What can I do?" Fik asked before Arik could answer her. "I want to help."

Arik looked stricken at the notion. "No, you stay here, be safe—"

"*Listen to me.*" He stared at Arik, using his slight height advantage to full effect. "I should have taken you with me five years ago, and I've regretted leaving you ever since. You almost killed yourself to save me. If you think I'm staying here while you march on Conota, you've lost your mind."

"You *did* hear me when I said I'm to be the new ruler, yes?" Arik replied, arching an eyebrow.

"And you heard me when I said you're still my little brother. Now, what's the plan of attack?"

Arik glanced at Janice but found no help there. "I don't have a firm plan. Get across, see what's happening, try to convince the armies to stand down. It's more of a big picture, really."

"Mm." Fik drained his water glass, then drummed his fingers on the table. "Your plan's lousy. There's strength in numbers."

"Well, I'm allegedly going to have a massive power boost as soon as I leave this realm—"

"Fine. Still looks better with a crowd behind you…and I think I know where we can find one." Turning to look over his shoulder at his wife, he asked, "If I put it forward, will Papa kill me in my sleep?"

"Papa will understand." Shifting the baby, she said,

"That bastard sent monsters to kill you. If not for Lily, I'd be first in line with a shotgun to let him know how I feel about that."

"Then it's settled." He crossed the room and tapped a panel on the wall—a communication device, I realized, hearing the voice of the friendly girl in the lobby. "Hello, Madeline," Fik said in his poorly accented Fae. "Would you please ask everyone to meet in the basement? I have news."

By then, the queasy expression had returned to Arik's face, and I patted his knee under the table to draw his attention. "This will be fine," I whispered. "Talk to them."

"And say what? 'Who wants to go with me and possibly die?'"

"I might phrase it a little differently. Leave out that last bit, keep it positive. People like motivational speakers."

"I'm no speaker," he protested. "I've never—"

"Then it's good that you're starting with a relatively small audience, isn't it?"

Arik stared at me, frustrated, but I just shrugged.

A few minutes later, we stood at one end of the basement recreational space while the rest of the Kentucky evacuees filtered in. The kids ran straight for the foosball table across the room and were soon cheering the players on, alternately shouting suggestions and taunts. Their elders, less distractible, regarded Fik curiously—Steve in particular, who came in on his daughter's arm, cane in hand. Once they'd pulled up the available chairs and yelled at their children to keep the noise down, Fik stepped in front of the sitting area and lifted a hand for attention. "I have an update," he began, but was interrupted by the bright flash of Ros's sudden appearance beside him.

"Hi, folks," she said as the settlers watched warily. "Fik, I'm going to save you some time and a lot of questions. Get over here, Arik." The men traded places, though Arik kept a healthy distance between himself and the glowing realm, earning a little smirk from Ros. "Here's the situation," she told the assembled. "Everyone remembers me from a few days ago?"

They nodded, a few mumbling in agreement. By then, even the foosballers had abandoned their game to pay attention.

"Great. So, I've had the, uh…I wouldn't call it *pleasure*, exactly, of chatting with my counterpart in Conota of late. This is his chosen king," she said, pointing to Arik. "He didn't know, and he's still not entirely sold on the idea, but he's going back tomorrow to try to stop that realm from tearing itself apart. Once there's some stability, or at least a fair chance that no one is going to aim more monsters at your neighborhood, we'll send you home. Okay, Arik, you can take it from here."

She vanished, leaving him stranded before the shocked room.

Seeing that he was on his own, Arik coughed to stall, then faced the waiting crowd. "The problem for you is Ketulm—Fik's father," he began. "Once he understands that Fik is no threat to him, the threat to *you* should end as well—"

"How are you the *king*? Aren't you a naffidar?"

I spotted the speaker on the right edge of the crowd, and from his lighter purple complexion, I assumed he was native to one of the settlements beneath Heluweya. His accent, at least, sounded more like Triple River than backwoods Kentucky.

Arik tapped a finger against his bare neck. "Collar's gone, isn't it?"

His face contorted with his incredulity. "And? That doesn't make you a man again."

Fik started to speak, but Steve beat him to the opening. "You know," he said, pushing himself upright with the aid of his cane, "I distinctly remember that we were given a chance to evacuate ahead of a pack of Hidden Ones. You were almost first through the gate, Rito."

A few of the assembled snickered as Rito's face began

to color.

"*He* stayed," Steve continued, pointing to Arik. "Kid could barely walk last time I saw him, and he stayed anyway. Now, if you want to make this about balls…"

The snickering morphed into full-blown jeers as Rito slunk back into his chair, and Arik waited until it subsided before resuming. "I wasn't consulted about this decision, and I don't presume to understand it, but for better or worse, I *am* the heir. Now," he said, slowly looking around the room, "for those of you not born in Iroja, I assume that none of you ended up in that realm by accident. You didn't decide to exile yourselves on a whim, right?" Weak laughter answered him, and he made a face. "Conota has a number of problems, and you don't need me to list them for you. I plan to do what I can to end some of the practices that brought us together here. Irojan concubines, for example. It's not uncommon among my people"—he paused, catching himself—"the cynaeli, I mean. The tennuwaya, of course, have a different variant."

I recognized the half-blooded tennuwaya woman, rendered bald and bluish without the magic necessary to hold her glamour together, who lifted a hand and nodded.

"That will end," he said, his voice growing stronger as he found his footing. "I don't know your customs as well as I should," he continued, addressing the tennuwaya, "but among the cynaeli, there's a practice of making arrangements for daughters against their will." His eyes met mine and held my gaze. "That will end as well. It may take time, but I promise you this."

"And naffidars?" came a voice from the back of the room. Arik peered toward the foosball table, where a young teenage boy—a strikingly cynaeli youth—stood with his peers. "My father did it to two of my brothers," he said, rubbing his elbow as the adults turned back to watch him. "They killed themselves."

"Korilki joined us about ten months ago," Steve explained. "He came alone."

Arik's mouth tightened as he considered the boy. "I thought that part would go without saying," he replied. Low laughter broke the tension of the crowd, but Arik kept his focus on Korilki. "I'm sorry for your loss. You're highborn?"

The boy shuffled, self-conscious with the attention. "My father is the paramount lord of Old Mother."

"*Tigal?* He's had three sons already?"

"Five, actually. And four daughters."

Arik whistled softly. "Let me be clear, then: what happened to your brothers will end." Regarding the crowd once more, he said, "But before I can do anything, I need to stop the coming war. Fik has indicated that he wants to return with me. If anyone else is interested…"

His voice faded as most of the room went to their feet—including, to my surprise, many of those who were far more human than not.

"That's…unexpected," he muttered. "Right…no children, no one with child, and thank you, Steve, but sit down."

"I'm a decent shot," the old man protested.

"And I believe it, but someone needs to see to the ones who stay behind. Besides," he added with a mischievous grin, "don't you and Coileán need to catch up?"

"Oh, not if we can help it. But yeah, I guess I could keep order around here," said Steve, sounding mildly disappointed.

"Thank you," said Arik. "All of you. The plan is to return to Iroja through Oklahoma so that Hope's mother doesn't kill me. For anyone coming with us, we leave in the morning. Take your rest."

With a last hug for Fik and a promise to get some sleep, Arik followed me out of the guesthouse and into the twilit park. As I dug in my pocket for my phone and Bonnie's number, I noticed motion across the far street: a tall, redheaded man and a petite blonde woman, locking the doors to their neighboring shops. "Quick, come on," I told Arik, grabbing his wrist, and intercepted the pair before they could reach the end of the block.

As they noticed us, the man's eyes widened, and he wrapped one arm around the woman, pulling her ever so slightly away from us. "Hope? I'd heard you were staying with Val."

"Hi, Kip. Amy," I said, nodding to the blonde, whose expression was much warmer than his. "Yes, we're about to go back, but, uh…I thought you'd want to know that most of us are leaving tomorrow. We're heading to Conota to stop a war."

He stiffened and gave me an odd look. "Since when are you good with combat magic? The Fringe is under the impression that it's not your specialty."

"Not exactly…"

"She will not be in the direct line of *anything*," said Arik. "Trust me."

"Hey, I'm not completely helpless," I griped.

"And last I checked, you weren't exactly a bruiser, either," said Amy, then extended her hand to Arik. "Don't think we've met. Amy Levey."

"Arik," he replied, briefly clasping it, then glanced at Kip. "Your husband?"

"Kip." He didn't move to extend the greeting, but he had the courtesy not to yank Amy away. "Friend of yours?" he asked me, raising an eyebrow.

"You could say that," I mumbled, trying to come up with an introduction that wouldn't result in bloodshed. "Uh…Arik, this is the fellow who gave us information on the Hidden Ones. Kip, um…Arik is our new king," I said in a rush.

"*What?*"

"And half human, and not genocidal, as far as I know, so, uh…"

Fortunately, Amy interceded. "Good luck, kid," she told Arik, and guided Kip past us while he sputtered.

Once they'd rounded the corner and their footfalls had

faded, Arik wheeled on me and jabbed a finger in the direction they'd gone. "*That* was the nikot? *Him?*"

"Kadalin," I murmured, unfolding the paper with Bonnie's number.

"But he...I mean..." He briefly floundered for the words, then managed, "But he seemed so...*normal.*"

"Yeah."

"We hunt *that?*"

I raised a finger to still him while I spoke to Bonnie, then put the phone away and walked toward the park to await the gate. "I'm putting it on my list," Arik muttered as he joined me. "They're intelligent, they can speak, we can't just kill them—"

"One fight at a time, hmm?" I replied as the gate crackled open, then nudged him through while he babbled, flabbergasted.

CHAPTER 15

Morning came too quickly—another meteorologically perfect day in Faerie, judging by the clear sky and light breeze. As Arik and I were finishing breakfast, I saw the flash of a gate in the courtyard from the dining room door, and out stepped Artur, followed by Beth and the Kentucky cohort. I was puzzled to see many of them bearing guns until Artur explained that she'd let them make a stop at their compound before bringing them by. "If they're going into battle, best that they bring weapons," she said with a shrug. "And a few of them wished to be certain that we didn't burn their houses down."

She left the villa soon after, returning with Frank, who was once more under the effects of a transformation bind. "I'm taking these two home," she explained as Beth rejoined them, having raided the breakfast offerings with the rest of our small force. "She's missed a week of school already, and—"

"And I haven't checked my mail in *days*," Frank finished. "Plus, there's New Zealand to prep."

"That there is," she agreed. "Maybe someone has taken the lead in our absence."

"Seeing as I'm slated to head up ground research for this one, I doubt it." He sniffed the air—the scavengers had yet to completely denude the buffet of breakfast meats—then turned his attention back to Arik and me. "All of that said, if it'll help, I'll go with you. Those two are useless across the border," he said, cocking his head at Beth and Artur, "but I don't mind pitching in."

"You're wonderful to offer," I said before Arik could reply, "but no, you've done more than we can repay."

"We'll manage," said Arik. "And yes, thank you again. Besides," he added with a sly grin, "what would Ione say if you were hurt?"

"Okay, first, *she* knows how to patch me up," Frank said, pointing to me as his enchantment-driven flush rose. "And second—"

"Ione would be upset, as would we all," Artur smoothly interjected. "Now, if Beth's finished inhaling her breakfast, it's time for dinner in Glastonbury. Good luck. Be careful," she said, clasping my hand and Arik's in turn, then offered under her breath, "If you need a sword, I'll return—"

"This is not your war," said Arik. "But I thank you, truly."

She gave him a curt nod, then opened a gate into a space I recognized as the den of Kitty's flat.

"You should get a picture of Ione for your desk," Beth told Frank as they crossed. "A nice frame. Maybe something with flowers, huh?"

"Do you or do you not have a death wish?" he retorted as the gate closed behind them.

When they'd departed, Arik said to me, "You know, in all honesty, I wouldn't have minded a dragon in the ranks. Flaming death from above is a nice touch when you're trying to make a statement."

"Granted, but do you want to try to shield him? I've seen what *jinoda* can do to him, let alone someone with talent…"

He grimaced. "Point taken. And as for them?" he asked, lowering his voice as he cut his eyes toward the breakfast scroungers. "I appreciate the enthusiasm, but how many of them are talented? Our natives, certainly, but what about Steve's children? His grandchildren? There's no way to test here, and by the time we get to Conota—"

"Optics," I murmured, taking his hands. "You may not

even need them. Remember what Nath could do."

"Not kill scintol, apparently." When I gave him a look, he sighed. "Nervous. Would you like to hear my grand plan? It's pretty technical: try not to get anyone killed."

"Maybe it could use a few details," I admitted, but another opening gate ended our conversation.

Eleanor stepped through first, followed by Coileán, who peered around until he spotted Valerius coming from his office...and a pair of peeved guards on his heels. "Sorry!" Coileán called across the courtyard. "We'll use the door next time, eh?"

"If you do, I'll drop dead of shock. You're not sorry," one of the guards protested. "You're *never* sorry."

Valerius smiled at the intruders. "And *that* is why Kiet is my captain. Come to see them off?"

"We thought it only proper, all things considered," Eleanor replied, unfazed by the guards' frustration. She peeked into the dining room, taking stock of the Kentucky group, then turned to Arik. "I understand that's your invasion force."

He spread his hands. "Unless someone here is willing to loan me an army that can enchant in Conota..."

"Fresh out, I'm afraid. Do be careful."

"And, uh...brace yourself," Coileán added. "Those first few minutes are uncomfortable—"

"They hurt like *hell*," Eleanor interrupted. "Just be prepared."

Valerius glanced at his colleagues, then looked at us with an expression reminiscent of a parent long accustomed to living with incorrigible children. "On that helpful and not at all terrifying note, shall we get on with this?"

Once the others had gathered with their knapsacks and weapons, Valerius said to me, "Your mother's house, correct?"

"If it's no trouble."

For a few seconds, I felt the sensation of another mind

invading mine, carefully flitting through my memories until it withdrew as gently as it had come. "No trouble at all," he replied, and opened a gate.

There before me lay Mama's backyard, a little space she'd tried to cultivate out of the wild fields around it with minimal success. The sod was patchy and dry, the bushes unkempt, the patio furniture dearly in need of cleaning, but my heart leapt to see it in the early afternoon sunlight and feel the blast of late August heat through the rift between the realms. I'd called Mama before breakfast and given her warning of our plans, which she liked not at all—well, nothing beyond the part where I returned to Pauline in one piece. But there she was, all the same, standing at the back door in shorts and a long T-shirt, regarding the gate much as she might watch an ill-tempered snake.

"*Mama!*" I called, running across the border, my carry-on bouncing against my legs as I sped toward her. She threw open the door and hurried out to meet me, and though she said nothing when we fell into each other's arms, the strength of her embrace spoke volumes. When she released me, she patted my face as if reassuring herself that I wasn't an illusion, then looked toward the waiting crowd in Faerie. "*That* is not an army," she muttered out of their hearing.

"It's all we have."

"Enogi will skin them alive." She wrapped an arm around my shoulders and squeezed. "Baby, I know you want to help him, but that's not a winnable fight. That's suicide, honey. You've done enough."

"Just wait," I told her, then motioned for the others to join us. They crossed singly and in pairs, men and women, some obviously Conotan and some passably human. Most carried shotguns or rifles, but all had at least a pistol on their hips. For those of us who'd been living in a magical drought for nearly a week, the relief upon entering Iroja was immediately evident—to me, it felt as refreshing as a cold plunge after a hot day's work, and I couldn't help but smile to see magic again in all its colorful splendor, even intermingled with its shadowy counterpart.

Finally, the only ones remaining on the far side of the gate were Arik, the Three, and Ros, who had manifested during the exodus. Arik, who seemed to be steeling himself to leap from a cliff, gave Mama a weak wave. "I'm *very* sorry about the trouble," he called across the border. "Um…"

"It's okay," I said, breaking free of Mama's protective arm, and walked to within a yard of the gate. "I'm here. Come on."

"Just don't touch him once the fireworks start," Ros cautioned, then gave Arik a firm pat between the shoulder blades. "Close your eyes," she told him. "Deep, cleansing breath…" Arik followed her instructions, and she asked, "Feel a little better?"

"A little," he mumbled.

"Good, good," she said—and without warning, she shoved him through the gate.

Arik stumbled as his feet hit a particularly brown patch of Mama's summer-dead lawn, but before he could do more than open his eyes and gasp, he fell to his hands and knees, screaming.

"Hope, do *not* touch him," Ros snapped as I instinctively moved forward to help. "Unless you'd like a quick and painful death, keep back."

Chastised, I forced myself to be still and watched as Arik convulsed and shrieked. Any magic near him flared with activation, then turned a brilliant white and seemed to flow into him. After a few seconds that felt like hours, he collapsed in the scrub and dirt, panting and still trembling with the aftershock.

"This is normal," Eleanor reassured me as I turned stricken eyes on the gate. "And…oh, Val, I think the healing enchantment broke."

"I'm not surprised," he replied, and studied my mending leg. "Hers is still intact, at least…"

But my focus then was on Arik, whose eyelids fluttered as he sought me. "Here," I said, kneeling beside him as lightning danced along his skin. "I'm here. It's over, you made it. How are you feeling?"

He answered me with a groan, then slowly eased himself upright until he was sitting. Swiveling his head until he spotted Ros through the gate, he muttered, "That was *low*."

She grinned. "Sometimes, you've got to push baby birds."

"Huh?"

"You're welcome," she said, and vanished.

"Give it a try," Coileán suggested.

Arik climbed to his feet and took a few staggering steps until he regained his footing. "You realize that I've done *nothing* with magic for five years, right?"

"So start small."

"The Frisbee," I said, and pointed to the bright green disc lodged in one of the larger trees on the edge of the yard. "I accidentally threw it up there in June. Think you can get it down?"

"I can try," he mumbled, giving it an uneasy stare, then held out his hand and slowly uncurled his fingers toward the tree. He started to curl them again in a beckoning gesture but aborted the attempt as the tree was yanked from the ground and sailed over our heads to land in a pasture.

While Eleanor and Valerius regarded each other in alarm, Coileán actually stepped out of Faerie and walked around the gate for a better look at the deep skid the tree had left in its rough landing. "Solid effort, slight overkill, didn't quite stick the landing. Six-point-five."

"Oh, my *God*," Mama cried, "my pecan tree!"

Arik cringed, then gestured the flight-loosened Frisbee into his hand. "Sorry, um...I could try to put it back..."

"Take a breather, kid," said Coileán as the tree floated overhead and landed in its hole. With a twitch of his finger, the disturbed ground settled and buried the roots, while the landing rut smoothed itself over. "How's that?" he asked Mama. "Does it need to be rotated?"

Mama, rendered momentarily speechless by the effortless restoration of a fifty-year-old tree, just shook her head.

"Oh, good." With that fixed, he gripped Arik's shoulder and said, "*Relax.* You remember how enchantment is supposed to feel, yes?"

"I...yes, but not like *that!*"

"Same principle, more oomph. Take it slowly and feel it out." Turning back to Mama, he asked, "How attached are you to your current landscaping?"

"*Move,*" said Valerius before she could protest. Coileán started to speak, but Valerius stepped into the realm and stopped him with a raised hand. "I dealt with Aiden, I know what to do. You and Ellie put out the fires."

"Fires?" Mama echoed.

He gave her a pitying look. "Really, child, grass can be salvaged."

It was, perhaps, unorthodox for three faeries to be teaching a cynaeli—or, rather, whatever Arik truly was—how not to blow holes through walls every time he wanted an object from across the room, but it seemed to be the best plan that day. The rest of us packed the house, watching TV and occasionally checking to see how many craters had popped up in the grass, and I restored my glamour and hopped in the car with Mama to pick up pizzas as the hours wore on. It wasn't as if we could have risked delivery.

The drive was quiet as we started down the old farm road. Mama gripped the wheel a little too tightly and stared straight ahead, and I said nothing as I tried to gauge her mood. I was back in a realm with magic—I could have simply looked at her thoughts—but that seemed unwise with everything else she'd witnessed that day.

Two miles down the main road, Mama softly said, "He's strong."

"Yeah."

"Stronger than your father ever was."

"He's the new Nath," I reminded her. "Strongest talent in the realm, remember?"

"I never met the woman." She flipped on her blinker and turned toward downtown Pauline. "Hope, honey—"

"If you're going to tell me not to go with him, you can save it, Mama. He needs me."

"To do what? You don't have physical abilities like that!"

I stared at her until she cut her eyes toward mine. "You know what I mean."

She was silent until she pulled into a parking spot by the pizzeria. "Yeah, I know," she murmured, not looking at me. "I just wish it wasn't you, baby. Let someone else take a turn at the heroics."

"Mama—"

"I don't want to lose you."

I noticed then the tears that she was trying to hold back. "Mama," I tried again, more gently, "he wants to make sure that what happened to you doesn't happen to anyone else."

"I know, but—"

"The only way to get to that point is to take power. That means stopping Father and Ketulm and anyone else who has ambitions for the realm. And if I can help him in any way, I will. This isn't just about Arik, Mama. It's about *me*," I said as she swiped at her eyes. "If Father wants me to return so badly, then I will—but not as a concubine. This is *my* choice."

I don't know what Mama saw in my expression when she looked at me again, but it was enough that she leaned across the emergency brake to hug me. "I love you so much," she whispered into my hair. "If something happens to you…"

"I love you, too, Mama." I pulled away, blinking back my own sudden tears. "Pizza? They're going to wonder what's become of us."

She wasn't happy—that was plain—but she pulled herself together and followed me into the restaurant.

By nightfall, Arik's impromptu tutors were satisfied, and Mama's yard looked better than it had in years with the addition of new sod, a hammock, much improved furniture, and a trellis covered in peach-colored roses that Eleanor assured her were impervious to the climate. As for the student, he seemed almost giddy, a child given the keys to a toy store the size of a city block. "It's so *easy!*" he exclaimed through a mouthful of pizza as he debriefed me at the patio table. "It was never like this before!"

"Glad to hear it." I peered into the shadows, studying the bushes. "Didn't there used to be a boxwood over there?"

"Is that the flat-topped one with the little leaves?"

"Yes…"

"Sorry," he mumbled, reaching for the garlic sauce. "Do you think your mother will notice?"

I glanced toward the restored pecan tree at Mama, who had gotten herself caught in a conversation about gardening with Eleanor. Judging by her enthusiastic gesticulations, the queen had landscaping *ideas.*

"She'll probably forgive you," I told Arik, and leaned back to consider the first stars in the wide, cloudless sky. "Any idea what the time difference is between here and Conota?"

"Middle of the night when I left, and there was daylight here on arrival, but more than that?"

"So there's probably still daylight across the border, isn't there?"

He stuffed the last of the crust in his mouth. "You're

suggesting that I should stop stalling and go home?"

"It's an idea."

"A good one," he said, pushing back from the table. "Let's move while my supposed army is happy and well fed."

Within minutes, we had tidied and grabbed our belongings, and Mama stood by with the Three while Arik, though bracing for an explosion, opened a gate into the prairie between Heluweya and the southern tennuwaya settlements, a grassy sea beneath the diffuse light of the eternally obscured sky. As our people filed through, I gave Mama a last hug and promised to be careful. She seemed resigned to my departure, but she still got Arik's attention and warned him in colorful terms of exactly what she would do to him if he failed to send me home alive. Even with his newfound power, Arik paled and assured her that this wouldn't be a problem, and he produced a new phone for me as proof that I would be in touch.

Before I could slip away, Flora appeared and ran between me and the gate. "Take care of yourself," she said, looking me in the eye. "I can't follow you there, child."

I know, I thought, and smiled for her. *Look after Mama for me, will you?*

"I will add her to my list." She stepped aside and gestured toward the rift. "Go, if you're going, and may fortune smile upon you."

With one look back at my unhappy mother—I suspected that the Three had remained in part to make sure she didn't run after us—I followed Arik home.

When Arik sealed the gate behind us, I studied our surroundings, trying to get a sense of where, precisely, we might be. I felt more energized than I had in a year—I'd adjusted to the lower level of magic in Iroja, and being back in its source realm reminded me of how much less I'd had to work with beyond the border. Seeing nothing but grass and the silhouette of a distant dragon flying toward the west, I sidled closer to Arik and murmured, "Where have you brought us?"

"Roughly the middle of nowhere," he replied. "When I was opening the gate, I asked Conota to send us about halfway between the major power centers. Nath built her stronghold firmly in tennuwaya territory. I want something more equidistant."

"*Conota* did you a favor?"

"Seeing as we're working toward roughly the same goal at the moment, he was amenable to it," Arik muttered, keeping our conversation out of the others' hearing. "And Valerius was right."

"About what?"

He tapped his temple. "The realm is in my head. Ros has a permanent link to the three of them, and Valerius warned me that the same might apply here."

"What's it like?"

"Weird. He's amused by my reaction, which *isn't helping*," he said, glaring at the sky, "but I suppose I have no choice but to adapt. Anyway, that's a matter for another time. Excuse me."

I frowned as he started off alone through the grass. "Where are you going?"

"To see about our accommodations for the night. You hadn't planned to camp, had you?" he asked over his shoulder.

Giving Arik all the space he wanted—I'd seen some of the larger craters he'd made in Mama's yard—I joined the others in a huddle near the place where the gate had been. My leg twinged with pain as I walked, and I noticed that the healing enchantment had dissolved, starved of the magic that had supported it.

Fik watched my approach with concern. "Still limping, Hope?"

"A moment." I sat, stretched out my bad leg, and constructed my own enchantment around it—*so* much easier a feat to manage in Conota than it had ever been in Iroja. Within seconds, the numbing component took effect, and I climbed back to my feet, a little grassy but feeling much better. "I can live with a limp," I told him. "Better that than a missing leg."

"Or worse," he agreed, and nodded toward his wandering brother. "What's he doing?"

"Something about accommodations, but he was sort of vague…"

My voice trailed off as the ground rumbled, and I grabbed Fik's arm for support as some of the others cried out in fear. "Earthquake!" one of the Brownfields yelled. "Get on the ground, don't fall!"

The ground *was* moving, but not from any natural cause. As I watched, the land around Arik rose and swelled until he was standing atop a hill several stories high, the tallest point for miles. The grass had ripped away during the rapid growth, leaving the rocky sides of the new hill bare and gray. The hill was capped not in a mound, but rather in a plateau—grassy still, but only for a moment before the turf gave way to stone walls that ripped upward like knives through paper. We stood there—or crouched—awestruck, as a massive castle grew around Arik, complete with turrets and a defensive wall. When the rumbling ceased, the result was beautiful, if austere from the outside, a fortress of gray walls and towers that seamlessly connected to the foundation rock below them.

"What the hell?" one of the younger Brownfields mumbled. "How did he—"

"*That*," said the tennuwaya woman, "is our king."

By the time the earthquake-fearing among us had risen, a door had appeared in the side of the castle nearest us, which opened to reveal Arik on the threshold. "Come in!" he called, his voice magically amplified to cover the distance. "Sorry, still working on the furnishings."

We trekked across the prairie and up the steps cut into the hillside, then walked through the flagstone-paved courtyard, staying close together as if fearing we'd wander off and accidentally find ourselves in a room in progress.

Before long, Arik poked his head out of a tower window and motioned for us to join him. "The door's right below me," he said, pointing to the archway. "Come up four flights, then turn right...I think. You'll find an entrance to the main part of the complex."

I hurried up the spiral staircase with the others on my heels, then passed through a wooden door and found myself in a spacious hall, carpeted with a deep violet runner and lined with high windows to admit the light. Following the corridor to its end, I opened the far door and gaped at the magnificent room beyond it. The room in which I was standing was merely a vestibule, but *that* room could have comfortably held Mama's house twice over. Larger windows of clear glass offered a view of the prairie around us on one side and the courtyard on the other, while a stone dais rose against the far wall. The carpet that began in the vestibule terminated at the foot of an imposing stone throne.

Slowly, I crossed the room, taking note of the circular chandeliers hanging from the rafters on black metal chains, each fixture as wide as a four-lane road. A door opened midway down the room onto a balcony overlooking the vista, and Arik hurried inside, beaming. "What do you think?" he asked. "Too much?"

"It's beautiful," I said, testing the thickness of the runner. My foot sank in the carpet halfway to my ankle. "When did you design this?"

"Just now. I'm sure I'll modify it, but the bedrooms are plentiful enough to suffice for the night. Here, let me show you the view."

I followed him outside, and he closed the door behind us. "Look," he said, taking me to the far-right side of the balcony and pointing to the distance. "See the smudge on the horizon?"

I squinted. "Yes..."

"Those are the tops of the tallest peaks of Heluweya. The balcony faces west, but it's large enough to give a decent view of north and south. I want to be able to see what's coming from either direction."

"Sounds wise." Seeing his slightly manic grin, I couldn't stop myself from smiling. "You're enjoying this, aren't you?"

"Immensely."

Peering over the railing, I traced the rocky hillside until it gave way to the grass far below us. "So, castle on a hill, huh? You didn't want to lay claim to a cave?"

"No. I plan to never live underground again. Maybe it's just the altitude, but I feel...I don't know, *freer* up here."

"Could have something to do with the lack of a collar."

"That's also a strong possibility." He hesitated, then cautiously wrapped his arm around my shoulders as I studied the land surrounding us. "Any suggestions? I'm serious, I won't be offended."

"At first glance? I mean, some trees would be nice. Maybe a decorative park with some fountains and flowers and such. When you're not fighting a war, of course."

"Duly noted."

When he said nothing more, I found him gazing up at the clouds, frowning in thought. Before I could ask what was on his mind, I detected his face's subtle movements—concentration, I mused, or else, a conversation. Deciding against interrupting him, I waited and looked again toward Heluweya...and then the light brightened. To my astonishment, the clouds above the castle were parting, rolling outward like an expanding ripple in a pond to reveal blue sky.

"What..." I whispered.

"Do you like it?" Arik asked.

"*How...*"

"I told Conota he owed me this much." His arm tightened around me, a comforting weight. "Still a few hours to sunset, I'm afraid, but in the meantime—"

"I love it," I interrupted, trying not to cry from the joy of seeing the sky above my homeland.

Arik left me on that balcony while he showed the others to their rooms. I was still there when the edges of the clouds colored and the sky darkened, and I wept alone when the first stars twinkled forth.

My room was palatial, a cavernous stone chamber dominated by a large, plush bed and laid with thick rugs. I was surprised at my fatigue once I dropped my belongings in the corner, but then again, my head was swimming with the time zones. Seldom does one witness two sunsets in one day, after all. Few of us were hungry, but Arik did his best to lay out a spread in the massive dining hall, which could have comfortably held Frank unbound. Arik's skill with food creation wasn't quite as refined as his skill with castle construction, but no one seemed eager to complain. On the contrary, those of the Kentucky group native to Conota smiled at the ease of enchantments long dampened by the Irojan ether, while the Irojan natives with any talent for our form of magic simply marveled at what they could accomplish. The Brownfield children could do little to nothing, their father having been a wizard and their mother half-blooded cynaeli, but most of them had married refugees like their mother, and many of their children exhibited more than the rudiments of talent. None of them could match even an average cynaeli in terms of combat magic, poor as our talents were in that regard, but I was heartened by their enthusiastic company.

As the evening wore on and my mind showed no signs of agreeing to sleep, I wandered through the castle, exploring and attempting to map the place. It wasn't easy—Arik had created rooms at random, many of which were still nothing more than bare chambers—but the exercise did me good and kept me from worrying about where he'd gone. I hadn't seen him in hours, and I hoped he wasn't hiding in a bathroom somewhere with a nervous stomach.

On that count, at least, I was mistaken. When I climbed to the top of one of the many towers, I opened the door to the last floor and found myself in a large office warmly decorated with a wide fireplace, more plush rugs, blazing candelabra, and ornately carved wooden furniture...including a desk in the same style, at which sat Arik, who looked up in surprise as I peeked inside. The wall behind him was almost entirely glass, and a door in the middle led out onto another balcony with what must have been an impressive view by daylight. Atop Arik's desk was a model of mountains and valleys, and I realized that I was seeing the local terrain rendered in miniature around the time that I realized I should have knocked.

Fortunately, Arik wasn't upset. "Hope! Come in," he said, rising to greet me. "I thought you might have retired by now."

"Restless," I replied, closing the door. "Shouldn't you get some sleep?"

He made a face. "Have you ever been too exhausted to go to bed? Plus, I have that to distract me," he said, gesturing toward the model. "A welcome gift, I suppose. It appeared shortly after I made this room. Here, take a look."

I approached the desk and studied the model, which was phenomenal in its intricacy. There, at the center, was Arik's new castle, perfect down to the stairs carved in the stone hillside. To the north, I could name the peaks of Heluweya, and I easily found High Vale, its towers melded with the protective rock around them. Beyond the mountains were the ruins of Foothold, and on the other side, the main entrance to the cavern system that contained Triple River, Old Mother, and the Fangs. At the southern end of the map, past the central prairie and another mountain range, I saw the valley where Nath had built her arboreal fortress—built on the ruins of Geheret's stronghold, or so the books said—though the trees that had contained her palace were nothing but blackened stumps. As I ran my fingertip over their edges, Arik said, "Some of the tennuwaya lords burned her palace when she fell. Nath wasn't the only one who didn't return alive, and a blood debt is a blood debt."

I gazed at the wild southern forests and the clearings where the tennuwaya made their settlements, which, freed of the constraints of the mountains, sprawled in wide patches. In the northeastern corner, I picked out the lakes where the kadalin made their homes…but then I noticed the pinpricks of light in the prairie to our north and south, which appeared as six discrete clusters. "What are those?" I asked.

Arik pointed to the three southern groups. "Tennuwaya, moving this way. And up here," he said, pointing to the northern set, "are the army from the Fangs, Ketulm's army, and your father's." His smile was grim. "No wonder Conota was in such a rush to have me back. The six contenders have made plans for a massive battle in the plain. Last lord standing takes all."

"You mean they're coming—"

"Here," he finished. "Roughly. They're due to engage in the morning. I suppose we'll be a surprise for them, won't we?"

"How do you feel?"

He paused, considering the question. "Terrified, but I'd appreciate it if you didn't share that."

I grinned. "You have my silence…my lord."

Arik snorted and flopped into his chair. "Only if I win tomorrow. What would you say if I dug a trench around us overnight and made a moat? Aesthetically pleasing but defensively useless?"

"I wouldn't say *useless*, but a few good bridges…"

When I saw that his attention was fixated on something over my shoulder, I stopped talking and turned to find a spirit standing just inside the doorway—a tall, pretty young woman with shoulder-length auburn hair and large brown eyes, a look common enough in Iroja but exotic among my people.

There's an English expression that had eluded me for a time: *You look like you've seen a ghost.* I gathered that it was meant to indicate that the subject was greatly surprised, but the saying had always seemed odd to me—I saw ghosts all the time, and it was never a shocking experience. With Arik, however, I finally understood how useful that phrase could be.

He stood again, his eyes wide and his hands faintly trembling. "Mother?" he whispered.

She nodded, smiling tightly. "Hi, honey. It's so good to see you again."

Though he swallowed hard, he managed to stutter, "I…I mean…I thought that you…"

"I am *so* sorry, sweetheart. Would you let me explain?"

He gestured toward one of the new couches, and as she took a seat, she gave me a quick inspection and smiled again. "Hope. Nice to see you, too."

The fact that she knew me took me aback. "I apologize," I began, "but have we met?"

"Not formally, though I've certainly noticed you. Leslie McWilliam. And *you*, my dear…well," she said, chuckling, "there's no introduction necessary. You are *known*."

"Is that a…good thing?"

"Good or bad, it's a thing," she said, and turned her attention back to her son. "Ketulm made me stay away."

His brow furrowed. "*How?* I didn't know he had that sort of—"

"Not physically," she clarified. "He threatened you. Told me that if I visited, he'd punish you—and he would know, since that goddamned collar stopped you from protecting your thoughts. That monster put you through hell, baby—I didn't want to add to it. That's why I haven't been to see you."

I could hear the tightness in his throat. "I…I thought that you were too ashamed—"

"*Arik.* Sweetie, *no,*" she insisted, her face softening. She rose from the couch and took a few running steps toward him before seeming to remember that any embrace from her would go right through him. "Please believe me, I am *not* ashamed of you. You survived. You risked your life for Fik—and since he's downstairs, it looks like you succeeded. Adrienne is overjoyed, by the way, and I'm sure she'll be along to tell you in person, but last I saw, she was heading straight for her son's room."

"That's fair," he said. "Mother, um…did you know?"

"About your father? Not until death," she replied, returning to the couch. "And he is *such* an impossible bastard. Ketulm can't stop me from doing anything I darn well please, but Conota…" She rolled her eyes and huffed. "He's made it quite clear that any discussion of his children's identities is forbidden. I can't even tell you what siblings you have out there—I don't know, and I couldn't say if I did. Sorry," she mumbled. "I've been nagging him for the last five years to break the collar, but he wouldn't do it. Said you had to figure it out on your own. I mean it," she said, slowly shaking her head, "neither of your fathers is worth a damn. I did my best, but I couldn't do more—"

"Thank you," he murmured. "Mother, I'm so sorry for not stopping him—"

"What, stopping Ketulm?" she interrupted. "You were *ten*! Honey, did you honestly think I'd hold that against you?" When Arik floundered, Leslie's shoulders slumped. "Tell me you didn't. That's not your fault, none of that is your fault…"

"I'm sorry. I'm really sorry."

"You have no reason to be. And if you can forgive me for staying away for the last five years, I'd like to check in on you again. I've missed you so much."

"I've missed you, too, Mother."

She smiled, then tilted her head toward me. "Now, aren't you going to tell me what Hope is doing here?"

The enquiry did nothing to make Arik less flustered. "She, um…Hope helped me find Fik, and, uh…"

Leslie gave me a knowing look. "Friends, hmm?"

"Something like that," I replied. "And seeing as there are six armies camped around us, Arik isn't being too picky about his friends right now."

He started to protest, but his mother beat him to the opening. "Sure," she said with a little smirk. "Speaking of said armies," she continued, turning to Arik, "what do you plan to do about them?"

Arik took a seat and rubbed his neck as he considered the terrain model. "Give them a show of strength. Prove that I'm the heir. Fik and his friends are willing to go with me for looks, but I don't know what sort of power they bring to the field." He paused, then asked, "If I killed Ketulm, do you think Fik would be upset?"

"Well, I can't speak for him," said Leslie, "but *I* wouldn't mind."

He began to smile. "Slow and painful?"

"Use your discretion, sweetie. As for tomorrow…would you like some reinforcements?"

"Reinforcements?" he echoed, frowning. "From where?"

She cut her eyes to me and grinned. "If you just need a show, I know some people who might be interested, especially if the result is punishment to certain lords and ladies. People who would love to have a word with some of the highborn. And since you count among your *friends* one of the greatest talents in this realm…"

Arik and I looked at each other, bemused, then at Leslie. "I think you have me confused with someone else," I told her. "I'm not even good at physical stuff."

But Leslie continued to smile. "You know, it's said among those who knew her that Lady Morgen of High Vale had an incredible gift for empowering the corporeally challenged. Do you know what they say of you?"

I shook my head.

"'Morgen who?'" With that, she stood and blew a kiss to her son. "Get some rest, Arik. You, too," she told me.

"You're going to need it."

Leslie disappeared, and I pointed to the door. "I, uh...I should probably let you wrap things up here, yeah?"

He rose and hurried around his desk. "Why don't I walk you to your room? I might remember the way."

"Mm." I waited while he extinguished the candles with a wave, then opened the door to the spiral tower staircase. "That's a very *friendly* thing of you to do, Arik."

"Mother knows, doesn't she?" he muttered.

"Oh, that's a safe bet," I said, and took his hand as we started down.

CHAPTER 16

Dawn found Arik and me on the throne room balcony, listening to the distant jangle of metal and pounding of hooves. Squinting, I could just make out the dust clouds of chinols approaching from the north and south. Surely, I reasoned, they would come to us—the patch of sky above the castle must have seemed like a beacon, a bright anomaly quickly shifting toward blue.

"I want you to stay in here when I go out," Arik said, clenching the bannister as he surveyed the land. "Be safe."

"I didn't come here to be safe."

"That may be, but I'd prefer it if your mother didn't murder me in my sleep, which she *will* if you're hurt on my account."

"Arik—"

"*Hope.*"

I sighed and rolled my eyes. "What, then, I'm useless now? Is that what you're telling me?"

"You know that's untrue. You've done more for me than anyone. But this time—"

"Arik!" came a faint shout from the ground.

Curious, he peered over the edge, then gasped.

When I looked down, I understood his reaction. There, standing in the field at the base of the hill, was a veritable army of the dead, a crowd perhaps fifty deep in places. From that height, it was difficult to make out details, but some of the spirits were obviously human—I picked out blondes, redheads, flashes of pale brown and dark black skin—while others seemed more cynaeli or tennuwaya.

More than half were women.

At the front stood Leslie, who waved up at us, then cupped her hands around her mouth to be heard. "I found some volunteers!"

He blinked in stunned silence for a moment, then mumbled, "That…is *incredible*."

Thinking of the optics, I had to agree. Sure, the Kentucky group came with weapons, but to be followed by a league of the dead…

…who were invisible to half the armies coming our way.

"Impressive," I told Arik, "but the tennuwaya won't be able to see them. I can fix that."

"Are you *insane?*" he said, sweeping one hand over the crowd. "You can't possibly—"

"You weren't at Glastonbury. I empowered an army to kill scintol. There's so much more magic here, it won't be nearly as taxing—"

"But—"

"But nothing. Can *you* empower them?"

"All at once? No," he admitted.

"Then I will." Leaning over the balcony, I waved back to Leslie. "Thank you! We'll be out soon!"

As I strode for the balcony door, Arik followed close behind, still trying to take control of the situation. "Hope, wait, we can do without them—"

I pulled him inside and closed the door for privacy, though the throne room would have echoed had I raised my voice about a near whisper. "Ketulm murdered your mother," I said, jabbing my finger into his chest. "I don't know how many others down there died like she did, but I guarantee that she's not unique. *All* of the humans in that group were held against their will. Now, they're offering to back you. They deserve justice. Recognition is the *very* least you can give them. So I'm going to go outside and handle them, and you're going to stop this war. Agreed?"

"Hope—"

"*Agreed?*"

Arik held my stare for a few seconds, but I didn't budge, and he backed down. "I'm leaving a guard on you," he said. "At least a few of the Brownfields. The ones with actual talent, I mean."

"Fine."

"And I still don't like this," he added as he followed me across the room.

"You don't have to like it."

He stopped me with a hand to my shoulder. "Aren't I meant to be king or something?"

I turned around and smiled. "You need to win this first, don't you?"

The tall grass was still dew-damp, but I didn't mind. While Arik's supporters gathered around to watch—the living with curiosity or concern, the dead with anticipation—I sat cross-legged, placed my palms on the ground beside me, and closed my eyes.

As I reached into myself to draw upon power, I could feel the slight tremors of the earth, the warning signal of approaching chinols, but I put the matter aside. The chinols and their riders were for Arik to manage. My focus had to be singular, my will unshaken. For an instant, I recalled the strain of Glastonbury, which had brought me to the edge of death, but I forced the thought from my mind. This was Conota, and magic was abundant. Still, I couldn't help but wonder if this was the moment for which Flora had been chiding me to conserve my strength. The notion made me smile, and then I drew deeply from myself and reached out to the dead.

I made contact first with Leslie, who stood only a few feet away, then with Adrienne, Fik's mother, and then on to the multitude I'd never met, my power flowing through them and connecting us all. Though I kept my eyes screwed shut—the strain allowed me to do little else—I could see the field from the spirits' perspectives, the surprised faces of the Irojan natives, the shock of the few tennuwaya as the rest of Arik's forces manifested. Arik started toward me, then seemed to understand what a bad idea it would be to break my concentration and stopped himself. "Protect her," he said, pointing to two of the Brownfield grandchildren and two half cynaeli. "If this fails, the gate to Kentucky is a short run to the east. Take her with you."

Before I could object, he was already walking away, and the others fell in behind him. I couldn't see what my guards thought of their assignment or my condition, and with the pressure on me already building, I didn't dare to look. I could, however, see Arik step to the head of the pack and square his shoulders as he waited for the approaching armies to arrive.

It wasn't a long wait. The first of the outriders arrived within ten minutes and drew up short, their mounts spooked by the mass of energized dead. Most retreated to their lords, who arrived a few minutes later with their armed, seasoned escorts. The chinols screamed and stamped if they stepped beyond an unseen perimeter, their dark scales glinting in the unfamiliar sunlight, and so the line was drawn: the tennuwaya lords to Arik's left, the cynaeli to the right, all tracing the outline of a rough semicircle around him and his unusual army.

Arik tapped his throat to amplify his voice, then addressed the contenders. "Lords of Conota," he said, slowly turning his head to stare at each in turn, "I am Arikol, and I am my father's chosen. Lay down your weapons and yield."

Perhaps convinced by the fact that Arik stood before a gathering of spirits the likes of which hadn't been seen in the realm in millennia, the tennuwaya were quick to do as he ordered. One by one, their lords dismounted, laid their blades and bows in the grass, and took a knee, and their followers did likewise. On the cynaeli side, though, only one was so wise: Lifiam, paramount lord of the Fangs. Father and Ketulm remained in their saddles, and Ketulm raised his voice in turn. "That is no king!" he said, pointing a ceremonial dagger at Arik. "This is mere trickery. *That* is nothing but a naffidar—I made it myself!"

Arik calmly opened his shirt, revealing his bare neck. "Not well enough," he said, then gestured with two fingers, flinging the holdout lords from their mounts and sending them sliding through the grass face-first to land at his feet. As they groaned, he studied Ketulm's cluster of supporters, then gestured again. I recognized Pimati as he was thrown down to join his father.

The men from High Vale and Triple River quickly did as their tennuwaya peers had done, and even Pimati had the good sense to stay down. Ketulm and Father were stubborn, however, and continued to struggle to rise. Each time one got a limb beneath him, Arik picked him up and slammed him into the ground, using progressively stronger force. Watching and listening through the hundreds of spirits, I could tell when their bones began to break—an arm there, a lower leg bent at the wrong angle, a rib cracked on impact. Only when the men were battered and bleeding did they finally yield, and both metal chains and binds of enchantments appeared around them, trussing them into submission. Pimati, too, was chained and left to lie in the grass as Arik considered the other four contenders. "Come forward," he told them, giving Ketulm an unsubtle kick in the stomach.

The other lords did as he bid, casting wary glances at their less fortunate opponents groaning at his feet. "I am given to understand that all of the ranking highborn have taken sides in this nonsense," said Arik. "Is that accurate?"

"Yes, my lord," said Lifiam.

Arik waited, then turned his gaze on the tennuwaya trio. "Shall I repeat myself?" he asked in their tongue.

"No, no, that's unnecessary," one of them replied, adding a hasty, "My lord."

"Then Lifiam speaks for all of you?"

The tennuwaya nodded. "He speaks truly."

"Good. Send word to your forces. The highborn will join us. *Now.*"

The lords slunk back to their waiting entourages, and I watched as riders headed away to where the bulk of the armies awaited the promised battle. Lifiam had sense enough to alert Father's and Ketulm's men as well, as their lords certainly weren't going anywhere. Within moments, the worried highborn, male and female, had come forward—all on foot, as no chinol would approach the dead. When they were assembled, Arik looked them over in silence, then simply said, "Inside."

He stood his ground as they passed, cringing and giving the spirits a wide berth. I heard a few shotguns racking, but there proved to be no need. Any cynaeli or tennuwaya knew what sort of pain the realm's chosen was capable of inflicting, and the bound lords at Arik's feet made it clear that he was in no mood for pushback.

The highborn hadn't come alone. Whether ordered to the front or simply curious, their fighting forces had neared and watched as their leaders were sent into the castle—a fortress that hadn't been there the day before, stretching toward an alien sky. By the time the last of the lords and ladies had passed Arik, the wisest of their men were on their knees, and more quickly followed their example. Arik waited for them to settle, then tilted his head as if he were engaged in an unspoken conversation. I couldn't hear his thoughts, especially not through the dead, but I surmised that he was speaking with the realm when he approached the kneeling soldiers and began to point. "You. You. Yes, and you," he said, making his way around the semicircle. "Come here."

The chosen joined him at a distance from the others, and Arik lowered his voice. "You are all half-blooded, are you not?"

They mumbled confirmation as a few of the spirits

behind Arik began to shout greetings to their sons and daughters.

"I'd like your assistance, if you'll give it. Security, crowd control, and the like." He glanced back at the dead, then said, "There are certain matters that should be addressed while I have everyone's attention. Will you join me?"

Perhaps it was fear, or perhaps it was the encouragement of their energized mothers, but all agreed. As they started inside, Arik motioned for the rest of his army to follow, then considered his prisoners. Father floated into the air and drifted after the last of the Brownfields, but Ketulm and Pimati were dragged by an unseen force behind Arik. Ketulm yelped in pain with the rough treatment, but Pimati held his tongue—and as a few of the dead waited for Arik to catch up, I saw the terror in Pimati's eyes.

I didn't break my focus when my father passed, though he spotted me behind my guards. "*Imaranta!*" he bellowed. "Stop this! What are you doing, girl? I order you to *stop!*"

"Oh, shut up already," said Fik, who silenced Father with a well-placed blow from the butt of his shotgun.

But Arik detoured from the procession to crouch in front of me before going inside. "Hope? Can you hear me?"

"Yes," I muttered.

"It's over. You can rest."

"No…it isn't," I managed through gritted teeth.

"What do you—"

"Let…them…*speak*."

He stood and looked at the waiting spirits, all of whom seemed far more substantial than they usually did, then turned back to me with a worried frown. "I can hear them without you. Come inside."

"It…matters."

"Hope—"

"I'm…fine."

Though he seemed unconvinced, Arik stepped back

and nodded to my guards, who took up their positions again. I watched through the many eyes to which I was connected as the last of them entered the castle, and then I saw myself no more.

While Arik proceeded to his new throne room, I took momentary stock of my situation. Yes, I was tiring, but with the volume of magic channeling through me, I almost didn't feel it. The difference between empowering the dead in Glastonbury and in Conota was like attempting to power a lightbulb with a potato versus flipping on a floodlight. Flora's warnings echoed in the back of my mind, but I was confident that I could do what the multitude of spirits were asking of me, and I trusted that Arik saw as well as I did that they craved a moment of confrontation. If Arik wanted to bring any sort of justice to the realm, then he could start with the victims to whom it had been denied.

I didn't have long to contemplate my own state. Soon enough, Arik took the throne and stared out at the crowd massed before him, and I focused my attention on the room. Father, Ketulm, and Pimati had been dropped in a corner and left with two of Arik's new guards, but the other highborn clustered together and waited in nervous silence. A few kept sneaking glances at the windows as if they were considering making a break for the balcony and leaping to safety.

Arik cleared his throat for attention, an unnecessary gesture, then said, "As king, my responsibility is to maintain order in this realm. When people are kidnapped, maimed, raped, and killed, then that order is disrupted. My predecessor was half tennuwaya, and were I feeling charitable, I might suggest that she was simply unaware of these petitioners." He paused to nod to the dead, who stood separate from the fidgeting highborn. "It's far more likely that she wouldn't have cared, had she known. While I am not, technically, cynaeli, my father shaped me to share many of their attributes, including an awareness of these people. What should concern some of you *far* more is that my mother is among them...and she is Irojan-born."

His smile held an edge, but I couldn't say I didn't like it.

"You," he said, turning to the nearest of the spirits, a brown-haired woman who seemed barely older than me. "What's your name?"

"Nicole Duvoisin," she replied, her voice high-pitched but strong.

"Human?"

She held up one beige, five-fingered hand and waved it back and forth. "Kind of obvious, right?"

"I didn't want to assume," he said, faintly grinning. "How did you come to this realm?"

"I was walking my dog one night. There was this weird anomaly out in the woods beyond my neighbor's house—a gate, I know now. My dog's hackles were up, and she wouldn't go anywhere near it. I'd picked her up and was about to turn back when this guy jumped out from the trees, grabbed me, and dragged me through. At least I dropped my dog first."

"Who grabbed you?" asked Arik. "Is he here?"

Nicole shook her head. "No, he was killed in a quarrel sixty years ago. He kidnapped me eighty-three years back."

"How old were you?"

"Fourteen."

"Why did you not return to your home? Your family?"

Her face tightened. "Because that bastard sold me to one of the lords of Triple River. As soon as he gave me the language, I begged him to send me home, but he kept me as a concubine." Her hazel eyes flicked over the agitated crowd. "He got me pregnant seven times. I miscarried all but the last time, and that little girl was stillborn. I tried to tell him that I needed rest, but he wouldn't leave me alone. He said he wanted a child with my eye color. Something *exotic*. But after the stillbirth, he got another concubine with eyes like mine, and after raping me one last time—one for the road, I guess—he killed me." Her mouth drew into a thin line. "He got the baby he wanted. A girl, in fact. But you know how humans age, yeah?"

Arik nodded in silence.

"The new concubine—that's Olga over there," she added, pointing to a pretty blonde—"hit thirty-five and started getting soft in the wrong places. He killed her, too."

"Is this true?" Arik asked her.

Olga stepped out of the crowd and looked at Nicole, who smiled reassurance. "It is," she said, her Cynaeli colored by an accent that sounded Russian to my untrained ear. "And that is my daughter." She gestured toward one of the two new guards watching the captives, who sneaked a quick wave to her mother.

Arik's face hardened. "This lord, is he here?"

"Yes," said Nicole. "Hetchol, the fat one hiding behind his wife."

A few of the highborn snickered as the flustered accused quickly ceased to use his wife as a shield. "What do you have to say for yourself?" Arik asked him.

"My lord," he began, spreading his hands, "they're just concubines—"

Before he could finish the sentence, he was bound and had joined the trio in the corner. Some of the assembled gasped and murmured among themselves, but Arik raised a hand, and they gave him their reluctant silence. "Thank you, ladies," he said to Nicole and Olga. "Now, who's next?"

One by one, the dead told their stories, most with a similar narrative. Some had accidentally crossed into Conota while hiking, while others were snatched. Some were sold as concubines for cynaeli lords or sent to a secret pleasure house deep in the Fangs, where they were used for sport until they aged beyond the point of desirability and were killed. Others were passed around the tennuwaya as servants, entertainments at the pleasure houses, or combatants in the great arenas, sent alone or in small groups to fight trolls, injured dragons, or other oversized predators. One man recounted being ripped in half by a pair of wolves.

Some of the highborn had clean hands, but the majority ended up with Father and Ketulm. I watched through a hundred eyes as five women named Father as their killer, though I wasn't surprised. Father was more than four and a half centuries old and had kept a changing roster of around fifteen concubines as long as I'd been alive—that he'd resorted to disposing of some of their predecessors was no shock. More appalling to me was the group that came forward to accuse Ketulm: Leslie, Adrienne, and ten others. As the last of them recounted the slow torture that had led to her death, another spirit appeared, a cynaeli man who pushed his way to the front and stood before the throne. "You're the new king?" he demanded.

The tennuwaya had to be confused, as I hadn't made the newcomer visible to them. "I am," said Arik. "And you are…"

"Naedim. The *rightful* paramount lord of Triple River."

Arik's eyes widened in comprehension. "So…that cave-in?"

"I was dead before the first rocks fell," he snapped, shooting a venomous glare at Ketulm. "My daughter's husband was my greatest mistake."

"He's lying!" Ketulm shouted, but his protest ended in a screech of pain when he wriggled one of his many broken bones.

By then, the number of guards on the accused highborn had grown to a dozen, some of them new volunteers who stepped up to offer assistance in the wake of their parents' testimony. The yelps from that side of the room came sporadically, a testament both to the guards' forceful bolts whenever someone tried to break free and to the prisoners' general sense of self-preservation. Arik was tiring—I could see it in his face, the strain of maintaining so many binds at once—but he persevered until the last of the dead had said her piece. Turning then to the remnant who had escaped accusation, he said, "If you wish to keep your titles and territories, you'll assist me now."

I watched as the accused were floated—or dragged, in Ketulm's and Pimati's cases—into the new castle's empty dungeon, carved into the solid rock of the hill upon which the fortress stood. Arik created five large cells and haphazardly tossed the captives inside, breaking their binds only once he'd enchanted the doors and walls against escape and made up a shift roster for the new guards. As an added security measure, he converted the metal bindings on each of the prisoners into leg chains, attaching them to the walls by short tethers. "Feed yourselves," he told them. "Heal yourselves, if you can. I'll deal with you later."

So caught up was I in observing the proceedings that I ignored my growing fatigue, which, even with all of the magic of Conota, was nearing a critical point. I could no longer feel my hands, but I didn't mind—hands were immaterial to the task before me. I couldn't feel the sun on my face, even the strangely direct sunlight over the castle, nor could I feel the light breeze on my skin. Whether I was hot or cold failed to register with me. I couldn't hear the voices of my guards, though I was taking in every sound from the crowd of spirits following Arik back upstairs, away from the cries of the newly imprisoned. Everything was perfect, flowing like music from a fine, well-played instrument, and...

Distantly—really, it didn't matter—I was intrigued to see myself in my mind's eye, then realized that Leslie was standing before me, her mouth an O of horror. "Hope, are you in there?" she yelled, a handbreadth from me. "Can you hear me? *Drop it!* You've got to let go!"

She had no reason to worry. I was fine. Everything was fine. The fact that I could now see her through *my* closed eyes was of no consequence, strange as it was.

"Hope." She knelt and lifted my chin in her hands—an oddity that should have been impossible, I noted, considering the matter with almost academic detachment. "You're *killing* yourself," Leslie said, punctuating each word with a tap on my cheeks. "You have to let go of us. Drop it *now*, honey. Come on, wake up! You don't want to die like this!"

I'm fine, I tried to say, but I couldn't locate my mouth.

"You are *not* fine! Let go!" When that produced no response from me—at the moment, I didn't see the point in fighting with a body that didn't wish to respond—Leslie sat back on her heels, sucked her teeth, then said, "I'm really sorry about this. Don't take it personally."

Her blow across my face came hard and fast, knocking my head to the side and almost toppling me into the grass. Ever so faintly, I tasted blood in my mouth—I'd bitten my tongue. Feeling a groan welling up inside of me, I forced my real eyes open and saw Leslie watching. "Let go," she begged. "Please, Hope, you've got to let go."

My cheek was beginning to sting and grow warm with the ringing slap, but part of me reasoned that it was good to feel any bits of myself again.

"You've done your part," she insisted. "*Thank* you. But you don't want to die today. Don't do this to your mother."

Mama.

My fuzzy thoughts flashed to Mama, envisioning her sitting at home in Pauline, waiting for her phone to ring. I pictured Flora standing near her, invisible to Mama but watchful all the same...

Flora.

Her warnings came rushing back to me, and with them, the memories of Glastonbury. I'd pushed too far again, I'd overdone it...

I felt more than heard a popping sensation when I cut the power and detached myself from the dead. Leslie grew less substantial before my eyes, but she seemed relieved all the same. "Good girl. You sit there, I'm going to get help—"

If she said more, I wasn't aware. I fell over and closed my eyes against the rapidly shrinking circles of my vision, and the last sensations of which I was conscious were rough grass on my skin and the smell of rich earth.

I awakened to the scent of clean linens and the feeling of light on my eyelids—not painfully bright light, but something warm and comfortable. After a brief struggle, I managed to coax my eyes open and tried to make sense of what I was seeing, shapes and colors without meaning that slowly resolved into walls and furniture. The walls were gray stone, so I wasn't in my bedroom at Mama's, nor was I in Valerius's guestroom...

"Hope?"

I rolled my head to the left, and the blob beside the bed came into focus with Arik's features. His face was drawn, and I detected an unfamiliar tension in his voice. "Hi," I croaked, and tried to smile. "Sorry, I think I fainted."

His shoulders slumped as he let loose a massive sigh. "You're alive," he said with undisguised relief, and smoothed my hair from my forehead. "Mercy in darkness."

"It was just a faint—"

"Three days ago. I was worried that you'd never wake."

"Three..." I paused, still struggling to pull myself together. "Still better than after Glastonbury."

"That may be, but Mother's been beside herself. If she hadn't checked on you when she did..."

He let that thought hang unfinished, but his eyes showed me all too well what was on his mind.

"I...may have overdone it. Flora would yell at me if she knew."

"Forget Flora—*Hayleigh* would flay me, were she here. I haven't called her, but your phone has been beeping," he added, cutting his eyes to the little black device on the dresser. "Once you're feeling better, maybe you could tell her you're still alive. You know, before she finds a gate and marches over here to see for herself."

"Can do." I glanced out the window at the afternoon sunlight, then slowly began to ease myself up from horizontal. "Just a minute, I—"

Arik caught me before I collapsed. "Easy, now," he murmured, holding me with one arm while he pulled the covers back. Someone had exchanged my clothes for thinner pajamas, and Arik, perhaps mistaking my bemusement for the beginning of outrage, hastily said, "Rin saw to your clothing. You remember her, the tennuwaya woman from Kentucky? She said you were drenched in sweat and cleaned you up when I carried you in. I didn't—I *swear*, I didn't—"

I chuckled at his flustered denials. "Never thought you the type to take advantage of an unconscious woman."

"Thank you," he mumbled, and hooked an arm around my knees. "All right, take your time, let's sit up..."

Ever so gradually, and with great support from Arik, I managed to raise my torso and swing my legs over the side of the bed, though the exercise left me shaking. "You're just weak," he soothed. "Let's get a meal in you, that'll help."

A wheelchair appeared beside my bed. "That's not necessary," I began, but Arik shook his head and lowered me to the seat.

"You pushed yourself beyond all sane limits," he said, tucking a blanket around my legs. "I should have kept better watch—I thought you would stop once you tired..."

"I really wasn't myself at the end," I murmured,

recalling Leslie's exhortations. "I felt fine at first, and then I suppose I...well, I..." I struggled, trying to find the words to convey to him what that moment of complete, serene detachment had been like—that moment of existing as a power conduit, seeing all and barely thinking. In my frustration, I felt his touch inside my mind, and when he saw what I was trying to say, he recoiled in shock.

"I need for you to promise me something," he said, crouching in front of my chair. "You will never attempt something on that scale again without people around to monitor you. Do you know how close you came to..."

I nodded. "But it's my talent. I have a responsibility—"

"You don't owe your life. *Certainly* not on my behalf." Standing, he said, "I spoke with Conota while you were healing. Do you know how many spirits the average cynaeli can empower at any given time? *One*. Maybe two, if he's trained. For a few *minutes*. And that's not something that should be attempted before you're at least fifty."

"So I'm ahead of my time," I said, grinning.

"You're a marvel," he replied. "But let's try to keep you alive, hmm? Maybe even standing?"

I attempted to hoist myself out of the chair, just to prove him wrong, but my legs barely wanted to move, let alone support my weight. He clucked his tongue at my poor efforts, and my nightclothes morphed into more appropriate daywear, a sleeveless red tunic over brown leggings.

Holding one hand over the side of my head, I tried to will my hair clean—a slightly tricky bit of enchantment for me, but something I'd been doing since late childhood. To my frustration, however, my hair refused to cooperate, and I pulled my hand away to stare at it, as if it merely needed a glare and a stern talking-to.

"Give it a few days," said Arik. "You drained yourself. I'd be surprised if you could pull together a glamour right now."

Ignoring him, I gave my hand a good shake and tried

again, with the same disappointing result. "I've lost my talent?"

"You're trying to draw water from an empty well. Let it fill." A twitch of his finger converted my dirty tangles into a manageable braid, and he knelt to put new leather shoes on my feet. "I'm told that this will pass. Conota has taken an *interest* in your healing," he muttered.

"What's that supposed to mean?"

"From what I gather, he finds you more entertaining when you're alive and moving on your own. Look more closely."

Squinting into my natural aura, I could just make out the fine, bright mesh of enchantment surrounding me. "That's, uh…impressive."

"Well, yes, we mustn't bore him." Standing again, he moved behind my chair and set it in motion. "Hungry? Thirsty? You should eat, build your strength."

"Surely you have more important things to do than nurse me back to health," I chided as he gestured open the door.

He bent around to look at me and smiled. "You're conscious. The rest can wait."

The castle was constructed with a distinct lack of wheelchair ramps, but Arik made do with a gate from the corridor outside my bedroom directly into a private dining room. "I'm afraid the food still needs work," he said as he pushed me to the wooden table, a four-seater decorated only with a pair of candlesticks—the least grandiose element of his castle that I'd seen. "I'm doing my best, but I think this is the sort of enchantment that comes only with practice."

A plate the size of Mama's Thanksgiving turkey platter appeared before me, piled high with roast meats, vegetables, and a sizeable portion of golden steak fries suspiciously like the ones we'd found in Kansas City. "Here," he said, willing a set of utensils into being beside the plate. "Tell me how to make it better."

I picked up the fork, silently grumbling at my hand for how heavy the little thing seemed to be, and stabbed a fry. "Not bad," I told Arik as I chewed. "Could use a little salt." A dish appeared within reach, and I sprinkled it liberally over the food. "Are you not hungry?"

"I had lunch," he replied. "Please eat. You must be famished."

In truth, I was ravenous, but my old tutor's admonition that a lady does not stuff her mouth like a feeding chinol kept me from inhaling my food. I was hardly a fair judge of its palatability—after several days without food, *everything* tasted amazing, and Arik kept refilling my water glass as I tried not to choke myself with rapid bites.

After a time, when my awakened stomach no longer felt quite like a bottomless cave, I asked, "What did you do with your prisoners?"

Arik grimaced. "Nothing yet. I'm still deciding how to deal with them." He plucked a forgotten fry from beneath a pile of spiced mash and chewed thoughtfully. "I've ordered the rest of the realm to be here tomorrow morning."

That almost made me drop my fork, though hunger overrode incredulity. "What, everyone?"

"I sent the armies home with a summons, so yes. I'll open gates back here from the major settlements at dawn."

"If you just wanted to practice your public speaking…"

He grunted and continued to steal my fries. "Hardly. If I'm to mete out punishment, then I want it to be clear what I'm doing and why—no rumors spread by people who weren't here to witness."

The word *witness* sent a shiver up my spine. "You're planning executions?"

"No. Not yet. I don't know." When my vegetables refused to reveal more fries, Arik solved the problem by creating a second helping, then resumed his snack. "I'm in a difficult position, Hope."

"Can I help? Possibly without giving you a legion of

the dead?"

He chuckled softly but sobered. "Here's the heart of the matter: I want to provide justice, but how am I to know what's just?"

I raised an eyebrow and attacked my meat, which was melt-in-my-mouth tender if somewhat under-seasoned. "Meaning?"

"What guidance do we, as a people, have as to permissible behavior? Where are the rules? *Are* there rules?" he asked, soaking a fry in a puddle of gravy. "Like...you and I agree that a lord shouldn't kill his concubines when he tires of them, correct?"

"Certainly."

"Ketulm disagrees. So does your father. The question is, as much as I dislike the practice, is there any rule prohibiting it?"

I had no ready answer for him. My tutors had offered me no formal instruction in legal matters—why would I need that when Father's word was law? "You *are* the king now," I pointed out. "If you don't like it, outlaw it."

"I already have a list, believe me," he replied. "But those rules are only good going forward." Seeing my bemusement, he explained, "Suppose I hated yellow shirts and decreed that wearing such a garment is a treasonous offense punishable by torture and death."

I ate a bite of vegetables, reminding myself that fried potatoes, although plant matter, didn't count. "Drastic, but I follow."

"Everyone knows that yellow shirts are forbidden, and I never see one again. But what if I receive word that someone once wore a yellow shirt, say a hundred years ago, and I summon him here and sentence him to death? How is that fair? Wearing that shirt wasn't a crime when he did it."

"Wearing a shirt and raping a kidnapped girl are hardly equivalent," I countered. "The former may be an insult to fashion, but the latter is clearly wrong."

"According to whom? You?"

"And you, I trust."

"Naturally. But as Conota continues to remind me, both of us are afflicted with the Irojan madness, are we not? Personally, I find it reprehensible to snatch someone and hold her against her will as a concubine or worse, but judging by my dungeon, a significant portion of the highborn find nothing offensive about it." He sat back and folded his arms. "So who's right? How can I be fair if we don't begin with the same set of rules and parameters?"

"Maybe we have some laws…somewhere," I offered lamely.

"That no one ever mentions?" Arik added his own glass of water to his non-meal. "If Nath made any beyond her few proclamations—or at least the few I heard of, she cared so little about our affairs—then I wouldn't know where to begin searching for them. Her fortress is ashes."

I found bread almost hidden beneath the meat pile— thick, nearly black, and soaked with gravy—and tried not to gobble it. Mama's cooking was fantastic, but I'd missed the flavors of home, and Arik's interpretation of them, though iffy, was close enough. "Not to bring up a difficult subject," I said between bites, "but have you thought about asking the realm?"

His nose wrinkled in disgust. "Honestly, I'd rather not."

"You don't have to like him, but what better option do you have? Especially if you want to do something about the prisoners in the morning. If there's anyone who can answer your questions, surely it's the realm."

Arik remained sulky about the notion, and I sighed and put my bread down. "Um…hello?" I began, unsure of where to look, and settled for addressing the arched stone ceiling. "If it's no trouble, did anyone ever try to make laws? Nath, Mab, someone before that? Anything that people might know about?"

Motion from the corner of my eye drew my attention

back to the table, and I saw Conota, fully materialized, pulling out a chair. "Interesting question," he said, planting an elbow on the table and his chin in his palm. "Why do you ask?"

I gave Arik a meaningful stare, and he reluctantly turned to his father. "You know why. Has it ever happened?"

While Conota's pair of eyes remained focused on Arik, his third flicked toward me and briefly closed—a blink or a wink, I couldn't say.

"Only once," he told Arik. "Your predecessors have been content to address problems as they arise, but for Geheret."

"*Geheret?*" I muttered.

"The boy was obsessed with the notion of conquering his mother's realm," Conota explained. "He made a set of laws in the hope that people would obey them and thereby decrease his duties here while he focused on his goal. Sent copies to all the settlements. I can't say whether it worked, as Geheret's reign was so brief. Little fool," he said with disdain. "He spent *days* in Iroja, trying to win the affections of that stupid girl. Everything hinged upon her—terrible plan, but would he listen to me? I told him that Faerie would never recognize him, but he refused to believe it. He thought I was *jealous*, of all the ridiculous notions."

I'd heard just enough about Geheret's short, disastrous reign to have an inkling of what Conota meant, but that wasn't the time to press him for details. "Did Nath do away with his rules when she took over?" I asked.

"No, though she never referenced them. Nath ruled by whim, and as far as she was concerned, if it didn't disturb her, then she wouldn't trouble herself. She made a few reforms among the tennuwaya, raising the marriage age and withdrawing some of the power that the highborn had taken through Geheret's apathy—and she did make that proclamation denying assistance to any who made unauthorized forays into Iroja after she was bested by that woman," he added. "Nath was never the cleverest of my children, though she had her moments. But as for the cynaeli, she really didn't care whether you lived or died, as long as you stayed to the north. Your little flight was the first time she found your people useful," he said to me with a smirk. "An affront to her sovereignty warranting a full invasion of Iroja. As I said, not the cleverest."

"So his laws are still in effect, then," I replied.

Conota shrugged. "Forty-six years, and they haven't been touched. Not enforced, but not erased."

"Where could we find a copy?"

He chuckled. "Good luck. There are a few copies deep in storage in some of the manors and towers. I suppose I could reproduce it...if Arikol had need."

Arik's patience had to be wearing thin, but he gritted his teeth and managed an almost civil tone. "I'd like to see it. *Please.*"

A long piece of paper covered in messy handwriting appeared on the table in front of him, and I leaned closer for a look. The document was written in Tennuwaya, but I could translate it with a moment's thought.

"The scribe?" Arik asked.

"Written in Geheret's hand and copied exactly," said Conota. "He didn't put an extraordinary amount of effort into this matter, you understand."

By the time we finished reading it, Arik and I were both smiling, though his seemed somewhat more predatory than pleased. "The one useful thing he ever did," said Arik, tapping the enumerated laws. "And I thought nothing good came of the Invader."

"You do realize that she was Valerius's mother, right?" I said.

"Fine. One decent thing."

"And Toula's. She's the one who loaned us the RV and crew, remember?"

"*Two* decent things. This makes three," he said, lifting the paper from the table. "Look at the list of prohibitions:

kidnapping to obtain concubines or bed servants for pleasure houses—"

"He had too many complaints," Conota interrupted. "That was intended primarily to keep lowborn daughters from being taken without proper arrangements."

"But he never stated that the rule doesn't apply to Irojans," said Arik. "And here, look—no killing unless authorized by him."

Conota snorted. "He thought he was going to end a century-long blood feud between two of the more prominent tennuwaya families. It's still ongoing."

"*This*," I said, pointing to a tilted line of Geheret's scrawl, and looked Arik in the eye.

Though he was sitting on the wrong side of the paper, Conota knew what I was talking about. "Oh, yes, *that*. Made him squeamish, for some reason."

I reread the text to be sure my interpretation was accurate: *Creation of naffidars is henceforth prohibited.*

"None of this speaks of punishment," said Arik, looking over the paper at his father. "How did Geheret intend to enforce these rules?"

Conota looked at him as if Nath had suddenly risen a step in the cleverest child ranking. "How else? *Death.* You break a rule, you're at his mercy."

"Death," he murmured, scanning the list again. "And these were made known to the tennuwaya *and* the cynaeli?"

"Delivered by hand to the lords and other highborn, and posted in every settlement for the lowborn to see. There was no Cynaeli translation, but—"

"Any cynaeli with a decent education can read this," Arik interrupted. "And that would certainly include Ketulm."

I won't say that Arik's smile was the most heart-melting expression I'd ever seen on his face, but I understood the hardness in his features.

"Do with that as you will," said Conota, rising from the table. "Oh, and Arikol?"

He glanced over the paper again and lifted an eyebrow.

"You should ask her for advice more often," he said, jutting his chin in my direction. "At least one of you has rudimentary sense."

Before Arik could retort, Conota vanished, leaving his son's exasperation unspoken. "Well, he's not *wrong*," I said, and squeezed Arik's shoulder. "Here, make more fries, will you? I'll share."

CHAPTER 17

Weak as I was, there was little I could do to assist with the preparations, and so I sat in my wheelchair on the throne room balcony, watching as Arik superintended the construction and arrangement of pavilions on the plain below. Having both experienced bad sunburns, he and I agreed that the canopies were a must, as the sky above us continued to be clear, a circular patch surrounded by a wall of cloud. The sky had cycled through its sunset colors—not as spectacular as the Irojan sunsets, but a fair substitute—and multicolored orbs hovered over the staging area, casting their light on the fluttering white silks.

Though I'd thought of waiting a few hours until morning returned to Pauline, I called Mama, deciding that she probably wasn't sleeping well after several days of silence on my end. "I'm alive," I told her after her frantic greeting. "Exhausted, but alive. It's kind of like Glastonbury all over again, but I'm on the mend."

She whispered, *"Jesus,"* though I couldn't tell whether that was a prayer or an expression of frustration with my life choices. "Come home, sweetie," she said as the microwave beeped in the background. I could almost imagine her standing in the kitchen in her bathrobe, reheating cold coffee. "Let's put you to bed, get a few good meals in you."

"I need to be here."

"Hope—"

"Father's in the dungeon."

After a brief silence, Mama said, "Arik has a *dungeon?*"

Leaving out the part about exactly how close I came to unintentional suicide, I recounted the events of the last days, then told her what Arik had planned for the morning. "I need to be here for this," I finished. "I *want* to be here."

Mama made no reply, and I was about to continue my attempt to convince her that I was doing the right thing when I heard her murmur, "Does Arik need more witnesses?"

"What do you mean?"

"I'll go back there. If I can bring Enogi down—"

"You still have *nightmares* about this place," I protested. "No one would ask—"

"I want to see that bastard go down. You tell Arik that if he does *anything* involving Enogi, then he'd better damn well let me watch."

Because I was a good daughter, I relayed the message when Arik came to check on me. And because Arik held a somewhat irrational fear of my mother, he immediately opened a gate, nudged her awake from her couch nap, and asked if she'd prefer to come over then or in the morning. After swearing that he would return to collect her at a decent hour, he left Mama to sleep and asked me to set a reminder on my phone.

As the stars came out and Arik tweaked the setup, the balcony doors clicked open, and I smiled to see Fik step out, an orb glowing in his hand. "Sitting in the dark?" he asked, tossing it to me.

I caught it and held it in my lap, a softball-sized sphere of yellow light. "Tried to make one earlier, but it fizzled. I'm still drained."

He leaned on the balcony, picked his brother out of the shadows, then turned back to me. "Glad to see you up again," he said in a low murmur. "He was terrified."

"Yeah, I know, I went too far. In fairness, no one's ever taught me how to empower several hundred people *safely*."

"I'm not sure there's a protocol for that." Examining the stars, he said, "They're not the same as the ones in Kentucky."

"Still pretty."

"Oh, sure, but…you know, it'll be good to go home."

That took me aback. "You're not staying? But you have nothing to fear here now. Arik wouldn't let anything happen to you."

"I know," said Fik, "but home to Janice is Kentucky, and to tell you the truth, I've grown attached to the place myself. Happy memories, see? Her family is there, and I wouldn't ask her to leave them. They've been nothing but kind to me, and I want our baby to grow up with her cousins." He scuffed his toe on the stone balcony. "Here, she's a half-blooded likdenfi's daughter. There, she's Lily. She belongs."

"Glamoured," I pointed out.

"That's a small price for safety." A second orb appeared in his open hand, and he tossed it up to hang above us. "Most of us are anxious to be off. Arik sent a group back to Faerie to reassure the others—"

"He can make gates into *Faerie* now?"

"I don't know. He got us to Kentucky, and I called Artur for a pickup from there."

"That's probably the more diplomatic way to go about it," I mused. "I would hate for someone on that side to get the wrong idea about intentions…"

Fik grimaced. "Considering how well our realms have interacted in the past, I'm all in favor of calling an intermediary. Anyway, Artur put us in touch with someone called Yolanda. She said she knows you…"

"Fringe coordinator, she's great."

"Glad to hear it. Once we're home, we're supposed to call her and set up a meeting—something to do with a network?"

"Nothing bad," I assured him. "The Fringe is a group for weak human adepts and lesser-blooded faeries and such, but they offered me their assistance when I was settling in. They take care of their own, and considering the composition of your settlement, I wouldn't be shocked if they extended an offer to you."

"That would be more than decent of them," he replied. "I doubt that Papa would be opposed, and if he supports it, the rest will fall in behind him."

Watching him fidget in the orbs' light, I quietly asked, "Nervous about tomorrow? Your father?"

His answer to that was a grunt. "Father can rot. I, uh...well, the thing is, Arik has asked those of us who exiled ourselves to give testimony. Some are lowborn, but I'm far from the only likdenfi in the group, if you follow me."

"If you'd rather not speak against your father, Arik will understand. Your mother certainly said her piece yesterday."

"Yesterday?" he echoed, grinning. "Try three days ago. You took a *long* nap."

Not trusting myself to stand unassisted, I settled for lightly kicking him in the shin. "You know what I mean."

He stepped out of range, his smile widening. "Care to try that again, or—"

"*Fikwed.*"

We turned and saw Adrienne standing near the doors, arms folded and scowling. "You be nice to that girl," she ordered.

He seemed to shrink a few inches. "Yes, Mother."

"And when is Janice coming? I want to meet her and my grandbaby before you run off again."

"Tomorrow," he said, and stepped around my chair to push me back inside. "For now, I think someone needs to eat dinner."

"I had a late lunch," I protested, looking up at him over my shoulder.

"You'll probably find an appetite." His eyes begged me to play along with the distraction.

I considered giving Fik a hard time, but I let it go. "You know there are no ramps between here and the dining rooms, correct?"

"Don't worry," he muttered, "I'll carry you."

Sleep left me feeling renewed, able to walk (if not run) and cobble together a respectable glamour. If Arik rested that night, however, I didn't know about it. By the first light of dawn, he had risen, dressed in a gray shirt, trousers, and silver-embroidered sleeveless robe more befitting his new station, brought Mama across with repeated reassurance that I would be myself again in a few days' time, and opened at least a dozen gates outside the castle. Mama and I stood on the throne room balcony to watch as crowds poured through from the various settlements—the highborn left behind for the aborted battle, the lowborn, the children, and a number of people who could be nothing but human. Most came on foot, though a few rode chinols. All stared in wonder at the exposed sky, and some took shelter beneath the pavilions.

Once the last of them had filtered in, Mama and I joined the Kentucky group at the back of the balcony while Arik strode alone to the railing. "Thank you for coming," he said in Cynaeli, his amplified voice echoing across the plain as the hubbub below quieted. "For those who haven't been here before, I am Arikol. I hope you took seriously my order to bring *everyone* here. It's my understanding that this has been done, but should that be proven inaccurate, know that there will be consequences."

After repeating himself in Tennuwaya, he paused to gaze down at the throng. "You should have noticed some of my guards standing at the base of the steps. They are there to maintain order, and they're not to be harmed. Again, there will be consequences if my words go unheeded. Now," he continued, "anyone of Irojan descent—natives, half-bloods, or less—is to come inside.

The rest of you will wait where you are. I'd advise you not to stare directly at the sun."

Arik had taken his throne, and the rest of us were seated on benches along the wall, when the first of the Irojan contingent arrived. Some of the obviously human came in costly attire, wearing flattering dresses and the silver collars of cynaeli concubines. Others were far too thin and seemed sickly, prematurely aged and weakened by years in the pleasure houses. Some shielded their eyes from the sunlight pouring through the windows, while others turned to face it even as they walked, soaking it in after their time underground. The men among them had generally fared worse, and none had any finery to speak of beyond items bearing the colors of one of the powerful tennuwaya houses. A few limped in with crutches or canes, victims of the arenas.

And then there were the half-bloods, tennuwaya with too few eyes or short hair instead of bald blue scalps, cynaeli with extra fingers or brown undertones to their purple complexions. I assumed that many were likdenfi, as none of them seemed to be starving. There were plenty of cynaeli concubines and tennuwaya bed servants among their number, mostly female…and then I noticed a few males among the pack wearing the type of collar with which I'd grown far too familiar in the last days.

They approached the throne, silent and wary, and Arik stood to address them once the doors had closed. "For those of you brought or held here against your will, I'm so very sorry for what was done to you," he said, once more beginning in Cynaeli. "You're free to go home."

He almost had to shout when he gave the Tennuwaya version to be heard over the uproar—gasps, exclamations, rapid conversations, and tears. He raised a hand for order, and the crowd gradually stilled, though the undercurrent of excitement remained. "I only ask for your patience. Give me a few days to make arrangements for your return…" He scanned the benches, then spotted me sitting with

Mama and pointed. "That's Hope. Tell her where you want to be sent. Has there been any word yet from the Fringe?" he asked me.

I lifted my phone as proof. "Yolanda and I have been in contact today. They're willing to assist with relocation and acclimatization."

"Wonderful. When you speak with her again, please thank her for me, and tell her I'll provide anything they can't produce—food, clothing, whatever is needed. I'm no expert on human fashion," he said to chuckles, "but I can take instruction."

"We've got room," one of the Brownfield sons called out—in English, no less, which led to the rapid turning of quite a few heads. "If you don't have any place to go back to, you're welcome in Kentucky. It's nothing fancy, but the offer's on the table." His siblings nodded emphatically, and Fik shared a brief smile with Arik.

The room had barely quieted again before a concubine stepped to the front of the crowd. "My lord?" she said, and waited until his eyes fell on her. "I appreciate the offer, but I can't leave without my daughter."

"Or my sons," another woman added.

Several of them spoke at once, and Arik again had to raise a hand for calm. "Your children are free to leave as well," he said, and looked around the room. "*All* of you. The drawback to living in Iroja is the necessity of using glamour, but if that's manageable and you want to make a life elsewhere, you'll have no repercussions from me. I only ask—and I'm sure that the Fringe would concur—that if you take young children to Iroja, make certain that someone has sufficiently glamoured them. We don't want to cause any problems in that realm."

As the crowd's rumblings surged, Arik raised his voice. "Before you go, would any of you be willing to testify as to what was done to you? Many of the Iroja-born dead have already made their complaints known, but I'd like a full picture. Abduction, rape, maiming..." He glanced toward the nearest of the naffidars. "I'd be most grateful if you would identify the ones who've wronged you."

"*Hell*, yes. Where do we sign up?" one of the concubines called out over the sudden crescendo of cheering.

Arik seemed momentarily thrown, then produced a piece of paper and a pen. "Hayleigh," he said, "would you mind?"

Mama's expression when she took the paper from him reminded me of a nature documentary I'd seen involving a pack of hyenas preparing to bring down a wounded zebra. "My *pleasure*, sweetie," she said, then climbed onto a chair in a less occupied corner. "Hey!" she shouted to the room. "Right over here, no need to shove."

While a large portion of the crowd migrated toward Mama, I watched as Arik stepped out on the balcony for a second time. "Any naffidars down there are to join us," he said simply, then returned to the room and slammed the door.

I counted four among the first wave, clumped together against a wall, avoided by the humans and other half-bloods. One of the guards escorted another five inside, fully cynaeli but cringing as if they anticipated a beating. While Mama continued to take down names and details, Arik beckoned the naffidars toward the throne and descended. "This won't hurt," he assured the nearest, placing his hands around the collar. The naffidar looked sick with fear, but I saw the pulse of enchantment Arik sent into the metal, overloading the binds and locks, then sending the force of the aborted explosion back up his arms to dissipate into the room. A sharp tug separated the halves of the collar, and Arik disintegrated them as the newly freed touched his bare neck with trembling hands. "Would you be willing to testify against your father?" Arik asked.

He nodded, nearly in tears, and Arik gripped his shoulder. "Never again," he said, and moved on to the next.

To no one's surprise, all of the naffidars added their names to Mama's list.

Arik was in no rush. He made more benches for the throne room, creating ample spectator seating on both sides of the aisle, then put out a modest table of refreshments near the door. "I apologize in advance," he said, "I'm new to food creation, and some of this is probably under-seasoned or worse. If something's terrible, just tell me how to fix it."

At that, one of the half-tennuwaya women got his attention. "I've worked in a kitchen since I was eight, my lord. If I could be of use…"

He nodded emphatically. "*Please*. Undo my mistakes."

While he discussed final arrangements with his guards, she went down the line, sampling and enchanting as necessary. No one mentioned to him just how many adjustments she made, but no one seemed to care about the quality of the offerings. The new king was trying, and for those in the room who were too thin to be healthy, the gesture was enough. The one dish his impromptu assistant left untouched was a bucked-sized bowl of fries—properly salted that time, I noticed—which some of the humans practically inhaled, their snacking punctuated by moans of happiness.

It had taken persuasion, but the mothers of small children in the room finally agreed to allow Arik to send the little ones to a separate hall to play, overseen by three of the guards. "No harm will come to them," he insisted, "but these proceedings are hardly appropriate for their eyes and ears." After a bit of cajoling, the children were herded together and led out with the promise of sweets— all but the infants, who remained in their mothers' arms, and a few girls who seemed younger than adolescents yet refused to leave. I soon learned the cause: all had been promised as concubines, though none were anywhere close to being of age. For them, Arik didn't insist.

The morning was to be a serious affair, but between the food and the unexpected camaraderie of other humans, the crowd was almost in a festive mood by the time the guards brought up the first ten prisoners. Apparently, Arik had already been down to the dungeon that morning, as his prisoners were both shackled hand and foot and bound by enchantment to prevent their escape. We watched from our benches as the lords were led down the runner toward the dais, where Arik sat and studied them: five tennuwaya, five cynaeli, some regarding him with defiance, others with barely masked fear. Arik waited until they were positioned before him, then flicked one finger toward his right. A copy of Geheret's laws, blown up to twice the size of a man, appeared in the air beside the throne. "Have you seen this document?" he asked the prisoners.

They cast quick glances at each other but said nothing.

"Don't bother lying," Arik told them, his tone almost conversational. "I can check your memories if you don't feel like speaking today, or you may answer my question verbally. Your choice."

"Yes," one of the cynaeli muttered. "Some years ago."

The others grumbled in the affirmative.

"Very good," said Arik, and pointed to the man who'd answered him first. "Lord Dakesht, we'll begin with you. You've been accused of holding two Irojans against their will and using them as concubines—"

"Four," a redheaded woman down the bench from me interrupted. "Add Emi and me to that tally." The petite, black-haired woman beside her raised her hand and nodded.

Arik looked to Mama for assistance. "Emi Nomura and Giselle Roy," she reported. "Emi was taken from outside Kyoto ten years ago, when she was thirteen. Giselle was taken from a town near Montréal nineteen years ago, at the age of *eight*."

"I've had two of his likdenfi," Giselle volunteered. "Emi's only had one, but he's impregnated her at least four times."

Though he appeared disturbed by that news, Arik continued. "Dakesht, you are also accused of killing two of your Irojan concubines. Does anyone want to add to that?" When the room remained quiet, Arik stared at the chained lord. "Are these accusations true?"

"And what if they are?" Dakesht retorted. "These creatures are of no consequence—"

The shouting from the gallery drowned him out until Arik stood to restore order. "I am the son of one of these *creatures*," he said. "Perhaps you should choose your words more wisely."

"Perhaps you should respect your betters, *naffidar*," he spat. "Ketulm told us everything. If you believe that the highborn will bow to you, then you're either an idiot or insane."

"Take the matter up with the realm," Arik replied, unruffled. "It was his decision, not mine."

"Then the realm is as stupid as you—"

The rest of that statement ended in a scream of pain as Dakesht's knees suddenly bent in the wrong direction. He toppled to the rug, writhing and howling, and Conota manifested on the dais beside Arik. "Argue with him, if he'll tolerate it," he said, cocking his head toward his son, "but *I* will not be insulted. Would anyone else like to question my choice?"

The nine lords left standing kept their mouths clamped shut.

"I thought so," he said, and vanished.

"Touchy," Arik told them with a nonchalant shrug, then reversed Dakesht's knees again and created a numbing enchantment around them. The injured man couldn't stand, but once he'd ceased his wailing, Arik resumed his speech. "The realm informs me that the accusations against you are accurate," he said, and gestured toward the blown-up copy of Geheret's declaration. "The punishment for any of these offenses should be death. I've decided to be merciful." He sat back and crossed his legs. "The penalty for kidnapping anyone, Conotan or Irojan, into concubinage, bed servitude at the pleasure houses, or any other form of sexual misuse is the loss of all lands and titles, plus a hand. The penalty for murder is the same. Dakesht…I suggest that you either work on your physical enchantment or learn to get by with your feet alone."

Dakesht started to protest, but Arik silenced him with a quick alteration of his bind. "Now," he said, eyeing the lord to Dakesht's right, "I do believe it's *your* turn."

Mere enslavement, as distasteful as it seemed to me, hadn't made Geheret's list of prohibitions. While Arik intended to include it in the revised version, he decided that he couldn't fairly punish those who had sent others into the arenas or condemned them to life servitude, nor could he offer justice for crimes committed before Geheret put pen to paper. Still, for most of the accused, that was no true reprieve. Most of the lords and ladies brought up from the dungeon were sentenced to lose at least one hand, many both—and without their families' long-held lands and status, they would be left at the mercy of their neighbors. As mercy wasn't a concept with which much of Conota had any true familiarity, I suspected that the kinder sentence might have been death.

Arik saved the worst for those who had broken the rule against creating naffidars, and I wasn't entirely surprised when he took into consideration those acts that occurred even prior to Geheret's reign. He watched with a hard smile as Ketulm and Pimati were brought in, the latter still bruised, the former limping on healing legs. After recounting the accusations against them and listening while several of Ketulm's likdenfi spoke, Arik repeated for them the penalties he had decided to impose. Pimati escaped with his hands, though Ketulm was slated to lose both. But before Pimati could relax, Arik said, "There's one more rule violation we should discuss, don't you agree? After all, I've heard several times this morning about how you told everyone in the dungeon what you did to me."

Ketulm's face, pale lilac already, seemed to go gray.

Arik pointed to the line on the list about naffidars. "I'm already going to take both of your hands," he told Ketulm, his voice dangerously soft. "What should I take for this?"

"Just kill me," he said in a rush, "you don't—"

"No, no, you won't *learn* anything that way. What is it you always told me? 'Learn faster and you won't be beaten,' yes? See, I've listened to you."

"*Kill me!*" Ketulm bellowed. "Be a man and—"

Arik's incredulous laughter interrupted him. "A *man?* Funny, I thought that's precisely what you *didn't* want me to be." Sobering, he said, "I could kill you now for what you did with the Hidden Ones. I don't know how many hundreds of innocent people they ate in Iroja, but all of that blood is your doing. Were I not limiting myself to Geheret's rules, I would be inclined to punish you for attempting to murder Fik. Instead, I'm going to make this a learning opportunity for you. You're going to learn what life is like as a naffidar."

Ketulm's sudden, frantic struggle against his binds was for naught.

"Oh, don't worry," said Arik with feigned concern, "it's not forever. A century should suffice. Of course, I won't be able to undo the physical modification after that time, but I suppose that's just the price you pay for an education." Grinning, he looked at Pimati. "You, too, my *dear* brother. I can think of no better way to repay you for being such a kind, compassionate master."

The two were dragged away screaming, and Arik waved at them before the door slammed. The other lords who had made naffidars fared no better, much to their abused sons' satisfaction.

Arik saved my father for last. Father walked in flanked by guards, his head held high even if he was dragging one leg, and stared coldly at the throne. After questioning him about Geheret's rules and reminding him of the accusations from the dead, Arik said, "I know quite well about the *arrangement* you made for Hope. I don't care if Geheret said nothing on the subject—I can't overlook that. But there's someone else who would like to speak before I pronounce sentence. Hayleigh?"

Father startled when he heard her name and realized who was sitting beside me, her face seventeen years older than when he'd last seen it. "Hello again, you sick son of a bitch," Mama began, folding her arms. "Miss me?"

His quickly regained his stoic façade. "Hayleigh. Time has been unkind to you."

"Oh, *fuck you*," she said, the curse in English but its meaning unmistakable. "You took my childhood. My innocence. You ripped my daughter out of my arms when she was the one good thing left in my life—the *one thing* I had to live for. And you know what everyone said when you finally dumped me across the border? They said I was crazy. That I'd cracked and made the whole thing up— you, Hope, High Vale, all of this godforsaken place. They almost made me believe it, too, until Hope found me." She paused to look down at me, and I nodded reassurance. "You ruined my life," she told Father. "My youth, my future..." Her eyes narrowed with her anger. "Can you imagine how anxious I still get every time it clouds up? Overcast skies put my stomach in knots. And men?" she said with a harsh bark of laughter. "Just the thought of being alone with someone makes me nauseated. Of course, that's not really a problem, seeing as my whole town thinks I'm nuts. Got you to thank for that, huh?"

Father was unmoved. "You said you wanted to return to Iroja. I gave you what you asked."

"You *kidnapped* me!"

"I traded with a dealer for you. He brought you into this realm, not me."

"And you could have sent me home then."

He shrugged. "The arrangement was fair."

"Not to *me*! None of this was fair to me!"

If she'd had a gun at that moment, Mama might have shot him. Instead, Arik thanked her for speaking and informed Father that he would be losing both hands. As the guards forced Father from the room, Arik said to Mama, "His title and lands are forfeit. If you want them, they're yours."

Arik spoke again to the throng gathered outside the castle as night fell, informing them of what had transpired and who had been stripped of power. He outlawed slavery of all kinds from that moment—well, aside from that of the soon-to-be naffidars—and decreed that the enslaved, whether kept for labor or as bed warmers, were to be freed immediately. Women who had been given as concubines against their will were permitted to leave their lords and entitled to compensation from their lands and fortunes. The pronouncement was met with an uproar, and once he'd quieted the crowd again, he suggested that they make camp for the night. He would hear complaints in the morning.

The line was out the door the next day. Some of the highborn not currently awaiting their fate in the dungeon wanted to lodge their objections to Arik's new laws, arguing that he was stripping them of concubines or property. To that, Arik simply suggested that they do as he said or lose more...and knowing what had happened the previous day, they slunk off, muttering. Two foolhardy young cynaeli men and three tennuwaya men—all highborn, I assumed—tried to rush the throne as a group, apparently having decided that the best way to deal with their new king was to remove him. Arik's guards leapt to his defense, but the fight was brief. Strengthened as he was by the realm's gift, Arik singlehandedly stopped his would-be assassins' bolts while striking down the attackers, and the guards made a point of dragging the five corpses from the room past the waiting crowd, just in case anyone else had considered regicide.

But by far, those who wanted an audience were the beneficiaries of Arik's rules, eager to have their claims approved. One by one, they stood before him and the full gallery, men and women bound to the pleasure houses, to the arenas, to the highborn. Fathers complained of daughters taken without proper arrangements being made; daughters complained that arrangements were made without their consent. Arik listened to each, and as I watched his face, I could tell when he was silently discussing the matter with the realm, who saw all and could reveal the truth of the matter. Some came before him, lied, and were threatened with severe punishment if they attempted something so foolish again, but the majority of the aggrieved spoke the truth, and Arik validated their claims, instructing them to return if their lords balked.

That evening, he descended to the basement with his full complement of guards and remained below for several hours. I found him in his office in the middle of the night, staring out the window at the campfires glowing like wild stars in the darkness around the pavilions. "Are you all right?" I asked.

"I will be." He beckoned me into the room, and I latched the door for privacy. "Speaking of brutal acts in the cause of justice is one thing. Committing them is another."

"You did it all?"

He nodded. "My rules, my reign, my punishment. The guards were there in case of emergency, but mostly as witnesses. At least I left them quickly enough when all was finished that they didn't witness me be sick in the corridor." As I took a seat on the couch, he said, "I did nothing to worsen the pain, and the prisoners are all sufficiently aged to tend to their own wounds, even the cynaeli. The tennuwaya, at least, should have little trouble managing themselves—I suppose they can compensate for the loss of a hand or two with enchantment. The situation may be different for the cynaeli, but that can't be helped. They'll find a way to get by. Probably go about with glamoured hands for appearances' sake," he added with a snort. "I suppose I could bind them to prevent glamours, but I'm exhausted after maintaining so many binds for even these few days," he admitted. "It's not a sustainable option in the long term, and honestly, the damage is done. If they want to salvage part of their dignity with magic, it's no harm to me."

Up close, he looked like he could use a week-long nap. "Have you made the naffidars?"

"Yes." He didn't smile, but his voice carried a hint of satisfaction. "All of them bound to me for the moment. I suppose I'll give them to their former naffidars tomorrow—seems appropriate, doesn't it?"

"So you'll be keeping Ketulm and Pimati, then? And do what with them?"

Arik rose and stepped to the window, motioning for me to join him. "Remember what you were saying about landscaping? A decorative park, perhaps?"

I grinned. "You've had ideas?"

"Well, once the crowd leaves, I was considering the aesthetic value of an ornamental lake, right about there. When Fik and I were small, we used to swim in one of the pools near the Fangs. I think I might like a lake of my own now. It'll give Ketulm and his son something to do."

My eyebrows rose. "Neither one has any talent for physical magic left, right? You *did* make dampening collars?"

"Oh, my yes."

I tried to imagine the scene: the pair of disgraced lords

toiling beneath the cloudless sky, one of them with no hands, attempting to dig a lake together.

"That'll takes ages," I told Arik.

He shrugged. "I'm in no hurry."

Weary as he was, Arik worked through the night. He tried to shoo me off to bed, protesting that I'd heal faster if I slept, but the castle was quiet, and something told me that Arik didn't need to be left alone to ruminate about the previous few days, much less the previous few hours. Though I caught a nap or two on his couch, I stayed with him as he pored over family charts, provided by Conota at Arik's mumbled request. From what I saw of them, they were accurate, tracing the major and lesser families throughout the realm and accurately depicting even the likdenfi's parents...though none of Conota's other children were marked as such. I'd gathered why their identities were kept even from Arik: any other king might be tempted to remove his competition, just in case they should somehow discover their true parentage and attempt to create a vacancy on the throne. Personally, I thought Arik had a right to know his half siblings, but Conota held his secrets closely, and not even Arik could pry them from him.

After breakfast, Arik summoned his chosen new lords and ladies into the office one at a time. Having stripped the convicted of their lands, Arik needed to redistribute them, and he did his best to keep them within their original families. But instead of calling the sons of the old lords—the wife-born among the cynaeli or the marital children of the tennuwaya, who took no concubines but made no secret of their trysts at the pleasure houses—he called their other children, the likdenfi, the sons and daughters of bed servants. Many of those summoned were partly human.

"If I'm to be thought mad," Arik had explained to me,

"then I want lords in power who are just as mad as I am."

"And ladies," I'd pointedly reminded him. "Not just among the tennuwaya."

He'd concurred and selected a mixed group—not quite evenly split between the sexes, but a beginning. The newly elevated were offered their disgraced parents' estates and towers and titles, and most accepted without hesitation.

There were, however, a few holdouts. Arik called Fik in as a formality, though he knew he couldn't convince his brother to remain in the realm. "I'm offering you Triple River," he said. "Paramount lordship. You could have the house and everything."

But Fik smiled and declined. "I appreciate it, and don't think otherwise," he told Arik, "but Kentucky is home for now."

"You'll visit?" Arik pressed.

"If you'll have us."

They embraced for a long moment in the middle of the office. "Gates work both ways," Fik said as they parted. "You're welcome with me, and if you don't make it over for Lily's first birthday, I'm going to be hurt."

One corner of Arik's mouth ticked. "There's an invitation for her sort-of uncle?"

"For her *uncle*, yes." Fik gripped Arik's shoulder, adding, "Blood only goes so far, little brother. Be well."

The Kentucky group left that morning with the majority of the released humans and even some of their adult children. Waiting on the other side of the gate was Yolanda, armed with a computer and five other Fringers, all of whom wore shorts in the afternoon heat and swatted at mosquitoes. "Right this way," I heard her say as the crowd filed through, "into the barn, let's get some names and details." Spotting me, she said, "Tell him I'll have a list of needed supplies tomorrow, once we get through with processing—"

"Hi," Arik interrupted, then underhanded a phone like mine through the gate. "Whatever you need."

She caught it and stuffed it into a pocket. "Arik, I take it."

"You must be Yolanda," he replied. "It's nice to meet you, Hope has said—"

"Likewise," she cut in. "Just do us all a favor and don't try to invade, okay? I've got enough headaches without *that.*"

Once the last of the departing had passed out of the realm, Arik returned to the task of redistribution. While only two of the naffidars had received their fathers' lands, Arik offered sizeable estates to the others. "I can't undo what was done to us," he told them, "but I *can* ensure that you'll never wear a collar again."

The last appointment of the day was with Mama, who glanced around the office uncertainly before I patted the spot on the couch beside me. "So," said Arik, folding his hands on his desk, "have you given any thought to my offer?"

"Enogi's tower?" she asked.

"The tower, the lands, and the title. Paramount lady of High Vale."

Mama smiled but shook her head. "That's sweet of you, but I wouldn't have the first *clue* what to do with it. Why don't you give it to Hope?"

That took me by surprise. "You don't want me to come home with you?" I asked.

"Oh, baby, *no,*" she said, rushing to squeeze my hands, "no, you're always welcome with me. I want you back in Pauline more than anything. But this isn't about me. You're not happy there."

"Mama—"

"It's okay," she insisted. "And it's nothing new. You've been adrift all year. I want you safe, but I want you happy, too…" Her eyes slowly shifted toward Arik, then focused on mine again. "I think we both know that you're going to be spending some time in this realm. I'd feel better knowing that you had a place to sleep over here—"

"That's not a problem. I have plenty of guestrooms," Arik interjected.

She gave him a *long* look. "A place to sleep under her own roof. Let's keep up the illusion of certain proprieties, huh?"

"*Mama*," I groaned, feeling the blood rush to my face.

"Hey, I'm not blind, and I'm not stupid. All I ask is that you call," she said, wrapping her arm around my shoulders. "And visit. Or let me visit here, I don't care."

After assuring her that this would be no problem, Arik returned Mama to her house, then closed the gate with a sigh. "So," he said, rubbing his forehead.

"So," I muttered, still feeling flushed.

"High Vale is yours."

"You're not going to ask if I want it?"

"I'm just following your mother's orders," he replied. When he looked at me again, I saw that he was as embarrassed as I was. "Uh…dinner?"

The castle was almost too quiet that evening. Arik's guards kept their voices low and patrolled the grounds in pairs, and anyone not on shift was asleep after a hard few days. The remaining human and half-blooded guests kept to themselves in a pair of towers, slipping out only to check the dining rooms for food. As for the prisoners…well, the thick walls blocked whatever noise they made in the dungeons.

Arik and I ate in the sitting room attached to his personal suite, a comfortable chamber with a fireplace and a pair of tall windows with a view of the plains. When our plates were empty but for sauces and crumbs, he produced two small glasses of iptof, a strong, pale yellow liquor made from the tuberous root of a semiaquatic cave plant, and we took them to the windows to enjoy the last of the sunset.

After a time, perhaps encouraged by the alcohol, Arik

stepped closer to me. "About what your mother said today…"

"I'm sorry, she's Mama, I—"

"No, don't apologize. You've done nothing to offend. It's, uh…" He drained his glass in a quick shot and set it on the stone window ledge. "I would love to have you here," he said, staring out at the night. "Or somewhere close. High Vale at most. But…"

"But?" I asked, watching his candlelit reflection twitch in the glass.

"*But*," he repeated, and sighed. "You know we can't be married, Hope."

"We've been through this, and I meant what I said. If you want me, tell me."

"Of course I want you," he replied, agitated. "But it wouldn't be fair to you to have you bound to someone like me."

I kept my silence for a moment, sipping my drink and gathering my thoughts. Finally, I asked, "Have you considered what *I* want?"

"What do you mean?"

"Don't I get a voice in this? If we're discussing an arrangement, then I'd like an equal vote in this matter."

"And if we were making an arrangement, I'd gladly hear your voice. But we *can't* make one. Collar or not, I'm still—"

"*Enough.*" I rubbed one hand over his taut back. "You are enough."

He turned to me with misery in his eyes. "We both know that's not true."

Putting my glass down, I took his hands and stared up at him. "I need you to understand something, all right? You don't get to tell me what I want. That's my decision."

"Hope—"

"I want *you*," I pressed. "Whatever that means. I want to be your wife…and I want that to be enough for you," I continued, taking confidence from the warming iptof. "No concubines, no bed warmers. I'm willing to fight for you now, but I won't compete for the rest of my life. *That* is what I want. If that arrangement suits you, then I'll consider the negotiations settled."

Arik blinked, momentarily silenced by my frankness. Cynaeli women, particularly highborn cynaeli women, did not make such demands—but then I wasn't entirely cynaeli, was I? I'd escaped my fate riding dragon-back, brought down a queen, and helped raise a king, and if Arik couldn't respect the version of me that was somewhat brasher than the girl he'd known in Triple River...well, I *did* have High Vale.

The silence between us was broken not by Arik, who seemed lost for words, but by Leslie. "You're not going to find anything better than that," she said, and we whipped around to see her standing by the fireplace, smirking at her son. "I'm serious, Arik. Listen to your mother, huh?"

"Mother," he said stiffly, his flush darkening his face to a rich violet, "privacy, please."

"Come on, it's not like your father isn't listening in."

"*Mother*," he repeated, almost begging.

"Fine," she said with a roll of her eyes. "Just trying to help."

She vanished, and Arik's iptof refilled beneath his hand. He drank it quickly, though it did nothing to calm his blush. As he toyed with the glass, I murmured, "If you don't want me, if you're not sure...tell me. I'll understand."

"You know I want you," he replied, cupping one hand against my cheek, "but that's selfish. You should have a chance at children, a normal family...I can't give you that. I don't want you to make any more sacrifices on my behalf, Hope—"

A loud, frustrated sigh made us jump, but instead of Leslie, Conota stood across the room, arms folded and top eye staring at the ceiling. "This is *tiresome*," he announced. "Try to be slightly more entertaining, won't you?"

From the corner of my eye, I saw Arik twitch, and a curious expression—equal parts surprise, fear, and excitement—crossed his face. "Uh…excuse me," he said, hurrying from the room.

His bedroom door slammed, and a moment later, I heard him yelp, "*Seriously?*"

I looked at Conota, whose third eye was definitely winking that time. "You fixed *that?*" I asked. "Faerie couldn't manage it."

"Unsurprising—Arikol is not fae, now is he? Even here, it would be nearly impossible, were I to attempt it on any ordinary one of my people. But he is of my *line*, and in this realm, with sufficient magic, under my direction…I can repair an amputation."

I arched an eyebrow. "And you could have done this at any point?"

"Yes."

"Unbelievable," I muttered.

With a low chuckle, he said, "You're welcome, Imaranta," then disappeared.

A moment later, Arik cracked open the bedroom door, flustered and even more deeply flushed than he had been. "Uh…Hope? Something—"

"I know." I crossed my arms and leaned against the window. "So, did you want to marry me, or do you need more time to think it over?" As he tried to stammer out an answer, I said, "Why don't I just come in there, and we can talk about this?"

He managed to nod.

"You know," I added with a little smile, "back in the RV, you *did* promise that you would help me try the techniques I've read about once Fik was safe."

"I, uh…I did," he croaked.

"Are you a man of your word, Arikol?"

He grinned back at me. "Yes, my lady, I am."

I could have sworn I heard distant laughter as Arik let me in.

CHAPTER 18

Cynaeli weddings are modest affairs by human standards: the man, the woman, possibly their parents, and an administrator, someone to make the appropriate records. If stripped of any ceremony, one can be accomplished in under ten minutes. But Arik didn't want to make ours a rushed affair—"I love you," he said, "and this should be a celebration, not an exchange of goods." That suited me well, meaning that I would remain unmarried for at least a season more while he put the realm in order.

I was in no hurry. With every day that passed, as he grew more comfortable and confident in his new role, the Arik I remembered began to show forth. He was quicker to laugh and as kind to me as he had ever been, though the man I watched recruit a small staff from the ranks of the remaining half-blooded and discuss logistics with his new guards wasn't the boy I'd known in Triple River. He'd grown both stronger and more brittle, and so many of his scars were still beginning to heal. Perhaps some never would.

But then, I wasn't the girl with the chinols anymore, quietly hoping for someone to give me a decent future without first asking me what I wanted. I'd grown stronger, too—and if I chanced to forget, Leslie was often around to remind me, fussing at me for pushing myself too quickly after my ordeal. In truth, whatever Conota had done to me had been far more effective than the Arcanum's techniques, and I felt almost like myself within a week— still somewhat drained, but once again able to access my talent.

While Arik dealt with the unpleasant issue of returning his prisoners to their home settlements, if not their homes, I took it upon myself to see to his guests. By then, the population of the towers had dwindled to twenty-three human women, all former concubines or bed servants, and their young children, some likdenfi, others half-tennuwaya castoffs destined for lives like their mothers'. I checked on them regularly and made sure that Arik's new kitchen staff of two remembered to put food out for them, but they were easy to satisfy. Though their backgrounds and experiences varied, the women shared an instant camaraderie, and I often heard laughter as I climbed through the guest towers. A few of the women practically moved into the courtyard during daylight hours, lounging beneath the blue sky and returning indoors only when necessary. "You don't understand," one told me when I asked if there was something amiss with their sitting rooms. "I was kept in Old Mother. I haven't seen sunlight in eleven years."

About a week after Mama returned home, she surprised me with a call in the early evening—at least midnight in Pauline, I estimated. "Are you okay?" I demanded on answering. "What's wrong?"

"I'm fine, baby," she quickly replied, and I relaxed when she didn't sound panicked. "Are you doing all right?"

"Sure, just busy. Why are you up so late?"

Mama hesitated, then asked, "Could I come over?"

"Of course. Let me find Arik, and I'll have him make a gate." Slipping on my shoes, I hurried out of my room and headed toward his office. "Is there something you want to talk about? Bored? Can't sleep?"

"Actually, uh…I was wondering if I could stay for a while."

I paused inside a stairwell and pressed the phone closer to my ear. "A while?"

"Yeah."

"Like...a few days? Few weeks?"

"I don't know. If that's an inconvenience," she hastily added, "don't worry, I understand—"

"No, no, Mama. You're welcome, I'd love to have you," I insisted, grinning to myself in the lonely stairwell. "But, uh...what about the store? Don't you need someone to run it while you're away?"

"The store can burn down, for all I care. There's nothing but memories for me here, and a lot of those I'd rather forget. Hell, most of this town thinks I'm nuts, and that's never going to change. I want to be close to my daughter. You're the best thing in my life, sweetheart, and I don't want to get in your way, but I *miss* you like crazy, and—"

"I miss you, too, Mama," I cut in as she began to choke up. "Hold that thought, I'm going to find Arik."

He was in his office with three of his guards when I knocked and let myself inside. "Mama wants to come back," I said without preamble. "You remember what her kitchen looks like?"

Arik didn't question me. He gestured a gate into existence, and within seconds, Mama had her arms around me and my face pressed against her terrycloth bathrobe. *Thank you*, I told him as I escorted her from the room, and I caught his smile before the door closed.

I started to take her back to my room, then had a better idea and led her to the guest towers, where we found a group of women talking and laughing over an informal dinner in one of the sitting rooms. Two of them recognized Mama from the week before and jumped up to welcome her, offering a plate and a description of the dishes on the sidebar. That most of them were younger than Mama and had yet to return to Iroja seemed to make no difference. She had been a concubine once, and so she was a member of the sisterhood.

When I left Mama that night, explaining that I needed

to check in with Arik, she was smiling. I returned to set up a bedroom for her, but Mama and her new friends had already arranged linens in a spare room and were chatting on the cushioned window ledges.

For the first time in many years, my mother had a community. I bade her goodnight and promised to see her for breakfast, my heart at peace.

Three days later, with the castle almost calm and Mama sunning in the courtyard with "the girls," Arik took me to High Vale to see my inheritance.

I hadn't planned on a homecoming to my father's tower. When I fled with Frank and Kitty, I'd never intended to return. And yet, there I stood on the ornamental bridge to the front gate, not just coming home but doing so as the paramount lady. In truth, I was too overwhelmed to fully consider the pressures of the position, but when my thoughts strayed to the matter, I took comfort in the fact that *all* of the towers of High Vale were now ruled by people of Arik's choosing. Maybe I wasn't exactly among friends, but I suspected that we could be cordial colleagues in time.

One of father's guards remained at his post by the gate, an older man who'd served the family for decades. He bowed low as Arik and I approached, then murmured, "My lord. Lady Imaranta, welcome home. Forgive us, we were unsure when you would be arriving, but I'll summon the others—"

"No need," I said, patting his shoulder as he straightened. "This is only a brief visit. Frankly, I'm surprised to see you here."

His head bobbed. "Some of the staff have left. Others of us thought we might find favor with our new lady…"

The notion that my favor was a commodity made me feel like cackling, but I held my composure. "Your loyalty is noted and appreciated. Who else remains?"

The guard squinted at the cloud-shrouded sky as he made his mental tally. "Your lord father took some of his personal articles and left with his wife—I believe that many in his situation have settled in Foothold."

"The ruins?" Arik asked.

"Yes, my lord."

"They don't fear the Hidden Ones?"

"I cannot say—Lord Enogi seldom shared his mind with me. But they went in that direction, over the mountains."

"His concubines?" I asked.

"Some never returned from the plains," he replied. "Where they went, I can't say. Three of the younger ones remain here with their children. Shall I summon them for you?"

I took him up on the offer and soon found myself facing the wary women in Father's former office. "The tower has ample space," I told them. "Stay here for now, if you like. I'd rather not leave my siblings homeless." Judging by their faces, the former concubines weren't thrilled with their new arrangements, but none of them complained as I dismissed them.

With that business settled, I started to give Arik a tour of the tower—he'd never been to High Vale, after all, and I *did* have a home to show off—but I paused in the entry hall and stared at Father's pair of mounted kadalin, his hunting trophies with their frozen snarls and upraised hooves. Arik stood beside me, considering them, then said, "Those are...um..."

I saw them and envisioned only Kip, who had the same brown skin and red hair. "Revolting," I muttered.

He studied them in silence for a moment longer, then offered, "Want me to dispose of them? It's no trouble."

"No. I need to make a call. Take me back to my room at your place, will you?"

He obliged, and after I switched phones—one ran on Conota's version of magic, the other on Faerie's, and the two weren't interchangeable—he took me to Mama's house, which was quiet but for the eternally blowing air conditioner. "This may take a moment," I warned him, and he rummaged through the pantry while I settled on the couch and called Yolanda. "Sorry to bother you," I began once I'd heard her cheerful greeting, "but could you give me Kip's number, please?"

There was a pause on the line. "*Kip?*" she asked. "As in—"

"That Kip, yes. It's, uh…it's sensitive."

Though she sounded uncertain, Yolanda sent me his number, and I held my breath as I dialed. After two rings, he answered with a cautious, "Hello?"

"Hi, it's Hope Lozano," I said in Fae as Arik came in with a sleeve of saltines. "Please don't hang up."

"Tell me he's not invading."

"No. *No*," I stressed, "nothing like that. He's sitting here in Oklahoma with me. I'm sorry to call so…late? What time is it over there?"

"It's only afternoon. The school year's just begun, and someone's already spilled water on three computers. I'm elbow-deep in repairs. And I assume this isn't a social call."

"No. Uh…hold on," I said, and put the phone on speaker mode. "So, um, I just took possession of my father's tower."

"Congratulations?"

I snorted. "Thanks. Slight problem: he hunted kadalin."

Kip said nothing for a time, and I'd begun to fear he'd hung up when I heard his voice again. "Are you saying…"

"Two, male, preserved and mounted. He's been using them as decoration at least as long as I've been alive."

I couldn't understand what he said next, but the tone suggested profanity.

"I don't want them in the tower," I said over his low curses. "Could you tell me what to do?"

"*Do?*"

"Should I try to return the bodies to someone? I know your people have settlements east of Heluweya...the Kint Porda area, isn't that what you call it? The bodies don't seem to have anything identifying on them, but do you think someone would recognize them? Help me return them to their kin?"

"If your father killed them," said Kip, "then they could have died centuries ago. It would be simplest if you burned them. That's what we do with our dead."

"Certainly. What do I do with the ashes? Do I say something, or is there a ceremony, or—"

"Take the ashes to a high place and scatter them to the winds," he interrupted, though his voice sounded warmer than it ever had in conversation with me. "If that's possible. If not, just be sure that the meat is burned away. Really, it's not the end of the world if you can't scatter properly—I mean, my brother never brought it up."

"*You* speak to the dead?" Arik asked.

"Only in dreams, and only when invited to do so. It's different with us." He hesitated. "Arik? Is that you?"

"Hello."

"Hi. I'm only going to say this once: if you go after my people, then I won't rest until you're back here before me, dead or alive. Maybe I can't kill you myself, but I know a few people who could."

Arik, who'd been reaching for the crackers, stilled his hand. "Actually, I was hoping to talk to you about that."

"What, assassination?"

"No. Your people." Shifting closer to the phone, he said, "Relations between us have never been good. I'd like to change that."

"If you think you're going to make yourself king over us—"

"That's not my intention. I'm after diplomacy, not domination. What happened to those two in High Vale shouldn't happen again, and I'd like to take steps to make sure it doesn't. Could we talk in person? In Faerie?" When

Kip didn't immediately respond, Arik pressed him. "I'm powerless to do anything but throw a punch in that realm. You have a head on me, and quite honestly, I don't want to brawl with you. It wouldn't be a long fight."

Faintly, I heard Kip snicker.

"If I can get permission, will you talk to me? Your time and place."

"No tricks?" Kip asked.

"My goal is to leave Faerie alive. No tricks."

"I suppose," he said after a silent moment. "Make the arrangements. I should have these machines up and running again by morning. And Hope?"

"Yes?" I said, leaning toward the phone.

"Thank you," he murmured, just before the line went dead.

I called Kitty, who spoke with Valerius, who ran the request past Ros before calling me to finalize the details with Arik. "No weapons, no one but Hope and me," I heard Arik say as he paced Mama's kitchen with my phone. "I'd be no threat to you."

Evidently, Faerie concurred with that assessment, as Artur met us at Mama's late the following morning—or late afternoon, Oklahoma time. If she minded chaperoning us at what had to be the middle of the night in Glastonbury, she didn't show it. "There's a couch in my office, a door that locks, and several rather dry books to go through before our next trip," she said when I apologized for the hour. "Don't worry about me."

The gate she opened dropped us on the sidewalk in front of Kip's shop—another lovely morning in Faerie, though the lack of magic after days back in Conota made my skin crawl. "Wish me luck," Arik mumbled, straightening his shirt, then opened the door to the jangle of a bell.

Kip was waiting behind the counter, stiff and ill at ease,

and watched in silence as the three of us stepped inside. Arik showed him his empty hands before approaching. "Thank you for meeting me. I don't want to take too much of your time—"

"Grab a stool," he said. "Hope, flip the sign, will you?"

I turned the placard on the door from *Open* to *Closed* as Arik dragged a seat to the counter. "Right," said Kip, settling onto his own stool, and propped his elbows on the countertop. "I've been thinking."

Arik took a small notebook and pen from his pocket before sitting. "Please."

"It would be nice if your people stopped murdering mine, but you're actually not our biggest problem. We lose more to raiders than we ever have to you, as far as I know."

He frowned. "Raiders?"

"That's the translation. We call them etalre. Uh…they come in packs on guronts, plunder and kill—does that sound familiar?"

"Jinoda," I murmured, taking a seat near Arik. To Kip, I added, "We know them well in High Vale. They've stolen our chinols for years."

"Chinols?" he asked.

"Our mounts—we breed them. What did you call them?"

"Guronts." He cut his eyes to Arik, who was taking notes. "If you could do something about them, I'd count it as a favor. They killed and ate my family."

His head shot up, a look of horror on his face. "I'm sorry, that's…"

"Something I'd rather not relive today," said Kip. "I have no love for the etalre, and it sounds like you don't, either."

"I'll work on it. They don't acknowledge me, but maybe a show of strength will convince them to limit their hunting grounds. I could post guards near your territory…"

Kip's laughter cut him short. "Oh yes, I see that going well. If your kind come anywhere near a kadalin village, we run."

"Which is why I need your help." Arik put down his pen and folded his hands. "I know nothing useful about your people. We're taught that you don't even have language."

"Well," Kip said dryly, "I hope we've all learned something here today."

"I need more than that. Teach me what I should know to reach out to your leader...leaders? Again, *ignorant*. Will you help me?"

His eyes narrowed. "So that you can explain who you are before you attempt to subjugate them?"

"Oh, for heaven's sake," said a voice behind us, and I turned to find Ros marching across the shop. "The kid means well. He's serious," she told Kip. "He wants to establish something like diplomacy with the kadalin. This isn't a trap."

"You're certain?" Kip asked her.

"Your paranoia is showing."

"It's not *paranoia*. They're deep dwellers!"

"It's fine," Arik interrupted. "Kip, you have no reason to trust me, I understand that. If our positions were reversed, I'd feel the same. But I can't improve the situation at home until I can convince the cynaeli and tennuwaya that the kadalin are...well, *people*...and it would help if I could carry on a civil conversation with them. Would you at least let me have the language?"

Kip studied him for a moment in silence, then looked again to Ros, who nodded. "If I trust you now," he said slowly, "and you betray that—"

"Then you'll hunt me until the end of time," Arik finished. "Understood." Turning to Ros, he said, "Can you transfer the language from him to me? I'm sorry to impose, but without magic..."

"It's no problem," she replied, smiling.

Kip watched from the far side of the counter as Arik reacted to the insertion of a new language—never the simplest of mental adjustments. After a time, he spoke to Arik in words incomprehensible to me, and Arik answered in kind before putting pen to paper again.

"This is going to be a long day," Ros murmured, ushering Artur and me back to the sidewalk. "Is there anything you need to do around here, Hope? I'll keep an eye on them."

"Not *here*," I said, and turned to Artur. "But if you have time, I could use a gate to Pauline. I still need to pack my things, and Mama left with the pajamas on her back. You could nap there," I offered.

"Or we could accomplish this quickly," she countered, and took me to Mama's house.

I'd intended to sort through my closet and drawers, decide which items I couldn't live without, and scavenge a bag or two from the garage for packing purposes. Artur's method required far less thought on my part. "Have you got a plastic bin?" she asked. "Something for storage?"

I dumped the Christmas lights from one such container and brought it to Artur for inspection. "Can you replicate that? I could put my shirts…"

My voice trailed off as Artur squinted at the den and the couch shrank to the size of doll furniture. "I learned this from Ellie," she explained, plucking the miniaturized couch from the rug. "Easy packing. Much simpler to transport stacks of books when they can fit in the palm of your hand, eh?"

The couch was barely as long as my index finger, and I tested the springiness of its cushion with a fingertip. "Remarkable…"

"And portable!" She placed it in the storage bin, then created little dividers, sectioning the couch off in a tiny room of sorts. "I'll handle the furniture. Why don't you empty the cabinets?" she suggested, glancing around the kitchen.

"Or I could start by emptying the fridge," I said, opening the door to a welcome blast of cold air. "*Ooh*, this milk has seen fresher days."

As I filled a trash bag with expired condiments and carefully set Mama's collection of hot sauces aside for packing, I noticed a flash of motion in my peripheral vision and found Flora standing beside me, all smiles. "Welcome back," she said. "It's good to see you whole. Are you healthy?"

Mending, I admitted. *I thought I would pack, save Mama the time. She's moved in with Arik and me.*

Flora's smile widened. "*Ah*. And you and Arik…"

We plan to marry soon. I couldn't help grinning, but it faltered slightly as a realization hit me. *I wish you could come. We're doing everything in Conota.*

"As you should."

Still, if you can find a way over, you'd be most welcome, my friend.

"Impossible, I'm afraid, but I appreciate the offer," she replied, then peeked around the wall into the den. "Artur seems to be having fun."

She thought it would be simpler to move everything in shrunken form.

"Hmm. Made small by magic, I assume."

Yes… I froze, then groaned and smacked my forehead. *Which means that everything will expand as soon as I take it across the border.*

"Tell Arik to duplicate what Artur has done," she said soothingly. "There's no need to panic." Chuckling as I flushed, she asked, "Are you happy?"

I am, I told her, pushing a jar of pickles safely away from the edge of the countertop. *It's exciting and weird and terrifying, and not at all what I expected, but I'm very happy.* Wishing I could give her a proper hug, I added, *Thank you for everything. I know I'm difficult, but you've been wonderful to look out for me.*

"It's been my pleasure, dear girl," she replied. "I

suppose you don't know when we might meet again."

I could visit, Arik makes gates, but...just in case I'm away for a long time, is there someone you'd like to speak with? Honestly, I feel strong enough. Surely there's some reason why you linger here.

Flora hesitated, nibbling at her lip, then murmured, "There is someone with whom I would love to speak again, but only if you have the strength. My husband. My son, too, if it's possible."

Tell me where to find them.

As she did so, I couldn't mask my surprise. "I saw you in Glastonbury last year," Flora reminded me. "I was not there by chance."

True, but... I pulled my phones from my pocket and selected the proper device. *What should I tell him? Would you rather this be a surprise?*

She considered her options, then said, "No, there's no need for that. Tell him, if you would, that Caecilia wishes to speak."

I frowned. *Caecilia?*

The corner of her mouth ticked. "I have several older sisters, all of us Caecilia. My mother called me Flora, but my husband always used my true name. As if I were the only Caecilia who mattered."

Noted. This may take a moment, I told her, dialing as Artur returned to the kitchen and gave me a querying look. When Kitty groggily answered, I said, "I'm so sorry. Is Marcus there?"

She grunted, and I heard the rustling of blankets and my muttered name while her phone was passed.

"Hope?" Marcus mumbled. "What's wrong?"

"Nothing," I said, "but I need you to do a favor for me."

"What's that?"

"Give your father a call. Caecilia wants to say hello."

The sun was rising over the island of Afallon when Artur

led me through the gate. Having overheard my calls, Artur had suggested that we wait for daylight in that time zone, particularly as I'd awakened Marcus from a sound sleep. "There's privacy on Afallon," she'd explained. "I mean, you could do it here, but…"

The kitchen clutter and lack of functional den furniture sold me on the idea.

Dawn came with a stiff sea breeze, but Artur showed me to a pavilion overgrown with climbing vines, set off in a modest copse that offered protection from the wind. She created a jacket for me while we waited, and Flora cast a worried glance at my bare legs, which had erupted in the bumps Mama called gooseflesh.

Are you ready? I asked Flora.

"Yes," she said, though the way she kept tugging on her dress belied her façade of serenity. "Remember what I told you—"

The crack of an opening gate a few yards away silenced her, and I looked up as Valerius and Marcus hurried through. From a distance, the two could have been brothers, similar as they were in build and coloration. Only when they neared could I see the weight of years in the king's dark eyes—that, and an expression somewhere between anxiety and full fear. I'd tried to reassure him once Marcus gave him my number that Flora didn't seem upset, but he still seemed prepared to meet the executioner. Marcus, by contrast, appeared merely excited.

I crossed the pavilion to meet them. "Thanks for coming," I said, and turned to Valerius—or Marcus Valerius, as Flora had explained. "I've been instructed to get the language from you before we do this. She wants a witness in case anyone misremembers in the future."

He didn't bother asking me which language I needed. After the shock had worn off and I'd tested the outcome with a brief conversation, I took a seat on the stone floor of the pavilion and pressed my hands against the ground. "Easier like this," I explained before they could ask why I was shunning Artur's nice furniture. "And in this realm, I could use the assistance. Are you ready?"

"Yes," said Valerius, though I saw him swallow hard before I closed my eyes and focused to draw upon the necessary power.

When I opened them again, I could tell that the men saw Flora, though neither spoke. She smiled and took a step closer, then softly said, "Salve, mi vir."

He stared at her, briefly speechless, then whispered, "Caecilia?"

As they drew nearer, he launched into uncharacteristically rapid babbling. "I'm sorry, I'm so very sorry, I didn't want to hurt you, and I thought that if I came home—"

"*Stop*," she ordered. "I understand."

"I didn't want to leave you, I didn't know what else to do—"

She reached up and pressed her hands around his face, unable to truly touch him but close enough to achieve the desired effect. "My dearest love, I forgave you long ago. You were trying to protect us."

But he refused to be consoled. "If I'd been there when Marcus was born, I could have saved you."

"Perhaps, perhaps not. You were much younger then. Besides, if you'd returned to me, what would have befallen us? The entire family might have been killed, or worse. I saw what Ordo Lucis did to my poor son."

I had no idea what she was talking about, but an unfamiliar voice to my left murmured, "Buried him alive for two millennia. His wife and his cousin betrayed him to a group of wizards because they were lovers, and he was in the way. He'd still be entombed if Kitty had not found him. I apologize for interrupting, but you looked perplexed."

The speaker was dead—that was obvious—but I didn't recognize him as one of the many who had come to me in the last year. He appeared as an old man, his face heavily lined, his hair white and thinning, his clothing of a style unfamiliar to me. *Can I help you?* I asked.

Before he could answer me, Valerius seemed to remember that his son was standing beside him and said, "Marce, this is your mother—"

"So I'd assumed," Marcus replied, and beamed at her. "It's nice to finally meet you."

"My sweet little boy," she said, beginning to reach for him, then stilled her insubstantial hand. "I'm sorry that I couldn't be the mother you needed, Marce. I would have paid any price, but—"

"Mater, please, you owe me no apology," he interrupted. "I'm grateful to see you."

"And I am so proud of you," she said, then looked at Valerius. "I'm happy for you both. You have each other now, and I can ask for nothing more...no, wait. There is one thing." Turning back to Marcus, she asked, "When you are you going to marry Kitty?"

The question took him aback. "I...um..." he stammered, "that is, I..."

"She's a lovely young woman, and I approve. Far better suited for you than Fabia ever was. I like her. Tell your sister that I like her," she added, pointing to Artur, who had taken a seat on a bench to my right.

I didn't know whether Artur understood them, but I made a note to pass on the message.

Reddening, Marcus looked to his father for help, but Valerius, still stunned to see his wife, merely laughed.

"I agree with her," the old man beside me quietly said. "Those two seem happy together."

While Marcus recovered from his sudden embarrassment, Valerius tried to touch Flora—an attempt that was met with a sad smile when it inevitably failed. "Hope is a wonder," she said, "but she can only do so much, and I know she's not as whole as she claims. We must be brief."

A sheen of panic appeared on his face. "But there's so

much…can you come with me?" he asked, making a desperate grab for her hand. "Please, whatever is necessary, I'll do it—"

"It's not within your power," she said gently. "But my dearest, this is not the end. I waited more than two thousand years before you returned to this realm. I waited for our son to be freed. Perhaps we may speak again someday, if Hope is willing. *And healthy*," she added, giving me a stern look I knew all too well.

"I'm indebted to both of you," I said. "Give me a few months to more fully recover—"

"And *you* have a wedding to plan," she added before turning to Valerius again. "I love you," she murmured. "I always will, and should the time come, I will be there to meet you. But for now, be happy. You have Marcus and Maria…and if there's another woman someday, I will understand."

"There's never been another," he insisted. "Momentary weakness, and I confess that, but I have loved only you…"

"I know." She held one hand against his chest. "Be happy, and do not mourn for me. There is so much I cannot tell you, but…" She smiled. "You know where to find me now. And as for *you*," she said, looking toward my companion, "I was wondering when you might show yourself."

The others frowned in confusion, and the old man said to me, "I don't want to cause you pain, but would it be possible? Only for a moment."

I nodded and stretched my power through him. Perplexingly, neither Valerius nor Marcus seemed to recognize him as he approached, though Flora took his hand and drew him closer.

"Hello, Pater," he said to Marcus, and nodded to Valerius. "Ave, I apologize for interrupting you and Avia, but when the chance presented itself…"

Marcus's flush blanched as the blood drained from his face. "*Publi?*"

Artur leaned down toward my ear and whispered, "Publius. That must be Marcus's son."

I shouldn't have been surprised—Maria was Marcus's and Valerius's distant great-granddaughter, and she had to have arisen from *someone*—but the contrast between the two men was striking. Marcus looked to be barely older than Arik, while his son was hunched with age.

"Marcus seldom speaks of his son," Artur added, perhaps mistaking the cause of my expression. "Ordo Lucis grabbed him when the boy was a few days old."

By then, Marcus was nearly in tears, struggling to produce words and managing only to apologize, over and over, until Publius intervened. "I know what happened," he said. "You did nothing wrong."

Marcus swiped at his wet face. "Your mother confessed?"

His son laughed incredulously. "*No*, never. Nor did Titus."

"Then how—"

"There are few secrets beyond death," he murmured, and Flora nodded along. "My mother died of a fever when I was five, and Titus raised me. Neither ever had other children. But Titus was very good to me, and he did feel guilt for what they did to you. He and I...we speak on occasion." His face briefly darkened. "That being said, I have little to do with my mother."

"I'm so sorry..."

"Don't punish yourself over me, Pater. I had a good life. A place in the senate, a wonderful wife, seven beautiful children, and twenty-eight grandchildren. And thirty-two dogs," he added, rubbing the back of his neck. "We started with three, and Cornelia kept finding hungry strays, and...I won't say it became a *problem*, but we never lacked for watchdogs. No matter," he said, pulling himself back from the tangent. "Put your fears to rest. Of course I wish I could have had you then, but I never suffered. Please stop worrying about me."

"I…" Marcus began, fumbling once more. "I…I just…"

"It's difficult, I realize that," said Publius with a little grin. "I fear that in some part of your mind, I'm frozen forever as an infant. Surely *this* is not what you remember," he said, pointing to his time-worn face.

"Not at all," Marcus admitted.

"Strange, I know. In truth, I've seen far more years than you, so if it's not too bold of me, may I offer you some advice?"

He spread his hands. "Anything."

"Enjoy your life, Pater, whatever it becomes. Don't waste time blaming yourself for abandoning me—*I* don't blame you. And, um…" A sly look creased his eyes. "Be happy with Kitty, yes? I never had a sibling. Perhaps you could rectify that."

"There, Marce," Flora interjected, "you see?"

I would have given them hours together—and perhaps I could have done so, had I made the attempt a few months later—but I was still healing, and within a few minutes, Flora called a halt. "It's time," she said, and brushed her lips as close as she could to Valerius's cheek. "Take care of my boy. I love you both. And husband?"

Valerius smiled sadly. "My lady?"

"Your father wants you to know that you have always been his son. The name you carry is yours by blood." With that, Flora nodded to me and took a step away from them, joining Publius.

I waited until the last goodbyes had been said, and then, with a sigh of relief, I dropped the power and closed my eyes. Feeling a hand on my shoulders, I looked up again to find Artur kneeling beside me, watching with concern. "Faint?" she asked.

"Not this time. Just exhausted." I let her help me to my feet and saw that the four of them remained where I'd last seen them, though the dead were once again invisible to all but me.

Seeing me standing on my own, Flora smiled. "Thank you," she said, and vanished. With a deep nod, Publius did likewise.

As I approached the others, Valerius hurried toward me and clasped my arms. "I cannot repay you for that—"

"It was my pleasure," I told him. "Flora's been protecting me for months. If she'd told me the connection sooner, then I would have made this happen long before now, but she's always been private about her past. Really, I owe her much more than this, and with all the trouble I've caused you and the Arcanum…"

I wasn't expecting a rib-breaking hug, but I patted his back until he released me, only for Marcus to continue the abuse. When he stepped back, his eyes were still moist and red, but he was smiling again. "What's this about you and a wedding?"

"Arik and I have made an arrangement," I replied, grinning back at him. "Once things are somewhat calmer in the realm, we'll see about the formalities."

"He has my sympathy for his current chaos," Valerius muttered, opening a gate to Faerie. "And you both have my best wishes. Is he still in town with Kip?"

"He was when we left him. I haven't received a call notifying me of his death, so I assume they're talking."

"Then let me escort you back. Artur, what's in the box?"

"Shrunken furniture…which Arik will need to re-miniaturize before they take it to Conota," she said, stepping through the gate. "And when should I tell Kitty to expect a marriage proposal, eh?" she asked Marcus.

Snickering as he sputtered, she walked me through the settlement as the streetlights flicked on, my mother's belongings tucked beneath her arm. Kip's shop was dark and locked, but before I could grow concerned, the adjacent door opened, revealing his petite crafter wife, Amy, bathed in the reddish glow of her work lamps. "They got hungry," she said, pointing down a side street.

"Giovanna's. It's lasagna night."

Artur and I found the place a few blocks away, a modest brick building with a plate-glass window beneath a red and white striped awning. Peering through the window, I spotted Arik and Kip sitting at a table near the front, half-eaten dinners and wine glasses between them, animatedly talking—and to my astonishment, they were *smiling* at each other.

"Well done, you," Artur murmured, squeezing my shoulder. "Shall we interrupt?"

"Let's," I replied, and opened the door to warmth and light and laughter.

ACKNOWLEDGEMENTS

Twelve times, now, we've met back here. Thank you for coming along on this strange trip with me! I'd love to know your thoughts—please feel free to reach out, and reviews are certainly appreciated.

As always, I thank the Novel Chicks for their friendship and support. Though he has much better things to do, Adam Domby continues to put up with me and offer his excellent feedback, for which I am most grateful.

And yes, here's to you, Mom and Dad.

ABOUT THE AUTHOR

When not writing fiction, Ash Fitzsimmons is an appellate attorney and an unrepentant car singer.

Find her online:
www.ashfitzsimmons.com